"Didn't you just say it was a mistake to expedite my healing?" Quinnlynn demanded, not listening to me at all. "Won't shifting do exactly that?"

Yes. It would.

And she wasn't wrong—I had just said that.

However, that was before I'd realized she'd denied her wolf for over *forty fucking years*. It was a miracle she hadn't disassociated from her animal yet.

Fuck. I'd sensed the shattered quality of her soul and the wounds she held deep within. I just hadn't realized the depth of the cause.

Four.
Bloody
Decades.

This female had been through hell.

But it would be nothing compared to severing ties with her wolf.

I could feel how frayed their relationship was now, how tenuous the bond between female and animal was within her soul.

"You need to embrace your wolf," I told her. "I was able to heal almost everything else, but not this. However, I will force your shift if I have to, Quinnlynn. Because it needs to happen—*to make you whole again*."

And if she spouted off some bullshit about me wanting her whole just to break her, I would growl. I would shut that beautiful mouth up by turning it into a snout.

"Don't make me the villain, darling," I warned. "It's a role I don't want to play in your life. But it's one I've mastered in many others."

BLOOD SECTOR

V-CLAN SERIES

To Rebecca

Congrats on your wedding!

LEXI C. FOSS

This is a work of fiction. Names, characters, places, and incidents are either the product of the author's imagination or are used fictitiously, and any resemblance to actual persons, living or dead, business establishments, events, or locales is entirely coincidental.

Blood Sector

Editing by: Outthink Editing, LLC

Proofreading by: Katie Schmahl & Jean Bachen

Cover Design: Jay R. Villalobos with Covers by Juan

Cover Photography: CJC Photography

Cover Models: Marcel Pospiech & Jenna Pospiech

Published by: Ninja Newt Publishing, LLC

Print Edition

ISBN: 978-1-68530-139-2

❁ Created with Vellum

To Fur Assistant Skoga, I could not have completed this book without you. Your typing "assistance" was extraordinary. I honestly have no idea why my editor deleted all your edits. I'm sure everyone would have loved your lkjaisfienfklj830f additions throughout the book! Love you muches, baby bear. Thank you for all your puppy cuddles and kisses.

PS—Bethany, Skoga was responsible for the andddd. You believe me, right?

BLOOD
SECTOR

A V-CLAN NOVEL

BLOOD SECTOR

Quinn MacNamara

Blood. Death. War.
A dynasty destroyed.
Leaving me as the ultimate prize.

I'm an unmated Omega wolf. A royal. And destined to rule. But the remaining Alpha Princes all want to claim me, their brutal methods terrifying and cruel.

I've spent the last century running, hiding in places where no one would think to look.
Only he found me. Prince Kieran, the most powerful shifter of them all.

Our game of hide-and-seek has come to an end.
It's time for me to submit.
Or to die fighting.

Kieran O'Callaghan

My little trickster escaped me once. She indulged in a dangerous game of chase throughout the sectors, but I've finally found my prize.

Poor little darling thought I valued chivalry and courting. I'm an Alpha Prince. I take what I want, when I want it, however I want it. And her sweet blood beckons the predator within me to destroy all her dreams of a happily-ever-after.

Let the Alpha Princes enjoy their Royal V-Wars.
As long as they bow to me as King of Blood Sector, I won't intervene.
Besides, I have a new pretty little Omega to tame. It's time to put a crown on her and make her my queen.

Author's Note: This is a standalone dark shifter romance with Omegaverse themes. Kieran is an unapologetic Alpha Prince, and Quinn is a feisty Omega Princess. It's a match made in literal hell, where the antihero is the king.

A NOTE FROM LEXI

Blood Sector is a standalone in the V-Clan universe. No other books need to be read prior to this one to follow the story line.

This is a shifter romance with strong Omegaverse themes. There are Alpha/Omega dynamics, nesting, purring, estrus cycles, and, of course, *knotting*. If you're unfamiliar with these terms, don't worry—they're explained throughout the book. ;)

Those of you familiar with my X-Clan series will notice these similarities.

However, you'll also likely notice that Kieran is a bit different from the Alphas of the X-Clan world. He's an Alpha male who understands the art of worshipping an Omega. And while his Quinnlynn has severely angered him, his idea of punishment is more sensual in nature.

He'll claim her because she belongs to him.

But he values consent a little more than some of the Alphas from my X-Clan world.

His approach creates an intoxicating combination of

dominance and reverence. However, it's still set in a universe littered with dark elements.

After all, this is the future.

And the zombie virus has destroyed over 90% of the human race.

Supernaturals rule the world in their various sectors and territories.

The V-Clan wolves are perceived by others as having gone mostly extinct throughout the years. That's a lie. They're just very good at hiding and tend to keep to themselves.

And *Blood Sector* provides an introduction to their secret world.

Enjoy! <3

WELCOME TO
BLOOD SECTOR

WHERE THE
ALPHA
IS KING

BUT HIS
OMEGA REIGNS...

KIERAN

Pre-Infected Era

"This is the breach to our security?" I asked, circling the Omega kneeling before me. "The one who slipped through our barrier?"

The alarms had sounded shortly after dawn, drawing me from my slumber.

I'd expected to find Tadhg or Lykos infiltrating my territory, or perhaps one of their pet assassins. But a beautiful Omega? That was certainly new.

Unless my fellow Alpha Princes had decided on more of a sensual threat than a physical one.

"Was she armed?" I crouched before the female, wanting a better look at her. But her hood hid most of her features from view. "Did she give you her name?"

"Quinn," a soft voice replied as a pair of midnight irises met mine from inside the black fabric. "And yes, *she* had a knife that she would very much like back."

My eyebrow arched. "A knife?" I glanced at Lorcan.

He dipped his chin in confirmation and held out the dagger for my review.

I reached for the lackluster metal blade and twirled it through my fingers to test the weight. While practical, it certainly wasn't very exciting.

"Is there a reason you left the cloak on?" The question was for both of my Elites—the two men who guarded me with their lives despite the fact that I could more than handle myself. Especially around a petite Omega wolf.

"She insisted," Cillian replied.

"And we bow to the demands of intruders now?" I countered.

Cillian shrugged. "She's not an ordinary intruder, my liege." A polite reply, but it lacked an apology.

Alas, I supposed he was right. This small Omega didn't really qualify as a threat.

Unless she was a Trojan horse of some kind.

How fascinating, I marveled. *What if she's an Omega assassin?* That would absolutely be a unique approach to taking down a fellow royal.

If I cared about politics and the territory disputes, I'd employ a similar concept.

But I chose to play within my own borders. For now.

"You crossed my boundary with a measly knife for protection," I mused, growing more intrigued by the second. "Not a wise decision, little one."

"I didn't come here to hurt anyone," she told me, her voice strong and matching the bold glimmer of her alluring gaze.

That remains to be seen, I thought, eyeing her curiously as I pocketed her blade. "Then why did you come here?"

"For asylum," she replied, pulling the hood back away from her head to reveal her beautiful face.

High cheekbones painted pink by the warmth inside my palace walls. Inky irises. Pert little nose. Full, fuckable lips. A head of dark hair that appeared to flow past her slender shoulders.

And a familiar black diamond crescent pendant hanging from her neck.

I reached for it. "Quinn," I murmured. "As in... Quinnlynn MacNamara?"

The flare of her nostrils and the slight widening of her gaze confirmed my guess. As did the overall familiarity of her features. She was the spitting image of her late mother. I should have recognized that the moment she'd revealed herself, her beauty too profound for just any wolf.

Cillian cursed. Lorcan merely narrowed his gaze.

"I guess you should have removed the hood," I said conversationally as I stood and held out my hand. "Stand, Princess. And tell me more about this request for asylum." I shouldn't entertain it. Accepting her into my territory would put me in the center of the war.

A war that had reached a peak when the MacNamara Dynasty had fallen, leaving behind an Omega Princess and a kingdom many Alphas wished to claim—*Blood Sector*.

It was the heart of the V-Clan world with its high-tech underground system and secure borders.

What had happened to Quinnlynn's parents was a tragedy. V-Clan wolves were immortal, similar to our vampire cousins. But we weren't indestructible, as Quinnlynn's parents had discovered after a freak accident involving their jet.

Quinnlynn stood of her own accord, refusing my hand, her head held high and regal just like the Queen she was destined to become. "I want to choose my fate."

I arched a brow. "Oh?" That wasn't how any of this worked, but I would indulge her. "Enlighten me, little one, on what fate you would like to choose."

"My mate," she replied. "I want to choose my mate."

"And you want me to help facilitate this choice?" I asked her, amused by the prospect. "I've stayed out of this war for a reason, little one. I'm content within my own territory and have no interest in battling over Blood Sector."

"Which is exactly why I'm here." Her dark eyes flickered with some hidden secret, some knowledge she didn't want me to see. "I choose you."

Very little shocked me in my old age. But those three words left me... speechless.

Because I had *not* been expecting to find a sweet little Omega in my territory this morning, let alone one offering herself to me on a platter laden with black diamonds.

"I'm not a participant," I reminded her, my voice miraculously steady despite the surprise flourishing inside my mind. *Is this some sort of trick? A game? A distraction of sorts?* I glanced at Lorcan and he nodded, clearly reading the warning from my gaze.

He disappeared from the room in a cloud of smoke, likely leaving to check our perimeters again.

Because this couldn't be real.

"That's why I'm here," she told me. "You're not out there killing innocents just to prove how big your knot is. And I want this war to end. So I choose you."

There were those words again.

"And if I say no?" I wondered aloud, my head tilting a bit to the side.

"You won't."

"I won't?" I repeated.

"You may not be fighting this war, but you're still an Alpha Prince. And Blood Sector needs a King. You can't deny that throne."

Her overconfident approach made me want to bend

her over and teach her a lesson only an Alpha could. However, that would lead to fucking.

Which would very likely end in me claiming her, as everything about this female screamed *take me.*

Not just because of her royal blood—an essence that made my canines ache with desire—but because of her persona.

She didn't act like an Omega.

She didn't bow or cower or beg. She stood up and made demands. Just as she should.

Omegas were rare. Prized jewels. *Exquisite diamonds.*

And this one was the brightest of them all.

"Is this a trick?" I asked her. "A trap of some kind?"

"How could I trap you?" she asked.

"That's not an answer, little one."

"I suppose it's not." She considered me for a moment. "Would agreeing to a betrothal bond help prove my sincerity?"

My eyebrows lifted. "You give your life away so willingly?"

"If it means you'll agree to my request for asylum, then yes."

"But you're not really asking me for asylum, Quinnlynn. You're asking me to become your mate and take over Blood Sector."

"Where you'll provide me with asylum within my territory walls," she replied. "And save me from the madness this war has created."

"An escape from your suitors," I translated. "That's what you're really asking me for."

"Yes. An escape from the Alpha Princes. An *end* to this war."

"You fancy me a hero?" I ran my gaze over her. "You come here uninvited and propose a mateship to an Alpha

Prince you hardly know on the basis that he's not participated in the battle for your hand. That's rather bold, Quinnlynn. And naïve."

"It's an opportunity," she countered. "And the risk is worth your rejection."

"It's about more than a mere rejection, Quinnlynn." I took an intimidating step toward her, forcing her to look up to meet my gaze. "I could take you right now, keep you as mine, and let your sector rot away to nothing. That's a rather large risk, yes?"

She studied me for a long moment, the first sign of uncertainty touching her striking features. "My alternative is to let these Alpha Princes murder needlessly in my name. I would rather put everything I have at risk to end the war than roll over and accept my fate."

"Or you could choose one of them."

"They're not worthy," she growled.

"And I am?"

"That depends on your answer," she replied. "Will you accept a betrothal vow?"

"You're asking for a lot more than acceptance, little one. You want me to mate you *and* take control of Blood Sector. And you seem to think this betrothal will end the war. But some of those Alphas won't accept your choice. They'll challenge me."

Her eyes flickered again with secrets, ones I could almost taste on my tongue.

She's definitely hiding something.

"You'll revel in their challenge," she told me.

"You say that like you know me and my motives," I countered, narrowing my gaze. "What makes you so confident in your assessment?"

"Tell me I'm wrong," she said instead.

She wasn't wrong. Which made me want to understand

her motives and knowledge even more. "Who have you been talking to, little one?" Because it seemed apparent that someone had shared details about me and my territory with her. How else had she crossed my boundary lines?

It also explained her assurance that I would accept this offer.

And her commentary regarding how I would react to a challenge.

Rather than reply, she merely smiled. "Accept my offer and maybe I'll tell you."

"If I accept your offer, you won't have a choice," I replied. Because mating her would give me full access to her mind.

Just as it would grant her uninhibited access to mine.

Which could be her goal.

But a mate bond would put her at a severe disadvantage—it would make her *mine*. Mine to fuck. Mine to own. Mine to control.

A dangerous connection for an Omega.

One she shouldn't be so willing to give to any Alpha, let alone one with my penchants.

Some ill-informed sod had told this poor girl that I was a hero.

She couldn't be more wrong about my proclivities or my desires in life.

Did I enjoy a decent challenge? Yes. Would I accept her offer and take the Blood Sector throne? Also yes. But would I be the Prince Charming she desired? The hero she deserved? Absolutely not.

I wasn't a white knight. I lived on the edges of darkness. I played with blood. I made deals that benefited me more than anyone else.

If this Omega thought to play me at this game, she would lose.

Rarity or not, I would destroy her.

And I let her see that in my gaze as I stared her down.

I am not your hero, I told her with my eyes. *I'm a blackguard. A scoundrel. A motherfucking villain.*

She shivered but maintained my stare with the confidence of an Alpha. *You don't scare me*, she seemed to be saying.

That's a mistake, little one, I told her with a look. "This is a dangerous proposition, Princess. One I'm not sure you've fully considered. So I'm going to give you a single chance to retract it." I moved even closer to her, oppressing her with my ancient energy and giving her a glimpse of the power that vibrated beneath my skin.

I'm old.

I'm an Alpha.

I will break you if you choose me.

"One chance," I whispered darkly. "Retract the offer, and I'll personally escort you back to your kingdom and leave you to your fate. But this opportunity expires in sixty seconds. *Choose* wisely."

"I don't need sixty seconds. I decided my fate the moment I left Blood Sector for your territory. I choose you."

My lips curled. "An unwise choice," I told her, my gaze falling to her mouth. "Especially if I find out this is all a ruse of some kind." Which I highly suspected it was. But if she wanted to play, I'd indulge her.

After all, it'd been a long time since something had intrigued me.

Might as well engage this little Omega and decipher her secrets.

She swallowed, confirming even more that she possessed a hidden purpose. "So we have a deal?"

Rather than reply, I slid my hand beneath the fabric of

her cloak to wrap my palm around the back of her neck. "How long until your next heat?"

Her body tensed, her pulse thumping wildly beneath my thumb as I drew a soft circle against her skin.

"It's a fair question, *dear intended*, yes?" I pressed. "To know when you'll accept my knot inside you? And my teeth in your pretty throat?" She'd come to me with this asinine plan. I'd offered her an escape. She'd naïvely rejected it. So it only seemed fair to demonstrate what she'd just agreed to.

Perhaps she'd beg me to reconsider now.

Beg me for that *offer* she'd so carelessly ignored.

"Two months from now," she whispered, her pupils flaring.

"And how long does it usually last?" I wondered aloud, my gaze falling to her luscious mouth again.

"Thirty days," she replied, swallowing once more.

"Mmm," I hummed. "And do you wish to try my knot prior to our proverbial wedding night? Or would you prefer that to be a surprise?"

She trembled, all signs of her confidence fleeing beneath the power of my grip and the potent energy swirling between us.

Now you understand, I thought. *Now you know why this was a terrible decision.*

"A-a surprise," she stammered.

"All right," I murmured, my thumb applying just enough pressure to her neck to be dangerous.

Cillian met my gaze over her head. We'd been together for so long that a single look conveyed my request.

He dipped his chin in reverence, then disappeared, giving me a much-needed moment alone with my *betrothed*.

"Are you still certain?" I asked, my chest brushing hers as I closed the gap between us.

9

"Yes," she breathed, surprising me. Her dark eyes met mine. "I still choose you."

For what purpose, I wonder, I thought, scrutinizing her beautiful face. "You may one day regret that choice," I warned her.

"Not today," she returned, making me grin.

"Today isn't over yet, Princess," I replied, my grip tightening on her neck as I lifted my opposite wrist to my mouth.

Some Alphas would make their Omegas drink from them in more innovative places.

But I was old-fashioned. I enjoyed courtship. I wanted her to beg me for the right reasons, not out of fear or despair.

She might have chosen me for nefarious purposes.

However, in the end, she would choose me because she craved me more than anyone else.

I sank my canines into my flesh, creating a river of blood along my tan skin.

Quinnlynn licked her lips in anticipation.

Rather than take blood into my mouth and feed it to her with my tongue, I merely held my wrist out to her. "Make your choice, Princess." If she wanted this betrothal, she would take it herself.

"I already have," she reminded me, leaning forward to latch onto my vein without a single second of hesitation.

One swallow of my blood would engage us in a betrothal bond—a link that could only be broken by Quinnlynn taking another Alpha's knot. And once I returned the favor during her estrus by biting her, our souls would forever be tied together.

It was a dangerous first step because it initiated the mating process, allowing me to sense her energy as she absorbed my own.

Which was why her eager acceptance confirmed what I already knew.

She's definitely up to something, I thought, my hand sliding from her nape and upward into her hair to hold her against my wrist as magic warmed the air around us. *I'll discover your secrets, little one. Then I'll make you pay in blood while I fuck you to oblivion.*

She couldn't hear me.

Not yet.

But she would be able to soon.

In two months.

When I knotted and claimed her.

During her heat.

CURRENT ERA

Alas, I'd never experienced Quinnlynn's delicious slick or indulged in her cries of pleasure.

Because less than a month later, my darling little trickster had vanished into the night without a trace, taking my blood and betrothal with her.

Leaving me to govern Blood Sector in her absence.

While I hunted her across the globe.

For over one hundred fucking years.

But now I've found her.

My devious runaway bride.

Ah, my sweet little wolf. Our game of hide-and-seek has officially come to an end.

You're mine now.

Forever and always.

Prepare to bleed...

QUINN

Come on, Savi, I thought. *Come on. Come on. Come on!*

She wasn't breathing, her throat having been crushed by that X-Clan Alpha while he'd knotted her like some sort of fucking doll.

He'd left her with a grunt, not noticing my presence at all.

Of course, they never noticed me.

My perfume reminded them of a Beta, not an Omega. It was a scent I'd perfected before coming here. A scent that had saved me from discovery thousands of times.

"Come. On." I voiced the words out loud as I pressed my palm to Savi's slender neck, my healing magic waning with each passing second.

I'd used too much of it on Blanca, not realizing that Savi would find herself in this position yet again.

Fuck. Fuck. Fuck!

"Heal!" I commanded in as loud a whisper as I could manage.

The Alphas rarely looked my way, but if they knew I was down here healing their Omegas, they would realize I was something distinctly *other*.

They already knew I was a V-Clan wolf—that part of my nature couldn't be hidden. However, there were supernaturals of all kinds in Bariloche Sector because Alpha Carlos harbored a penchant for collecting Omegas of all supernatural types. So being a V-Clan wolf didn't make me special, even if I was the only one in existence in this sector.

Although, if they realized I was an Omega, I would be in trouble.

Then I'd be forced to shadow my ass out of this place.

But until that happened, I was determined to help as many Omegas as possible.

Including Savi.

With a low growl, I shoved even more energy into her, demanding her lungs *work*.

She responded with the tiniest gasp, making my heart thud wildly in my chest.

And silence.

"Shit!"

I need more power. I need more energy.

Tears gathered in my eyes, failure licking at my conscience.

No. No. No.

I would not give up.

I would fix her.

I had to.

I... I couldn't just let her die like this. Not after everything she'd been through. "Please, Savi. Please breathe." I pressed my lips to her ear. "Joseph is alive. I can feel him in your blood, your bond, your *soul*. You have to survive to find him. To become whole again."

I'd told her this before, but she was so far gone mentally that she rarely heard me. The only one who could truly mend her broken spirit was Joseph.

And he was locked up in Alpha Carlos's dungeon.

I'd shadowed in there on countless occasions, trying to use my magic to heal the snarling beast of an Alpha. But Joseph was just as broken as his mate.

Fucking Carlos, I snarled.

I wanted to slit that bastard's throat for doing all this. But he was only at the tip of the proverbial iceberg. Yes, he commanded everyone in this godforsaken sector. However, his minions were all too eager to do his bidding.

Which meant I'd have to kill a lot more than Carlos to fix this shithole.

There was only so much I could do. I'd come here to save whatever Omegas I could. And that had been over four decades ago.

I hadn't left because there were just so many I needed to help.

Omegas like Savi.

Omegas like Kari.

My heart panged at the thought of Savi's sister. I hadn't been able to save her. She'd been sent to Winter Sector as a wedding gift for Alpha Enrique.

At least she'd been relieved about it. The pair shared a special bond, one that protected her from his lust. Enrique was Joseph's brother, which sort of made him family to Kari. Not that he'd ever openly acted like her brother.

However, I'd never seen him rut. He'd only ever taken Kari into a room to purr for her.

More secrets, I thought. *Secrets I don't have time to debate right now.*

Because I needed to save Savi, to force her—

A jolt of familiar energy sizzled down my spine, stilling the air around me.

Oh, no… Not now!

My hands froze against Savi's neck, my exhaustion leaving me only two choices. Run and leave Savi to die. Or stay and let *him* find me.

Kieran O'Callaghan's presence washed over me like a hot wave of furious power, making me shiver with longing. *More*, my soul whispered. *I need more.*

It'd been several decades since our souls had last touched one another.

Nuuk, I thought, shuddering with the memory. He'd been so close to capturing me then, to discovering every secret I held dear.

Secrets he may already know, a part of me whispered, reminding me of why I'd fled. *Secrets he may exploit the moment he finds you.*

Fortunately, I'd escaped before he could put his paws on me.

And I'd fled south.

All the way to Bariloche Sector, where I'd remained ever since.

Before that chance meeting in Nuuk, there had been another in Atlanta, shortly after the Infection had begun— the zombielike virus that had taken out ninety percent of the human population, leaving supernaturals to rule the world in their absence.

I'd been hiding with a group of terrified mortals while working through the logistics of the Sanctuary with another Omega. *Kyra.* My best friend. My *only* friend.

But the moment I'd felt Kieran's power, I'd fled.

Just like I'd done the two times before that.

Shadowing came naturally to me.

But today… today I couldn't shadow.

Not just because of my exhaustion, but because of Savi. I... I couldn't leave her. "You have to heal," I whispered, resigned to my fate.

It'd been over a hundred years since I'd betrothed myself to Alpha Kieran. One hundred years since I'd handed over the throne to my kingdom and named him the Prince of Blood Sector. One hundred years since I'd run without a single glance backward.

I swallowed, my eyes closing as I pushed every ounce of energy I possessed into Savi's still form. Kieran would force me to leave.

Hell, he'd do more than that.

He'd punish me in ways I didn't even want to think about.

But everything I'd accomplished in the last century was worth the pain of his fury.

"Come on, Savi," I whispered. "We don't have much time."

I could feel him approaching, his dark cloud of power growing stronger with each passing second. It brushed my skin like a whip of pure energy, searing my insides and making my soul ache with need.

My attraction to him had never been an issue.

He was an Alpha supreme, a worthy mate that made my inner wolf want to purr with excitement.

However, my animal didn't understand the politics behind our betrothal or the potential for his betrayal.

But I did.

"Don't trust the Alpha Princes. Not until you find out the truth, mo stoirín."

My mother's final words whispered through my mind even now, the reminder of my purpose a stamp upon my heart.

Her warning, and my legacy, was what had always guided my purpose.

My betrothal to Kieran had never been meant to lead to a true mating.

I'd needed his rare gifts. His ability to *heal*. And I'd acquired them through the engagement bond.

Just as my own powers had been bolstered as well, such as my ability to shadow around without detection.

The sole reason he could sense me now was because of our link.

And that only worked when we were in close proximity to one another.

I tried to harness some of his ability—if he was going to be here, I might as well use him—to help Savi. But he seemed to have built a wall between us, throttling my capability to absorb energy from him.

Fine, I thought, gritting my teeth. *I deserve that.*

I'd abandoned him a month before my heat, leaving him with the intense responsibility of maintaining Blood Sector in my absence.

Well, I'd done a lot more than that.

I'd betrayed him in the worst way, fleeing before he could consummate our mating. He'd probably taken on a harem in my absence just to satisfy his knot.

My jaw clenched at the notion.

I wouldn't fault him for it.

Maybe he'd found someone he preferred and would release me of our betrothal.

That would be a suitable punishment. Of course, he'd lose Blood Sector as a consequence. Because my bloodline still trumped his, even if I found his abilities profoundly more powerful than my own.

All V-Clan wolves maintained their own unique

supernatural talents via the magic running through their veins.

And Kieran's was impressive, as most of the royal families' powers were.

But I was a MacNamara, the sole heir to the diamond dynasty.

My father had been the most powerful Alpha in existence. His traits ran through my veins. I might not be able to tap into all those abilities, but my progeny likely would.

And *that* was what made me valuable to the Alphas of my kind.

My womb.

Something told me that wouldn't be enough to protect me from Kieran's flavor of punishment. He hadn't struck me as the "I want a pup now" type. Unlike some of the other Alphas of our kind.

I swallowed, thinking about all the ways Kieran could hurt me as I tried futilely to save Savi. I was running out of time. His essence grew sharper with each passing second, his focus on my energy signature clear and resolute.

It wouldn't be long now.

I could practically taste him in the stale air.

Feel his heat wrapping around me like a cloak of darkness.

Sense his anger like a whip to my senses.

His footsteps whispered along the slick stones of the underground tunnels, his presence a darkening shadow that seemed to snuff out the minimal light around me.

He paused to murmur something I couldn't quite hear, making all the hairs dance down my arms in response. This was my last chance to disappear.

But Savi's condition held me captive.

Her lungs had flexed just a little beneath my last blast of power, her lips parting on another sharp inhale.

More, I told her, pushing another wave of dwindling energy into her. *Please, Savi…*

Kieran resumed his journey, his minty scent swirling around me in a claiming stroke. *Mine*, his animal seemed to say. *You are mine.*

If I shadowed now, he'd follow, his power hooking into me like a sharp claw as he commanded my wolf to heel.

A whimper nearly escaped my throat, but I refused to bow. Savi mattered too much to me. Her life was important. Precious. She deserved so much better than this fate.

I slid my palm to her heart, shoving another tendril of power into her, trying my damnedest to give her everything I had left before it was too late.

As Kieran entered the room.

Dark, intense eyes.

No smile.

Just a severe expression and an imposing aura that made my knees shake with the need to kneel.

"Help me," I begged him, his energy full and thriving around him like a beacon of hope. "Please help me heal her first." All I needed was a little push from his spirit, a warm stroke of vitality, and I could shove it right into her being.

"You felt my arrival," he murmured, ignoring my request.

I nodded, helpless to his will. *I stayed for her*, I nearly said. *I stayed to save her.* But admitting that out loud would give him a weakness to exploit.

And I would never forgive myself if he punished me by killing Savi.

"You chose not to run," he mused, his midnight gaze

sliding from me to Savi as he took in her poor condition. "You put her life before your own."

I gathered up more energy inside me, my reserves empty apart from a little flicker of flame that kept trying to refuel my spirit. With a nod in response to Kieran, I sent a final gust into Savi's chest, expelling everything inside me once more and willing her to *breathe*.

But all she gave me in response was another feeble inhale.

"Admirable." That softly spoken word wrapped around my neck like a noose as Kieran reached for my wrist to pull me away from Savi.

"Kieran, please." I was too exhausted to keep the emotion from my tone. *I've failed her. She's going to die because I couldn't save her.*

"It would be a suitable punishment to make you stand there while she dies," he informed me in a velvety tone that wrapped around my heart and *squeezed*.

A plea rose to my lips, my insides crumbling to dust in the wake of that lethal threat.

But one look at Kieran's dark eyes held me captive and still.

I wasn't in a position to negotiate.

His will overrode my own.

His dominance forced my submission.

His desired punishment would be my fate regardless of how much I begged.

"Fortunately for you, I'm not that cruel," he murmured, his grip tightening on my wrist as his opposite palm went to Savi's chest.

Energy rippled around us as he engaged his superior ability, the cool air suddenly warm and alive with *life*. My breath caught in my lungs, my heart thudding wildly in my chest in response to the display of enigmatic power.

Savi's lips parted on an exuberant inhale, the sound bringing tears to my eyes.

He's saving her. He's really saving her.

And he wasn't holding back, either.

He was giving her everything she needed to *thrive.*

I stared up at him with a mixture of shock and gratitude swirling inside me, his benevolence not at all what I'd expected from him in this situation. It made me want to go to my knees and praise him. To bow to his authority. To… to *submit.*

But his grasp on my wrist made moving impossible.

He'd woven some sort of spell around me, keeping me immobile beside him, forcing me to remain here. Making it so I couldn't shadow away. Trapping me in this tunnel. Securing me *to him.*

I could fight it.

I could twist away from him and shadow out of the underground, take him on a chase through all of Bariloche and into the Andes Mountains.

However, I would risk Savi in my wake.

I would risk everything I'd done here.

And I was so *tired* of running.

"Hmm," he hummed, glancing down at Savi. "You must be Kari's sister."

My eyebrows rose. *He knows Kari? How?*

But I wasn't given time to ask before another presence made himself known. *Lorcan.* One of Kieran's Elite.

Because of course he'd come here with Kieran.

It didn't matter that the Alpha could handle himself; his pet bodyguards refused to leave his side.

Lorcan and Cillian.

I hadn't seen them in over a hundred years, but I remembered them clearly.

Lorcan and his intimidating silence.

Cillian and his charming facade.

Both were deadly and two of the biggest threats I'd ever met with only their leader topping them.

"This one goes to Andorra Sector," Kieran said. "She needs more treatment."

Andorra Sector? I nearly asked.

But Lorcan was already moving forward, his arms scooping Savi up into his chest with a tenderness I hadn't known the big Alpha possessed.

Then he disappeared into a shadow, leaving me to blink up in confusion at Kieran.

"Hello, Quinnlynn. This game of hide-and-seek is growing tiresome, don't you think?" Kieran spoke casually, completely ignoring the fact that he'd just finished saving Savi's life.

Always so calm and collected, I thought, blowing out a breath.

"I don't know," I replied flippantly, playing his game. If he wanted to pretend that he hadn't found me in a dungeon full of Omega slaves, then who was I to correct him? "It took you a few decades this round, so I think I'm getting better at it." At running and hiding, I meant. "Shall we go again for a century this time?"

His resulting smile was all arrogant wolf. "No, little trickster. You hid and I caught you." He tugged me into his arms, his gaze holding mine. "Game over, Princess. I win. Now it's time to go home. Again."

"Sure," I replied. "Just as soon as you explain why Savi is going to Andorra Sector."

"You think to command me, little one?" He almost sounded amused.

However, he didn't give me a chance to reply, instead choosing to engage his shadowing ability and whisking me out of the dungeon.

And to the waiting jet outside.

My heart immediately froze at the notion of stepping onto a Blood Sector–sanctioned aircraft. A completely inept response. One driven by my past. By *fear* of what I knew could happen if it crashed.

Or explode, I thought numbly.

If Kieran noticed my reaction, he ignored it, his power wrapping around us again and taking us right into the bedroom of the plane.

"Strip," he said. "*Now.*"

KIERAN

Quinnlynn's fear suffocated my senses, leaving me almost as dizzy as her dreadful perfume did. I wanted to scrub her clean, remove that filth from her skin, and return her to her diamond-like glory.

She should not be this weak.

This dirty.

This *broken*.

Her movements were jerky as she obeyed my demand, her inner wolf whimpering beneath my Alpha compulsion.

Yes, I'd used it on her to force her submission.

No, I didn't feel bad about it.

My errant betrothed had run from me for over a hundred years, leaving me to manage her throne in her absence while engaging me in a chase throughout the sectors.

That ended here and now.

Because I'd caught her.

And she sure as fuck wasn't going to escape me again.

I wrapped my power around her just a little more, ensuring she couldn't shadow.

I'd given her freedom once, trusting her at her word,

allowing her to lead me around by my knot even while knowing she was hiding something from me.

But I'd never expected her to fucking disappear.

Just thinking about it infuriated me all over again, the memory of waking up to a too-quiet sector an event that haunted my nightmares.

At first, I'd thought someone had kidnapped her. It had taken nearly five years of hunting the various V-Clan sectors to realize she hadn't been abducted; she'd *fled*.

That was when the real hunt had begun.

I'd found her twice. But the mischievous little deviant had vanished just as quickly as I'd sensed her.

And then the Infection had happened.

I'd worried needlessly about Quinnlynn while also feeling completely incapable at the same time. What kind of Alpha loses his intended mate?

Not being able to protect her had been bad enough.

But the associated connotation of weakness had nearly emasculated me.

It was an infuriating combination of feelings— disappointment in myself as a leader and a mate, anger at my Omega for running, worry over her well-being, and *pride* at her ability to outmaneuver me.

Even now, standing before her as she undressed beneath my command, I was torn between beating her ass raw and fucking her to oblivion.

I had never been so attracted to and enraged at one single being in my entire goddamn life.

She swallowed, clearly feeling my conflicting emotions.

Or maybe it was being on a jet that bothered her senses.

When I was done with her, she wouldn't be thinking about her surroundings. She would be solely focused on me. On *us*.

Her jeans whispered along her legs as she tugged them down and kicked off her dirty shoes. I wanted to ask her how she'd ended up in Carlos's little play camp. I wanted to ask her why she hadn't just shadowed out of it. I wanted to ask her if playing in Bariloche Sector was truly that much more enjoyable than the pleasure I'd offered her back home.

Fuck, I wanted to ask her a thousand different things.

Just like I yearned to do a thousand different things *to* her.

But I needed to ensure she was all right first. Simply touching her wrist had told me so much about her current state. She'd expended all of her energy on healing Savi. However, her pain and suffering went deeper than that.

I could practically taste the toxins in her blood.

In addition to that disorienting perfume.

Removing her clothes didn't help. She merely stood before me naked and surrounded by a cloud of wrongness. My wolf growled inside, furious at her current state.

How could she degrade herself in this manner?

How had I allowed this to happen?

I felt inferior. Broken. *Wronged*. Witnessing her in this state threatened to undo over a thousand years of self-control.

Because it made me feel *weak*.

I wrapped my palm around the back of her neck and sent a blast of healing power through her, needing her to feel restored, needing her to feel *whole*.

She gasped in response, her back bowing and causing her breasts to touch my chest.

My liege, Cillian whispered into my mind, his gift for telepathy not one he often engaged with me, as he knew I despised the sensation of having another voice inside my head. *Apologies for the intrusion, but we await your command.*

Are all the Omegas secure? I asked.

Yes.

And Carlos's compound?

Currently being destroyed by Ander, Sven, and the other X-Clan Alphas, Cillian reported. *I dismantled all the traps waiting for them as well. There will be no more accidents.*

I nearly snorted at the not-so-subtle reminder of Alpha Sven stepping on a land mine shortly after our arrival.

The X-Clan wolves could be useful in some matters, but they were severely inept when it came to surveying their surroundings.

Or perhaps my vision was skewed by my enhanced abilities.

They can handle the rest from here, Cillian continued. *They'll need to do several shipments with the Omegas, so they may call in a favor or two.*

If they do, do as they ask, I replied, giving him complete authority to cooperate. This wasn't how we usually operated. But I was making an exception due to the circumstances surrounding our little field trip to Bariloche Sector.

When Omega Riley, an old friend of mine from the initial phase of the Infected Era, called me for a favor, I'd accepted out of curiosity. She'd claimed she had an Omega wolf that she couldn't heal.

Her despair over the situation coaxed me to board a jet.

As it turned out, the whole meeting was a happenstance of fate.

Because the Omega who had needed to be healed was Kari. And she knew my Quinnlynn.

That had led me and my Elites here.

We'd helped the X-Clan Alphas infiltrate Bariloche Sector to take down Carlos and his generals. Mostly so I could find Quinnlynn. But also because it was the right thing to do.

A fact that caused me to mentally add, *If any of the Omegas need my brand of healing, let me know. I'll do what I can.*

I'll inform Omega Riley, my liege.

Good. Take us to the sky, Cillian.

Yes, Sire.

The engine roared to life as I continued to hold Quinnlynn, thus allowing me to feel her shuddering response to the sensation of the jet powering up for takeoff. *I need to focus on my errant betrothed,* I told Cillian with a sigh.

We're here if you need us, was his reply.

Silence followed, allowing me to give Quinnlynn my undivided attention as the jet lifted into the air.

Her eyes rounded.

"Technology has changed over the last one hundred years," I murmured. "Enhancements have been made to ensure safety, among various other things."

Perhaps later we would discuss the stealth capabilities of our fleet.

But not right now, not when I could feel just how weak she'd become.

It was a miracle she'd been able to stand after transferring so much energy into Savi's broken form.

Quinnlynn swayed before me, her pulse skyrocketing in time with the jet.

"Have you not flown recently?" I asked, curious.

"Not for several… decades," she rasped, her eyelashes fluttering.

I caught her as her knees gave out, her terror zapping the final reserves of her energy as the jet soared vertically toward the clouds.

No runways required.

But it did take some getting used to.

Which was why I probably should have buckled Quinnlynn in for this, as evidenced by the way her eyes rolled into the back of her head now.

Lifting her into my arms, I carried her to the bed, my stability perfected after decades of playing on these upgraded aircrafts. My animal side helped, my sense of balance an innate part of me that I'd honed over my very long life.

I barely even noticed the change in the air.

But Quinnlynn certainly had.

I laid her on the mattress and cradled her head against the pillows. "You are in need of a bath, little one," I told her.

As she'd lost consciousness, she couldn't actually hear me.

Which made any sort of discussion moot for the moment.

Sighing, I stretched out beside her on the bed and balanced on one elbow while I used my opposite hand to continue healing her.

She was severely underfed.

Too thin.

Bordering on emaciated.

That perfume tainted her sweet scent.

And those suppressants, I thought, sensing the toxin running through her veins. "*Fuck*, Quinnlynn," I growled, furious at the taste of them in my mouth. "What the fuck have you been doing to yourself?"

Her insides were a mess, her soul fractured to a point of obvious pain.

This was going to take me days to properly heal.

Starting with her depleted energy.

"Oh, little trickster," I sighed, my palm skimming her abdomen as I delved into the harm she'd done to herself.

V-Clan wolves healed naturally. We were immortal.

But she'd been pumping something very unnatural into her veins. She'd been dousing herself in poisonous scents as well. *And* she'd clearly been using all of her energy to heal everyone other than herself.

"It's like you court death," I whispered, both infuriated and saddened by the concept. However, I could feel her will. Her feisty air. Her desperate need to survive.

So this wasn't about self-harm.

This was about survival.

I just didn't understand what had forced her to such extremes.

"You could have escaped from Bariloche Sector long before I found you there." I studied her pale face. "You chose to stay. And it seems you've been there a while. Why? To help the Omegas there?" It was a guess based on what I'd caught her doing upon my arrival.

The extensive damage to her body and spirit suggested she'd been doing it for quite some time as well.

Decades? I wondered. She'd said it'd been decades since she'd last ridden on a plane.

How many decades?

And was that because she'd been here the entire time?

It certainly wasn't somewhere I'd thought to look. No Omega would willingly go to Bariloche Sector.

Of course, Quinnlynn wasn't a normal Omega.

I drew my touch upward to her sternum, my movements clinical as I traced the area over her heart, feeling for the steady beat. She shuddered as I sent a jolt of electricity into her, my need to heal her trumping my desire to punish her.

She'd clearly been through hell.

That realization wasn't enough to satisfy my anger, but it tempered it for now.

I would heal her first. Then I would reassess the situation and go from there.

However, I would be adding a leash of sorts, too. Something to keep her from shadowing out of my reach.

A cruel mechanism, but a necessary one. Because I would not risk losing my Omega again.

"You're mine," I told her, still very aware that she couldn't hear me. "And you won't be escaping me this time."

I'd learned my lesson.

And soon, she would learn hers.

But not tonight.

I flattened my palm against her chest and created a steady stream of vitality to begin the process of gradually healing her soul.

Blasting her with consecutive hits of power would heal her faster. But it was a more painful method.

Creating a flow of energy ensured she still healed while remaining comfortable.

Something she probably didn't deserve, but I refused to let her suffer.

"Because I'm not cruel," I mused aloud, reiterating my words from earlier. "At least not with you." For as angry as I was at her for everything she'd done, I couldn't torture her.

Which was why I relaxed beside her and lulled her deeper into a sleep state, as it was clear she hadn't rested much recently, if at all.

"My errant little mate," I murmured, studying her profile. "We're going to have a serious discussion about proper care when you wake. Then I'll give you a lesson on heeling." I drew my thumb along her collarbone. "I'm going to enjoy watching you kneel for me."

Just as I was going to enjoy kneeling for her.

But that would come in time.

Assuming I succeeded in taming my devious intended.

I smiled. "You once told me I was the type to enjoy a good challenge." I leaned forward to press my lips against her cheek before drawing my nose along her skin toward her ear. "Well, little one. I think you just might be my favorite challenge of them all."

My palm warmed as I sent more energy into her chest.

Then I relaxed beside her once more.

And sighed.

"Sleep well, Princess. You're going to need every ounce of strength I give you for what's coming."

Because I intended to destroy her in the best way.

By making her truly mine.

QUINN

I woke with a start, my body tingling with magic.

It warmed my veins, leaving me with the sensation of floating. *Bliss.* I sighed, reveling in the heat and allowing it to lull me into a state of extreme comfort.

Until my mind began to question the source.

What's happening? I wondered dizzily, my thoughts swirling around in a serene cloud, escaping me for a moment before the words repeated in my head.

It was an odd sort of contentment that was followed by a tickle of confusion before drowning me in a calming sea again.

In and out.
Up and down.
Sigh.
What's happening?
Where am I?
Happy.
Content.
Sigh.

I attempted to claw my way to awareness, but another ripple of energy had me relaxing once more.

On and on it went.

A war I didn't quite understand because the second I started to grasp something important, it disappeared into an ocean of soothing power.

My nostrils flared, inhaling a healthy dose of mint and man, the combination instantly reassuring. *Safe*, my wolf purred. *I'm safe.*

But something about that thought kept nagging at me. I hadn't been safe in over a hundred years. Why did I suddenly feel that way now?

Where am I? I asked for the thousandth time.

My eyes finally responded by opening and allowing me to see the tall canopy of dark silk above me.

A bed. I swallowed, noting the striking posts and obsidian engravings etched along the dark wood spires. The headboard behind me boasted a similar design.

And around me was a cloud of dark fabric.

Fabric that matched the gown I now wore.

I fingered the sleek material, the black color making my skin appear even paler than usual.

The lower lighting didn't help my alabaster glow, either. I appeared almost ghostlike in this sea of darkness.

I inhaled, catching the scent of mint and man once more, my mind working overtime to process this change. *Why is that so familiar?*

How did I get here?

Where am I?

I hated that question because it kept whirling in my thoughts.

The windows were covered by black shades, making it impossible to see outside. So I studied the furniture instead, noting how the dressers and nightstands matched the dark wood of the bed.

But the seating area framed by obsidian drapes across the room was all leather and glass.

A set of French doors opened to a hall on my right, which I assumed led to a bathroom because the carpet changed to marble at the entryway.

Which meant the hallway roughly thirty feet away from me probably led to an exit.

Except the plush carpet also gave way to dark tiles at the threshold there, too.

I sat up slowly to take it all in again while stroking the soft material flirting with my thighs. *Definitely not Bariloche Sector*, I decided, my fingers tracing up my sides as I evaluated the healing energy running through me.

It wasn't mine.

But it felt familiar. Actually, it reminded me of—

I gasped.

"Oh." *Ohhh.* "Kieran."

His name left my mouth in a whisper, my hands freezing near my breasts as I fought to understand how that was possible.

Did he find me?

When?

Where?

How?

I grabbed my throat on impulse and froze again as I felt the pendant hanging from the chain around my neck. *Shit.*

I knew without looking at it that it had belonged to my mother. *The Blood Sector Pendant.* A crescent moon glittering with black diamonds.

It was a family heirloom.

The Blood Sector equivalent of a crown.

"This is a token of power, mo stoirín. And it's yours now. Wear it for us. Wear it for you. Wear it when you kill our betrayer."

I swallowed, my mother's urgent tone carrying a memory with it that bruised my heart.

I'm home. I could sense it now, the familiar currents in the air, the magic of the underground, the icy chill of the Icelandic weather.

The memory of Kieran finding me in Bariloche Sector started to filter through my thoughts, how he'd saved Savi before shadowing me onto the plane.

I remembered little after takeoff, the concept of being airborne striking fear into my heart and shutting down my mind.

But the warmth that had followed from Kieran's touch remained.

He'd healed me.

I lifted my bare arm and scented the fresh soap on my skin.

He'd bathed me.

Running my fingers through my hair, I confirmed that he hadn't just bathed me—he'd *groomed* me.

For the first time in decades, I smelled like *me*. Like an Omega. The sweet perfume made me feel relieved and terrified at the same time.

I'd missed being me.

But being me meant I was no longer disguised.

Except…

I pressed a palm to my abdomen, searching for the suppressants I knew thrived in my system. Some of them were still there, but the healing magic was dutifully working through each foreign speck in my blood and removing the essence from my body.

My eyes rounded. *What will happen when it's completely gone? What if he removes it too fast?*

I hadn't experienced a heat cycle in over forty years.

How could he remove this without considering the consequences?

I pushed back against his magic, trying to stop the assault, but he slithered around me like smoke, easily overtaking my block and continuing his process.

A growl rumbled inside me. *Stop that.*

But I couldn't.

No matter how hard I tried to push back, his power overwhelmed mine.

I nearly screamed. Partly in frustration, but also in fear. Because I had no idea what this would do to me, and he'd just left me in here... in this room... to what? Go into estrus alone?

Is that my punishment?

I blinked, startled by the notion.

I'd always known Kieran would punish me the moment he put his hands on me. But like this? To force me into heat *alone?* After over forty years of suppressing my urges?

My lips parted. *He wouldn't.*

I'd already gone a century without a knot.

A century of agony every single year when my heat had hit me.

Suppressing it had almost been a relief.

But to undo all of it now, all at once?

I might go into estrus for a year...

My body might feel compelled to compensate for all that missed time.

My wolf certainly felt compelled to shift. To run free. To finally feel my paws on the ground.

It'd been so long since my last shift. Nearly as long as my last estrus.

Tears blurred my vision as I realized that this was very

likely meant to be my punishment—a fancy isolation surrounded by black drapes and Kieran's scent while I suffered my heat alone.

I hate you, I wanted to tell him. *I loathe you.*

And yet, I couldn't blame him either.

I'd betrayed him in the worst way possible. It didn't matter that my reasons were noble. He wouldn't care about that. He was an Alpha. I'd betrothed myself to him to borrow his power, then I'd fled and left him to lead my sector.

My heart ached at the memory.

I hated myself for that choice.

Yet I would make it again if required.

Because what I had achieved after leaving him far surpassed the pain of my broken soul. It left me unapologetic.

Yes, I'd hurt him. Yes, I deserved some measure of punishment.

But this was brutal.

Kieran had no idea what would happen when the suppressants wore off.

He had no idea what this would do to my body.

It was almost as bad as him pumping me full of a drug to induce my heat—which I'd seen done multiple times in Bariloche Sector. Several Omegas had almost died from the experience.

But I'd saved them.

Now who is there to save them? I frowned. *Wait. Didn't Kieran mention something about Andorra Sector to his Elite?*

Lorcan had taken Savi, but Kieran had never clarified his intention or what would happen to her. Or why she was destined for Andorra Sector. I knew they had advanced medicine, which could help Savi heal.

But Kieran had never confirmed or denied his plans for her.

He'd simply shadowed me onto his jet—which had operated more like a rocket ship than a plane—and had taken me home.

Are the other Omegas here? I attempted to trigger my ability to shadow on instinct, wanting to search for the other Omegas, or maybe even Savi.

Only to feel a sharp tug in response.

A tug that kept me here.

In this room.

Thus confirming my imprisonment.

He leashed me.

Of course he'd fucking leashed me. He wouldn't want me to escape again.

Annoyance clawed at my mind, but it was quickly chased away by confusion. Because I hadn't even considered escaping. I'd... I'd just sort of sat here, accepting my punishment without a fight.

What the fuck is wrong with me?

Perhaps it was the healing haze I was still lost in that kept me from wanting to react negatively to Kieran's form of castigation.

Or maybe... maybe he'd done something to me to keep me compliant.

The thought had my blood going cold. *He wouldn't.*

But that wasn't true. I knew he would. Powerful V-Clan Alphas were blessed with the ability to *compel*. Just like he'd compelled me to undress on the plane.

I remembered it clearly now, the whip of his command forcing my movements. I hadn't cared, though. Being naked in front of a shifter meant very little to me.

But to make me complacent in my punishment?

That was a whole new level of low.

Unless he'd done it as a gift to dull the impact.

However, even then, it was cruel. I could handle many forms of reprimand, but mental manipulation was not one of them.

How long did he expect to control my reactions? Throughout the entire heat cycle? Would I be imprisoned beneath this facade of calm even while my body burned for a knot?

Oh, moons…

That…

What if my heat lasts for months? Years?

I palmed my belly, willing the sensation to stop. Futilely pushing back against his power once more. *No, no, please! Not like this!*

A month of being emotionally throttled while lost to my estrus would break me in a way I wasn't sure I'd recover from. Maybe with time.

But if my heat lasts longer…

That'll damage me irrevocably.

I growled again and used every ounce of power I possessed to create a wall inside me to block Kieran's energy.

But he shadowed right through it like it wasn't even there.

"*Fuck.*"

"What's wrong, little trickster?" Kieran's voice rumbled down the hallway before me, preceding his entry into the room. "Having trouble shadowing?"

He sounded amused.

Pleased, even.

It made me want to claw his eyes out. Scratch up that too-handsome face. *Hurt him* for thinking up this torturous punishment.

Because I hated him.

I wanted to destroy every part of him.

Yes, I'd betrayed him.

Yes, I probably deserved this fate and worse.

But I couldn't let him degrade me into nothing but a fuck sleeve. Because that was what I'd become if he forced this punishment upon me. My brain and spirit would never recover.

All I'd be was a breeding slave.

Just like some of those Omegas in Bariloche Sector.

"I chose you because I thought you possessed a shred of decency," I seethed. "I see now that you don't."

He paused a few feet away from the bed. "Excuse me?"

"Surely you could think of a better punishment than forcing my estrus while mentally handicapping me," I continued, ignoring his expression and the oppressive energy wafting off of him.

I was too furious to focus on anything other than my blossoming rage.

"I deserve better. I'm Queen of Blood Sector. It's *my* bloodline you need for an heir. So what will you do? Reduce me to a fuck sleeve, breed me, and then what? I won't be able to mother our heir if you destroy me."

Another thought struck me quickly, the realization deflating some of my ire and spearing my chest with an icy hot blade.

"You'll have another Omega raise the child..." Because of course—he probably already had one picked out as my replacement.

That would explain his cruelty, how he saw no problem with leaving me here to suffer for months, maybe even years, while my psyche broke beneath his power.

"I hate you," I breathed, my hand curling into a fist against my abdomen. "I knew you could be cruel, but this..." This was more than I could ever have anticipated.

"What is it exactly that you think I'm going to do to you?" Kieran asked, his tone lacking his earlier amusement.

"Don't play games, Kieran. I can feel your compulsion, forcing me to relax even when I should be losing my mind. Especially with my heat coming. Forty years of pent-up suppression. It's going to…" I couldn't finish, the pain spreading from my mind to my heart.

Yet my pulse remained miraculously *calm*.

Because of *his* control.

"I didn't even think to try to shadow until I remembered Savi," I whispered. "You've suffocated my instincts entirely."

"I dulled your senses to protect you from the pain of healing," he bit back. "I was doing you a favor. I wanted you to rest."

Something unhinged inside me, some sort of band shattering around my soul and forcing a sharp inhale from my chest.

His compulsion.

He's… he's releasing me from his compulsion.

"And you've been taking suppressants for *forty years?*" He cursed. *Loudly.* "Were you trying to kill your wolf? When was the last time you shifted?"

I was too overwhelmed by all the sensations slamming into me at once to respond.

His healing energy pulsed inside, the fiery embers licking at my veins and shooting pangs of discomfort to my mind. *Fuck, that hurts.*

I no longer felt warm and relaxed.

I felt tight and sore and *tired*.

"What did you do before the suppressants? How did you handle your heat? With a Beta, perhaps?"

I snorted. As if I'd have risked my betrothal bond by

letting any male or female touch me in such a way. I'd needed Kieran's power too badly to risk shattering the link.

"I hid," I ground out, my voice far more gravelly than moments ago. "Then I started"—I paused for a much-needed inhale—"the suppressants. In Bariloche."

He was suddenly beside me on the bed, his palm covering mine against my lower abdomen as more energy vibrated from his touch.

I flinched in response and he hushed me.

The power seemed to change, the pulsing slowing in my belly to a low ache. "I've had you in this state for seven days. I tried to expedite the process today to finish your healing, but I see now that it was a mistake."

"So eager to make me suffer?" I asked, panting beneath his power.

"Eager to make you *whole*," he returned.

"Why? So you can break me yourself?"

He grunted. "You've been spending too much time around X-Clan Alphas, Quinnlynn. Otherwise, you would know that my punishment for you will be much more inventive."

"Locking me up in a room, disabling my ability to react, and forcing me into a prolonged heat without access to an Alpha or any sort of relief isn't inventive enough for you?" I wasn't sure why I felt the need to goad him, but I still wasn't over what he'd done to me when I'd woken up. I never wanted to feel that sort of mental manipulation again.

Even if he'd claimed it was for reasonable means.

Kieran's palm encircled my throat, and his thumb nudged my chin upward to force my gaze to his. "I put a leash on your shadowing abilities, yes. But I haven't locked you up. And you're in *my* room, Quinnlynn. You will not be alone for your heat. You will have me. *Your intended mate.*"

He squeezed a little to guarantee that I not only heard him but also *felt* him.

I swallowed.

And blinked.

"You're not punishing me?"

"Oh, I fully intend to punish you, darling," he promised silkily. "But not like this. *Never* like this." He held me for another beat, then lowered his palm to my stomach again. "When was the last time you shifted?" he asked again.

I cleared my throat, but no sound escaped me, as I was too stunned by the abrupt shift in my mind from anger and fear to confused understanding.

This was the Alpha I remembered.

Dominant yet nurturing. At least where I was concerned.

It hadn't been easy to leave him.

It wouldn't be easy to leave him again, either.

But my life required sacrifices.

His gaze narrowed as though he could already read my mind. "You won't be escaping me again."

We'll see, I thought.

But rather than voice that reply, I responded to the question he'd asked prior to his statement. "Since around the time of my last heat cycle."

He growled, and the sound caused every hair along my arms to dance.

"Shift. Right fucking now," he demanded. However, his words lacked any hint of compulsion. He also didn't use his Alpha control over me to force the movements.

Although, I caught the desire to command me lurking in his dark eyes.

If I didn't comply, he would make me shift.

And that would hurt.

But so would shifting in general. Especially after so many years… *decades*… of denying my wolf.

I swallowed. "Kieran…"

"I'm not debating this."

"If I shift, my metabolism—"

"Will very likely finish the job of ridding your body of those suppressants and send you into heat. Yes, Quinnlynn. I'm fucking aware. *Now shift*."

"I'm not ready," I told him. "I'm not ready for—"

"For me to knot you?" He arched a brow. "For me to claim you? A century wasn't long enough for you, Quinnlynn? Do you need *more time?*"

He pushed away from the bed, his dark jeans whispering against the silky sheets.

Then he ripped his shirt off over his head.

"If you don't shift, you risk permanently disassociating from your wolf when you go into heat. Which will likely happen within the next twenty to thirty hours. There isn't *time* to debate this, Quinnlynn. Now *shift*."

KIERAN

"Didn't you just say it was a mistake to expedite my healing?" Quinnlynn demanded, not listening to me at all. "Won't shifting do exactly that?"

Yes. It would.

And she wasn't wrong—I had just said that.

However, that was before I'd realized she'd denied her wolf for over *forty fucking years*. It was a miracle she hadn't disassociated from her animal yet.

Fuck. I'd sensed the shattered quality of her soul and the wounds she held deep within. I just hadn't realized the depth of the cause.

Four.

Bloody

Decades.

This female had been through hell.

But it would be nothing compared to severing ties with her wolf.

I could feel how frayed their relationship was now, how tenuous the bond between female and animal was within her soul.

"You need to embrace your wolf," I told her. "I was

able to heal almost everything else, but not this. However, I will force your shift if I have to, Quinnlynn. Because it needs to happen—*to make you whole again*."

And if she spouted off some bullshit about me wanting her whole just to break her, I would growl. I would shut that beautiful mouth up by turning it into a snout.

"Don't make me the villain, darling," I warned. "It's a role I don't want to play in your life. But it's one I've mastered in many others."

I allowed her to see the severity in my gaze, the very real threat my inner Alpha posed to her Omega.

She swallowed in response and slowly slid off the bed.

The black silk resembled cascading water over her curves, flowing beautifully against her alabaster skin. I wanted to taste her, to *know* her, to make her mine.

But not yet.

Not after everything she'd just accused me of wanting to do to her.

Was I angry? Absolutely.

However, I would never subject her to such torment. And the fact that she thought for a single moment that I was capable of such cruelty just proved how little she knew about me.

Omegas were meant to be adored, not broken.

And this Omega clearly needed that lesson more than most.

Considering where she'd just spent the last *forty years* of her life, I wasn't surprised.

Bariloche Sector had been burned to the ground after we'd left, and rightfully so. Alpha Carlos didn't deserve his land, let alone his fucking head.

Quinnlynn swallowed, her hands fisting in her dress.

I arched a brow, curious at her delay. I'd already removed my shirt, my intent to shift with her clear. *Would you like me to disrobe you?* I nearly asked, but the words stilled in my throat as she slowly pulled the fabric up her shapely legs.

I didn't bother hiding my admiration.

She was a stunning creature, one I'd missed very much these last hundred years.

I'd never been afforded the opportunity to knot her, or even kiss her.

All because she'd *fled*. From me. Like I was some sort of monster who had intended to keep her locked up or worse.

Or perhaps it had been her plan all along to run.

I didn't know.

But I was determined to find out.

Quinnlynn huffed a breath as she tugged the dress over her head. Her dark eyes met mine in acute challenge, making me smile. "You can test me all you want, little trickster," I informed her. "I enjoy winning."

Her jaw ticked. "I'm not testing you."

"Hmm," I hummed, neither agreeing nor disagreeing.

She huffed again and closed her eyes.

Energy swirled around her as she engaged her wolf, the warmth of her spirit seeming to brush mine.

Ours, my inner animal purred. *This female is ours.*

She'd remained untouched, or had implied that, anyway. While she could have fucked a Beta or even another Omega, she definitely hadn't been with another Alpha. Had she been knotted by another Alpha, our betrothal would have shattered and her link to my abilities would have died with it.

Is that why she remained faithful? I wondered. *Or was it something else?*

Quinnlynn winced, drawing my focus back to her wolf.

Or lack thereof.

I frowned. *Something is very wrong.*

I could sense her trying to shift, the soft hum of familiarity kissing my soul and urging me to change with her. But she wasn't changing at all.

She lowered herself to the floor in a graceful manner that suggested she was about to see it through. However, nothing happened.

She merely remained on all fours in human form, a position I would find useful and even alluring in most situations—particularly as she was doing this right next to my bed—but the pain rolling off her had me kneeling in front of her rather than behind her.

"Quinnlynn, are you—"

"*I'm trying,*" she growled, flinching with the words and lowering her forehead to the floor in supplication.

"I can feel you trying, darling," I said softly, my palm going to the back of her neck. "Is your wolf refusing you?"

"I don't... I don't know." The words sounded pained, making me want to heal her.

But I didn't want to be accused of "suffocating her instincts" again.

So instead, I purred, my wolf needing to do something to placate his intended mate.

She stilled beneath my hand, the energy from her shift dissolving around her.

I didn't comment or push her, just provided her with a hint of comfort.

She eventually lifted her tear-filled gaze to mine, her brow pinched in confusion. "What are you doing?"

"Waiting," I replied.

"For what?"

"For you to calm down and try again," I answered simply, my purr a steady thrum beneath my words.

"You're not going to force me?"

"I would prefer not to," I told her. "But I will if you ask

me to." Or if she refused to try again, then yes, I would make her. Because she clearly needed this. She'd gone too long without a shift.

Four decades.

I might never forgive her for that.

Fuck, her *wolf* might not forgive her. And *that* was the true concern here.

What if she's even more disassociated from her animal side than I realized? I ran my thumb along the column of her throat. *If she is, then we have a lot of work to do.*

I stroked through her aura with my healing gift, caressing the frayed strands linking her to her animalistic soul. They were damaged, but not broken. She should be able to shift.

But as she engaged her gift again, I felt the bands straining inside her, threatening to snap. My purr increased, her agony shredding my heart and making it nearly impossible to ignore my instinct to *help*.

She cried out and fell forward again, but this time her forehead went to my chest instead of the floor. I held her to me and continued my soothing rumble, trying to calm her down, and she shook in response. "*Kieran.*"

"Shh," I hushed, my purr intensifying as I pulled her shaking form up against mine.

Quinnlynn wrapped her arms around my shoulders as she buried her face in my neck. Sweat dampened her spine, her skin taking on a glistening sheen from her efforts.

Her trembling increased, her breaths coming in pants from the exertion of trying to shift.

I stroked my hand up and down her back while my opposite palm remained against her nape, holding her to my neck as I tried to calm her with my rumbling chest.

"It's okay, little one," I whispered. "We'll fix it."

"I didn't know," she replied. "I didn't realize…"

"It's okay," I repeated.

It really wasn't okay. It was the opposite of okay. But we'd worry about that *after* I helped her.

Chastising my mate in this condition would only prove to damage her more. What she needed right now was my support, not castigation.

I lowered all the way to the floor and pulled her into my lap. She curled into my chest on a shudder, her cheek damp from her tears.

This was why I hadn't wanted to force her shift with a growl—it would hurt.

But it seemed her trying to shift on her own had hurt as well.

Perhaps I should have just growled, I thought. Only then I would have felt like an ass for abusing my power over her. I'd meant what I'd said—I didn't want to be her villain. I would happily be a villain *for* her, but never *to* her.

I continued to run my hand over her back, my purr a steady thrum in my chest.

She eventually started to quiet, her tremors dissipating beneath a few heavy sighs as she melted into my chest.

This is what we should have had from the beginning, I nearly said. *But you ran. You left me. And I still have no idea why.*

I drew my touch up from her neck to run my fingers through her silky, dark hair. Petting her. Learning her. *Soothing* her.

She didn't pull away, her inner wolf starved for the attentions of an Alpha. And not just any Alpha, but *her* Alpha. Because while the woman might have fled, her animal knew mine. Our souls were linked through the betrothal bond.

Which was part of why I couldn't punish her now.

Even if she deserved it.

51

"Why?" she whispered, her voice a rasp of sound that caused her to clear her throat.

"Why what?" I replied, my fingers still combing through her hair. My other palm had paused against her lower back, the position meant to make her feel secure and safe.

"Why are you being kind?" Her voice was a bit stronger now, but still low.

"Because you're mine," I answered simply.

"But you're mad at me."

"Very," I agreed. "However, I already told you that I would never punish you in a harmful way, Quinnlynn. I'm not one of those Bariloche Sector X-Clan Alphas."

"They weren't all X-Clan Alphas," she muttered, the words so soft I nearly missed them.

I froze. "There were other types?"

"Visiting Alphas," she confirmed.

I fisted her hair and tugged her back a little, wanting to see her face. "What types of visiting Alphas?"

She winced, telling me my tone and touch had been a bit too rough. But what she'd just said suggested something I hadn't expected—other Alphas had visited Carlos's little playground at Bariloche Sector.

"Were there V-Clan Alphas?" I demanded. Because that went against the core of our existence. V-Clan Alphas protected and revered Omegas. *Always.* And there was nothing *protective* or *reverent* about the fuckery I'd seen in Carlos's sector.

"One," she admitted.

"Who?"

She shook her head. "I never saw him. I hid when he visited."

"And he didn't sense you?"

"I hid outside of the sector," she clarified. Which

confirmed what I already knew—Quinnlynn could have left that place had she desired to. Yet she'd chosen to remain in that hellhole over coming home.

"Was it really so much nicer there than here?" I asked, miffed by her choice.

She stared at me, her dark eyes giving nothing away. "They needed me."

"The Omegas?"

"Yes."

"I would have helped them," I pointed out. "Had you asked me."

She moved farther away, her gaze narrowing in the same challenging manner as it had earlier. "By sending them to Andorra Sector? Like you did for Savi?"

"Among other locations."

"Then go back and save the others," she told me. "Go back and help them."

I stared at her for a long moment, debating on how much I wanted to tell her. On the one hand, I could withhold the information and perhaps use it as a bargaining chip later. On the other hand, I could relinquish the truth and gain some favor.

That latter was better than she deserved, as it was truly *her* favor that I was owed, not the other way around.

Alas, that slight quiver in her lip had me sighing. Because this clearly struck her heart. *"They needed me,"* she'd said. That statement was important. Not just to her, but to our situation. She felt protective of the Omegas. It was a trait we shared.

"They're already saved, Quinnlynn. Bariloche Sector was burned to the ground. And all the Alphas there have been left without a home." Only a handful would qualify for asylum in other sectors. But not many.

She sat up a little straighter. "The Omegas are here?"

I frowned. "No. Most of them were taken to Andorra Sector."

Her jaw clenched. "To a sector filled with Alpha wolves and very few Omegas."

"To a sector run by a respectable Alpha," I corrected. "With a state-of-the-art health facility that happens to be run by an X-Clan Omega."

"Riley," she growled, the vehemence in her tone surprising me. "Your former partner."

My eyebrow lifted. "My former *research* partner, yes."

She snorted. "Sure."

I smiled, the stench of jealousy seeming to percolate around her. *How sweet,* I thought. "You're worried I fucked her." I cocked my head. "I didn't realize you cared."

"The only thing I care about is the unfairness of the betrothal bond that forces the Omega to remain faithful to her Alpha and not the other way around," she snapped.

"You could have fucked a Beta," I offered.

She snorted. "Like it would've been enjoyable."

My smile grew, amusement stroking my chest. "It wouldn't have been, no."

"Yet you've probably fucked your way through the Omega population here," she muttered, her focus shifting away from my face.

And there went my smile.

I tightened my grip in her hair to force her gaze back to mine. "It would have been my due, considering my betrothed left me before our mating," I informed her flatly. "If you wanted me to remain faithful, then you should have stayed."

She narrowed her gaze. "So this is how you're punishing me, then? By fucking every other Omega available? Will you do it in front of me, too?"

"Would it prove a point?" I asked her.

She pushed away from me, or attempted to, anyway, but my palm on her lower back held her in place. When she tried to shift sideways off my lap, I grabbed her nape and forced her to look at me.

The rage in her irises made me hard.

Because it meant she didn't want to share me at all.

Which was probably a result of our betrothal bond and her wolf's link to my soul, but I could work with that.

"Why do you think I would punish you by fucking another Omega in front of you, Quinnlynn?"

She clenched her jaw, her expression mutinous.

"Would it punish you?" I pressed. "Would it make you feel bad for running? Or would it make you feel *justified* in leaving me without a word?"

That chin of hers jutted out stubbornly, the female refusing to reply.

"I think it would make you feel justified," I continued. "Which would defeat the purpose of the punishment, wouldn't it?"

I gave her nape a little squeeze while I studied her face intently.

Her nostrils flared just a little, but it was enough to confirm my suspicions.

"I've had many offers," I continued. "I've even had Omegas beg me to fuck them."

She grunted, but the scent of her jealousy and anger flooded the room. Because her wolf knew I belonged to her. To proposition me—the Princess of Blood Sector's intended mate—was a direct insult to Quinnlynn. A show of disrespect to her throne. Because no one should consider trying to take me from her.

Except she'd run.

And she was in for a rude awakening when she greeted her people later.

"Do you want to know how many of them I've fucked?" I asked her, my gaze dropping to her mouth before slowly returning to her eyes.

"No," she gritted out. But her wolf disagreed with a low growl that made Quinnlynn wince.

That was part of their disassociation.

Her animal wanted out. However, she'd refused to make an appearance when Quinnlynn had tried to shift because she hadn't wanted to honor her human half.

Yet *now* her wolf wanted out to teach *me* a lesson.

The reaction made me smile.

"Are you sure?" I asked her. "Maybe I should tell you how many offers I've received instead? Start listing names, hmm?"

The growl grew and Quinnlynn snarled. "*Stop.*"

"Why?" I kept my voice flippant, purposely goading her wolf. "You left me, darling. I'm an Alpha with needs. You might not want my knot, but plenty of other females do."

"*Kieran.*" The rumble underlining my name told me she was close to shifting and lashing out.

I was probably going to take a claw to the chest.

But it would be worth the pain if this worked.

"What, Quinnlynn? Do you want the details? How their slick smelled? How they drenched me in their Omega need? How they *moaned* my name?" I gave her my best nonchalant look. "I'm not tied to the same requirements as you, right? That's what you said. So how many women do you think I've fucked in the last hundred years?"

Another ferocious sound left her, making me impossibly harder. *Goddamn, I need this woman. I want her. I crave her. I intend to* claim *her.*

But I wasn't done.

She had to shift.

So close, darling. We're so close.

"How many cunts do you think I've knotted?" I pressed, purposefully using vulgar words to push her over that edge. "Think about them squeezing around what was supposed to be yours. Raking their claws down my back. *Biting* my neck. Maybe I'm betrothed to them now. Can you smell any of them on me?"

She leaned forward to sniff, her wolf clearly owning the action as her chest released another animalistic sound.

"Maybe I plan to claim one of them instead of you," I said against her ear. "Would you like that, Quinnlynn? Would you prefer I take one of them as my mate? Accept one of the several *dozen* offers I've received?"

Her teeth skimmed my pulse, confirming her wolf's presence on the surface.

"Maybe I should tell you how many of those offers were given in this very room, in *my bed*." I nipped her earlobe. "With my knot buried——"

Her hand slashed out at my chest, the fingers having morphed into claws.

And then she screamed as the shift took over, her bones snapping from years—*decades*—of disuse. I blasted her with a wave of healing power, needing to help ease her shift despite my reservations to the contrary. She could accuse me of dulling her sensations later. I'd prefer that over the agony I felt rippling through our bond.

But it wasn't just from her change.

It was the thought of everything I'd just said.

Knowing it bothered her made me feel victorious in a way, mostly because I would feel the same about her with another male.

She was mine.

And I did not share.

Her wolf snarled, her beautiful black coat gleaming beneath the lighting of my room.

I grinned, pleased with her appearance.

Until she lunged for my neck, intent on ripping my throat out.

Which I deserved to an extent—I had been goading the sweet creature with my words. She might not have fully understood them, but she'd understood Quinnlynn's jealousy. Which was enough to coax the beast out of hiding.

I caught her muzzle with my hand before she could make a meal of my throat and wrapped my opposite arm around her middle to roll her onto her back with me hovering over her. Her paws came up to claw at me, the sharp edges catching my skin.

"*Calm down, Quinnlynn*," I demanded, my wolf sending a blast of dominant energy through her and forcing her to obey.

She whimpered in response, her animal wounded by my stern tone.

I released her snout and drew my fingers through her soft fur. Other than being a bit thin, she seemed healthy enough. Likely from my ministrations this week.

Her dark eyes glared up at me before shifting to the side in clear submission.

Even in human form, I could best her.

But I didn't want a docile mate.

Or a broken one.

Which was why I pressed my lips to her ear and said, "I'm going to tell you how many offers I've accepted since you left, Quinnlynn. How many other women I've *fucked*."

She stilled beneath me, her breath seeming to stop.

This would be the moment I could be cruel, a moment I could truly punish her.

However, that wasn't me at all.
I was a strong wolf. A male of restraint. *A good mate.*
All facts she would now understand.
With a single word.
"*None.*"

QUINN

Kieran's reveal left me frozen beneath him.

"*None.*"

He hadn't been with anyone since I'd left.

Truth or a lie? I wondered. But he didn't smell foul or untruthful. He… he smelled like a sexy Alpha in *need*.

A need I'd felt growing beneath me when I'd been sitting on his lap.

A need that seemed to be echoed within me now as my wolf inhaled his minty scent.

His lips whispered across my forehead as he moved off of me.

"We're going for a run," he informed me, his hand moving to his jeans. "Then afterward, we'll discuss your heat."

Those final few words made my stomach twist.

But not in revulsion.

In *expectation.*

Shit. It's already started. I could feel my interest in him mounting by the second. Because my estrus was imminent.

And his reveal…

He's not been with anyone else.

That showed an incredible amount of restraint. And devotion. And...

And other qualities I really wanted to ignore.

Yet couldn't.

He remained faithful.

He didn't knot anyone else.

He only said all that to coax me into shifting.

Not as a punishment or to be cruel. But for me. To help me.

Kieran had never been particularly rude or unlikable. If anything, he'd proved *too* likable. But that hadn't meant I could trust him.

It also didn't mean I could trust him now.

He might have proved himself capable of handling Blood Sector, and from what I could tell, he hadn't gone near the Sanctuary, but that didn't make him innocent.

No one is innocent.

A killer lurked among the V-Clan sectors.

An Alpha of unknown name and origin.

An Alpha who killed my parents.

That was the part no one knew—the plane crash hadn't been an accident. It'd been an attack.

An attack that had left me as the sole heir.

The sole V-Clan royal.

The sole *protector*.

The Sanctuary needed my magic to thrive. Which made me the literal key to their survival.

As well as a potential key for entry.

Kieran had been the only Alpha who hadn't tried to compete for my hand after the death of my parents. Which had marked him as the safest suitor. Because surely whoever had gone after my parents would have wanted me as well.

However, for all intents and purposes, he hadn't wanted me at all.

Until I'd shown up in his territory and made him an offer I knew he wouldn't refuse.

He might not have enjoyed the political arena or the notion of leading the capital of our world, but he was an Alpha who had always thrived on the concept of challenge. And I'd offered him the biggest one of all—a throne to defend.

In return, I'd inherited his ability to heal, which had been quite useful over the last century.

If we finished our mating, I would inherit a hell of a lot more power.

But he'd also be given access to the true heart of our kind.

And *that* wasn't a gift I could give lightly. Or ever. Not until I solved this puzzle.

A puzzle I'd been trying to piece together for over a hundred years.

That puzzle had led me to Bariloche Sector as well. Among other things. *Like Kieran finding me in Atlanta.*

He kicked off his boots and jeans, giving my wolf a nice view of his firm ass. I told her not to stare, but she ignored me and released an appreciative noise instead that sounded suspiciously like a hungry huff.

Stop that, I told her.

However, she sat on her rump and openly appreciated her intended mate just as he glanced over his shoulder. He gave me a knowing little smirk that I really wanted to swipe off his face with my clawed paw. But my animal was apparently in charge right now because she just gave him a little pant in response.

"At least I know you're easily tamed," he murmured,

his tone holding an annoying touch of amusement. "Want to see what you've been missing?"

My wolf practically melted at the sound of his deep, masculine voice. She would probably do anything he asked. Including supplicate.

Traitor, I muttered at her.

Then he faced me fully, giving me an eyeful of his impressive manhood.

Fuck. Feeling it against my ass had been one thing. Seeing it? Seeing it was entirely another.

Because I'd never actually seen him naked before. We'd never shifted or run together. Mostly because it was a rather intimate activity and I hadn't been interested in truly getting to know him before. He'd been a means to an end.

He's still a means to an end, I thought.

A good end, my wolf seemed to be thinking. Because she had practically swallowed her tongue when he'd faced us.

And now she was solely focused on his knot. Something he seemed to be ensuring we obtained a very good, long look at.

"All yours," he murmured, his comment reminding me of his celibacy. "After our run."

My stomach flipped with the promise underlining those three words.

I'm going into heat.

And he's going to knot me.

Then claim me.

Which would give him access to—

I froze as his beast came out to play, his magic a ripple of power that left me breathless as he shifted to all fours in what felt like a blink.

So fast.

So strong.

So mine.

I shook my head. *No. Not mine. Not really.*

Not yet, another voice seemed to say.

Not ever, I snapped back.

But my wolf had other ideas.

She immediately rolled us onto our back to show our belly as she gave him a lopsided, playful grin.

He snorted in reply to her not-so-subtle request to play.

She whined at the obvious rejection, the sound so irritatingly needy that I felt sick to my stomach. *How about you let me lead this dance?* I suggested.

Not that she could truly understand me.

And even if she could, I suspected her reply would be something like, *You throttled me for over four decades. Fuck off.*

Which, yeah, I probably deserved that.

Kieran snorted again, drawing my gaze to where he stood watching me with an expectant expression. My wolf gave him another toothy grin.

He leaned down to give my nose an affectionate lick, which caused my animal to practically purr in response.

Then he cocked his head in a movement that said, *Let's go.*

She immediately rolled back onto her paws and hopped up in excitement.

He rewarded her acquiescence by gently bumping his much larger snout against mine. My wolf nipped at him in reply, apparently in the mood to play.

Kieran grunted and took hold of my scruff with his teeth. I froze inside, the dominant gesture one that made me feel a little too safe in his presence.

Then the air began to shift as he shadowed us out of his den and to a street outside.

My wolf waited patiently for him to release us while I tried desperately to survey our surroundings.

He held us for a beat longer than necessary—something I suspected he did to make a point that if I tried to run out here, he'd catch me and drag me back by my scruff. When he finally released us, my wolf did a little circle, her legs clumsy from a lack of use all these years.

I took advantage of that moment to review our surroundings.

Reykjavik. Not the center of the city, but the outskirts. Away from the harbor and closer to land that would lead us to the mountains.

Everything appeared much more modern than I remembered, the buildings newer and rebuilt since the Infected Era had begun.

Blood Sector had always existed here, the wolves having a symbiotic relationship with the surrounding humans. Our kind needed blood—mortal or otherwise—for our magic to thrive. Similar to our vampire cousins in a way, but not nearly as intrusive.

However, we did have limits on how long we could go without—something I'd experimented a lot with over the last century.

I could go about a month without a drink and feel fine.

But two months was pushing it.

Three months depleted almost all my energy.

And four months left me feeling no stronger than a human.

An Alpha Prince like Kieran could probably go four months without and still thrive. His need would kick in after six or seven months.

So our kind had developed a system with the Iceland locals—we protected them for a blood tax.

And Kieran had more than upheld his part of that bargain.

The Infection had never reached Iceland—something I

knew because of discussions with Kyra. She'd kept a close watch on Blood Sector for me, among other things. She was my rock.

And might just be my ticket out of here.

Kieran had put a leash on my ability to shadow.

But not hers.

I just needed to find a way to send her a message. Or perhaps this run today would be message enough. She would hear through the rumor mill about my return and reach out.

She might even already know I was here, especially if what Kieran had said about Bariloche Sector was true.

I hope it's true.

I hope the Omegas are safe.

But Andorra Sector? I wasn't so sure about *that* being safe. Although, he'd mentioned that Riley ran the research labs there. Which meant they were at least in good hands.

Even if I didn't much care for the pretty Omega doctor.

"*Former research partner,*" Kieran had said. Followed by his pronouncement that he hadn't knotted anyone else while I'd been gone.

"*None.*"

That might have been my new favorite word.

Which wasn't exactly something I should care about, but I did. It meant something to me. Something... powerful.

Something I shouldn't feel.

Kieran bumped my side, drawing me back to him and the sidewalk beneath our paws.

I hadn't been paying attention at all, letting my wolf lead. But it seemed she'd stopped circling. I glanced around, curious as to what had seized her focus now.

Packmates.

My heart skipped a beat. Several of them had appeared like ghosts from my past, standing across the street in the shadows cast by the moon and surrounding buildings.

I wasn't sure what I'd expected upon my return—in truth, I hadn't thought about it, as I hadn't been ready to consider coming home yet—but it certainly wasn't this.

They stared at me as though I were a stranger. And perhaps I was to them. It'd been over a hundred years. I'd lived through a lot since then, as had they.

Kieran bumped me again, then used his snout to gesture in the direction he wanted to run.

A few of the others snorted at the display, making me frown inside.

He ignored them.

As did my wolf.

She was more taken with the big Alpha at her side— the one she wanted to claim as hers—and leaned over to nip at his snout again.

He grunted at her and started forward.

She immediately followed, her obedience resolute.

You're an embarrassment, I thought at her. *We don't need him to escort us. We could just go for a run to the mountains on our own.*

But she had no desire to leave him, as evidenced by the way she kept rubbing against him while we walked.

He didn't return the gesture, something that seemed to irk her. She continued to touch him, stroke him, and *mark* him with her scent.

When we reached the outskirts of the city—after having been observed by several more packmates who had shadowed onto the street without any type of formal acknowledgment—Kieran pounced.

My wolf made an excited sound as he tumbled us to the ground with his big body over ours.

He released a growl that had my wolf simpering while I groaned inside. He knew what that sound would do. My veins immediately lit up with an uncontrollable fire that only he could extinguish.

With his knot.

I hadn't experienced a heat in so long that I'd almost forgotten this obnoxious *need*. But it hit me square in the abdomen now, causing a quake to ripple out from my center to my limbs.

He licked my snout in response, clearly pleased with my wolf's reaction.

She melted even more.

I hate this. I hate you, I thought at him.

His dark irises sparkled as though he could hear me. Perhaps he could see the anger in my gaze.

But then he released a playful yip and jumped off me. I frowned—or at least I did mentally. *What is he do—*

My wolf leapt up and took off after him at a dead sprint, her legs seeming to work just fine now that she'd had a bit of a warm-up through the city.

The wind hit my coat as familiar scents assaulted my nose. *Home,* I thought, my eyes nearly closing. *I'm home.*

Visions of the past assaulted me as we ran, the scenery much less changed out here beneath the trees and fields.

Snow.

Black sand.

Ice tips.

Stunning.

My father used to run with me along this same path, taking me to the mountain range for a bit of exploration on our way to the family estate hidden deep within the trees.

Has Kieran maintained it? I wondered. *Are the palace grounds still intact?*

His den was in the city, likely a penthouse of a tall building, given the view I'd seen from his windows.

I preferred the wilderness and waterfalls and trees.

I preferred *snow*.

My wolf did as well, something she proceeded to drive home as she found a particularly soft patch in the plains to roll in before chasing after Kieran once more.

He had slowed his pace to let her play and gave her time to catch up to him now before continuing onward.

Is he taking me to my parents' home? Because we were following the right path for that to happen.

I picked up my pace—or rather, my wolf did—our minds falling into sync as excitement settled over us.

Home. Home. Home.

Each step felt more sure, more powerful, more *me*.

I miss this, I thought. *I miss this place. This world. My sector.*

I'd spent so many years forcing myself to forget, to ignore the call in my very soul, but now that I was here, I couldn't ignore it. It made me feel whole. Alive. *Complete.*

The wind was right. The scents were right. The snow felt right. And the scenery was right.

Home. Home. Home.

My soul rejoiced, my wolf finally backing off a little to let me lead, our spirits seeming to join in harmony once more, making me *connected*.

This was the disassociation Kieran had feared—my inability to shift or to control my wolf. I hadn't even realized how close I'd been to losing my animalistic soul.

Now I knew.

Now I understood.

And the realization terrified me.

How had I allowed myself to become so lost? I'd been consumed with the need to *heal* and to *protect*. I'd all but given up my search for my parents' killer, mostly because my being in hiding had more or less protected the Sanctuary anyway.

However, at some point, I'd lost sight of the end goal— to return here. To return to a mate. To return to *Kieran*.

His dark fur glittered beneath the moonlight, his body long and lean and powerful. *Like a sleek panther*, I appraised. *Only he's a wolf. A very long black wolf.*

My wolf.

He ran with expert ease over the ground, his paws sure and his stride confident. This was a male who feared nothing. Bowed to no one. Took what he wanted whenever he desired it.

And yet he'd remained faithful to me.

To my throne.

To the crown.

Maybe he'll prove trustworthy after all.

Or maybe he'll prove to be the ultimate villain.

But I'd chosen him because he was the least likely suspect.

However, he'd agreed rather quickly, too.

Which left me conflicted all over again regarding his innocence.

I'd followed a trail to Bariloche Sector—specifically, the signature of an unknown V-Clan Alpha—but I'd never *seen* him. And he'd only ever returned twice.

Rather than try to pursue him more, I'd stayed to heal the Omegas who'd needed me.

And I'd forgotten my true purpose—*vengeance.*

Being back here was a bit of the wake-up call that I needed, a reminder of the importance of my former pursuit. *I need to get a message to Kyra, then I…*

The thought trailed off in my mind as I followed Kieran around a familiar corner, one that revealed the perimeter of my parents' estate.

Only…

Only it wasn't right.

It wasn't right at all.

There were overgrown trees. Unkempt bushes. Too much snow. No… no path…

My brow came down as my paws slowed across the ground, my wolf's uncertainty rivaling my own. She didn't want to follow this path anymore. It felt wrong. Cold. Too unused.

But I had to keep going. I had to see their home. To check on it. To taste the air, inhale the scents, roll in the familiar ground, and revel in my memories.

However, my wolf refused. She dug her claws into the ground beneath us, her response resolute.

Well, that's too fucking bad, I thought at her. *I'm in charge, not you. Now run.*

I forced us to take a few steps forward, only for her to yank at my control and jerk us backward.

Stop that, I demanded, pushing her again.

Only for her to backpedal again.

I growled, furious. *You are not in charge here!*

Like fuck I'm not, she seemed to say as I fought her for control.

How the hell has this even happened? I marveled, the two of us spinning in a whirl of fur as we battled each other.

She kicked me back.

I punched forward again.

And onward we twirled, my mind fracturing beneath the onslaught of confusion and the sense of being ripped in two.

A sharp growl entered the chaos, but I was too deep into this debate with my wolf to heed the warning that underlined that sound.

I'm busy, I thought at it as I tried to yank on my wolf's reins again.

She snarled in fury.

I snapped back.

And my soul lost the sense of equilibrium from before, my heart seeming to pound for an entirely new reason now.

Every part of me ached.

My insides burned.

My world... *spun*.

Because we were literally running in a frantic circle, resembling a cyclone of black fur as my wolf refused to give me the control I desired.

Another growl sounded, this one even more powerful than before.

My wolf started to submit.

But I refused. I wasn't done. *You will not submit to that sound while you defy me*, I told my animal. *I'm in charge.*

I yanked again at the controls and spun us in the direction I thought might be home but landed on my rump instead.

A sharp pang split through my middle, my stomach cramping with a sudden blast of *need*.

Oh, moons. Not now. Please not now.

But another spasm shot through me in the next minute, drawing a whine from my throat.

Estrus.

I was going into heat. And quickly.

My wolf curled into a ball, shivering violently. *We need to shift*, I told her. *I need you to let... let me... let me out.*

It was as though she couldn't hear me. Like I was speaking to a wall and not my inner self.

Shit!

My soul felt shredded. Lost. *Incomplete*. The opposite of how I'd felt however many minutes ago.

"*Quinnlynn*," Kieran said, the impatience in his tone telling me he'd been saying my name for some time now.

What's happening?

I couldn't see. My wolf had shut her eyes.

Open them, I said.

She ignored me and curled into a tighter ball.

Kieran growled, the sound one I recognized. *A command to shift.*

And I screamed in response.

Because I couldn't. My wolf wouldn't listen to me. *She's fighting me!* I wanted to tell him. *I... I...*

He growled again, this time more harshly than before, and the agony spread through every corner of my being.

My wolf started to convulse, the combination of his command and my impending heat creating an inferno of torment inside us both.

But she didn't give me back control.

It was like she couldn't even feel me.

A third growl from the impatient Alpha made her howl, our shared agony nearly knocking me unconscious.

I can't shift.

I'm trapped.

And... and I'm going into heat.

KIERAN

"Fuck!" I shouted as Cillian and Lorcan arrived with murder in their gazes. They immediately searched the scene around us, looking for the cause of Quinnlynn's anguished cries.

Her howls could likely be heard from all over the damn sector.

I knelt beside her, my fingers in her fur. "You have to shift, Quinnlynn." Her estrus had begun, and I couldn't help her like this. Not in wolf form.

But my growl wasn't working on her because she'd completely disassociated from her animal. I'd taken her this way because I'd thought she might want to see her old home.

She'd seemed quite eager with the notion, following along with a panting grin the whole time.

Until something had happened.

Something that had her wrestling with her wolf until the two of them had completely separated.

I could feel the fracture inside her, along with her suffering. My growl had only worsened the pain because her wolf hadn't seemed to know *how* to shift. Like she was too disconnected from her human to even sense her.

Another of those chilling cries left her snout, making my heart skip several beats.

"*Fuck*," I repeated, furious with Quinnlynn for causing this problem, but also infuriated with myself for making it worse.

I ran my hands over her quaking form, trying to find a way to help and doing the only thing I could do—*purr*.

Her wolf quieted a little, the shift away from my growl seeming to help.

But as soon as another spasm rocked her, she cried out again.

"I can't knot you like this, little one," I said. "That's not how it works."

We could fuck as wolves, but it wouldn't help her heat. She needed my knot, which I couldn't use as effectively while in my animal form.

Well, it would be effective.

But it wouldn't be right.

"I won't take you like this, not with you in a dissociated state." It could worsen her situation. She might have accused me of wanting to break her, but I didn't. Not really.

Punish her, yes.

However, not like this.

Never like this.

She howled again, the sound reminiscent of a scream.

"There are others coming," Cillian warned. "How do you want us to handle this?"

"Tell them all to fuck off. This is about me and my mate." They would probably assume this was my version of castigation, which they all would agree was my due, but I didn't want to deal with them all right now.

And I especially did not want to see anyone finding pleasure in my intended's pain.

Because she'd left more than a few furious wolves in her wake, something that had been hinted at a bit during our walk through the city.

However, she hadn't seemed to notice.

And I was thankful for that right now. She didn't need more pain. She was in enough already.

I ran my hands over her, my purr intensifying as I evaluated my options.

She hadn't approved of my tampering earlier. But I wasn't sure she would have a choice now.

I couldn't just let her suffer, not when I had the ability to soothe her.

Her wolf released another cry as her body quivered, her womb likely cramping with the need for a knot. I could feel her yearning curling around me, begging me to fix her, to *help* her.

But it would damage her even more.

"You've completely disassociated," I whispered, my fingers curling into her coat by her nape. "I can't fuck you like this." I wasn't sure if her human side could even hear me. But I kept repeating myself just in case she could.

Then I gathered her into my arms as the first of the pack members began to arrive.

I'll be in my den, I told Cillian. *Stay close in case I need you.*

Yes, Sire.

I didn't bother conveying my intentions to Lorcan. We'd been together long enough that he probably already knew my plan. He was also my cousin, which meant we often approached situations similarly.

Quinnlynn released a sound of discontentment as I engaged my shadowing ability.

Then she jumped out of my arms and went straight for

my bed—muddy paws and all—and started digging at my sheets.

"I already told you—I'm not fucking you like this," I said as she frantically shuffled the fabric around on my mattress. "And now you owe me a new silk sheet set."

She ignored me, too busy creating a new bed for us to fuck on.

Or rather, a *nest* for us to mate in.

I leaned against the bedpost, allowing her this moment —particularly as it seemed to calm her. After several minutes of clawing and mouthing the sheets, she sat with a triumphant sound.

Only to fall over on a whimper that made my heart hurt.

She wasn't producing slick because she wasn't in human form.

But she was clearly in need.

And as her eyes met mine, I saw the plea in them for me to help her.

"The only way to help you is to force you into another healing coma," I informed her softly. "And that will feel like hell if I don't dull your senses again."

She blinked at me, and I couldn't tell if the human inside her was listening or even there.

She was all wolf right now.

"Fuck it," I muttered to myself. "You can hate me later." Because it was the only way to help her through this and I had promised to see her through her heat.

I just hadn't expected it to be like *this*.

Her wolf immediately presented her rump as I pushed off the post, telling me to mount her.

Instead, I stroked my hand down her spine and gave her a little tap near her tail. "Not yet."

She growled.

I nearly growled back at her, but I didn't want to risk sending her into another painful spiral.

So I just combed my fingers through her fur once more and unleashed healing energy from my touch. She mewled in response, her rump collapsing as she lay down. "Yeah, you like that now. But you'll probably yell at me the moment you shift back into human form."

Her legs stretched at the back and front, her wolf making a grumbling sound of what I assumed was pleasure, not disagreement.

I increased the flow of energy and stretched out alongside her, a purr resuming in my chest.

"That's it, little one," I murmured. "Let me help you relax."

She rolled into me in response, her fur soft and welcome against my torso.

I weaved more vitality into my touch, lulling her into a state of calmness that eventually led to her falling asleep beside me.

Once I was certain of her healing state, I numbed her reactions again. "I hope that's enough to keep you somewhat comfortable," I told her. "It would never be my choice to force you to endure your heat in this manner, Quinnlynn."

I could accuse her of bringing this on herself—because she had with her foolish actions.

But that wouldn't help the situation, nor would it fix it.

I preferred to focus on solving the problem, not worsening it.

"Try to rest, Princess," I said, pressing a kiss to the top of her head. "I'll figure out how to put you back together. Then we'll discuss our future."

Assuming I could determine a way to help her shift.

My growl should have fixed that problem immediately.

But it seemed her relationship with her wolf was even more damaged than I'd feared.

Foolish female, I thought, thinking through the last one hundred years.

I loved her tenacity, but she'd done irreparable damage to herself and to our sector.

And I wanted her to answer for that. I wanted her to explain it, too.

Soon, I thought, petting her and pushing more of my healing essence into her through my fingertips. *Just as soon as I finish healing you.*

Assuming I could.

Disassociation wasn't something I typically healed.

But for Quinnlynn, I would try.

"For you, I would do just about anything," I confided softly as I curled myself around her. "You just haven't realized that yet."

Perhaps one day she would.

Maybe then she'll stop running…

QUINN

Hot.

Cold.

A land of fire and ice.

Fitting, considering my birthright. But it *hurt*.

A volcano erupted across my skin only for a blanket of ice to overwhelm me in the next breath.

Kieran, I thought. *He's... he's doing something.*

Healing, perhaps.

Or is this torture?

Awareness stirred around me, the scent of his minty aftershave invading my senses.

Followed by a rumble that had me sighing in contentment. *Alpha purring. More.* I tried to snuggle into his chest, but my limbs refused me, my body no longer my own.

I felt imprisoned in this torment of extreme temperatures. *Lava. Ice. Inferno. Blizzard.*

I shivered, but only inside. Because outside, I was all fur and wolf.

"Do you want to try shifting for me, little one?" Kieran

asked, his deep voice a kiss to my senses that had my stomach churning with *need*.

Alpha.

My Alpha.

Take me.

Oh, moons, I need you to knot *me.*

The visions of him fucking me assaulted my mind, my fantasies spinning with reality. *What's real? Is this real? No. I would feel him if it was real.*

But all I could feel was that calming rumble against my back.

All I could taste was his magic.

All I could hear was his voice begging me to shift.

My eyes were blind, my wolf refusing to let me *see*. She was in charge, belittling me to a puddle of nothing inside my mind.

Is this how you felt all these years? I wondered idly. *Imprisoned inside me?*

I'd gone too long without a proper shift, denying my wolf side and hiding from my Omega instincts. She was punishing me now by forcing me to endure my estrus in this overheated cavern.

I whimpered, the sound seeming to echo through my mind.

"Shh," Kieran hushed. "I'm here, Quinnlynn."

Can you hear me?

Or did my wolf release my whimper?

"Sleep," he said. "I'll see how you feel about shifting in a few hours."

Sleep? But I... I...

Darkness swirled around me, sucking me into a vortex of nothingness.

And spitting me out into a fiery pit once more.

I screamed, only to be doused in Kieran's healing

power. My lips parted on a moan only I could hear, my heart hammering in my chest.

His lips were against my ear again, whispering words I couldn't understand.

But his purr steadied me.

That sound was a beacon of hope, a comfort I craved more than oxygen itself. I breathed it in, allowed it to wrap around me in a blanket of protection, and let the repetitive hum overwhelm every inch of my being.

The darkness ascended again.

Followed by more fire and ice.

A spiral of insanity.

One that threatened to destroy the very core of my being. I felt isolated. Alone. *Broken.*

Except for that purr.

"Come back to me, little one," Kieran murmured. "I need you in human form again."

My body remained still, my wolf stubborn in her control. It was as though we were two separate beings trapped in animal form.

I was her consciousness.

She was my existence.

Please, I whispered to her. *Please let me shift. I promise not to suffocate you again.*

She ignored me.

And another cloud of obsidian overwhelmed me.

The cycle continued for hours.

Days.

Maybe even weeks.

But Kieran remained a steady presence beside me, his purr seeming to chase after me into my dark oblivion.

He woke me with a growl.

My wolf mewled in response.

"You need to shift," he said, a dominant thread underlining his tone. "Give your human control."

My animal grumbled in reply, then cried as he unleashed another growl.

I tried to obey, to grab hold of his command and force myself back into human form. But I couldn't reach him. I couldn't reach my wolf. I couldn't take control. She had the reins and refused to let me in.

I lost myself in the swirl of mixed temperatures, my body weeping for Kieran, for my intended, my mate.

Everything felt so futile in this state. So inconsolable. So *moronic*.

I had a purpose. I knew I did. I'd left for a reason. However, I couldn't define that reason now. All I felt was anger, fear, and a sense of loss that left me devastated.

I'm sorry, I whispered. *I'm so sorry.*

The words were for my wolf.

Maybe even for Kieran.

For *everyone*.

I failed, I thought numbly.

I couldn't say which task I'd failed, just that I felt like a failure. Like I'd let everyone down. Let myself down. Let my *spirit* down.

Another jolt of heat lashed at my veins, causing my stomach to cramp violently. Kieran's essence quickly chased it away, but the residual ache made me weep inside.

This is worse than any punishment I could have imagined.

Yet I deserved it.

Every ounce of agony.

Not because of what I'd done to Kieran—which had earned me a different sort of punishment—but because of what I'd done to my wolf. My other half. My true partner in this life. *My fucking soul.*

"*Quinnlynn.*" Kieran's voice pierced the fog of my mind,

drawing my focus to him. "Stop feeling sorry for yourself and *fight*."

My brow wanted to crinkle. *Fight? Fight what?*

"Demand that your wolf heel," he continued. Or maybe that was a reply.

Has he already claimed me? Can he hear my thoughts?

No.

No, I would feel his claim, and I'd be able to talk to him, too.

"*Now*," he snarled.

My animal whimpered in response to his ire, her spirit seemingly bruised. Dejection swirled in my heart, the source of it caused by my wolf.

She felt rejected.

She kept offering her rump to him, and he kept denying her.

I hadn't been aware of it, or the fact that my eyes were now open, but she was begging him for his knot and he kept saying no.

Why? I thought, delirious. *Why are you rejecting us?*

His palm tapped the base near my tail. "Give your human control, and I'll give you what you need."

My wolf growled in response.

Causing Kieran to growl right back, the sound so domineering that the very essence of my being quivered beneath the weight of his power.

"I've tried this the kind way, little one," he said. "You're hurting yourself by doing this. And I won't allow that. Now *shift*."

A scream left my throat as my wolf tried futilely to accept his command, but she didn't know how.

I didn't know how.

We were lost.

Separated.

Completely disassociated.

Kieran grabbed my scruff and forced me to look into his eyes as he growled again.

Stop! I wanted to beg. *Please stop!*

But I could see the pain reflected in his gaze, his nostrils flaring as my wolf cried out in response to his command.

However, whatever he saw in my eyes made him sigh and press his forehead to mine. "You're killing me, Quinnlynn," he whispered. "I need you to fight, baby. *Fight.*"

My insides clenched once more, his nearness, his *scent*, drugging my mind and making me groan internally. *Want. Need. Knot. Please.*

"No," he said, his voice holding a touch of reprimand. "I won't fuck you like this. Tame your fucking wolf, Quinnlynn."

The world descended into darkness again, my mind drowning beneath an avalanche of intense need and a scalding wave of anguish.

No ice.

No healing energy.

No Kieran.

I whimpered. *Why? Why are you doing this to me?*

Of course, it was what I deserved. But it had my wolf spiraling in confusion and sadness as well, a sense of despair settling over us both. She didn't understand why our Alpha wouldn't satisfy us. We were in need. This was his job. Our *purpose.*

A fresh trickle of flames flourished inside me, the world seeming to light up from within. I'd denied my cycle for so long that I'd forgotten what this agony felt like, and to be trapped inside my mind, inside this dark, obsidian space, made it so much worse.

My animal vibrated with shock, incapable of

withstanding the stark need burgeoning between us. We needed our Alpha. We needed Kieran. But he'd rejected us. Left us to burn.

Alone.

In the dark.

Except... I wasn't alone. I was with my wolf. My other half. We were in this hell together, trapped beneath a blaze of fiery energy, melting from the feverishness of our collective *need.*

I groaned inwardly, craving the healing touch of my intended mate while seeking solace in my inner self. *We need to work together,* I told my wolf. *We can't do this to ourself.*

Reality surfaced again, or some measure of it, because I suddenly felt suffocated by Kieran's scent. *Mint. Masculinity. Alpha dominance.*

His skin was hot against my fur.

His knot a presence I could almost taste.

Except all he did was pet me.

And growl.

Demanding my heat. My slick. My *need.*

A whine caught in my throat, his presence no longer soothing, but excruciating. My wolf wanted to nuzzle against him, to beg for him to shift and fuck us. But he held us down with a sturdy arm and leg, pinning us to the bed, keeping us contained beneath his virile form.

This is torture! I wanted to scream at him. *What happened to helping us?*

What happened to his claims of never punishing me like this?

Perhaps this was the real Kieran. The devil beneath the handsome mask. The villain he'd warned me about.

I knew he could be cruel.

But this stretched beyond cruelty to sadism.

My wolf growled in agreement, furious that our

intended was treating us this way, tormenting us with his delicious scent while refusing to knot us.

We needed to make him pay. To hurt him like he was hurting us. To declare him unworthy of our mating because no good Alpha would do this to an Omega.

The fury inside me mounted with each passing second, my animal seeming to be in full agreement of our wrath. *He betrayed us. He hurt us. He doesn't deserve us. He needs to pay.*

His growl increased with the sounds of my wolf snarling.

Commanding us.

Punishing us.

Harming us.

But our strength was no match for his. He held us down with ease, controlling my snout and body without so much as breaking a sweat.

I hate him.

I want to maim him.

I want to make him bleed.

Because every part of me screamed in agony. I needed his knot, but I didn't want his knot. Not anymore. Not after what he'd done to me and my wolf.

Maybe he felt I deserved it.

But no crime merited this sort of anguish. This burning need. This dissatisfaction. This taunting behavior followed by a lack of action.

Evil. Vile. Savage.

Behavior that needs to be reprimanded.

Behavior that makes him no better than me.

A howl left my mouth as my wolf gave me control, letting me take charge to voice the fury inside us. She wanted me to scream. To yell. To scold our Alpha. To make him hurt with words. To make him *see reason.*

Because we needed him.

Yet he was denying us.

And it no longer mattered why that was, or how he felt this was okay.

All that mattered was our need to heal, to feel whole, to be *complete*.

I shuddered as my transformation crawled across my body, turning my fur into skin and leaving behind a sheen of sweat. It created a beautiful sort of torment inside me, the bliss of my shift underscored by the painful contortion of bones and shape.

Too long, I thought, panting. *Too long since I last did this.*

The other day—or whenever that was—hadn't been enough. My animalistic spirit needed so much more. Daily shifts. Hourly. I wasn't sure. But I would give her whatever she needed to properly heal.

Never again, I promised her. *I'll never deny you again.*

Some part of her understood my vow, her hackles immediately soothing as she purred with contentment beneath my skin.

For that single second, I felt complete. Happy. At peace.

Only to inhale and remember *why* I'd shifted back to human form.

Kieran O'Callaghan.

"*You*," I snarled, my voice hoarse as I rolled beneath him, my nails digging into his bare shoulders and biting into his skin.

His dark irises captured mine, his intense expression stealing the breath from my lungs and the words from my head.

What…? What had I been about to say, again?

I blinked, trying to break whatever spell his presence seemed to weave over my being. But it clung tightly to my heart and my mind, holding me hostage beneath him.

My chest began to burn, the subtle reminder telling me to breathe.

Burn, I thought. *Fire. Agony. Inferno!*

I growled, the memory of my ire hitting me full force, only to vanish as I inhaled more of his delicious scent.

Oh...

Kieran's presence cooled me almost immediately, his energy roaming over every inch of my naked body and claiming me intimately.

His purr vibrated my chest, his palms sliding up to cup my cheeks. "Welcome back, Quinnlynn."

KIERAN

Eight. Fucking. Days.

But to have my Omega staring up at me—*in human form*—meant everything.

It'd taken me five days to realize what she'd needed—to heal herself. My helping her had actually been hurting her. Because it had given her a safe place to hide. A calming energy field to survive the heat overtaking her fragile form.

Things had begun to shift once I'd taken away my power.

The sounds her wolf had made would haunt me to my fucking grave, but it'd worked. That was what mattered now. My Omega was whole again. Connected to her animal side.

And glaring up at me with a ferocity that set my blood on fire.

More, I thought. *Give me more.*

"Welcome back?" she repeated, her voice a rasp of sound. "From hell, you mean?"

I ignored the accusation in those four words and reached for a bottle of water. She dug her nails into my shoulders again, an action I ignored in favor of bringing the drink to her mouth. I curled my free hand around her nape to help lift her off the bed, not wanting her to choke, and said, "Swallow."

She glowered at me in response.

I unleashed a growl that made her lips part on a moan, her estrus still very much thriving inside her. She sputtered as the water touched her tongue, then she began to swallow like I'd redefined the meaning of life.

The contents all but disappeared, causing me to grab a second bottle for her.

She drank it down as her eyes rolled into the back of her head.

When I held up a third drink, she shivered, her eyes closing. I set it aside and drew my thumb along her bottom lip. "Hungry?" I asked, my natural lilt stronger after having spent over a week in bed with an Omega in heat.

An Omega meant to be mine.

An Omega I couldn't *fuck*.

An Omega I now needed to care for to ensure she didn't revert back to her disassociated state.

She hummed, her nostrils flaring as she inhaled deeply.

"That's not an answer, little one," I told her. "Are you ready to try eating something?" Because she hadn't eaten anything in eight very long days. Her shifter heritage, coupled with my ability to heal, had kept her healthy. At least during the first few days until I'd realized what I had to do to fix her.

The moment she'd shifted back, I'd hit her with a wave of healing power, which she seemed to be reveling in now. She murmured something about ice, her lips curling into a lazy smile.

I frowned at her. "Ice?"

She leaned into me, nuzzling my throat. "Mmm, Alpha."

"Yes," I told her. "*Your* Alpha."

She started to nod, then paused and shook her head. "No. Not my Alpha."

That deepened my frown. "What did you just say to me?"

"You *hurt* me," she whispered, either not hearing me or ignoring me. Her brow furrowed as she pulled back to glare at me. "You hurt *us*." Her nails bit into my shoulders again as she unleashed a sound that was all pissed-off wolf.

Well, at least you're both on the same wavelength again, I thought as her palm connected with my cheek.

Another animalistic sound left her mouth as she started to throw a tantrum beneath me.

Nails.

Hands.

Teeth.

"*Enough.*" I caught her wrists and pressed them to the pillow on either side of her head and used my lower body to pin her hips and legs to the bed.

"*You rejected us.*" The words came out on a hiss, her wolf staring at me through her eyes.

"I don't think you want to talk to me about rejection, little trickster. Because I'm not the one who *left.*"

"I thought you wouldn't punish me like this," she retorted, making me wonder if she was even listening to me. "You *lied.* You hurt us."

"I *fixed* you," I snapped back at her, my tone holding a touch of dominance because I needed her to fucking *hear* me. "You disassociated from your wolf, Quinnlynn."

She snorted, her nostrils flaring.

But she didn't speak.

Which I hoped meant she was finally understanding me.

"Making you endure your estrus brought you back. It forced you to *feel* as a unit, not separately. Because the agony of going through your heat alone is something you both understood."

Her obsidian eyes glittered, her wolf seeming to taste the truth in my words. She might not have understood me, but her human half did.

I settled more firmly between her splayed thighs, my grip on her wrists lessening. "Now you're whole again. You're *you*." I ran my nose across her cheek to her ear. "You're safe. You're mine. And you're still in heat."

She shivered but remained silent. *Because she's finally hearing me.*

"I've numbed you from the impact again, but the moment I release you from my healing energy, you'll be in agony like you were before. So you have a choice to make, Quinnlynn."

I pressed a kiss to her skittering pulse before pulling back up to stare down at her.

"I'm going to knot you," I told her.

There was no debating the inevitability of our situation. She'd chosen me over a hundred years ago, even after I'd warned her of the consequences.

Running hadn't changed our fate. She'd been mine from the moment she'd swallowed my blood.

I'd spent a century chasing her, and I'd finally won our game of hide-and-seek.

Now it was time for me to finally taste her. To knot her. To fuck her to oblivion. To make her *beg* for my claim.

But I would allow her to decide *how* I took her.

"You…" Her voice was barely audible, but my

enhanced hearing allowed me to hear her with ease. "You'll knot me?"

I narrowed my gaze. "Yes. You're my intended mate. And I think I've waited long enough, Quinnlynn." Not only that, but I'd more than proved myself worthy of her. "This game is done. I won. You're mine."

"Yours," she whispered.

I leaned down until we were nose to nose. "*Mine.*"

"You didn't reject us." The words were a statement, not a question. "You fixed us." Her phrasing told me just how close her wolf was to the surface. She was still in a very fragile state, her shifter soul wounded from decades of ignoring her instincts.

Which was why I confirmed her claims by saying, "I would never reject you, Quinnlynn. I hunted you for over a century because you're mine." That word felt like a brand on my tongue, one I wanted to stamp into every inch of her being until she submitted.

Until she claims me back just as fiercely, I thought, correcting myself.

"We made a vow to each other, Princess," I added softly. "And while I may be a lot of things, dishonorable isn't one of them."

Her wolf seemed to blink away from her gaze, leaving just the female behind. *My* female.

She stared up at me with a mixture of curiosity and wonder, her pupils widening as she searched my face for some sort of answer. Some clue. Some hint at a question I couldn't read.

This Omega contained so many secrets and hidden truths, all of which I was dying to know.

Why did you run?

Where did you go?

What have you been doing?

Do you plan to run again?

I wouldn't allow the latter to happen. I'd leashed her firmly, my power an invisible rope around her neck.

She wouldn't escape me again.

But it didn't stop me from wondering if she would try. Part of me rather hoped she would so I could teach her a proper lesson. The other part wanted her to stay willingly. To *choose* to be mine for the right reasons, not as some unknown ploy.

"You're suppressing my heat," she said, her wolf seeming to blink in and out of her gaze. It wasn't the response I'd expected in answer to what I'd told her, but she appeared to be struggling to truly focus.

"I'm not suppressing your heat," I murmured. "I'm numbing you to the overwhelming impact of your estrus."

"That's why I'm cold."

I frowned. "You're cold?" I pulled back some of my healing energy, concerned by her statement. "You shouldn't feel cold."

Her nostrils immediately flared, her pupils dilating as I allowed her to feel some of the force of her estrus. "*Kieran.*"

I regulated my power again, trying to pull back enough to keep her steady, but she arched into me in response, her thighs clamping around my hips.

My name left her mouth again, the plea going straight to my groin. "*Help me,*" she begged. "S-suppress…"

"Numbing," I corrected her again as I doused her with even more of my energy.

She shuddered beneath me, her thighs relaxing marginally around my hips. "*Thank you,*" she breathed as another shiver overwhelmed her.

"I can't keep doing this for too much longer, Quinnlynn. You're fighting your natural instincts, which is precisely what landed you in this situation with your wolf."

She swallowed, nodding. "I know."

"Then choose," I told her. "I can knot you as you are now and slowly ease you back into your heat. Or unleash you entirely and fuck you into oblivion."

Because a man could only have so much patience.

And I'd certainly gone above and beyond that requirement.

Something I allowed her to see now in my gaze. We wouldn't be negotiating this. She'd willingly swallowed my blood. That made her mine.

My wolf. My mate. My Queen.

"I promise to see you through this," I said, releasing her wrists and grabbing her neck, my grip gentle but sure. "But you need to tell me which way you prefer, Quinnlynn. Slow or fast."

Her throat worked beneath my palm as she tried to swallow again, her midnight eyelashes fanning her porcelain cheekbones.

I didn't rush her decision, just continued to stroke her throat while my power kept her from drowning beneath the sea of lust. It wasn't natural. But I couldn't make her suffer. Not after witnessing the last few days of her torment as she'd fought her wolf.

However, I would push her headfirst into her heat if she started to disassociate from her animal again.

Fortunately, she didn't appear to be trying to fight her instincts so much as considering how she wanted to embrace them.

I drew my nose along her cheek and inhaled her sweet scent. I'd bathed her several times over the last week, including when I'd taken away my healing energy. She hadn't seemed to notice at all, but she might one day realize what I'd done and appreciate it.

Or she might lose her mind to her heat and never

remember these moments again.

Regardless, I knew.

I'd taken care of my intended. And that was what mattered most.

Her eyelashes parted to reveal her wolf once more, the animal staring up at me through her beautiful dark irises. That look told me they were communicating as one and connected appropriately.

But she didn't speak.

Instead, she pressed against my shoulders.

I allowed the movement, granting her the space she appeared to be requesting, and rolled to my back. She stole a deep, calming breath, her chest rising and falling with the motion.

My purr intensified instinctually, my need to protect her overwhelming my being. There was no one else in this world that I felt these urges for, not even my closest friends and family.

Only Quinnlynn.

She'd become my heart the moment she'd imbibed my essence. And while I'd barely known her then —*fuck, I barely know her* now—she was still the core of my soul. A cherished jewel deserving of my care and devotion.

A weakness, a cynical part of me acknowledged.

However, Quinnlynn had proved to be one of the strongest Omegas of my acquaintance.

Devious, too.

Intelligent.

Full of secrets.

Several of those secrets brimmed in her midnight gaze as she went up onto her elbow to gaze down at me. Her sensual mouth parted to reveal her tongue as she dampened her bottom lip.

It took physical restraint not to reach for her and take charge once more.

But I wanted her to *choose*.

"Quinnlynn?" I prompted, my voice deeper than before.

She hummed something unintelligible back at me as her eyes roamed over my naked form, taking in every inch of my torso before lowering to my throbbing knot.

I tucked one of my arms behind my head and reveled in her open admiration.

She placed her palm on my abdomen, her focus homed in on that single touch. Her pupils pulsated, her wolf very much in control of this moment.

I didn't comment, instead observing as she explored me with her hand.

First she traveled up to my pec, her nail scraping across my nipple. It stood at attention in response, something that made her lick her lips. Then she leaned down to sniff my neck, the action more animalistic than human.

A female scenting her mate.

I tilted my head back to give her more access, my purr rumbling in my chest in reply to her clear appreciation.

She nuzzled my throat, her hand flattening on my chest before moving down to my abdomen again.

Where she traced every rigid muscle.

Slowly.

Carefully.

As though memorizing the feel of me.

"If this is your version of foreplay, darling, I approve," I told her, my purr adding a deep vibration to my tone.

She ignored me, her hand still roaming.

Her fingertips danced along my hip bone, her thumb tracing the indent above it, causing my thighs to tense in anticipation. It'd been far too long since a woman had properly touched me. Yet I couldn't recall any of them ever doing this.

Mostly because I usually took charge.

I hadn't played with females in the past; I'd fucked them. But for Quinnlynn, I would play. I would play all night. All week. All damn month.

Especially if she kept shuddering against me like that.

She stole another deep breath, her breasts pillowed against my side. Her lips tasted my skin, causing my wolf to stir beneath the surface. He recognized the touch as coming from her animal, her instincts too feral to be human.

He wanted to indulge in her in kind, to push her to her back and hold her down while I devoured her slick with my mouth.

Because fuck, her arousal was potent, the sweet fragrance permeating the air and drowning me beneath a sea of need.

Her need.

But her movements were measured and slow, her exploration incomplete.

I didn't want to leave her unsatisfied.

Not now. Not ever.

So I waited as her hand ventured downward to my groin. *So gentle and tentative*, I thought as her fingertips feathered across my pelvic bone.

And straight to the base of my cock.

To my *knot*.

I didn't bother hiding my growl of approval, the sound echoing from my chest. "*Fuck*, Quinnlynn."

That touch threatened my control, something she didn't seem to realize because she started nuzzling my neck while wrapping her palm around my shaft.

My insides ignited with a dark need to take her, my

century-long celibacy riding me hard.

I'd been patient.

Waiting.

Telling myself that it would be worth it in the end.

And as she started licking a path down my neck to my pecs, I realized that I'd been right. This intensity. This fiery yearning. This indecent craving. It all made the fight—the *hunt*—worth my sacrifice.

Her lips skimmed my pec, tracing the touches of her fingertips with her tongue. This was all her wolf, leading each caress, demanding that the human inside her explore and learn her mate.

But Quinnlynn was still aware, her presence evident in her eyes as she glanced up at me from my abdomen.

Her irises reflected the same dark craving I felt in my spirit, our animals in sync with our shared passions. However, there was a hesitancy there as well. A curiosity that needed to be sated.

"I once asked you if you wanted to try my knot before our proverbial wedding night," I reminded her. "You chose to wait. But it seems that you want to try it now, hmm?"

She replied by circling my belly button with her tongue.

"I can't tell if you're stalling or genuinely enjoying yourself," I admitted.

Her palm squeezed my knot, making me groan.

"But feel free to continue," I encouraged her. "I'll have my answer in the end."

Then I would knot her.

Repeatedly.

Until she begged me to stop. But even then, I might not.

Because an Omega in heat was insatiable.

And fortunately for Quinnlynn, so was I.

QUINN

This is never going to fit, I thought, my hand squeezing Kieran's knot again.

My wolf had initiated this game, wanting to explore and taste our mate.

And now I wasn't sure what to say or do.

He'd freed me from his energy, causing my body to immediately go up in flames and leaving me panting and needy in response.

Then he'd offered me a choice.

A choice I still hadn't truly made.

But my wolf needed this. She wanted to know our intended mate, to explore the contours of his masculine form and taste the saltiness of his seed.

His blood had run through me for so long that my soul felt intimately connected to him. And yet, he was a stranger. A being I might not even be able to trust.

But if that's true, then why give me a choice? Why not just release me to my fate and claim me?

I shivered, the questions making me dizzy.

Because the moment this game ended, he would mate me once and for all. He would lay claim to my mind and discover my every secret. He would *own* me. He would own the Omega Sanctuary. He would become the true King of Blood Sector.

This was always an inevitability between us. I'd chosen him for this path. But I'd made a fatal error in that choice.

I'd selected him because he hadn't seemed interested in Blood Sector. That had made him less of a threat in my eyes because he clearly had no desire to be King.

However, he'd proved to be the biggest threat of them all.

Because my wolf desired him.

And now that I'd let her off her leash, she was taking me for a ride.

A ride on Kieran's oversized cock.

All Alphas were well-endowed, their size dwarfing everyone around them.

And despite our much smaller frames, Omegas were built to take an Alpha's knot and whatever brutality he wished to dispense.

But seeing Kieran's arousal throbbing in my hand had me second-guessing everything I instinctively knew.

Kieran must have sensed my concern because he reached down to brush his knuckles across my cheek. "You're looking at my cock like you've never seen a knot before."

"I haven't," I admitted, my voice hoarse from, well, *everything*. My heat. My curiosity. My fear. My *need*. "Not this close…" I swallowed, unable to elaborate.

Fortunately, he seemed to understand—I'd never been with an Alpha before. Something I was pretty sure I'd already told him but maybe I'd only stated the obvious: that I hadn't been with one since our betrothal.

Regardless, this was my first time.

With an Alpha, anyway.

I'd experimented with an Omega male a few times when I was younger. Then he'd been happily claimed by a female Alpha from Lunar Sector. And, well, like most Alphas, she didn't like to share.

"Quinnlynn." He grasped my chin, forcing me to stare up at him. "Are you a virgin?"

I shook my head, causing his hand to drop.

"But you've never been with an Alpha." He worded it as a statement, not a question.

Still, I felt the need to say, "Only with another Omega."

His eyebrow arched at that. Probably because he would be able to guess who I meant. Omegas were rare. Male Omegas were even rarer. And I'd grown up with one of the only male Omegas in existence.

"I see." He brushed his knuckles against my jaw again. "Then tell me, little one, do you want a slow introduction? Or would you prefer to be so out of your mind with lust that you don't feel anything other than pleasure?"

He was reminding me of my choice, just phrasing it differently. I could remain in this numbed state and let him ease me into my heat, or I could fall headfirst into the inferno that awaited me.

My focus returned to the hard bundle at the base of his impressive manhood.

That's going to be inside me soon.

But I couldn't possibly understand how.

Will it even fit in my mouth?

My hand barely wrapped around him; he was just so thick and long and *pulsating*. A bead of precum glistened at the tip, distracting me from my thoughts.

Taste him, my wolf demanded. Not necessarily with words, just urges.

Urges I was helpless to ignore.

Because I wanted to taste him, too. I wanted to see if he would fit. I wanted to... to... "Take it slow."

Or maybe that was my wolf just taking control.

But it didn't matter. We were operating as a single unit now, working together rather than against each other.

"Slow it is," Kieran murmured, his deep voice and seductive purr coaxing me into action.

Taste.

Lick.

Suck.

All natural instincts.

All actions I craved.

All desires I could no longer ignore.

I parted my lips and angled his head toward my mouth. *It'll fit*, I decided, suddenly hungrier than I'd ever been before. *It has to fit.*

Because I needed to experience this. *Him. Us.*

The taste of his precum exploded on my tongue, causing me to moan around his cock as I forced him deep into my mouth.

"*Fuck*," Kieran cursed, his fingers suddenly in my hair. But rather than tug me off him, he urged me to take more of him.

I tried and gagged around him, tears springing to my eyes.

He pulled me back until just the tip met my lips.

"You have to relax your throat," he said, his voice low and deep and guttural and sexy and hypnotic to a point where I almost forgot what we were doing.

But then his knot pulsed beneath my hand and more of that precum appeared.

I licked it off him on impulse, making him shudder.

"You're going to fucking kill me, Princess," he said, groaning. "Take me again. But relax. Don't force it. Just do what comes naturally."

He didn't give me a chance to reply, his palm already urging me forward.

"Relax," he repeated. "That's it, little one. Just like that." His head fell back, his muscles seeming to strain beneath me as I took him as far as I could into my mouth. "Now massage my knot with your hand."

I did, and more of that delicious essence seeped from the tip. I sucked it down, swallowing while I still had him in my mouth.

He released a curse in Irish, his accent thickening.

"*Again.*"

It was a command I had no trouble obeying. He rewarded me with more of his salty essence and a feral sound that called to my inner wolf.

She encouraged me to do more.

To slide my lips up and down. To suck. Swallow. Repeat. All while fondling his knot and reveling in the way it pulsed in response to my actions.

"Is this your way of thanking me, darling?" he asked, his Irish lilt more pronounced than I'd ever heard it. "Or are you apologizing?"

His base practically vibrated beneath my touch, his cock leaking precum as though he were already orgasming. But I knew this wasn't his climax. His dark eyes were too shrewd as he lifted his head to stare down at me.

"Or maybe you think this will save you from my knot." His obsidian irises swirled with knowledge. "A distraction, Quinnlynn. A way to delay the inevitable. Is that your goal? Because if that's the case, I'm about to teach you a lesson you'll never forget."

I shivered. *Is that what I'm doing? Trying to distract him from knotting me?*

Perhaps.

But I also just wanted to experience him.

To taste him.

Know him.

Fulfill this desire for my wolf.

She wanted to make him ours, to prove our worth as his mate. So maybe it was a display of gratitude or a way to apologize for everything we'd done.

I wasn't sure.

All I knew was that I needed to make him come. To truly experience his pleasure. To *swallow* his seed. Make him mine intimately.

To mate.

My stomach panged with the notion, my need to drink from him suddenly ravenous.

He's easing me back in, I realized as heat licked at my core. *Letting me feel the delirious notions associated with estrus. Turning me mindless.*

But I didn't care.

I needed this. I needed *him*.

My wolf had felt so rejected. *We* had felt rejected. And while, on some level, I understood that it was what I deserved, I couldn't bear the thought of being turned down by this Alpha. *My* Alpha.

Fuck, I'm a mess.

There's a reason I left.

But right now... right now, all I want... all I want is this.

I stared up at my intended mate and let him see the yearning throbbing inside me. *I'm hungry, Alpha. Feed me. Give me what I need. Please.*

"*Fuck.*" His grip tightened in my hair. "Keep looking at me like that, Quinnlynn. Don't you dare stop."

I had no intention of stopping anything.

I wanted more. No, I needed *more*. And I proceeded to demonstrate that by swallowing him down until I couldn't breathe.

More Irish expletives fell from his lips, his irises smoldering as he held my gaze. "Eyes on me, Princess," he said, a warning in his tone. "I want to watch you while I come down that pretty throat. A century's worth of torment, Quinnlynn. A century's worth of *waiting*."

Those words sounded more like a threat than an admission. He was about to destroy me, drown me in his agony, and I could tell by the way he held my hair that he expected me to swallow.

Good, I thought, staring up at him. *Give it to me.*

Because I wanted it.

I wanted him.

And if we were going to do this, then we were going to do this the right way.

My wolf growled in agreement, the sound touching my chest and rolling off my tongue.

Kieran's nostrils flared, his lips curling into a wicked grin. "You can't top me, little wolf." A growl accompanied his statement, the sound going straight to my abdomen and lighting a fire deep inside. "I'm the Alpha here."

My inner animal practically purred with excitement. *Then give it to me*, she seemed to say. *Stop teasing and let me really taste you.*

Maybe those were my words. My desires. My *needs*.

I couldn't tell. Everything was convoluted and twisted.

Hot. Yet not uncomfortably so.

Because of Kieran.

He was still numbing me and allowing me to be here in the moment.

But what would happen when he finally erupted?

Would his control snap? Would I drown in a whirlpool of lust?

He pulled me back to the tip, his dark eyes holding mine captive. "Deep breath, darling. You're going to need it."

I inhaled through my nose, my wolf practically panting inside me in stark anticipation.

Anticipation that I saw reflected in Kieran's gaze.

"Eyes on me," he said again. "Now squeeze my knot."

My palm obeyed before my mind even comprehended the command.

Then he thrust deep, hitting the back of my throat on a growl that shook me to my very core.

Oh, moons...

My thighs dampened with a gush of slick, my abdomen pulsating with a demand for satisfaction.

Except the seed I desired was flowing down my throat, not into my womb.

I swallowed on instinct, the decadent flavor unlike any I'd ever experienced. *Ambrosia. Alpha essence. Mine.*

My throat worked around his girth, my eyes watering from the intensity and the need to keep watching him. To observe as this powerful male fell apart beneath me.

It energized me. Gave me new meaning for life. Revitalized my spirit.

His grip left my hair, his palm falling to my nape as he growled my name. More slick spilled from my core, my body going up in flames.

But he wasn't done coming.

He was drowning me in his seed, spilling endlessly into my throat.

He hadn't been kidding about me needing air.

I could feel my lungs beginning to burn as I fought to keep swallowing, my eyes wet from the onslaught of tears.

His irises bored into mine, forcing me to maintain our stare.

But I was starting to see spots.

I tried to move back, telling him I needed to breathe, and he pushed in deeper instead, his hand controlling me via my neck.

I grabbed his thighs, my nails biting into his skin.

He caught my wrist and brought my fingers back to his knot. "One more squeeze," he told me.

I wanted to bite him instead. Yet my body behaved as though I were a puppet.

And more of his cum hit my throat.

I swallowed because I had no alternative option.

I swallowed because I *wanted* to.

I swallowed because it made his nostrils flare and his growl rumble louder.

I swallowed because it was Kieran. My mate. My future.

I swallowed because I needed more.

"So fucking good," he whispered, pulling me off him.

The world shifted, my back suddenly hitting the sheets as he positioned himself over me.

I inhaled sharply, my lungs screaming with *need*. It almost hurt to breathe. Or maybe it hurt from being slammed against the mattress.

No, from almost choking to death on his seed, I thought dizzily.

"We'll work on your stamina for breath play," Kieran said against my mouth. "But for our first time, that was very well done, Quinnlynn. Thank you."

He didn't kiss me, something I was almost grateful for, as I was already struggling enough with inhaling and exhaling. Yet some part of my mind registered the loss as his lips moved to my neck and then down to my breasts.

"I've waited an eternity to worship you." His reverent tone drew my gaze down to where he hovered just above my chest, his lips a mere inch from one of my nipples. "Now you're going to learn what it means to be mine."

KIERAN

QUINNLYNN'S TEAR-STREAKED cheeks darkened to a luscious pink shade, her breaths still coming in pants.

I'd tested her limit, wanting to see how far I could push her before she fought back. And my darling little deviant didn't disappoint in the slightest.

Fuck, I was still hard and more than ready to knot her.

But first, I wanted to taste her.

I wanted to trace every damn inch of her with my tongue, torture her with orgasms that weren't climactic enough, and make her beg for my knot.

It would be too easy to release her from my numbing energy. I wanted a challenge. I wanted to dominate. I wanted to *claim*.

Because it was very clear to me that I couldn't properly bite her. Not yet. Not until I knew for sure that she and her wolf were fully healed.

So I would mark her in another way.

Possess her body and soul.

Make her mine in every way that mattered, and maybe then her wolf would be ready.

I closed my lips around her rosy tip, my tongue laving her skin as I held her watery gaze.

My hands skimmed her sides, determined to pet her, know her, *own* her. Just like she'd done with me.

Because that performance with her mouth had been an act of possession.

One she'd more than mastered.

Her ministrations had been unpracticed, confirming everything she'd said about having never been with an Alpha before. I loved being her first.

I wished that she could have been mine.

Alas, I'd helped several Omegas through their heats over time. Not since meeting Quinnlynn, of course, but before her. *Long* before her. During a time when I'd never planned to take a mate. All it took was a pill to keep me sterile during the heat cycle, allowing me to fuck without risking a pregnancy.

But this devious little trickster had changed everything.

One unexpected agreement and all my aspirations had shifted.

The thought of impregnating Quinnlynn very much appealed to me. Not that I would do so during her first heat—I'd already taken my pill to ensure that wouldn't happen—but eventually, yes. I wanted to watch her belly grow with our child. *Our heir.*

And it all came down to a simple cause and effect—this daring female had chosen me.

Then left me.

I switched to her other breast, my teeth skimming her supple flesh and nibbling just enough for her to feel the sting before chasing it away with my tongue.

She moaned, her thighs splaying wider beneath me. "*Kieran.*"

"Oh, darling, I'm only just getting started." I caught

her taut peak between my teeth and pinched it before sucking it deep into my mouth.

Quinnlynn cried out in response, her hands landing on my shoulders. "I... I..."

"You what?" I asked with a grin against her nipple. "Do you need more?"

"Yes," she hissed, arching up into me and soaking my lower half with her arousal.

"Mmm," I hummed. "An invitation." I nipped her rosy little bud once more, then began a path downward to the slickness between her thighs. "An invitation that I accept." I spoke the words directly against her clit.

No point in delaying.

My mate wanted pleasure.

And my wolf wanted to lick her.

My palms went to her thighs to widen her even more, then I gave in to the impulse to *taste*.

She moaned as I drew my tongue along her damp seam, downward to her entrance, and slid inside. My name fell from her swollen lips, her heat slowly overcoming the numbness as I continued to gradually pull back my healing essence.

She wanted slow.

I'd give her slow.

And by the time I was done, she'd be pleading for me to stop while demanding that I knot her at the same time.

It would be a delicious conundrum, one I couldn't wait for us to experience together.

But first, I needed to take the edge off, to give her a little reward for the pleasure she'd bestowed upon me.

It wouldn't take much, her body so primed and ready to explode that all she needed was a small push.

Except I didn't believe in doing anything partway.

With Quinnlynn, I was all in.

Something I showed her by taking her sensitive bud into my mouth and growling at the same time.

She screamed in response, her orgasm immediate. Overwhelming. *Intense.* I could see it in her eyes, in the way her cheeks reddened, in the way her body broke out in a sheen of sweat. And I could *hear* it in her cries of pleasure.

I didn't stop.

I kept suckling. Licking. *Torturing* her clit.

Driving her straight into a second climax that had her shrieking my name.

"Beautiful," I praised in Irish. "So fucking beautiful."

She shuddered violently, one of her hands going to my head. Her fingers wove through my hair as she tried to pull me away from her sensitive flesh.

But I latched on with my teeth, forcing her to accept *more.* Just like she'd requested.

I slid one palm up her leg and drew two fingers through her slick heat. Her thighs clenched around me, a word of protest falling from her lips—a word that ended on a groan as I slipped two fingers into her tight sheath.

"Shh," I hushed her. "You need this."

Because I needed her loose, wet, and ready to take my cock.

If I took her now, it would hurt her. And that was unacceptable. She wanted to be eased into this, and that was exactly what we were doing.

I laved her thoroughly while releasing another strand of my power, lulling her back into her estrus with expert strokes of my tongue.

She vibrated beneath me, her body shaking from the onslaught of pleasure and the intensity of her heat. "Are you burning, baby?" I asked softly, my words a hum against her damp flesh.

"*Yes,*" she hissed as her legs tensed again, another climax rolling through her in a violent wave.

I grinned, my purr long replaced by a steady growl meant to coax my intended into a mating frenzy. By the time we were through, she would regret having left me in the beginning. We could have been doing this for a century.

Instead, I had to take out over a hundred years of lust on her now.

Thank fuck she's in heat, I thought. Because the things I wanted to do to her couldn't be done outside of a normal cycle.

Well, they could be done.

The activities would just exhaust her more.

At least she could keep up during her estrus. Hell, it would be on *me* to keep up with *her.*

A challenge I happily accepted.

For however long it lasts, I thought as I added a third finger. Quinnlynn had once told me her typical heat lasted thirty days. But there was nothing typical about this cycle. It was a forced estrus after decades of denying her body's instincts.

It could end tomorrow.

It could end six months from now.

That was another reason why claiming her was risky. *What if it caused her to disassociate again?* The question rolled through my thoughts, the lack of a clear answer making me pull back from my desire to bite her.

I'll convince her to stay with me by giving her an experience she won't soon forget.

I'll make her choose me.

And I'll keep her leashed until I'm certain she won't try to run again.

"*Kieran.*" My name resembled a curse as her fingers yanked on my hair. "I can't. I can't... Stop. No more."

I smiled against her pulsing nub. "One more," I told her.

"*I can't.*"

"Trust me, darling. You *can.*" Which I proved to her with my fingers and tongue, all the while ignoring the burn against my scalp as she pulled on my hair.

It took a little coaxing.

And a lot of growling.

But I sent her spiraling into yet another climax that left her panting and crying and *begging* me to stop.

"*Knot,*" she breathed. "I... I can't... I need... *Fuck,* Kieran. I hate you." She shook her head, her eyes closed as she fought her desire-induced state. "No, I... I want you. But... but I hate... *Kieran.*"

My growl overwhelmed her complaints, my energy unwinding from her being while leaving a few tendrils behind to keep her grounded.

"Please," she begged. "Please, Alpha. *Knot me.*"

I pressed a kiss to her throbbing cunt, earning me a scream in protest and a moan of unadulterated desire. The perfect combination. "You're stunning," I murmured. "My perfect little deviant."

My fingers left her tight sheath, causing her to groan in disappointment.

I silenced her by bringing the digits to her mouth. "Suck, Quinnlynn," I murmured as I crawled up her flushed form. "Let me feel your tongue."

She eagerly complied, her mind and body almost entirely lost to the need humming through her veins. That sense of cognitive loss was why Omegas had to be protected in this state. They became consumed with the need to fuck, their sole purpose becoming a desire to *mate.*

Some Alphas went into a rut in response, unable to control the urge to satisfy the female, their need to breed too strong. I could feel the pull at my conscience, demanding I follow that path and fuck my Omega until both of us were too satiated to move.

But I forced the inclination down.

This was about her.

About taking care of my Quinnlynn.

My intended.

I settled my hips against her, pressing my knot right along her hot center. She arched into me, her legs wrapping around me in immediate welcome.

Until the head of my cock kissed her clit.

A harsh sound left her throat, the vocal reaction trembling around my fingers in her mouth.

"Sensitive?" I asked, rubbing against her.

Her thick eyelashes fluttered to reveal twin pools of liquid black around her pupils. She appeared to be at one with her wolf—*for now*—the pair of them furious and undeniably turned on at the same time.

I stroked myself against her once more, loving the way she both growled and moaned in tandem.

"Sensitive and ready," I clarified, no longer asking, but telling her how she was feeling. Because I could see it in her expression, could *sense* it against my groin.

So wet. So swollen. So perfect. So mine.

"You're going to cry," I warned her, aware of how intense the knotting experience would be for her. "And then you're going to tell me to never stop."

Her expression cleared just enough to convey that she understood my words.

That was why I continued to feed her a few final strands of healing energy, my desire to have her somewhat aware for our first time a driving need to keep her stable.

I pulled my fingers out of her mouth and palmed her cheek. "Don't close your eyes," I told her. "I want to see your every reaction to taking my knot. Understand?" It was another way to keep her grounded, to ensure she remembered this moment.

She shuddered, her nostrils flaring as she pressed up against me in wanton demand.

"Tell me to fuck you, little one," I said softly. "I want to hear you ask for it." She'd technically already said it, but after everything I'd gone through in pursuing this little trickster, I wanted to hear her say it again. To hear the eagerness in her tone. The demand. The *need*.

Because she was mine.

I had her now.

Beneath me.

Wet against my cock.

Writhing with a need for *my* knot.

"Kieran." She swallowed, her fingers still locked in my hair. "I... I... *please.*"

"That's not telling me to fuck you, Quinnlynn. I want to hear the words." I nuzzled her nose before skimming her cheek with my mouth on my way to her ear. "I want to hear you *beg.*"

A violent quake settled through her, the tremble seeming to erupt from her slick center. It kissed every part of me, making me want to drive into her and take her to oblivion.

But not until she admitted her need again.

Not until I heard the words from her beautiful lips.

"Say it," I encouraged her. "Say it and I'll reward you with my knot."

Her grip tightened again in my hair, her opposite palm going to my shoulder and then to my back, where she dug her nails into my skin. *That* was her wolf, demanding she make me bleed for prolonging their torment.

"Mmm, good little wolf," I murmured. "Now tell me what you want."

"Your knot," she said, arching into me. "*I want... your... knot.*"

I pressed an open-mouthed kiss to her thundering pulse. "What do you want me to do with my knot, little one? Do you want to milk it with your mouth and fingers again?"

"*Kieran.*"

"Tell me," I demanded. "Admit what you want, and I'll give it to you."

She growled, the stubborn female showing me her claws and teeth. *Literally.* Because she sank her nails into my back again as her teeth bit into my shoulder.

A purr escaped me at the beautiful claim, her wolf clearly at the helm of this embrace.

But it was Quinnlynn who snarled.

Quinnlynn who pulled back with my blood on her lips.

Quinnlynn who looked me in the eyes and said, "Fuck me, Kieran."

I replied with my hips instead of my mouth, my cock finding her entrance and sliding home in one harsh thrust.

She bowed off the bed with a scream that went straight to my groin, exciting my rutting instinct. But I paused inside her, wanting to give her a moment to acclimate.

Another one of those violent trembles vibrated along her skin, and her tight cunt squeezed the life out of my shaft. The instinct to bury my head against her neck overwhelmed me, but I refused to break eye contact. Especially since I'd told her to maintain it—something she seemed to be doing instinctually after I'd broken it to whisper in her ear.

Her cheeks reddened.

Her lips parted.

Her pupils dilated fully.

And her breaths came in pants again.

But I caught the moment when she started to relax, the moment her shock transformed into rapture. She gave a tentative little shift, then moaned at the sensation below.

"Hold on to me," I told her. "And don't stop staring up at me. I want to watch you fall apart. I want to remember this moment before oblivion captures you. Before your heat becomes all-consuming insanity."

She sank her nails into my skin again, a note of challenge in her gaze. "Knot me."

My lips curled. "With pleasure."

QUINN

Kieran's dark gaze held me captive as he began to move, his body mastering mine with a skillful twist of his hips that left me dizzy and inconsolable.

I was on fire.

Burning.

Dying.

Needing his knot.

But he appeared to be hell-bent on making this devastating oblivion last. And I couldn't truly hate him for it, not when each stroke of his thick cock heightened the intensity.

He grabbed my hip, angling me to a position that allowed him to go even deeper. I moaned, the pleasure-pain driving my need for him that made me burn even hotter.

His name left my lips, my vision darkening from the onslaught of sensations.

"Eyes open," he reminded me, the command underscoring his tone causing me to clench tightly around him.

This male was all Alpha.

All wolf.

All feral shifter goodness in an exquisitely handsome package.

Fuck, I was losing my mind.

Yet some part of me held on, remaining present for each thrust, feeling every inch of Kieran's power, experiencing the overabundance of lust flourishing to life between us.

His gaze locked on mine, his hunger a stark force of nature that touched my very soul. I could almost taste his craving for me, his dark need to *claim*.

This was the male who had remained faithful to our bond for over a hundred years.

The male who had chased me across the globe.

The male who had finally caught me and tethered me to his essence.

Yet he made no move to bite me. No move to even kiss me. He merely fucked me with deep, powerful flexes of his hips.

When are you going to bite me? I wanted to ask him. *When are you going to claim me?*

Only, the words were never given a chance to leave my lips because, in the next moment, he did something with his lower half that had me seeing stars.

A subtle twist.

A purposeful move.

A sharp sensation.

Right against my clit.

"*Kieran.*" His name left me on a growl, or perhaps a snarl.

And he responded in kind, only his rumble utterly destroyed me. It stirred a pulsating maelstrom in my belly that refused to abate, the desire clawing at my consciousness and demanding that he finish this. Finish me. "*Please.*"

I wasn't even sure what I wanted. His knot? His teeth? His kiss? His tongue? His hands? His everything?

He hushed me.

Which resulted in my wolf springing forward to protest.

But another growl from the Alpha had me whimpering beneath him and melting into an incoherent version of myself.

I wanted to weep.

Scream.

And moan.

All at the same time.

Instead, a flurry of words left me that didn't make sense. Something about Kieran. His knot. Need. *More.*

"I've got you, Quinnlynn," he vowed, his palm going to my throat and giving it a little squeeze while his opposite hand remained against my hip. "Now keep looking at me. That's a good girl. Just like that, little one."

My veins resembled liquid fire, the source of it seeming to come from my core. Every punishing twist of his hips only worsened the flame, stirring an inferno deep inside that made it difficult to breathe.

I'm dying, I realized. *He's killing me with his fucking knot.*

"Shh," he hushed. "Stay with me, Princess. Eyes up."

I wanted to glower at him, but I couldn't. I was too busy moaning and throbbing and pressing up against him and *begging him to anchor me.*

My whole being resembled a blazing mess of nerves, nerves that were going to explode if he didn't complete me. *Bite me. Knot me. Make me whole.*

His hand squeezed, drawing me back to him. I couldn't breathe. He'd cut off my airflow. I parted my lips to tell him, but the cruelty in his gaze told me he knew exactly what he'd done.

No. Not cruelty.

Passion.

But with him, it was one and the same. A dark mix of intrinsic sadism coupled with incredible intelligence and underscored with alpha aggression.

My mate.

No. My intended.

I felt dizzy all over again, lost to his punishing thrusts, his feral need, his *rutting* instincts.

Oh, but those *eyes.* They were like obsidian diamonds, glittering with intent and holding me captive. *Stay with me. Stay in the present. Enjoy this.* His voice was loud in my head. Or perhaps he'd spoken out loud. I couldn't really hear anything beneath the primal growls of my wolf. His wolf. *Our* wolves.

A tribal dance.

A mating founded on an ancient embrace.

Our souls commingling, our animals dancing, our bodies *joining.*

Except he was still staring down at me. Not biting me. I shook my head to clear it, confused, only to be dragged back under his intoxicating presence with a low growl that had my vision darkening once more.

He didn't demand my eyes again.

Maybe because I hadn't closed them.

Maybe because I was too far gone to hear him.

But a spasm in my lower belly drew me right back to our embrace, his low rumble of approval ripping through me and demolishing the thick fog threatening to take over my being.

His dark gaze ensnared me, forcing me to see his

pleasure as his knot erupted from the base and secured our bodies together in blissful agony.

My lips parted, the scream refusing to leave me. Not because he was still strangling me, but because I no longer knew how to make sound. It was too intense. Too passionate. Too *incredible* to process.

All I knew was weightlessness.

Sensitivity.

Quaking.

Insanity.

My clit pulsated, the sensitive part of me still sore and abused from his earlier ministrations yet thriving with a euphoric throb I couldn't ignore.

It forced an animalistic sound from my chest, reminding me of a groan mingled with a cry for leniency. Because it was too much. Yet not enough.

I needed more.

I wanted to milk his cock with everything I owned.

Take him inside me. Claim him. Make him *my Alpha.*

I raked my nails down his back, my instinct to bite him hitting me hard in the chest.

So I leaned forward and sank my canines into his throat. He growled and my wolf cheered. *Swallow. Satisfy. Mate.*

The last vestiges of reality seemed to fade into the fringes of my mind, the world spiraling into the depths of depravity.

I needed to be fucked.

Knotted.

Over and over again.

To taste his cum. Lick him clean. Possess him with my mouth. *Drink his blood.*

I scratched at him again, demanding more.

Because something was missing. I couldn't define it. I

wasn't even sure it was a real need. My body was a mess of nerves and desires and pent-up lust.

My wolf leapt forward, driving my actions, her yearnings more feral than my own.

Yes, yes, I thought as we bit Kieran again. This time it was on his pec. We were on top, riding him, taking what we wanted from him. He stared up at me with amusement in his gaze, his dark eyes still glittering.

I wasn't sure how I'd ended up in this position or when I'd started this game, but I liked it. I liked having my teeth in his chest, tasting his blood on my tongue.

Except, in the next blink, I was under him again with a bottle of water pressed against my lips.

I'm losing time, I realized as I swallowed hungrily. He'd done something to the water. Flavored it somehow. And I wanted more. So. Much. More.

I closed my eyes and swallowed, swallowed, swallowed.

And opened them to find his cock in my mouth, my hands around his knot.

More time lost, I thought, delirious.

I was exhausted yet invigorated.

And I couldn't ignore that inkling that something was missing. I wanted to ask, but I was too busy imbibing his essence to speak. *Moons, he tastes so good. Like Alpha. My Alpha. My wolf. My chosen male.*

Dangerous words.

But I couldn't ignore them, not while beneath him. *Wait...* I'd moved again. I was on all fours, my nails scratching at his bedding as he fucked me from behind. Noises I barely recognized left my lips, my wolf still running the show and demanding more with harsh little growls.

Growls that Kieran intensified, his snarl reminding my wolf who was in charge here.

Him.

Alpha.

Kieran.

Mate.

But not… I shook my head again and stirred in a pile of pillows, blinking. *What…?*

The sun was up, the golden rays bathing Kieran's room in warm tones. His lips were against my neck, his cock inside me from behind, moving slowly, keeping me sated, while we rested in this position of intimacy and safety.

I sighed, my rump pressing back against him in a request for more.

He moved inside me in long, languid strokes, his teeth grazing my neck on his way up to my ear. "You're starting to come out of your heat," he whispered. "I can feel it."

I shivered, the sensation of wrongness still stirring within me. *Too soon,* I thought. *It's ending too soon.*

"Yes," he said. "It's only been a few days."

Did I say that out loud? I wondered.

"You did," he kissed my throat again, his cock still sliding in and out of me in that slow, measured way. Goose bumps pebbled up and down my arms, his motions stirring heat in my lower abdomen—a heat that spread through my being until I felt like I was burning from the inside out.

But he didn't pick up the pace.

He maintained his unhurried movements instead, gliding all the way to the hilt before pulling out to the tip. I had one leg draped back over his hip, keeping me fully exposed.

"Touch your clit," he told me. "Make yourself come on my cock."

My hand moved as though pulled by a string, my fingers finding my bundle of nerves and stroking me to completion in a matter of minutes.

"Again," he demanded as my body still shook from the aftermath of my explosion.

I whimpered in response but did as he demanded, my body bowing back into him as my too-sensitive nub protested my motions.

But it only took a few strokes for the heat to reignite, my estrus still lingering heavily inside me.

"It's only been a few days." His words echoed in my mind. *How is that possible?* My cycle was usually thirty days long.

And... and I'd been out of it... for eight, right?

Oh... My legs tensed as my pleasure surfaced once more, my body igniting in a ripple of ecstasy that forced Kieran to follow, his knot lodging deep inside me and pulsating as he bathed my insides with his seed.

Yes, yes, I panted. *My Alpha. Inside me. Scorching me. Fucking me.*

I closed my eyes to revel in the euphoria, only to open them again to find the night sky staring back at me. And an empty space behind me.

A *cold* empty space.

Frowning, I rolled to my back and reached for the other pillow. The silky fabric chilled my fingertips, confirming that Kieran had left some time ago.

But his scent still lingered all around me.

Because this is his room.

The evidence of our fuck-fest saturated the sheets as well, making my brow furrow. *This still doesn't feel right.*

It also didn't smell right.

What's missing?

I pressed a palm to my belly, immediately aware of my non-pregnant state. Omegas instinctively knew when they were with child, and thanks to Kieran's healing abilities, I was even more in tune with my body.

Is that what's missing?

I ran my thumb along my flat abdomen, my eyes on the ceiling.

No. That's not it.

I didn't want a child yet. It was something else. Something important.

My wolf paced inside me, her agitation making all the hairs along my arms stand—

"Ah, you're awake," Kieran murmured as he materialized by the bed with a tray in his hands. "Just in time to eat something."

My nose twitched at the savory scent of fresh meat.

But that sense of wrongness only grew.

I couldn't shake it.

Not even when presented with a plate of salted salmon and cheese. Kieran set it down beside me, then handed me a bottle of water. "Drink that."

I sat up and moved back against the headboard, my body aching with the movements.

Kieran eyed me carefully. "Sore?"

I nodded, then winced as I realized just how sore I was. I seemed to be lost in this afterglow state where my mind processed things slowly.

Maybe that's why I feel wrong, I thought while drinking the water. *I'm just struggling to process.*

The last few days—weeks?—were a blur.

I remembered coming together with my wolf after living in unspeakable agony.

I remembered why Kieran had done that—to force my animal and me to rejoin.

I remembered him torturing me with his mouth… after I swallowed, like, a gallon of his cum. *Fuck.*

And I remembered him fucking me.

Repeatedly.

But not necessarily all the details.

I rubbed my forehead with my free hand, then tried to drink more water. It tasted different from the last bottle I recalled imbibing.

I pulled the bottle back to read the label, confused.

"What's wrong?" Kieran asked.

"Tastes different," I admitted, my voice gravelly. *Moons, it feels like I ate a bucket of rocks.*

"Because it's just water. The other bottle had my cum mixed into it," Kieran said, startling me.

"Oh." My cheeks warmed at the memory of how fast I'd finished that bottle.

His lips merely curled in response, obviously amused by my antics.

I'd been in heat.

Hell, I still felt like I was on the vestiges of that heat because just looking at Kieran made me want to mount him again, to finish what we'd started, to make him—

Wait... My eyes widened. *That's what feels wrong.* "You didn't bite me." *What the hell?* "You didn't *mate* me." The words were followed by a growl from my wolf, her irritation overwhelming and *loud*.

That was why she felt so unsettled. Why nothing smelled right. Why I hadn't nested—something I just now realized. Why nothing seemed right.

"Why?" I demanded, no longer hungry. "Why didn't you mate me?"

Except...

Except I already knew why.

It was such an obvious answer.

"To punish me," I breathed. "You... you promised not to punish me with my heat yet decided to punish me by not completing the mating?"

My voice was shrill, my mind spinning with a thousand questions and accusations at once.

Nothing made sense.

Some part of me tried to speak up, to remind me of something important, but my wolf's chaos overwhelmed my ability to process anything other than *anger*. And betrayal. And *hurt*.

"How could you?" I demanded, tears rushing to my eyes. "Did I not *beg* enough for you?"

"Quinnlynn—"

"No. I get it. You helped me through my heat. Got your knotting fix in. And now it's time to punish me by truly rejecting me." Because I'd run away. Because I'd betrayed him.

Now he wanted me to know what it felt like to be on the receiving end of a rejection.

He'd used me for my heat just like I'd used him for the power in his blood.

Only, I'd used his power for good.

While he'd only used me for a good fuck.

He'd played with my body and my emotions and *my wolf* just to satisfy his own needs. That wasn't the same as what I'd done. I'd sacrificed everything for a greater cause. I'd given up my own chance at happiness to save others. I'd fulfilled my obligations to the crown.

While all he'd done was fuck me.

Use me.

Knot me.

To punish me.

Which meant he'd lied to me. He'd said he would never punish me during my heat. But not claiming me was a punishment, one that damaged my very soul.

My wolf whimpered inside, feeling lost without his claim.

And that only made me angrier. It made my blood boil so fiercely that I couldn't even hear what he was saying right now. Because the whooshing in my ears was too loud. My heart hammered like a broken drum in my chest, the thuds uneven and pained.

This punishment is wrong.

Everything about this connection is wrong.

My heat is tainted. Ruined. No longer safe.

I hate him.

How could he do this to me? To my wolf? Does he really think I deserve this agony?

My stomach cramped, the residual pang a result of my waning heat. I wasn't even technically done yet, just coherent enough to understand the *wrongness*.

He rejected us. Again.

Before, he'd claimed that it was to help me heal.

But it seemed that had all been for the benefit of making me whole just to fucking break me. Which I'd suspected had been his goal all along.

I won't let him win.

He can't—

"*Quinnlynn*," he snapped, his angry tone breaking through the fog in my mind. But I didn't want to *hear* him. I wanted nothing to do with him!

I threw the empty bottle at him. "Get out!"

His eyebrows flew upward, his dark eyes widening. "Excuse me?"

"Get out!" I repeated, enraged now. "Leave me alone! I *hate* you!"

Some part of me tried to rein in the anger, to force me to see reason.

But my animal was weeping, sad and alone and shattered over our mate's rejection. And I had to protect her. To *avenge* her. I'd hidden from her for too long. I wouldn't do it again.

Kieran huffed a laugh, the sound lacking humor, but it made me see red regardless of the intent.

I screamed, the sound one of agony and fury, and I lunged at him, claws ready.

Only to be shoved back down onto the bed with a growl from the now infuriated Alpha. "*Calm. Down.*"

"Fuck you!" I felt manic, my grasp on reality seeming to slip as my wolf demanded retribution in the form of blood.

He wronged us.

He berated us.

He rejected us.

The words repeated over and over again, drowning out his voice until all I heard was his growl.

Ferocious. Commanding. *Cruel.*

I whimpered, the anger in that sound forcing me to submit despite my own vivacious fury.

I hate him. I want to end him. I want to—

"I didn't claim you because I didn't want to risk you disassociating from your wolf again," he said, his tone exasperated yet *loud*.

His words stilted my thoughts.

Made me blink.

Silenced everything except for his voice.

It was as though he'd hit me with a bucket of ice, the impact cooling my ire and freezing me in place. *Wh-what?*

"But you're welcome for seeing you through this hell, *Omega*," he added before abruptly releasing me. "*Fuck.*"

He took several steps back, his hand in his hair as he glared back at me.

Then he shook his head as a string of words in his ancient tongue fell into the air, the language one I didn't understand. Yet it drove home how old this Alpha was, just like the billowing energy around him confirmed his abundance of power.

"Kieran…"

He held up a hand to silence me.

Then he disappeared into the shadows.

Leaving me alone in his room with only the plate of food by my side.

KIERAN

"I HATE YOU."

Those three words rioted in my mind, agitating my wolf.

Disrespectful little brat, I growled to myself.

While I understood that she was still a bit sensitive from the final stages of her heat, I couldn't shake my irritation.

She'd done nothing but disrespect me throughout our entire courtship. First by running away. Then by questioning my every motive. And now by being angry with me for not claiming her after she'd made it perfectly clear through her actions that she hadn't wanted to mate me to begin with.

Well, maybe I didn't want to mate her either now.

A lie.

One I felt to my very soul.

But it didn't make me any less infuriated by her behavior.

I'd been trying to *help* her. Yet she'd accused me of *rejecting* her.

As though I hadn't wanted to bite her.

Fuck, it'd taken enormous strength not to claim her these last twelve days. I wanted to access her mind, to know her secrets, to ascertain her true feelings.

Yet if all I was going to hear from her were words about *hate*, then maybe I didn't want that access after all.

I ran my fingers through my hair and gripped the strands. I'd shadowed from the room before I said something I'd regret later.

My wolf needed freedom.

A moment to growl away from his intended.

Some fresh air.

Perhaps even a run.

I pulled off my shirt and let it fall to the ground, not caring at all about where it landed. My wolf panted in agreement, ready to be set free, to sprint through the underbrush and forget all the weight on my shoulders.

Just for five minutes.

Sire. Cillian's telepathic call interrupted my movements, making my hand pause on my belt.

"Apparently, I can't even have five fucking seconds," I muttered. *Yes?* He wouldn't bother me unless he needed something important.

Omega Riley has requested a phone call when you're able. I believe she wishes to provide an update.

I'll call her after my run, I replied, my hands resuming their disrobing mission.

There's more, Cillian murmured, making me stop again.

Yes?

Word has spread regarding Quinnlynn's return. Several of the Alpha Princes are demanding proof of claim.

I growled, that term—*claim*—the source of my agitation.

Prince Cael has temporarily calmed the masses by stating that he's sure you plan to reschedule the official coronation soon.

How kind of him, I muttered, my hands fisting and falling to my sides.

This was all inevitable.

Quinnlynn had disappeared shortly before our formally announced coronation ball. It'd been the perfect time, as the sector had been thrown into chaos to prepare for the massive event.

And she'd used that distraction to slip through the barrier unnoticed.

Or I assumed that was how she'd done it, anyway.

Not this time, I thought at her, my mind automatically tugging on her leash. *You might be a brat, but you're my brat.*

Sire? Cillian prompted, likely overhearing my mental commentary.

Rather than acknowledge it, I merely said, *I loathe politics, Cillian.*

My head fell backward to take in the night sky, the northern lights bright and colorful overhead.

Despite the beautiful sight, I sighed.

I'd never desired this life.

I did it all for *her*—the female who *hated* me right now. The one who'd fled without a backward glance, leaving me to run her fucking sector alone for a hundred years. The female who had engaged in a game of chase across the sectors for reasons unknown.

Fuck.

Without her tempting little offer, I'd still be prince of my own sector. Content on my idle throne. At peace with my chosen path.

Or that was what I'd like to think, anyway.

But the truth was that she'd walked into my life with an offer I couldn't refuse—unlimited power and a tight little Omega pussy to fuck for the rest of my life.

An opportunity to create an heir. My heir.

How could I deny such an intriguing opportunity?

But with that opportunity came responsibility.

Leadership was one of my natural traits. I didn't actually mind protecting Blood Sector or the wolves and humans within my boundaries.

However, Blood Sector was so much more than just a territory. It was the heart of V-Clan kind. The king of all the sectors.

And that required me to play political games to keep all the other princes satisfied.

One wrong step and they'd try to take my destined throne. *And my female along with it.*

The battle for this kingdom and the right to knot the blood dynasty's heiress might have paused when Quinnlynn had chosen me, but it was still very much alive.

I'd thwarted several attempts on my life over the years, more than proving my worth for the title of King.

But if my betrothed didn't announce that to all the princes in a formal venue—during our coronation ceremony—I would never truly be respected as a monarch.

Her fleeing all those years ago had undermined my power and position.

What Alpha Prince loses such a prized jewel?

How could I, Prince Kieran O'Callaghan, let this happen?

I'd entertained numerous accusations and comments, indulged in hundreds of conversations, and allowed several insults to roll off my back.

Because I'd considered Quinnlynn's behavior to be a challenge. One meant to test my strength as an Alpha.

It'd also been a betrayal, but I didn't let the others see that. I'd told them all it was a game—a game I'd finally won.

And now they wanted to see my prize. My *Queen*.

Which meant Cael was right—I had to move forward

with the coronation ceremony. Blood Sector had gone without a proper Queen and King for too long. It was time for Quinnlynn and me to take our place on the throne. *Together.*

If I may, I have a suggestion, Cillian said softly, his tone polite as always.

I bent to grab my shirt from the ground and pulled it back on, my plans for a run obviously canceled. *Where are you?* I asked him, temporarily ignoring his comment.

In Lorcan's den reviewing some messages, Sire.

Rather than reply, I shadowed to the location in question and peered at the screens over my cousin's dark head. Lorcan had a penchant for technology, which I found entertaining.

As my closest living blood relative, he was exceptionally powerful—an Elite who should actually consider being a Sector Prince. But he'd always preferred his enforcer-type role over leadership.

I studied the images he appeared to be reviewing, noting the communications between Alpha Lykos and Alpha Cael.

"Those don't appear to be addressed to me," I said, slightly amused. "You wouldn't be spying on our neighbors, now would you, cousin?"

Lorcan grunted, the man notoriously silent. While he looked a great deal like me with his dark features, tan skin, and similar height and build, our personalities were quite opposite.

Which was what made me a better leader and him an excellent Elite.

Cillian, however, was the most diplomatic of our trio. We weren't related, but we had grown up together. Which made him family in his own right. He also had darker features, so he could easily pass as a relative.

But blood didn't matter as much as honor and respect, something Cillian had demonstrated countless times.

"It seems Cael and Lykos have decided to open trading between their territories," Cillian said conversationally. "We're simply doing our job by overseeing the agreement, making sure it's fair to the other sectors and all that."

"Hmm," I hummed, fully aware of the real reason they were sifting through their messages—they wanted to see what kind of alliance the two princes were forming.

Alliances could be dangerous when created to pursue a common enemy.

And in this case, *I* could be that enemy.

There were several princes who didn't feel I was worthy of this position. Most hadn't done anything more than send a few assassins my way. But Quinnlynn's return changed things.

I had no doubt my competition had searched for her over the century, hoping to be the prince to take her home and change her mind about mating me—either by persuading her gently or forcing her to accept fate.

While most of my kind valued consent, there were those who didn't.

Which was what had made our bond so tenuous—the potential for another Alpha to break the betrothal with his knot.

That had concerned me from the moment I'd learned of her disappearance, initially because I'd thought someone had kidnapped her.

And when I'd realized she'd left of her own accord, I'd worried that another Alpha might find her first.

At least until she'd proved too difficult for me to catch her.

That was when it'd become clear that the others wouldn't stand a chance in pursuing her. My little trickster was too clever for us all, a devious Omega with the ability to hide better than anyone else I'd ever met.

It had all been a serious risk—hence the need for her punishment—but I'd always firmly believed that high risk yielded great rewards.

Quinnlynn had already validated that opinion, and I'd only just begun tasting my reward over the last few days.

But the game was done now. She wouldn't run again, or the consequences would be severe for her.

Because I wouldn't let her make me look like a fool twice.

Once, I'd been able to explain away as an Omega testing her mate. Not that everyone had believed me. But I just hadn't entertained alternatives to that reasoning.

However, a second time would indicate a deeper issue. And that wouldn't be as easily explained. Nor would it be tolerated.

Fuck, most Alphas wouldn't have allowed or accepted it the first time.

But I wasn't most Alphas, something my unruly mate should appreciate a hell of a lot more than she seemed to.

"Do you want to read the messages from the other Sector Princes?" Cillian asked.

"No need. I know what they all say—they want to see Princess Quinnlynn." I met his dark gaze. "Cael is right. We need to plan a new coronation ball. But you mentioned having a suggestion?"

He nodded. "Yes. I recommend hosting another betrothal dinner."

I arched a brow. "Oh?" I'd already planned to host one, but my reasons likely differed from those of my second-in-command. Which made me curious as to his thought process and what had led him to voice this suggestion.

"It will help unite the sector prior to the visitors arriving."

"Are you suggesting that they're not united at present?" I asked, wondering about his take on the general mood of my wolves. I'd tuned most of them out over the last few weeks while dealing with Quinnlynn. Perhaps that had been a mistake.

"On the contrary, their loyalty to you has never been stronger." He gestured to the screens. "There isn't any chatter of Quinnlynn's heat. As far as all the Alpha Princes are concerned, you and your bride-to-be have been busy reacquainting yourselves."

Reacquainting, I thought with a snort. *Leave it to you, Cillian, to give fucking such a formal name.*

He didn't reply or acknowledge my mental comment, but I knew he'd heard it.

"Only a handful of wolves were nearby when Quinnlynn's estrus began, but the scent traveled. Yet there hasn't been a single mention of Quinnlynn's state."

"Meaning none of my wolves betrayed our privacy," I translated, nodding. "Yet you still feel a formal event is needed?"

"Yes. Because it's their due, Sire. They need to see their future Queen." He paused, his expression telling me he wanted to add to that statement.

"Don't hold back on my account, Cillian. Tell me what you think."

"The sector is *owed*, Sire. She needs to face her people to regain their trust."

I smiled, but the amusement didn't reach my heart. If anything, it was just a reflex.

But Cillian's words told me we were on the same page, as per usual.

I dipped my chin, acknowledging his wisdom, and

added, "Respect is earned." I knew that better than anyone. "My intended has a lot of work ahead of her."

Which I didn't think she understood yet.

But she would.

Poor Quinnlynn thought I meant to punish her by withholding pleasure and denying her my bite.

Alas, her punishment would be far more severe.

And while I might help orchestrate it, I wouldn't be the one delivering it.

"Please announce to the sector that we will be hosting a betrothal feast in seven days. That should give our darling princess enough time to recover."

"Will you be hosting in the new entertainment venue?"

"I think that would be appropriate," I replied. "It will give her an idea of the upgrades we've made. Perhaps she'll appreciate them."

Although, I doubted it, considering she hadn't shown much appreciation for anything I'd done. Perhaps she would approve of the name—The MacNamara.

Her family history was etched into the glass walls, the words ones that had been drafted by Blood Sector wolves. Most were cherished memories of her parents, making the building a memorial of sorts.

But her name didn't appear very often.

Perhaps discovering that detail would make her realize the impact her disappearance had had on her people.

Another form of punishment, one that might seem cruel. However, she needed to understand the results of her actions. And it was up to her people to demonstrate the pain inspired by her abandonment.

Cillian held my gaze for a long moment, his mind likely analyzing thoughts similar to my own. "I'll announce the betrothal feast, Sire. I'll also arrange for a dressmaker, as I imagine Quinnlynn will require a gown."

I considered that for a beat. "No. Don't arrange for it. I'll ask Ivana to help her." Because it would serve as another lesson, one Cillian immediately recognized, because his eyebrow lifted.

Or perhaps it was the mention of the petite white-haired Omega that piqued his interest.

"Do you think that's wise?" he asked, his voice holding a note of caution.

"I wouldn't suggest it if I didn't," I replied.

His expression told me he wasn't sure, but he didn't push it.

"I'll have a word with Ivana before I tell Quinnlynn," I added. "Unless you'd like to do it?"

Darkness settled across his features, his jaw ticking at my suggestion. His silence spoke volumes.

I arched a brow. "No?" He remained silent, his refusal loud and clear. *Coward.* "All right, then I'll ask her."

He stared at me for a long moment before changing the subject with, "What about the coronation ceremony?"

One of these days, we're going to discuss Ivana, I thought at him.

Not today, Kieran, he replied flatly.

Kieran, not Sire, I mused. *Touchy.*

He merely narrowed his gaze.

Goading my oldest friend was always entertaining, but I needed him on my side right now. So rather than tease him further, I focused on his coronation question. "Let's set a tentative date for three weeks from now. Add a note that it's pending Quinnlynn's availability. Make it suggestive."

"Suggestive, Sire?"

And just like that, I was *Sire* again.

Cillian never remained angry for long.

Unless I really pushed him.

But he was right—today was not the day for that.

"Yes, suggestive," I said, replying to his clarification inquiry. "Quinnlynn didn't experience a proper estrus." Something that was rather obvious since I was standing in Lorcan's den instead of actively knotting my Omega

He dipped his chin in understanding. "It was short."

"Which is why she'll likely go into heat again," I added, the words a warning more so than a promise. "So imply that her cycle is forthcoming."

Cillian studied me, his dark eyes thoughtful. "Shall I make it suggestive in that your *reacquaintance* is creating some irregularities?"

V-Clan Omegas only went into heat once a year, so I understood his clarification—he wanted to make the reasoning believable.

Because this wasn't a typical cycle period for our kind.

Estrus typically occurred during the summer months, giving us cause to hibernate during the longest days of light.

"Don't explain it," I replied. "Let them think what they want."

"Of course, Sire."

"At a minimum, this will give us an excuse to postpone the ceremony, should we need it," I added, explaining my logic in case it wasn't obvious.

The flare of his pupils told me how he felt about the potential for postponing again. Because there was only one other reason for that to happen besides Quinnlynn going into heat, and that reason was her potential disappearance. *Again.*

Fortunately for us all, I had no intention of allowing that to happen. I'd learned my lesson. It was time for my mate to learn hers.

"It will also allow us to monitor the chatter," Cillian

said after a beat. "We made a list of those who witnessed the scene, but as I said, the scent carried."

I nodded. "Who is on the monitoring list?" I wondered aloud. "Who saw Quinnlynn go into heat?" I'd been so focused on her that I hadn't bothered to identify the approaching scents.

Cillian listed seven wolves.

Only one stood out. "Myon was in the city?" Or near it, anyway. Near enough to be running on the outskirts of Reykjavik. "How long has he been back?"

He was an Alpha who used to guard Quinnlynn's family. I hadn't welcomed him—or any of the others—into my Elite guard because I didn't know them. Nor did I trust them.

Had Quinnlynn remained, she might have kept a few on for herself.

Which meant there might be some anger or disappointment because of her actions.

And considering Myon had been the head of the guard, he would be the most bitter. He'd chosen to take a guard post far away from the main city, his choice being to live in solitary rather than be close to the regime change.

Others had chosen to stay and prove themselves. Several of them had since been promoted.

But not Myon.

"His return is recent. He's always expressed wishes to see Quinnlynn to make sure she's okay," Cillian said. "I've denied the request so far."

"Good." I would ask my betrothed if she wanted to see him and go from there. "Keep monitoring him and the others."

"We will. And on the off chance someone shares intimate secrets, we'll know based on the reactions we receive and intercept."

"Yes," I agreed. "It'll give Lorcan something to do."

My cousin snorted, his black hair falling in unruly waves over his ears as he tilted his head backward to look at me. He didn't speak, just told me with his obsidian eyes what he thought of my "joke."

I'm never bored, he seemed to be saying in that stoic way of his.

Oh, he could speak. I'd heard his voice before. He just preferred silence.

"Let me know if you see or hear anything unusual in the communications," I told him seriously.

He grunted again. That was Lorcan speak for, *I always do*. He didn't call me *Sire* the way Cillian did.

And Cillian only addressed me that way because he insisted on following V-Clan etiquette practices.

It was when he called me *Kieran* that I knew I'd done something to piss him off. Otherwise, I was always *Sire* to him.

"Anything else?" I asked as Lorcan went back to his screens.

"Omega Riley," Cillian murmured.

"Right." I glanced at my watch. "I'll call her back after my run." Because I still had a lot of agitation to work off before I returned to my intended mate.

She had food and shelter. And I had her on a leash. She'd be fine alone for a few hours.

Perhaps it would help her calm down and see reason.

Or maybe it'll make everything worse.

Whatever the outcome, I'd handle it.

You can challenge me as much as you want, Quinnlynn. Just know, I always win. Which means that you, my darling little deviant, will heel. I vow it.

QUINN

I PACED KIERAN'S ROOM, the silk robe—one I'd found hanging in his bathroom—whispering against my thighs.

The residual elements of my heat still lingered, the need a simmering presence inside my lower belly that was driving my inner wolf wild.

He left us, I thought. *He left us when we still needed him.*

But I couldn't blame him.

I'd behaved irrationally. *Stupidly.*

My hands fisted on my hips as I growled at my own idiocy. *What the hell is wrong with me? I don't even want to be claimed!*

Yet I'd felt inadequate, wronged, and *rejected* by his lack of a mark.

Which was ludicrous. I should be thrilled and celebrating the fact that I'd managed to make it through my estrus without falling into his clutches. And I probably would feel that way if it weren't for the dejected state of my wolf.

She hadn't been able to process his explanation, his

disappearance only seeming to add to her sense of rejection rather than heal it.

However, my wolf sensed my calmness regarding Kieran's lack of a claim, which kept her somewhat caged. Had his words not calmed me down, my animal would have fallen into a state of despair and likely ruined all the furniture in his room.

I could feel her pull to do just that, her instinct to act out making her a bit of a brat.

Not that I could fault her. I probably would have done the same thing if he'd left without an explanation.

Yet he hadn't.

He'd left after dropping a bomb on me in the form of a statement.

"I didn't claim you because I didn't want to risk you disassociating from your wolf again."

A selfless reason. One I admittedly respected. A lot.

And that just made me even more confused because he'd yet again proved himself a worthy Alpha. Meanwhile, I'd essentially presented myself in the worst way possible as an Omega mate.

I'd disrespected him at every turn. He'd helped me through my estrus in the most magnanimous manner possible, seeing to my pleasure, ensuring I was safe, helping me reconnect with my inner animal, and I'd thanked him by raging at him.

I gritted my teeth and let my head fall back to glare at the high ceilings.

None of this was right. This fractured connection. My being here. This insatiable need.

The distance growing between us.

My eyes fell closed on a grimace, my heart seeming to stutter in my chest.

I'd spent so many years devoting my life to a cause that

superseded everything, including my own happiness. But Kieran had introduced me to something these last few weeks, something I hadn't realized I'd been missing.

And now I wasn't sure how I would walk away from it.

Fuck, I wasn't even sure I *could* walk away from it.

I yanked on the invisible leash holding my shadowing abilities captive and sighed. *Yeah, definitely can't walk away, let alone teleport away.*

My wolf growled, irritated by her restraint. Rather than hold her back, I allowed the sound to rumble past my lips, only to be met by a much deeper growl in response.

"Running already, darling?" Kieran asked, his silky tone a hot presence at my back.

I blinked at the ceiling, then whirled around to face him, an explanation on my tongue.

Until a sickly-sweet scent slapped me across the face. *Unmated. Omega. Female.* My eyes widened. "Where the fuck have you been?"

His eyebrows shot upward. "Excuse me?"

That was the second time today he'd said those two words to me in that same incredulous tone. But I ignored the subtle warning in them and prowled toward him. "You heard me. Where the fuck have you been, Kieran?"

My wolf snarled inside me, ready to shred him and the potential competitor for *our* mate.

Except he wasn't *ours*.

Because he hadn't claimed me.

Something I understood, but my animal didn't, and her renewed despair made me dizzy with confusion.

I... I wanted to maim him.

No... I want to... to hug him.

Beg him.

Kneel for him.

Tell him the truth.

Become one.

So many competing desires. And that *fucking scent* wasn't helping matters. I grabbed his shirt and ripped it down the center, my claws having come out to play and leaving a track of blood behind.

"*Quinnlynn,*" he snapped, the fury in his voice rivaling my own.

"*Where were you?*" I demanded back at him, my wolf overwhelming me with the need to check every inch of him for proof that he was untouched. But that fragrance drugged my ability to see reason.

Check him.

Scent him.

Claim him.

My hands went for his jeans, my claws having retracted, as my nose met his chest. I inhaled deeply, my eyes closing in euphoria. *Minty. Masculine. Mine.*

The Omega hadn't touched him here, his skin fresh.

But that wasn't the place that mattered most.

My wolf had to know, to ensure he was still hers. *Ours.*

Except not ours.

But I couldn't... I didn't... *Stop thinking.*

His zipper whispered downward, my name leaving his mouth again.

However, I wasn't listening to him. I was listening to my instincts. *My animal.*

I went to my knees, my nose tracking down his abdomen along the way, inhaling, scenting, *ensuring* he smelled right. Until I reached his groin, which still carried *my* aroma. My slick. My Omega imprint.

Because he's mine.

My male.

My Alpha.

My knot.

It pulsed near my lips, my nose pressed scant inches away as I breathed in Kieran's familiar scent. My wolf purred, her instincts driving mine. *Want. Need. Lick.*

I drew my touch down to the tip of his hardening cock and took him into my mouth while pushing his pants the rest of the way down.

My wolf wanted to thank him, to tell him how much she appreciated him returning to us rather than indulging the other Omega.

Competitor, she seemed to be saying. *Must prove our worth. Must please our Alpha. Must show gratitude.*

Or maybe that was my voice. My thoughts. My *desires.* I wasn't sure, but I swallowed him down, my eyes lifting to his smoldering ones.

He didn't appear pleased. He appeared angry. Furious, even.

Must do better, I thought, wrapping my palm around his knot and massaging it like he'd taught me.

"Is this your version of an apology?" he asked, his words reminiscent of the first time I'd done this.

Only, he didn't seem amused now.

He seemed pissed.

Maybe because of the raw scratch marks down his chest and the blood painting his skin.

Kieran wrapped his palm around the back of my neck. "Because you're going to have to try a lot harder than that, *Princess.*"

My animal growled inside, the sound carrying to my throat and vibrating around his cock.

His eyes narrowed in response, but he didn't return the rumble. He simply observed as I drew my teeth along his shaft, all the way to the tip.

Is this an apology? I thought. *No. This is a claiming.*

And I proceeded to demonstrate that by taking him

even deeper into my mouth, my urge to breathe disappearing behind my need to please him. To own him. To *master* him.

As well as to thank him for returning to me. To us. To my wolf. *Unmarked. Unscented. All ours.*

Minus that subtle female perfume that still lingered, the fragrance coaxing my actions and driving me onward with a vigor that had his nostrils flaring in response.

His grip tightened, his abdomen clenching.

Yet his face remained a mask of annoyance.

I want to change that, I decided. *I want to make him lose control. Force him to fall apart. Make him realize I'm better than that other Omega. Whoever she is.*

Just thinking about her made me growl around him again.

He squeezed my nape. "You want to try to distract me from punishing you? Then stop growling and do your fucking job."

My nostrils flared at the crudeness in his words and the darkness underlying his tone. This had nothing to do with distracting him and everything to do with *claiming* him.

"What? Too cruel?" he demanded, his grip shifting to pull me off his cock.

But I fought back, my mouth latching onto him and sucking hard in protest.

When that didn't do it, I dug my nails into his hips, drawing blood.

"*Quinnlynn.*"

What? I tried to say with a glare. *What are you going to do, Alpha? Take away your knot? Mate another Omega? Was it all a lie? A way to placate me before delivering the ultimate punishment? Because I don't fucking accept.*

He couldn't hear me.

But I knew he would understand the challenge in my actions.

I skimmed his sensitive skin with my teeth, warning him not to make me stop, telling him to let me finish, *demanding* that he accept my offer.

Was it insane? Yes.

Was it a little desperate? Probably.

Was it counterintuitive to all my goals? Absolutely.

However, it felt right. I needed this. *He* needed this. And I proved that by taking him as deep as my throat allowed, all the while *growling* at him to accept me. Accept this. Accept *us*.

His wolf took over his gaze, his irises resembling obsidian stones.

My inner animal peered right back up at him, her emotions uninhibited and pure. Whatever he saw made him stop trying to tug me away from him.

I swallowed around him, my chest burning with the need to breathe. But I refused to back down. He had to understand, to *know* that I was worthy of this. Of *him*.

He considered me for a long moment, his thumb idly brushing my pulse while I fought the need to release enough of him to inhale.

I won't back down.

I'm your intended.

You will not take another Omega.

"All right, little one," he said, his voice less severe than before. "But I'm going to drown you in my cum." Those twin dark orbs flicked down to my shoulders. "Lose the robe."

I shifted enough to let the silk fall from my body, then I grabbed his thighs.

My eyes had begun to water, the lack of oxygen making me dizzy.

But I was determined to hold on, to *win* whatever battle I'd started with my mouth.

"Breathe, Quinnlynn," he demanded, his fingers sliding into my hair.

He narrowed his gaze and let me see his waning patience, but he didn't try to yank me off him. However, if I didn't comply, he'd demand my submission.

And his expression told me he would ensure that I wouldn't *enjoy* submitting.

I drew my teeth along his shaft again, warning him that if he tried to force me to stop again, I'd bite.

The action had him arching a brow.

I flicked the tip of his cock with my tongue, the head still in my mouth as I inhaled, then I went back to swallowing him again while my hand massaged his knot.

He observed with a cool stare, but the slight change in color on his cheeks told me I was starting to dismantle his ire.

Good, I thought.

Although, I couldn't really decide why that felt good, or why I even felt the drive to do this, but I ignored all that and focused on his satisfaction.

On watching his muscles tense.

Tasting the hint of precum.

Feeling his arousal pulsate in my mouth, elongating impossibly more, *heating* beneath my tongue.

Yes, yes.

His knot throbbed against my touch, causing me to massage him with a firmer grip, the experiences from my heat driving my knowledge and improving my technique with each passing second.

He drew his fingers through my hair, his wolf still heavy in his gaze. "I'm not going to hold back," he warned me. "I'm angry, Quinnlynn. But you chose this. And now I want to cover you in my seed and ensure that you understand who you belong to."

His voice had lowered to a deep tenor, his Irish accent pronounced once more.

I loved it.

Loved that I'd done this to him.

Loved that he was talking about claiming me.

Because that was the goal—to ensure he understood my worth.

That's not the goal, some part of me whispered.

I ignored it, my focus on Kieran and the way every inch of him appeared to be strained as he fought the urge to give in to me. That slight tension in his limbs made me feel powerful, as did the subtle dilation of his pupils.

He was trying to fight me.

And losing.

Because I'm in control here, I realized. *My mouth is dictating everything. This feeling you're experiencing, Alpha, is because of me.*

My name left his lips, this time with a subtle hint of reverence.

Or perhaps I was making up that note in his voice.

But the way his knuckles brushed my neck seemed to accentuate his tone.

Only, he grabbed my nape in the next moment, his grip unyielding. "Inhale," he demanded, the change in his voice sending a jolt of electricity down my spine.

Angry Alpha. Powerful male. Hungry mate.

I stole a deep breath, aware of his impending explosion, then took him all the way down again.

He held me in place, a low rumble thrumming from his chest. "You're going to swallow until I decide otherwise, little one. Then I'm going to bind you to the bed and keep you there until you stop trying to shadow away from me."

Wait, what?

But there was no time to ask what he meant, or to even consider his words, because in the next second, he exploded down my throat.

I swallowed, my throat aching from the abundance of his essence and the power of his climax.

"Don't stop squeezing my knot, little deviant," he gritted out, his voice guttural with the pleasure of his release. But his grasp on my neck was resolute, his thumb pressing against my pulse as he continued coming in hot, thick waves of ecstasy.

His eyes closed, cutting me off from his pleasure as he tilted his head back.

I growled, annoyed by the dismissal.

But he ignored me, instead choosing to indulge in his orgasm and act like I wasn't the one *swallowing every drop.*

I released his knot and grabbed his hips, my nails digging in again to draw blood.

His wolf released an animalistic sound that would have dropped lesser beings to the floor in immediate supplication.

But I wasn't a lesser being. I was his fucking intended, and I would not be disregarded or ignored or *tossed to the side in favor of another Omega!*

I raked my nails down his thighs, drawing his furious stare to mine.

His palm left my nape, his fingers fisting in my hair instead and yanking me off of him even while he continued to come. His opposite hand went to his knot, the veins along his forearm bulging as he gave himself a firm squeeze, causing more of his essence to spurt all over my face.

I gasped, the influx of air burning my lungs.

But he wasn't done.

He continued the action, his seed spilling all over my

neck, my breasts, and again on my face.

He covered me in his semen even while I dug my nails into his skin.

And then he shoved himself inside my mouth again to unload more into my throat.

By the time he finished, I was panting, enraged, confused, and so damn turned on that I could hardly think straight. But one thought registered above all the others —*need*.

I scored my claws down his thighs again and lunged for him. Only, a guttural growl forced me to the ground on a sharp intake of breath, the sound ripping through me and sending a fresh wave of slick pouring over my thighs.

I moaned, the need inside me escalating to the point of pain as he did it again.

And again.

His rumble of power causing me to roll onto my back in immediate submission. "*Alpha.*" The word left my mouth on a plea as tears leaked from my eyes.

But he didn't release me from his spell. He growled again, the action punishing me in the worst way.

"*Kieran.*" His name left on an agonized sound as I curled into a ball on the ground, my insides *burning* harshly from his mating call.

Because that was the purpose of this growl—to prepare an Omega for the knot. But he hadn't used it like this during my heat. He'd chosen to prepare me with his touch, with his tongue, with his *words*.

Not this way.

Not like I was a meaningless fuck toy to wind up for his pleasure.

But he just came down my throat like that, I realized. *He closed his eyes. He cut me off. I could have been any Omega to him. Not his mate. Not his future Queen.*

"Get on all fours, and I'll give you what you need," he demanded, his tone harsh, the words a lash against my senses.

I shook my head.

Not like this.

He had promised not to punish me like this. Or had that only applied to my heat?

I didn't understand. I couldn't think. And as he growled again, all I could do was curl tighter into a ball and cry.

"Why?" I whispered. "Why are you...?" I trailed off on a painful moan as a spasm hit my lower belly with the sharpness of a blade.

"Why am I what?" Kieran spat at me. "Why am I reminding you of your place? Perhaps because you just tried to *shadow* and *escape* after I spent the better part of the last three weeks trying to make you whole again."

What? "I didn't—"

His unexpected—yet highly anticipated—touch startled me, his arms winding around me as he lifted me off the floor.

Only, he didn't cradle me or offer me solace.

He growled *again* and tossed me onto the bed. "On all fours, Omega. *Now.*"

I trembled, at a loss for his callous treatment. "N-not like this," I begged. "Please." Maybe that made me weak. I deserved his wrath. I'd been lucky not to experience it yet.

But after the last few days together, I... I wasn't sure I could handle his ire. Not right now. Not tonight.

"Please," I whispered again. "I wasn't... I didn't want to shadow. I just... I just wanted to know..."

"Know what?" he demanded, his voice more furious than I'd ever heard it. "Know if you'd been convincing enough for me to unleash you after your shortened heat?

Know if you can escape yet? What, Quinnlynn? What did you want to *know*?"

"If I could still shadow!" I cried out, my mind fracturing beneath his Alpha growl. He'd uttered every word with such potency that I felt like I was about to break.

Or maybe I was broken.

Because I felt inconsolable.

Alone.

So fucking hot.

Yet so utterly used. And worthless. And the complete opposite of what I'd wanted when he'd returned.

I'd wanted him to see me as powerful, as a worthy mate.

And he'd propelled me into this useless state where I could hardly see beyond the water coating my eyes.

"I didn't want to escape." The admission sounded hoarse, my body and mind exhausted. "I was thinking about not being able to walk away from this... from... from *you*. And just th-thought about shadowing. So I tried to... to see if I could."

I curled into a ball on the bed, terrified of whatever came next.

After a century of fending for myself, of surviving unthinkable conditions, I'd been brought down by the one male who should never hurt me. *My intended mate.*

Yet I'd hurt him.

I'd run without an explanation.

And now he was ensuring I knew how that felt.

I deserve this, I thought, shuddering. *I deserve his ire. His castigation. His* rejection.

I hadn't been a good mate to him. Hell, I still wasn't living up to expectations. I'd *attacked* him and made him bleed just for smelling like an Omega.

An Omega who hadn't touched him.

After he'd already told me about his celibacy.

Of course, that could have all been a lie. A way to lull me into a state of comfort just to rip it all away.

Did I really deserve any better?

No.

Because Kieran had no idea why I'd left. Maybe if he did, he wouldn't hate me.

But I wasn't sure I could trust him.

Or perhaps I was too scared to try.

Which makes me unworthy.

Mates should trust each other.

However, our entire betrothal was founded on a lie.

We've been doomed from the very start.

No wonder he hates me.

Even now, I wasn't behaving the way a mate should. He'd given me a command, and I'd ignored him. No, I'd *refused* him.

That wasn't how this worked. He'd called for my slick with his growl and then told me what position to assume.

"On all fours, Omega. Now."

His earlier demand pummeled my heart and mind, forcing my body to unfurl. I owed him at least this—my submission.

I'd used him. I'd betrothed myself to him and left him to handle everything in my absence. All the while borrowing his power to aid in my quest to protect others while seeking the truth.

Now it was his turn to use me.

I went up onto my hands and knees like he'd demanded.

Bowed my head.

And whispered, "I submit."

KIERAN

Quinnlynn's voice and body told me I'd pushed too far.

When she'd come at me with her claws, demanding answers after I'd felt her trying to escape, I'd snapped.

After everything I'd done for her, she'd chosen to thank me by shredding me with her claws and trying to top from the bottom by sucking my cock?

I'd been furious.

All that on top of how she'd treated me earlier, and I'd been driven to the conclusion that my Omega needed a stern lesson in hierarchy.

But this…

Seeing her shaking on her hands and knees, head bowed, tears falling to the bedding, and the soft hints of her sobbing silently before me, was not what I wanted at all.

And her comments about shadowing—about how she'd just wondered idly if she could, hence why she'd tried —had struck me in the heart.

I'd assumed she'd wanted to run.

An assumption I should have reevaluated when I'd realized she was wearing nothing but a robe.

Maybe she'd intended to run in wolf form—which could explain the robe—but her reactions to me proved she wasn't fully recovered from her heat.

Trying to escape in this state would be a terrible decision, and after chasing Quinnlynn for over a century, I knew she wasn't the type to flee without thinking through every detail.

She was too strategic to run in this condition.

I knew that.

Yet I'd reacted aggressively, without thought, and had jumped to a conclusion driven by a century of frustration.

Fuck.

I drew my hand down her spine, my insides cracking at the way she flinched in response.

She hadn't done that these last few days. She'd craved me. Trusted me. *Enjoyed* me.

But not now.

Right now, she feared me.

And that just wouldn't do.

My palm left her skin so I could remove what was left of my clothes.

She'd destroyed my shirt, left blood to dry against my skin, and haphazardly yanked down my pants.

I'd thought she was desperate to distract me, to make me forget how she'd just tried to run.

But now that I'd calmed down enough to properly think, I realized the true cause of her actions—*possessive need.*

"Where were you?" she'd demanded.

I'd assumed she was playing a role to aid in her distraction, which had further infuriated me—because how fucking dare she use our betrothal in such a disgraceful manner. But now it was clear that it hadn't been an act; she'd meant every word.

Her whole performance had been her way of establishing worth.

And I'd essentially responded by degrading her on the deepest level imaginable.

I knelt on the bed beside her, stirring an array of goose bumps along her skin. Not the good kind, but the frightened kind.

Rather than speak, I pressed a kiss to her shoulder and started to purr.

She shuddered, her elbows bending as though she could no longer hold her own weight. "You're torturing me," she breathed. "I… I know I deserve it… but…"

I hushed her, my lips ghosting over her shoulder again before I gripped her nape. "I would never torture you, Quinnlynn."

Fuck her into submission, yes.

Hurt her intentionally, no.

My purr intensified as I lay down beside her, my hand still on her neck. "Come here," I told her, my palm squeezing gently to give her the dominance I knew she needed. "I promise not to growl again."

She didn't move. "I don't… I don't understand."

"I'm apologizing," I admitted softly. "I misunderstood your intentions, and I reacted the wrong way. Your wolf felt threatened, but I thought you were just trying to distract me from your escape attempt."

"I wasn't trying to escape," she whispered.

"I know." I applied pressure to her neck again, not cruelly, just enough to give her support. "I'm sorry, Quinnlynn. You didn't deserve any of that."

"B-but I did. I do. I… I used you for your power. I left you here. I'm a bad mate."

I frowned. "You used me for my power?" Was that the real reason she'd chosen me all those years ago? To have access to my healing abilities? "How did you even know about my ability to heal?"

"I… I didn't. Not exactly. I knew a little. Learned a lot." Her arms and legs were shaking, the sweet scent of her slick a reminder of what my growls had done to her.

She wouldn't be able to stay like this for much longer.

"Quinnlynn—"

"I'm sorry," she interjected with a sob. "I'm sorry I left. But there was no other way. I had to pursue my lead, Kieran. And your ability to heal… it *helped*. But it also distracted me. I lost myself. I lost time."

Her words almost sounded drunk, her aroused state stirring comments from her that seemed important yet didn't make sense.

"*Please,*" she begged, her forehead going to the bed. "Please stop torturing me. I'm sorry, Alpha. I'm—"

"I'm not torturing you, Quinnlynn." And yet, that clearly wasn't true. Because she appeared to be in a lot of pain, thanks to my cruel behavior.

I couldn't knot her the way I'd intended to; it would be too unfeeling and would further damage our connection.

But I couldn't leave her to suffer either.

"Roll onto your back," I told her. "I want to see your eyes." Because that was what we needed—our connection.

Except she didn't move.

She stiffened instead, almost as though she hadn't heard me or perhaps thought she'd misunderstood me.

"Quinnlynn," I murmured, my palm slipping from her nape to trace her spine. "Lie down next to me. I want to see you, little one:" I returned my hand to her neck. "Please?"

I punctuated the request with my purr, causing her to shiver almost violently.

"Kieran?" The distrust in her tone slayed me. I'd

broken our fragile connection by misunderstanding her intentions.

"I thought you were running again," I murmured, my fingers drifting up into her hair to comb through the knotted strands. "And I thought you were using your wolf to distract me from correcting your behavior."

None of it was meant as an excuse, simply an explanation.

"I was wrong. I'm sorry." The two words burned my tongue, my ability to apologize rusty after never really having a need for it. But here I was uttering the phrase for a second time in the span of minutes.

"I'm sorry," I said again, prepared to repeat that phrase as many times as Quinnlynn needed me to.

I would apologize to her for an eternity so long as it made her look at me again.

Only it seemed three times truly was the charm as she slowly lifted her head.

And destroyed my heart in the process.

Her tears mixed with my cum, her face a saturated mess of angry passion and fear.

"Oh, Quinnlynn." I gripped her nape again and pulled her to me, my purr intensifying.

She quivered in response, her face wet against my neck.

I wrapped my arms around her and lent her my strength. I'd expected her to fight me, not fall apart.

But I should have known better. She was still on the fringe of her heat. That made her vulnerable, leaving her wolf wildly in control. And given everything she'd been through, of course my punishing growls had shattered her protective walls.

I kissed the top of her head and held her while she cried, my purr offering her more comfort than my knot ever could.

Well, maybe not. I'd revved her up so intensely that she probably needed me to fuck her. But I couldn't. Not like this.

Comfort and protection came first. I'd damaged our connection, and now I had to repair it.

Cillian, I called, opening the telepathic link he'd established with me over a thousand years ago.

Yes, Sire?

I need someone to quietly start a bath in my quarters. Can you ask Vin or Shiv to shadow in? I don't want to be disturbed, but I also can't release Quinnlynn at the moment.

He was quiet for a beat. *Is she all right?*

She will be, I vowed. *She reacted to Ivana's scent, and things spiraled from there.*

I see. Those two words held the full weight of his accusation. I could hear him thinking, *I told you so,* even without him voicing the words.

Cillian.

Sire.

I need your help, please. And it has to be Vin or Shiv. They were both Beta males. The last thing I wanted to do was risk Quinnlynn scenting another female in my suite, let alone an unmated Omega or a virile Alpha.

Please? That's a new term for you.

Cillian, I said again, a hiss underlining his name.

I'll sort it, Sire. For her. Not for you.

I nearly growled in response to that, but on some level, I knew I'd earned that comment. He'd expressed his hesitation earlier over my idea of having Ivana help with the dress.

Thank you, Cillian, I murmured, choosing to go the grateful route.

Gratitude? His shock was palpable. *You really did fuck up, didn't you?*

I clenched my jaw. *Cillian.* This time I added the requisite warning to my tone.

And the bastard chuckled in response. However, he didn't say anything else, which told me he was working on the arrangements I'd requested.

Within minutes, I felt the presence of a Beta in my suite.

Quinnlynn stirred, but I pressed her head back down to my shoulder and whispered words in my ancient dialect. It was one she wouldn't understand, the language having died out long ago. Cillian and Lorcan could converse in it, but not many others could.

We were part of an old tribe.

Which had been my territory prior to agreeing to Quinnlynn's betrothal.

I'd taken my people with me to Blood Sector, initially temporarily. However, my former Irish home had been destroyed during the beginning of the Infected Era.

Humans had thought bombs would solve the zombie infestation problem.

It hadn't.

And they'd soon been without their precious explosives, leaving them with only one option—find a cure.

It was something they should have done from the start, but the leadership of the world had wasted too much precious time blaming each other.

By the time the survivors had come together to pay attention to the research, they'd already lost most of their teams.

The few who'd remained were predominantly supernatural, such as myself, and we'd cared more about stopping the mutation of the virus at that point.

Blood Sector had become my permanent residence as a result of it all, which I supposed was a stroke of fate.

Because now that I'd tasted Quinnlynn, I would never be able to leave. Not that I'd ever truly wanted to. I'd merely planned to manage both V-Clan sectors.

And I supposed I was doing that, just within the same boundaries now rather than on two separate islands.

Sire, Cillian said, drawing me back from my idle thoughts. *The bath is ready.*

Thank you.

I'm not sure if I should be fearful of this change or amused by it.

Fearful, I told him. *Because it comes with a side effect of violent possession.*

I have no interest in your intended, Sire.

Hmm, I hummed, dismissing him with a soft growl.

I knew Cillian would never betray me or Quinnlynn. He was loyal to a fault. Just like Lorcan.

However, apparently I didn't display my gratitude frequently enough. Perhaps I'd change that by thanking them daily for a few weeks, see how long it would take for them to demand that I stop.

And in the interim, I would work on earning my Omega's forgiveness.

Starting with a bath.

KIERAN

Quinnlynn had fallen asleep against me in the bath, her small form seemingly exhausted from the emotional trauma of the last few hours.

Her intense estrus had already depleted her energy, in addition to the complications with her wolf. She was due a long sleep.

Only, she started to stir as I wrapped a towel around her, her dark eyelashes parting to reveal distrusting irises. It seemed that not even her dreams could help her escape our reality.

I palmed her cheek and kissed her forehead, then lifted her to sit on the counter. It helped free up both my arms to properly towel-dry us.

I'd only marginally struggled to bathe her, the water having helped move her fluidly around as I'd gently soaped up and washed off her skin. I'd shampooed her hair as well, then used a comb to brush conditioner through her strands.

The water was filthy now and draining.

Which was why I'd ended our experience with a quick rinse in the shower.

None of that had woken her up.

But the moment the warm cloth had touched her skin, she'd stirred.

She watched as I ran the towel over my limbs and torso, her gaze going to my groin. I was hard, something her nearness automatically caused. But I wasn't necessarily aroused. Taking care of her took precedence over everything else.

I finished drying her off and set the towels to the side. The wariness didn't leave her gaze, the obvious unease a heavy weight on my heart.

However, when I reached for her, she buried her head against my chest, her wolf clearly seeking more of my purr.

Which was exactly what I gave her, my rumble a steady rhythm between us as I gathered her into my arms to carry her back to my bed.

Someone had come in to change the bedding, but they'd left the soiled linens in a basket, just in case Quinnlynn wanted them for nesting.

Except she didn't even seem to notice.

She was too busy clinging to me as I settled us beneath the clean sheets.

I rolled her beneath me, bathing her in my Alpha strength as I brushed her spirit with my healing power. She jolted in response, then sighed with such stark contentment that I did it again.

"Thank you," she breathed, her nose going to my chest as she inhaled.

I gave her more energy but couldn't sense where she truly needed it. Which was strange because she seemed to be absorbing it in abundance.

Her hands went to my shoulders, her lips ghosting across my skin as she tried to pull me impossibly closer. I settled my hips between hers and unleashed my vitality upon her, all the while considering what she'd said to me before our bath and shower.

"I used you for your power."

"I had to pursue my lead, Kieran. And your ability to heal… it helped."

Helped what? I wondered. *What lead?*

She soaked up my energy now as though she were a sponge, her body replenishing hidden reserves and storing the power for future use. I nearly cut it off, aware that this clearly wasn't a good sign, but I couldn't seem to stop *giving*. I wanted her full of me, of our intended bond, of my *essence*.

"Quinnlynn," I whispered, my lips in her hair. "Why did you need my power?"

"For the Omegas." Her voice sounded dreamy, almost as though she wasn't quite cognizant of her surroundings.

A better man wouldn't take advantage of this state.

But I wanted answers.

And it was past time she gave me a few.

"Which Omegas?"

"My Omegas," she murmured, causing my brow to furrow. "I tried to save them all. But I couldn't. I wasn't you. I don't have this power. It's yours."

"Do you mean in Bariloche?" I asked, pulling back to look down at her.

She blinked up at me, her eyes a little hazy but clearing quickly.

So I blasted her with more of my energy, drawing her back into her dreamy state where she sighed happily and stared at me with stars in her eyes.

Much better than fear or wariness, I decided. "You used my ability to help the Omegas in Bariloche Sector. Is that why you went there?"

Her eyelashes fluttered as she sighed again, lost to my healing touch. "That's why I stayed. To help them. But you could help so many more. This power... this power could ensure the safety... of all of them."

"All of the Bariloche Sector Omegas?"

She started to shake her head, her lips curling down. "More. The Sanct..." She trailed off, her brow coming down. "Hmm, no. You might be him." Her grip on my shoulders tightened, her eyes opening again as some of that earlier wariness crept back into her gaze. "What are you doing to me?"

"Comforting you," I told her. "Making you feel good."

"For information?" She pushed against me a little, her face seeming to clear. "You're... you're making me drunk... on *power*."

"Only a little," I admitted, cupping her cheek. "But your soul seems to need it even though you don't feel wounded or hurt anywhere. So why are you so hungry for my energy?"

Or perhaps the better question would have been, *How are you so hungry for my energy?* Because I'd given her more than enough these last few weeks, yet I could feel it filling her and being instantly sucked out by some invisible pull.

Her nostrils flared, her palms pushing harder against me now. "Stop."

I didn't fight her, choosing to let her win this round because I'd so badly fucked up the last one. "All right, little one." I rolled onto the bed to lie beside her and took my power away with it. Then I settled against the pillow and tilted my head to watch her, waiting for her to make another move.

I might have wanted answers.

But I wanted my feisty mate back more than anything else.

So if it meant lying here and waiting for her to recover, I would.

Her chest rose and fell in rapid succession as she tried to fix herself, her hands still up in the air as though my shoulders were still beneath her palms.

Then she slowly looked at me and blinked. "You stopped."

I arched a brow. "Yes."

"Why?"

I frowned. "Because you told me to."

"I didn't expect you to listen."

I snorted at that. "I won't force you to accept my comfort, Quinnlynn." Of course, I was still purring for her, but that was more my wolf than me. And that hadn't been what she'd wanted me to stop doing.

"But you didn't get your answers."

"No, I didn't," I agreed, studying her and the secrets brimming in her gaze. "But your mind will tell me what I want to know when we're mated. I've waited a hundred years. I can wait a few more weeks."

She froze, my words clearly striking a nerve.

What is it you're hiding that you don't want me to know? I wondered. *Does it deal with why you chose me? Are you worried about how I'll react to that information?*

I went to my side and balanced my head on my elbow to stare down at her without touching her. She was barely breathing

Yes, I definitely struck a nerve.

"What are you so afraid of me knowing?" I asked, studying her intently.

"A hundred years?" she repeated back at me, ignoring my question. "You... you've waited a hundred years for... for my secrets?"

"I've waited over a hundred years for a lot of things, Quinnlynn. Your secrets being among those things, yes."

The hairs along her arms drew upward, her fear seeming to rise with each passing second. "You... you're..."

I raised a brow. "I'm what?" I asked. "Your intended mate?"

She swallowed, her skin paling. But she didn't reply.

"Quinnlynn." I couldn't help the sigh in my voice. "We've been betrothed for over a hundred years. I warned you from the beginning what it meant, that you may one day regret that decision. I gave you an out, too. You chose to ignore it. Then you ran. I caught you."

She stared at me, still saying nothing.

"And now, we'll finally be mated," I concluded. "Word of our betrothal dinner has already spread to the sector. We'll be celebrating in one week."

Her nostrils flared. "One week."

"Yes. I asked Ivana to help you find a dress. She'll be by in two days to do so."

"Ivana?" she repeated, her voice barely a whisper.

"The Omega you smelled on me earlier."

That brought some color back into her cheeks. "You want me to go shopping with one of your whores?"

My eyebrows lifted. "Ivana isn't a whore, Quinnlynn. She's an unmated Omega by choice. And I don't have *whores*." I leaned toward her, my eyes narrowing. "I told you how many women I knotted in your absence—*none*. Remember?"

The clenching of her jaw told me she recalled the details just fine but was feeling too stubborn to admit it. "Let me guess—she's one of your *many* offers?"

"Actually, no. Which is why I chose her for this task." I

reached for her chin to hold her gaze. "*You* are my intended. And I find it insulting that you don't take my faithfulness to you seriously. Do you know how hard it was to go a century without the comfort of a woman in my bed?"

"How terrible for you," she deadpanned, disrespecting me all over again. "Must be like going into heat without a knot."

"A choice *you* made for yourself," I pointed out, refusing to feel bad for her. "Regardless, my point is that I remained faithful when I didn't have to. And you're treating me as though I lied."

"You did lie," she snapped.

"About what?" I demanded, my fury mounting. "I've been nothing but truthful with you, Quinnlynn. Something you can't claim for yourself, now can you?"

"Why?" she demanded, ignoring my rhetorical remark. "Because you told me from the beginning that I would regret this? That I pretty much ignored the signs of who you were and went through with this anyway?"

Now it was my turn to blink. "What the fuck are you talking about?"

"You know what I'm talking about. You've been waiting a century for my secrets! And you almost pulled them from me by using the very essence you know I *need* to succeed." She sat up and moved away from me, anger and fear wafting from her petite frame. "I will never give it to you willingly. Not after what you did to my parents."

I gaped at her. "Your *parents*?" I had no idea what she was talking about.

"Moons, how could I be so blind?" she asked, her hands going to her head as she curled her knees into her chest. "I... I thought... You weren't a contender. Because you knew I would come to you?"

"Quinnlynn," I said, sitting up and joining her against the headboard.

But she wasn't listening to me now; she was too busy puzzling something out loud.

"How did you know? Or were you planning to fight and surprise them all?" She started massaging her temples. "I don't… I don't…"

I reignited my purr, the sound having disappeared after she'd insulted my integrity. But I sensed her need for it now, her fragile state of mind evident in her actions and words.

"Tell me about your parents." I voiced it softly, rather than as an order, but the demand was implied. "Tell me what you think I did to them."

Her hands dropped from her face, her gaze murderous as she glared at me. "Like you don't know."

I really don't, I nearly said. Instead, I decided to push her a little. "If I already know, then it won't hurt to say it, right?"

"You're going to make me say it?"

"Yes, Quinnlynn. I am." *Because otherwise, I'll never know what the fuck you're talking about.*

"You really are a monster," she whispered, the accusation and hurt in her voice nearly undoing me.

But I had to know what she thought I'd done because it was clearly linked to why she'd run.

"Am I?" I asked softly. "Am I a monster, Quinnlynn?"

"You want me to say that you killed my parents out loud as some sort of sick and twisted enjoyment. So yes, Kieran, you are a monster."

My eyebrows flew upward. "I *killed* your parents?" In what fucked-up nightmare world had I done that? "They died in a plane crash."

She rolled her eyes. "Right. Except my mother sent me

a message that night." Her hand went to her bare neck. "When she sent me this…"

Her pupils dilated, her fingers roaming all over her throat and down to her naked breasts.

She glanced around, her heart rate accelerating.

"Quinnlynn?" I prompted, my purr automatically heightening.

"Where is it? Where's my pendant?" She started frantically searching the sheets. "What did you do with it? Where did you hide it?!"

She started clawing at the blankets, forcing me to grab her.

Which made me her next target, her actions violent and borderline psychotic.

Because she thinks I murdered her parents. "Quinnlynn," I snapped as she fought for her life beneath me. I didn't want to risk hurting her or her hurting herself, so I caught her wrists and pinned them to the bed. Then slammed my hips against hers to keep her from trying to kick me. "Calm down."

"I won't calm down! You killed my parents!"

"Why the hell would I kill them?" I demanded.

"Where's my pendant?" She shouted the words, completely ignoring my question.

"In the jewelry box on the dresser," I hissed. "I took it off after you shifted back the other day." I hadn't wanted to risk damaging it during our frenzy.

"I've… I've been so blind," she whispered, not hearing me at all. "You warned me from the beginning, said I'd regret…"

"Not because I killed your parents, Quinnlynn. They died in a plane crash. An *accident.*"

"Liar," she whispered. "My mom sent me a communication about how you sabotaged the plane."

"How *I* sabotaged the plane?" I repeated incredulously.

"An Alpha Prince." She blinked. "*You.*"

"Not me."

"What?" Her brow furrowed. "But… but you've been waiting a hundred years for my secrets. The ones from my parents." Some of her confusion seemed to disappear as she uttered the accusations. "I'll never tell you. I'll die first."

I gaped down at her, my purr still thrumming in my chest, as it seemed to be the only thing keeping her somewhat sane. "What secrets could I possibly want from your parents?"

"About the…" She trailed off, her lashes rising and falling as she appeared to be thinking hard about something. "You know."

"No, Quinnlynn. I don't. Because I didn't kill your parents." I gathered her wrists beneath one palm and used my free hand to cup her cheek, forcing her to meet my gaze. "They died in a freak accident, little one. They weren't murdered."

She started to shake her head, her gaze seeming to darken with memories. "Not an accident."

"Something you know from a communication?" I prompted, referring back to her statement regarding her mother sending her a message about sabotage.

"Yes. They told me it wasn't an accident."

"That an Alpha Prince killed them," I reiterated.

She nodded.

"Not me specifically."

"Not you," she replied, blinking again like she was trying to clear some of the fog from her mind. "But you've been waiting a hundred years for my secrets."

"Yes. To know why you chose to mate me," I told her.

Which now didn't make any sense. If her parents had told her someone had fucked with their plane, thus killing them, and she knew it was an Alpha Prince, then why had she picked me?

Because I didn't fight for her hand, I realized after a beat. *I didn't join the battle for Blood Sector King.*

Making me a *safe* choice.

She'd also wanted my energy, my *power*—and I still didn't know how she knew anything about that—for something as well.

And she'd left… "To pursue a lead," I breathed.

"What?"

"That's why you left. You were pursuing a lead on your parents' murder."

Her expression cleared almost immediately, but she didn't reply. Because she didn't need to. I understood now.

"I had to pursue my lead, Kieran. And your ability to heal… it helped. *But it also distracted me. I lost myself. I lost time."*

"How did my power help you? What did you use it for?" However, the answer came to me almost instantly. "The Omegas." In Bariloche Sector, she'd used my gift to heal them.

But she'd made it sound like she'd mated me for my power, too.

Perhaps she'd meant it was a benefit she'd chosen to *use* after leaving me, thus *using* me for my power.

No. There's something else here. Some underlying piece of the story—a secret—that she hasn't yet shared. I could see it lurking in her gaze now, as well as scent the fear of discovery along with it.

She wasn't ready to tell me.

And for once, I didn't want to push her for the knowledge.

Because she'd already revealed a rather large secret

regarding her parents, one I would need to corroborate. Although, I wasn't sure why she'd lie about the cause of her parents' death. But I understood her not announcing it.

"You haven't told anyone because you don't know who did it," I said, thinking aloud. That was why she'd just accused me of it. "Why didn't you tell me, Quinnlynn? I'm your intended mate. I could have helped you find out the truth."

"Or ensure no one ever finds out," she whispered, her terror a potent scent between us.

My lips parted at her words, the underlying truth of them striking me right in the heart.

She doesn't trust me. Of course she didn't; she'd never given me a chance to prove my innocence or my true worth to her.

That was the heart of our issue—a lack of faith in one another. My distrust in her had been earned through her actions, while her distrust in me was just a natural response to her situation.

Both were forgivable offenses.

It was how we moved forward from this moment that mattered most.

Because my devious trickster had just given me a way to win her over.

If I was able to find out who had murdered her parents, I'd secure her faith in me in the process.

Alas, I had no idea where to begin. Her parents had died over a hundred years ago, and the plane was long buried beneath the waves of the Arctic Ocean.

I would begin looking into it tomorrow.

After I helped pull my intended out of this bizarre mental state.

"I didn't kill your parents, little one," I said, releasing

her wrists. "And the only secrets I've wanted from you are the real reasons why you betrothed yourself to me."

She swallowed, her expression remaining uneasy, that scent of terror still lingering between us. She remained utterly still beneath me, seemingly too terrified to move.

"I've known you had ulterior motives from the beginning, Quinnlynn. And I don't take kindly to betrayal. But I'm starting to suspect that your reasons were noble, so I may show you some leniency. However, the sector won't. Which is why we'll move forward with the betrothal dinner." I slid off of her and back to my side.

She still didn't move; she barely even breathed.

"I'll postpone your trip with Ivana by two days, unless you decide you're ready to go sooner." Which didn't seem likely, given her shocked state right now.

When she continued her silence, I simply purred.

And brushed her with my healing energy.

She'd revealed something that clearly meant a lot to her, and she didn't know how to proceed. Rather than push her, I decided to lend her my strength and support.

And wait for her to make the next move.

I'll be right here, little one. No matter how long it takes.

QUINN

I EXISTED IN A CLOUD.

Floating.

Drifting.

Surfacing again.

Only to roll into a blanket of heat that vibrated with power and affection.

I nuzzled into the comfort of that sound, the proverbial anchor that kept me grounded in this bizarre version of reality.

A reality where Kieran O'Callaghan purred. And purred. And purred.

So more like a dream. But it was a dream I didn't want to wake up from.

Which caused me to float again, the current taking me into a land of sleep where my fantasies mingled with nightmares.

A cool breeze whirled around me, the air whispering notes from my past. *Words. An alarm. A sharp pang in my chest.*

I tried to massage the hurt away, but I felt trapped. Unable to move. *Lost.*

"This is a token of power, mo stoirín. And it's yours now. Wear it for us. Wear it for you. Wear it when you kill our betrayer."

My mother's voice drifted in and out of my mind, the image of her on my wall one I'd imagined hundreds of times.

An urgent communication.

One that had stirred me from a cold, dreary night.

No sun today. No light. It's January. Mom and Dad should be home soon.

"Quinn."

I rolled away from the soft voice, determined to continue sleeping.

"Quinnlynn."

My father's tone coaxed one eye open. "Hmm?" I hummed, not fully ready to commit to waking up yet.

"We need you," my father said, the whisper in his voice one that made me frown.

"What?"

"Look at us, mo stoirín," my mother begged. "Please."

I muttered something in response, the memory slipping into reality as I rotated into a wall of hot male. *Purring.* I pressed my nose into his bare chest, inhaling deeply. *Mint. Man. Mine.*

But that dream... *memory*... still lingered.

"What's wrong?" I asked, my eyes trying to focus on the image that was no longer there. Only skin. *This isn't right.* I rolled again, the wall before me made of glass. "Mom?" It came out in a whisper, her visual strong inside my mind. And yet... nonexistent.

The necklace.

I grabbed my neck, my fingers immediately curling around the pendant at my throat.

"Mom," I whispered, my eyes closing as I thought back to how the necklace had appeared.

An enchantment.

A delayed broadcast.

A warning from my parents that had appeared *days* after their death.

I'd been in the middle of mourning them, my mind foggy, but their words had remained.

"Don't trust the Alpha Princes. Not until you find out the truth, mo stoirín."

I repeated the words aloud now, my voice hoarse from my fitful sleep.

"Someone bespelled the plane," I said, blinking at the windows. "My parents didn't have a choice. It was either them or…" *Or risk the Sanctuary.*

Because the plane would have led the betrayer right to the heart of the Omega world.

The only way to ensure the culprit couldn't follow the lead had been to destroy the link. Which had required the power of both of my parents to do.

"They crashed the plane," I whispered, a tear falling from my eyes. "Because of *him*." So perhaps that made them martyrs, not exactly *murdered*. But I didn't see the difference.

They'd died because of someone they'd trusted.

An Alpha Prince.

Not Kieran, I thought, recalling his behavior last night. Or had that been earlier today? Yesterday? I couldn't say. Time didn't make sense here, my heat having distorted my mind and thoughts.

But one aspect had remained constant—the male at my back.

And his purr.

I rolled into him again, my nose returning to his chest, breathing him in as though he were my source of life. He folded his arms around me, his warmth a blanket I craved more than the sheets around us. I pressed myself against him, determined to join us together indefinitely.

Such a stark difference from weeks ago when he'd found me.

Years ago when I'd run.

However, it felt right. *He* felt right.

I'd spent a lifetime fighting alone. Maybe it was time to let him in, to let him *help*.

He wants our secrets, a small part of me reminded.

Yes, but he explained that.

He could be lying.

I don't think he is.

It was a conversation between two sides of my psyche, one that longed to welcome him as a partner and the other that was terrified of trusting anyone besides myself.

I shivered, then jolted as he flooded my veins with his healing essence again. *Yes, yes.* A sigh escaped me, my soul rejoicing in Kieran's powerful energy.

He could be using it to lull me into a placative state again, but I wasn't sure I cared.

Except he didn't speak.

He didn't *push*.

He just let me revel in his presence.

I don't deserve him, I thought sleepily. *I haven't been fair to him.*

That thought chased me into the darkness.

And when I woke, it was to light streaming in through the windows.

I winced and shied away from it, only to come up against a muscular leg instead of a torso. My lips pulled down. "Kieran?"

"You need to eat something, little one," he said, his

purr drawing my gaze upward to find him still naked but with a tray on his lap. "Will you let me feed you?"

He lifted a strawberry for me, making my inner wolf practically salivate.

I lunged for it, except my body was too sluggish to execute the motion, so I sort of wiggled instead, and my head landed harshly on my pillow.

He arched a brow. "Was that your version of a yes?"

I opened my mouth in response.

His lips twitched, and he brought the berry to my lips.

Then he gave me some water.

Followed by more fruit.

Until I was somewhat stable enough to sit up and join him.

Everything from the last few—*uh, hours? Days?*—sort of blurred together, but I recalled most of the important bits. Including my admission about my parents and Kieran's initial punishment that he'd never actually finished.

As well as the way he'd just offered me comfort for what felt like weeks.

Taken care of me.

Been a true mate.

And had shown extreme amounts of patience.

It could be because he wants access to the Sanctuary, I reminded myself. I hadn't kept that secret for this long to just give it up to an Alpha Prince after only a few weeks together.

But I could admit *wanting* to tell him. To share the full truth. To have a partner.

Most of the energy he'd fed me had gone straight to the enchantments surrounding the Sanctuary. I was their primary source, my magic protecting them from potential discovery and keeping their location off the proverbial map.

However, I'd spent so much of my essence on helping Omegas that I'd allowed myself to deteriorate to a point where I'd almost completely lost my wolf.

I wasn't naïve; I knew Kieran was the only reason I hadn't completely disassociated from my animal soul. Had I tried to shift while in Bariloche Sector, I probably would have become feral. I wouldn't have had the energy I needed to control the beast, and I would have been lost to her control.

Which meant I would have lost the Sanctuary, too.

I'd taken on too much, trying to save too many others at the expense of myself and my family dynasty.

Kieran hadn't just saved me; he'd saved us all. And he had no idea.

Maybe I should tell him, I thought, glancing at him as he held some meat up to my lips. *Maybe it's time to trust him.*

He pressed the water bottle to my lips again, his gaze dropping to my mouth. "Ivana will be here in a few hours to take you shopping. I prolonged it for as long as I could, but our betrothal dinner is tomorrow. And you need a dress, Quinnlynn."

"T-tomorrow?" I repeated. "I thought..." Hadn't he said it was in a week?

"Yes. We've been in this bed for... a very long time." He set the water and tray aside, revealing that he wasn't actually naked but wearing a pair of tight black boxers. "While Cillian's comments regarding our *reacquaintance* are great for my ego, it's time for the sector to see you."

Reacquaintance? I repeated to myself.

"Your wolves need you, Princess," Kieran continued. "They need to know their future Queen is truly home."

Is that what I am? Truly home? I wondered. My wolf certainly felt at home, especially with Kieran by our side.

However, his words also left me uneasy.

Because his mention of the betrothal dinner reminded me of the coronation celebrations that I'd missed over a hundred years ago.

If Kieran had rescheduled the dinner, then he'd probably rescheduled our coronation, too.

Which meant the Alpha Princes would be arriving soon.

And among them was the culprit—the one who'd killed my parents.

"When is the coronation?" I whispered, wondering how long I had to prepare myself mentally for the ceremony and the visiting Alphas.

"Two weeks from tomorrow," he replied, his gaze studying me intently. "And you will remain tethered to my side the entire time, so don't even think of trying to shadow."

I swallowed, my gaze falling to my hands as I clasped them in my lap. I was sitting naked beside him, something that should have left me feeling inferior. But it was his words that hurt me more.

And yet, I deserved them.

Because I'd run once, and there was a good chance I would try to run again.

Except he knows now, I thought. *He knows the truth about my parents' murder.*

"One of those Alphas killed my parents," I told him softly. "And you're inviting them all into Blood Sector."

"I am," he agreed, his palm sliding up my arm to wrap around my nape as he pulled my attention back to him. "And we're going to use it as an opportunity to learn more about them, see if anyone gives anything away."

I blinked. "We are?"

"We are," he murmured. "You mentioned something about the plane being enchanted in your sleep. Is that what caused it to crash?"

There was a slight edge to his tone, giving me pause.

I couldn't remember how much I'd revealed in my dreamlike state. Everything had been a mix of reality and nightmares.

Lying to him now would defeat the purpose of trusting him. It would also serve as a dishonor when all he'd truly done the last few weeks was respect me.

What will it hurt to tell him the truth? I thought. *Not everything, but enough for him to prove his worth?*

Because even if he was the culprit, then he'd already know all of this anyway. And if he wasn't the culprit, then perhaps he'd meant it when he'd said we would work together to solve this puzzle.

"Someone enchanted their jet," I explained slowly, making up my mind to put a little faith in him. *A peace offering*, I thought. "The only way to break the enchantment was to crash the plane."

"Why not just land it?"

That question alone told me he wasn't guilty. Only someone who didn't understand the end goal would ask such a thing.

"Because landing the jet was the desire of the enchantment," I told him. "The Alpha Prince wanted my parents' location. Which he would have obtained if they'd landed, and they couldn't afford for him to know where they were."

And there hadn't been enough fuel for them to land elsewhere. They'd been surrounded by ocean and glaciers for hundreds of miles. It would have been too obvious had they landed in Greenland.

So they'd flown deeper into the Arctic Circle, away from their initial destination.

And crashed as far away from the end goal as possible.

All the while enchanting a message to arrive with the pendant that now hung from my neck.

"Because wherever they were headed is related to your parents' secrets," Kieran replied softly.

I swallowed, nodding.

He studied me for a long moment, his dark gaze intense. "I'll learn those secrets eventually, Quinnlynn."

I know, I thought, unable to voice the words. *You'll learn them as soon as we're fully mated, and not just because of my mind, but because of my family's magic.*

"But I won't push you for them today," he continued, his thumb brushing my pulse as he leaned in to press a sweet kiss to my lips.

The tenderness in that action surprised me, in addition to the fact that I was fairly certain it was our first kiss.

But he pulled away before it could become anything more. "Ivana will be here soon. You need to shower and dress warmly. It's cold outside."

"She's coming here?" I asked, my hackles immediately rising. "To your rooms?"

He smiled. "As much as I would enjoy provoking your possessive side, no. She'll be in the living area downstairs with Cillian."

"Cillian?" I repeated, frowning. "She's unmated."

His eyebrow winged upward. "Yes. I believe we've already discussed that at length, Quinnlynn."

"Right... You said she's unmated by choice?"

"She is."

"And that's... that's allowed?"

He lifted a shoulder. "I'm not going to force an Omega to take a mate. But I have taken it upon myself to protect her from unwanted suitors. Which is probably why she's still unmated—no one has tried to court her."

"Because she doesn't want to mate, or because she wants to mate you?" I asked, my wolf pacing inside me again, itching to growl and stake her claim. *Our male. Not hers. She's not welcome here. I'll kill her.*

Kieran sighed, his hand leaving my neck before drawing his fingers through his hair. "You'll need to ask Ivana her reasons, but she chooses not to mate. Period."

"Not because she's waiting for you?" I asked, my nails sharpening to claws.

"Even if she was, it wouldn't matter," he replied, his wolf flashing in his gaze. "I'm very much taken, Quinnlynn."

"That doesn't tell me if she's disrespected my claim or not," I pointed out.

"She's never expressed interest, Quinnlynn. Not in me, anyway."

My brow furrowed. "But she has in someone else?"

His lips curled into a half smile. "Not my story to tell, little one. Now put your claws away and go take a shower before I decide to bathe you myself." He leaned forward, his fingers snatching my chin. "And I won't be bathing you in water."

A quiver rippled from my belly at the promise in his words, causing a hint of slick to dampen my thighs. His nostrils flared in response.

"Shower," he growled. "*Now.*"

I scrambled off the bed, determined to obey, mostly because I didn't trust myself to stay.

Because bathing in his cum could be fun.

Then I'd be saturated in his scent and his claim, something I would very much enjoy wearing in front of Ivana.

And then what? You'll parade around the sector in his cum? Go try on dresses while covered in his essence?

Not a bad plan.

I paused at the doorway to the bathroom and turned to look at Kieran.

His eyes narrowed.

Then he slowly slid out of the bed and started toward me, his growl one filled with warning and promise.

My feet rooted themselves to the floor, my wolf refusing to run from her prowling mate.

He caught me by the hips and lifted me without breaking stride, but rather than take me back to the bed, he took me to the shower.

Set me inside.

And turned on the water.

Before stiffly walking away.

I frowned at his back. "This isn't what you promised to do."

"No, it's not," he agreed, his voice low and filled with dark promises. "But I don't reward disobedience, little one." He glanced over his muscular shoulder, his gaze smoldering. "And it seems you like the idea of being drenched in my essence just a little too much for it to be a punishment."

With those silky words, he disappeared, leaving me shivering beneath the lukewarm sprays.

They quickly heated.

But they did little to dispel the chill of disappointment cooling my veins.

My wolf had wanted to play.

As had I.

"I don't reward disobedience, little one."

Then what do you do when a wolf behaves? I wondered, still staring at the vacant doorway. *Maybe we'll find out later.*

Or maybe I would learn more about his punishment preferences instead.

Because I had a century of "bad" behavior to make up for.

And I doubted Kieran had started forgiving me for any of it.

QUINN

Omega Ivana was stunning.

So, naturally, I hated her before she even spoke.

"My Prince," she greeted, her long white hair touching the ground as she curtsied.

It was an elegant move that appeared even more regal as a result of her porcelain features.

She was my complete opposite, all light colors where I was dark.

Ice-blue eyes. White eyebrows and eyelashes to match her hair. Pink lips.

She looked right at home in this opulently furnished room. It was a seating area of sorts with a pair of pristine elevators framed in marble along the back wall.

I'd just been inside one of those gold-plated boxes, Kieran having chosen to descend from his penthouse down to the ground floor via the standard transportation rather than shadowing.

"Hello, Ivana," he greeted politely, his palm going to my lower back while he spoke. "I don't believe you've had the pleasure of meeting our future Queen, but this is Quinnlynn."

Ivana didn't speak at first, her eyes peering up just a little to look at me. "Princess MacNamara." Her flat tone and cold formal title had me raising an eyebrow.

I glanced at Kieran, but he was too busy narrowing his gaze at Cillian, the two males seemingly engaged in a private conversation.

Telepathy, I thought, recalling Cillian's unique talent. I'd never met a V-Clan wolf with that ability, but he came from an ancient bloodline. Just like Kieran. Both of them were almost equal in power, making their friendship rather intriguing.

Most Alphas refused to bow.

But Cillian clearly conceded to Kieran's will, as evidenced now as he slightly angled his head in agreement to whatever they'd just been discussing.

Kieran shifted his gaze to mine, his lips curling just a little. "Cillian will be your guard today. Try not to run. He's in a mood."

I frowned. "Where would I run to? We're on an island." And I couldn't shadow, thanks to the leash Kieran had wrapped around my spirit.

He lifted a shoulder. "I'm sure you could get creative where it counts."

That almost sounded like a compliment, but I suspected he meant it as more of an insult. "I'm not very interested in running right now. Maybe I'll revisit the notion later."

"Hmm," he hummed, his palm sliding up my back to wrap around my nape. He stepped in front of me, giving Ivana and Cillian his back, his lips going to my ear.

"Maybe I'll join you on that run *later* in wolf form."

The words were soft. However, his grip on my neck certainly wasn't gentle. "But only if you behave."

His words from earlier echoed in my mind. *"I don't reward disobedience, little one."*

And now it seemed he would reward me with a run if I behaved. *By taking me for a run*, I thought, my eyes narrowing. "I'm not a dog, Kieran."

"No. You're just my devious intended," he whispered, his nose nuzzling my throat. "I won't be far. Cillian will call me if you need me."

A threat lingered in that statement, one I chose to ignore. Because I had no intention of *running*. Yet I understood why he continued to suggest otherwise.

I deserved it.

Just like I probably deserved the cool look in Ivana's gaze now.

Or maybe that look was a result of her being jealous.

Kieran was certainly a prime Alpha candidate, one many Omegas would crave. But he was mine. And to even consider him as a mate served as an insult to me—their future Queen.

I caught his hip as he started to move away, my eyes lifting to his curious ones.

"I'm not going anywhere," I told him, the words underlined with possession. Because I needed this Omega to understand that this Alpha belonged to me. And while that claim might be temporary—*should* be temporary—it felt needed.

"Wrong, darling." He gave my nape a squeeze. "You're going dress shopping."

That was not what I meant and he knew it, but I played along anyway. "Right. And then I'll return for our run."

He arched a brow.

I arched one back.

"So you plan to behave."

"I plan to reign," I corrected him, feeling bold. *I'm a royal. I don't kneel. I don't* behave. *I rule.*

His lips curled. "I see." He pressed his forehead to mine. "Then find a dress worthy of a Queen." He shadowed before I could respond, leaving me gripping nothing but air and facing an inquisitive-looking Ivana.

There was no jealousy in her icy irises, nor did I see any of the earlier annoyance or spite. Just... interest.

Um, okay. That's not what I expected.

She seemed to be reconsidering me, her irises flicking over my boots, jeans, and sweater before returning to my face.

I lifted my brow again, this time to challenge her. "Well?" I prompted. "Do I live up to your expectations, Ivana?"

She considered me for a long moment. "Not quite," she answered.

Then she turned with a flourish, her long, silky hair flowing in her wake like a cape, and started across the room, her booted heels clacking against the obsidian stone beneath her.

"Excuse me?" I demanded, not used to being treated so rudely, and especially not by a fellow Omega.

Everything I did in this world was meant to protect them. To *help* them.

Of course, Ivana didn't know that. She seemed to be pretty well cared for under Kieran's guard, but not all Omegas were so fortunate.

Ivana paused to look back at me, her expression exuding supreme confidence. "You asked. I answered." She shrugged. "If you don't want honesty, don't ask questions." With that, she started walking again.

I gaped after her, stunned by her easy candor and rudeness. And yet, impressed by it at the same time.

"It's going to be a bloody long afternoon," Cillian muttered.

"I heard that," Ivana called back to him.

"I wasn't trying to hide it," he replied, glancing at me. "After you, Princess."

Rather than comment, I moved forward, pursuing Ivana. "And what are your expectations?" I asked, honestly curious as to what she *expected* of me.

"A princess who doesn't flee at the first sign of trouble, for one," she replied without missing a beat. "But I suppose you haven't tried to run yet, so there's that."

"I didn't *flee* at the first sign of trouble."

"Oh?" She stopped by a pair of heavy wood doors and gave me an incredulous look. "So you didn't disappear during the zombie apocalypse?"

"It wasn't a zombie apocalypse," Cillian interjected.

She waved him off. "Yes, yes, the *Infected Era*. But they're zombies. And she"—Ivana pointed at me—"ran, leaving us all to fend for ourselves."

My eyebrows flew upward. "I did not. I left several years before that happened."

"And didn't come back," Ivana drawled. "Yes, *Princess*, I'm aware of the historical account of your life." She pushed through the threshold and stepped into a grand hallway I didn't recognize. Windows lined the corridor, reminding me a bit of the glass wall of Kieran's room.

Rather than focus on that, I gave my attention to Ivana.

"Tell me more about my *historical account*," I requested, genuinely curious about the rumors. Ivana was clearly young, maybe twenty-five at most, and therefore she hadn't even been alive when I'd *fled*. "What stories have they told you about me?"

"Does it matter?" she asked, leading the way with a knowledge and confidence that told me she visited here often.

We'll circle back to why *you're so familiar with my intended's home later*, I thought, studying the light-haired woman again. "It matters because I requested it," I told her. "And you promised me the truth. So indulge me."

"I didn't promise you shit," she replied.

"Ivana," Cillian warned.

"What?" She met and held his gaze without flinching. "I'm doing this as a favor for Kieran because he asked me to help his *intended* find a dress. He never told me I had to be kind about it."

"Fine, then I'm telling you to be kind." And his tone suggested she should listen to his command.

But all the Omega did was smile. "I'm respectfully *declining*."

His eyes narrowed, his Alpha energy warming the air. "*Ivana*."

"What are you going to do? *Growl* at me?" she demanded, arching one delicate eyebrow.

He clenched his jaw.

"Yeah, that's what I thought." She gave me a look that I couldn't decipher and pushed onward toward the exit. "Come on, Princess. The stores close in two hours, and I doubt any of them will stay open late for you."

My eyebrows were in my hairline again.

And Cillian looked ready to murder the mouthy Omega.

These two clearly had a history, one that had me wondering if that little private chat earlier between Kieran and Cillian had something to do with Ivana and not me.

I followed the fiery Omega into a foyer and toward the front doors—which were all glass, just like the hallway walls—and out into the street. We were along the harbor here, right in the center of Reykjavik. I had already guessed that based on the view from his room, but it was nice to orient myself on the ground.

I stole a deep breath, enjoying the familiar scents of home.

Unfortunately, the clicking of Ivana's high-heeled boots on the sidewalk told me she was already walking.

And it wasn't toward the water.

Sighing, I turned to follow her, my heelless boots silent against the concrete. Cillian was also quiet, his large form prowling alongside us with a lethal grace that defied reason.

Just like Kieran, I thought, imagining my intended's panther-like stride. *It's a wonder they haven't killed each other yet.*

Not all Alphas desire war, Princess, Cillian replied, making me jump.

Because those words hadn't been aloud, but *inside my mind*.

He smirked at my obvious discomfort. *If you don't wish to converse this way, might I suggest lowering your mental tones?*

How does one "lower a mental tone"? I asked incredulously.

By modulating your voice, he suggested.

I gave him a skeptical look. *Or you could try tuning me out.*

I usually do, he admitted. *But there are particular words and names I listen for, Kieran and my own being among them.*

Then you must overhear a lot of thoughts, I deadpanned.

I do. His dark eyes went to Ivana a few steps ahead of us. *But I've learned how to pick and choose.*

Maybe you can choose not to hear mine.

Only when you're with Kieran, he replied. *Otherwise, it's my responsibility to protect you.*

Protect me, I repeated, snorting. *Or do you mean guard me to make sure I don't run again?*

My job is to protect you. Kieran is responsible for everything else. His nearly black irises met mine. *It's his job to ensure you don't run, not mine.*

I considered his words while we walked, his comments providing a sense of ease.

Because Kieran hadn't assigned him to me to ensure I didn't try to escape; he'd assigned him to me as a protection detail.

But why? I wondered. *Why do I need a bodyguard here?*

Cillian didn't reply, just glanced at the sidewalk across from us.

I followed his gaze, my lips curling down. Several humans and wolves had paused on the sidewalk, or perhaps had just walked out of their respective homes and buildings, but none of them were making any move to approach us.

I swallowed, the hairs along my arms dancing with discomfort.

Because they were all murmuring amongst themselves.

And watching me.

Two more shifters stepped out, one of whom I recognized immediately. *Myon.* My heart skipped a beat, my feet almost angling toward him.

Except he stopped me with a scowl.

My lips parted at the disgusted expression coloring his pale features, surprise nearly causing me to trip over my feet.

Myon had been my father's Elite, the equivalent of what Cillian and Lorcan were to Kieran. He'd always treated me like a daughter, doting on me and protecting me from afar.

However, his soured look now told me that things had

definitely changed between us. He no longer saw me as his *little princess*—as he'd once fondly called me—but something else. *Someone* else.

As I glanced up and down the street, it became apparent that he wasn't the only one looking at me like that. Almost everyone shared his obvious distaste.

My gaze lowered, my shoulders seeming to pull forward as I longed to be able to shadow. But Kieran had taken it from me. He'd forced me to walk these streets as a mortal would without the ability to disappear.

This is my punishment, I realized, the pain of it striking me through the heart. *He's making me feel the sector's wrath, to know how disappointed they are in me for leaving.*

Cillian didn't reply, but he didn't need to. And my comments weren't meant for him anyway. They were meant for me.

I'd expected the worst from Kieran, some sort of sexual torment or public declaration of our severed betrothal. Perhaps a forced knotting, or even making me carry his heir to term so he could be rid of me forever.

Continuing the royal line without having to mate me in the process, I thought darkly.

But no.

He'd chosen a far more appropriate punishment, one meant to teach me a lesson.

Except none of them, not even Kieran, knew the truth about why I'd left. *Would it change their opinions if they did?* I wondered. *Or would they be furious with me for keeping such important truths from them?*

The Sanctuary was a long-standing secret, one only my family line knew about.

However, the world had changed drastically over the last century. Perhaps it was time to share the secret.

Perhaps it was time… to talk to Kieran and tell him everything.

Can I trust him? I asked myself as I followed Ivana around a corner toward an open street. *Can I…?* I trailed off, the scene before me momentarily distracting me from my thoughts.

There were several more pack members gathered here, all of them standing in silence as we moved by them.

No one greeted me.

All they did was stare.

No, not even that. They *glared*.

"Doing our prince's bidding, Ivana?" a female asked, her voice sickly sweet.

"You're just jealous he didn't ask you, Miranda," Ivana replied in a matching tone. "Of course, he never does, does he?"

The dark-haired woman—*Miranda*—narrowed her equally dark eyes. "You don't know anything."

"I know enough." Ivana smiled. "Just like I know he'll never accept your offer, or any of the others." She looked pointedly at the group around Miranda.

Omegas, my wolf told me with a sniff. *Fertile. Unmated. Omegas.*

These are the females who have propositioned my intended, I realized in the next beat, my gaze narrowing. *The disrespectful wolves who dared to touch what is rightfully mine.*

It served as a slap in the face to my position, a proverbial insult to my very throne.

But as much as I wanted to put them in their place and remind them of my superiority, I couldn't. Because I'd brought this fate upon myself. I recognized that now, understood the disdain my fellow wolves were throwing my way, and accepted their hatred.

Because sometimes leading meant making sacrifices for the betterment of our world.

I knew that better than anyone. I'd made countless sacrifices for those weaker than myself, for those who *needed* me more than my own people.

Blood Sector had Kieran.

The Omegas I'd saved only had me. My parents only had me, too. I was the only one who could find out what had truly happened to them.

One day, my people would understand. Just as soon as I could tell them the truth.

Until then, I'd accept their judgment. I'd accept their anger. I'd accept their disrespect.

Cillian glanced at me curiously, his eyebrow lifting upward.

Stay out of my head, I warned him.

Too late for that, Princess, he murmured as we stopped before a shop. *But I don't make a habit of sharing what I overhear unless I feel it's a threat.*

Oh. I wasn't sure what to say to that because I wasn't sure how much he'd truly overheard.

And while I think you're absolutely a threat to Kieran, it's the kind of threat I think he deserves, he continued as he reached around me to open the door. *So your secrets are safe with me, Princess.*

"Ivana," he added out loud, pulling her away from the ensuing conversation with the Omegas. I hadn't been listening, too caught up in my discussion with Cillian.

"Yes, Ivana," the one called Miranda said. "Do what the Alpha tells you, and maybe he'll finally knot you. Oh, wait... that hasn't worked out very well for you, has it?"

"About as well as you begging Prince Kieran for his knot," Ivana shot back, entirely unbothered by the word play. "At least I don't try to seduce mated males."

"He's not mated yet," Miranda sniffed, her liquid brown gaze boldly meeting mine. "Is he, *Princess*?"

I stared at her for a long moment, momentarily at a loss for what to say. Omegas never spoke to me like this.

Alas, our situation here wasn't typical. I'd abandoned my wolves, something they would all see as unforgivable.

Yet I'd returned to a position of power solely because of my blood.

And only because Kieran had found me and forced me to return home.

That wasn't going to endear me to these shifters very quickly. Several of them—including all the Omegas standing on the street before me—were new to me. While my family name and destiny might be renowned throughout the V-Clan world, these wolves didn't actually *know* me. Very few people did.

So while Miranda and the others had clearly disrespected my rule by trying to seduce my mate, I couldn't find it in myself to be rude to them. Not over this. Not after I'd abandoned them.

It didn't matter that I'd done it all for the right reasons. Until I could explain that, they wouldn't understand.

Which meant I needed to earn their forgiveness and respect through other means.

"No," I finally said, thinking through my answer as I voiced it. "No, he's not mated yet."

Her eyebrows shot upward in obvious surprise at my calm reply, an expressive response that made me smile.

"But he will be soon," I added. "And then I will become your Queen, and he will be *my* King."

With those words sweetening the air between us, I turned toward Cillian and the door he still held open for us.

Only to be stopped by Ivana grabbing my shoulder.

I shifted my focus to her, my eyebrow arched in question.

"I stand corrected," she said, her gaze running over me with interest. "Now you're starting to live up to my expectations."

She smiled.

Then led the way into the shop.

KIERAN

Sire.

I stopped typing my email to Riley and leaned back in my chair to mentally answer my Elite. *Yes, Cillian?*

Myon has been trailing us. I just caught him lurking outside the shop.

I ran my palm over my face and sighed. *He's probably just worried about her. He and her father were close.*

Quinnlynn's father had left numerous notes behind, all of which suggested a closeness to Myon that rivaled my own with Cillian and Lorcan. It was a closeness I'd identified almost immediately upon meeting the older shifter as well.

Myon had made his disapproval of me evident from the beginning, his dislike of my betrothal to Quinnlynn palpable and obvious in the way he'd addressed me. It hadn't been a jealous sort of disdain, but a fatherly one, suggesting he had not approved of our mating.

That was one of the many reasons I hadn't allowed him to remain on as part of my personal Elite.

I couldn't afford to have someone at my back that I couldn't trust.

He wasn't exactly warm when he saw her on the street, Cillian replied. *He radiated disapproval.*

Hmm, I hummed. *Sounds familiar.*

There's more, he continued.

Isn't there always? I drawled.

He ignored my comment. *Miranda made herself known.*

I considered that for a long moment. *How did Quinnlynn react?*

Like a Queen, he murmured, approval evident in his tone. *She made it very clear that she intends to make you her King.*

Did she now? That intrigued me. *And you believe her?*

Yes.

Did you overhear something? I wondered, even more curious now.

Many things, Sire. Many things.

And you're not going to share them with me, are you?

No, I am not.

Because you're still sour over this assignment? I guessed. *Punishing me for making you spend an evening with your intended?*

Ivana is not my intended, he retorted without missing a beat. *And no. I'm not sharing the information because I promised Quinnlynn I wouldn't. You need a challenge, Sire. It's how you thrive, right?*

My lips twitched at the memory of Quinnlynn's *proposal.* That was clearly the memory he meant to play on, and it worked. *You're either fucking with me, Cillian, or truly testing my patience.*

Perhaps a bit of both, he admitted. *But your Omega needs you, Sire. So try to reserve some of that patience for her.*

I frowned at that. *Are you on your way home?*

Yes, we're almost there. And all the wolves on the street are presenting Quinnlynn with their backs.

Fuck. I closed my tablet and stood.

You knew this would happen, Sire.

I did, but that didn't mean I enjoyed being right. Without her ability to shadow, Quinnlynn would be forced to face them all. *I'm on my way.*

Let her finish her walk, Cillian said before I could teleport to him. *She's holding her head up high and taking everything in literal stride. Don't ruin her moment by making her appear weak.*

I swallowed, my fingers curling into fists. *You told me this to punish me, didn't you?* Because he would know how much I'd long to go to her, to pull her into my arms and purr the pain away.

No, Sire. I'm ensuring you receive my full report, as requested.

I snorted. *A basthaird mór.*

A term I believe I used only hours ago to describe you.

You called me a gobdaw. Essentially a pretentious fool.

Close enough, he replied. *But you're insulting my mam by calling me a bastard.*

I just shook my head. *I hate these games.*

As do I, Sire. As do I.

And yet he was playing one with me right now.

We're almost there, he told me. *She's not spoken a word.*

What is she thinking?

Ask her when you see her, he suggested.

Of course he wouldn't help me. He'd know I didn't actually want to know. Because I'd prefer that she open up to me willingly.

I shadowed downstairs to wait for her near the doors, just inside my building.

There were several wolves standing right outside, their backs all presented to the sidewalk. Word must have spread of her outing, causing half the damn sector to come out to display their disappointment in their Queen.

Cillian was right—I'd known this would happen.

I just hadn't expected it to bother me this much.

Perhaps I felt this way because I now knew that part of

the reason she'd fled was to find out more about her parents' death. It was a noble cause, one I wished she would have shared with me prior to leaving. But trust had to be earned, something she was now experiencing firsthand with those under our rule in Blood Sector.

I watched from the shadows as she moved down the sidewalk, Ivana nowhere in sight. *What happened to Ivana?* I asked.

Quinnlynn thanked her for her assistance, then told her she would handle the walk back on her own.

How did Ivana take that?

Ivana nodded and said, "Like a Queen should." Then she left.

So they got along? I pressed.

So it would seem.

Good. I had hoped that would happen. Ivana was a strong Omega, one who voiced her demands and accepted nothing less in response to them. Very similar to my betrothed.

Because, like Quinnlynn, Ivana had also chosen her mate.

Only, unlike Quinnlynn, Ivana's choice had denied her.

Because he's a stubborn arse who refuses to allow himself to be happy.

Fuck you, too, Cillian said, clearly listening to my thoughts.

Eavesdropping has its consequences.

He didn't reply, instead choosing to meet my gaze through the windows. I was still hidden in the shadows, but he could sense me. Quinnlynn would be able to as well if she tried, but I suspected she was too caught up in holding her emotions in check to search for me.

Three shifters blocked her entrance to the building, their faces masks of stone as she paused behind them.

It took serious restraint not to growl and demand that

they move for my intended. But this was her task to fulfill, not mine.

Because Cillian was right—I needed to let her finish this walk on her own.

She considered them for a moment, giving me a chance to scrutinize her features. Other than a slight tug on her lips, she appeared completely unfazed by the display outside. But that subtle tightness around her mouth told me this all bothered her a lot more than she let on.

I pulled the shadows more tightly around myself to ensure I remained hidden, the instinct to take charge making me doubt my control.

But then Quinnlynn smiled, the expression unlike anything I'd seen on her since her return, and it quite literally took my breath away.

"It's nice to see you all supporting one another." Her voice was soft, but it carried through the glass, my enhanced hearing allowing me to catch every word.

"I wish this demonstration of unity wasn't at my expense," she continued, "but I understand your anger and frustration. I accept it. And none of this will make me love you all any less."

She turned to take in the wolves across the street, giving me her back in the process.

"Blood Sector is my home, and I know my actions have been perceived as dishonorable. But I've returned. And I fully intend to reclaim my family's throne with Kieran O'Callaghan by my side."

"You think you're still worthy of him after all that you've done?"

I narrowed my gaze as I sought out the owner of that question. It came from across the street. Feminine, but not soft.

"Maybe we don't want you on the throne," a second

female said. "Maybe we would prefer that Kieran take a more appropriate mate."

"She's heir to the throne," a male replied. "Her bloodline must thrive."

A series of snorts followed that statement.

"She can provide an heir for us to raise. Then run away again to hide." That came from the second female voice. *Florence.* I identified her only because she turned to reveal herself as she finished speaking.

Several others followed suit, their expressions all hard and filled with fury as a series of malicious statements spilled from their lips.

"We don't want you here."

"We don't accept you."

"You abandoned us."

"I won't call you my Queen."

"Your parents would be ashamed of you."

"You've tarnished the MacNamara name."

"Go back to wherever you came from. You're no longer welcome here."

Quinnlynn didn't move, her shoulders rigid as each hurtful word graced the night air.

The three males blocking the entrance to my building finally moved, but it was only to face her, not to grant her entry.

"You're a disgrace," one of them said. "An Omega unworthy of your own genetics."

"Kieran should breed you and kill you."

I can't let this continue, I warned Cillian.

But he was already moving, ignoring my comment and focusing on the Beta who'd just insulted me and my mate. He grabbed the bastard by his throat and shoved him up against the doors.

"You dare dishonor your future King and Queen with

213

such blasphemy? To call for the *death* of your Queen by the King's hand?" he demanded.

Quinnlynn reached for Cillian's shoulder. "It's okay," she whispered, her voice not nearly as strong as before. "Everything they've said is true."

"No. Everything they've said makes me question the leadership I've provided to this sector," I corrected as I materialized beside her, no longer able to keep my distance or observe this cruelty.

Several of the wolves gasped in surprise.

Others immediately bowed their heads.

And a few wore expressions of shame, including the Beta Cillian still had pinned to the doors.

"Blood Sector thrives on unity," I added. "But also on mutual respect and forgiveness."

I looked at each wolf on the street, allowing them to feel my shame and disappointment in their behavior.

To give Quinnlynn their backs was one thing.

But this? To smother her in cruel statements? This I would not allow.

"We value support and respect," I reminded them all. "Yes, Princess Quinnlynn broke our faith in her, but she's returned. And I fully intend to repair our connection. Because we made a vow to each other once, and I trust her to see it through."

I held out my hand to my intended mate, my gaze finally meeting hers.

"Am I right to trust you?" I asked softly, my words meant for Quinnlynn, not for the others.

Hell, this entire display of devotion was for her.

I wanted the wolves to know that I believed in giving her a second chance. Therefore, they should, too.

Because I suspected her reasons for fleeing went beyond what I already knew about her parents.

Which made her actions noble.

Once she shared her story, those here today would be apologizing to her, not the other way around.

Her dark eyes glimmered with unspoken emotion as she evaluated my words and stance.

My offer wasn't meant to belittle her. Nor was it a power play. This was about standing together as a team, sharing our strengths, and demonstrating our promise to each other.

If she understood me at all, she would know that.

Submission required kneeling. That wasn't what I'd asked her to do. I'd asked for her trust instead.

And she gave it to me by accepting my hand. "Yes," she said softly. "We can trust each other." The emotion in her eyes grew with that statement, telling me that this embrace served as a pivotal moment between us.

So small, yet so incredibly large at the same time.

I pulled her into me, my purr automatic as I pressed my lips to her hair. She shivered, her exhaustion a palpable presence that I attempted to soothe with my strength.

She'd been so strong walking along these streets, accepting the rejection of her home, absorbing all their barbed comments, and taking my hand for all of them to see. Pride blossomed in my chest, my wolf utterly pleased with his chosen mate.

"Did you find a dress?" I asked her softly, aware that we still had an audience.

Let them see us. Let them know us. Let them understand us.

"Yes." She nuzzled into my chest, her hand releasing mine as her arms encircled my waist. "He's making some alterations. It might end up being covered in blood or ripped to shreds, though."

"Cameron won't do that," I promised, my lips at Quinnlynn's ear. "He knows how important tomorrow is."

Quinnlynn didn't reply, just inhaled deeply and allowed my energy to embolden her own.

I wrapped my arm around her lower back, securing her. Then I grasped her nape with my free hand and gave it a gentle squeeze of reassurance.

It was a touch that said, *Mine,* and it was one I wanted everyone to see.

Because I intended to mate this female.

The pack might not have found her worthy, but I did.

And my opinion was what mattered most.

I lifted my gaze to the wolves around us, ensuring they all saw and understood our embrace. This wasn't about mastering Quinnlynn or demonstrating my power over her. This was about displaying our power *together.* And I could see that acknowledgment blossoming throughout the crowd.

We are your royals, your leaders, your future. We are united. I forgive my intended mate, and so will you.

"Think about what I've said," I told our observers, my voice holding a note of command. "We'll see you tomorrow."

I glanced at Cillian. He still had the Beta by the neck, his grip unyielding. *You can make an example out of him if you want,* I murmured to my Elite via our mental connection. *But don't kill him. He deserves the right to grovel.*

He insulted your honor by suggesting you would breed and kill your own intended. He deserves death, Cillian argued.

Then make it hurt. But teach him a lesson he can remember and learn from, yeah? I didn't wait to hear Cillian's agreement, instead choosing to wrap my intended up in shadows and take her back to my room.

She didn't move, her face still buried against my chest as we materialized beside my bed.

I purred louder for her, giving her a moment to

acclimate and accept my strength in private. She shuddered in response, her arms tightening around me as she absorbed my energy. It wasn't the same as healing, just an exchange of power that kept us grounded.

It was an exchange that would intensify when we officially mated.

But that was a conversation for another day.

Right now, my mate needed my support, and she'd more than earned it with her performance outside. "Do you still want to go for a run?" I asked softly.

KIERAN

QUINNLYNN DIDN'T IMMEDIATELY REPLY, her arms still clutching me as though I were her lifeline. But she eventually tilted her head back, allowing me to see her beautiful eyes. She stared up at me with a mixture of confusion and wonder and *need*.

That last emotion came from her wolf, the animal inside her peering hungrily at me through her dark pupils.

My inner beast growled in approval, ready to play as soon as our mate asked.

But the human part of Quinnlynn was still very much in charge. "Why?"

I frowned. "Why do I want to go for a run?" Had she forgotten our conversation from earlier?

"No, I mean why did you interrupt?" She studied me intently. "I deserved their ire, Kieran. I abandoned them. They've earned the right to chastise me."

I considered her for a long moment before saying, "A few weeks ago, I would have agreed. However, while I don't know all the reasons you left, I now suspect those reasons are noble."

She swallowed, her eyes still searching mine. "But they have a right to express their anger."

"Yes," I agreed. "Except the pack will never forgive themselves if they find out they ridiculed you unnecessarily. It'll rip them apart, Quinnlynn."

"Assuming I can ever tell them."

"Why can't you?" I wondered aloud, my thumb tracing the column of her neck. "Don't they deserve to know the truth about your parents?"

"The truth requires me to find out who killed them. It also might necessitate admitting the reason it all happened —the reason why their jet was enchanted—and I don't know if I can do that."

I arched a brow at that. "Because you don't trust the sector?"

"Because it's a family secret that's been guarded for generations," she whispered, her expression shuttering. That look alone told me she wasn't ready to trust me yet with that secret, which meant she didn't consider me family yet.

"That's the primary reason you ran," I mused out loud. "You didn't want me to know this secret."

"I've already admitted that," she replied.

I nodded. "Yes, when I was providing comfort and you accused me of trying to lull you into a state of submission to gain information."

She swallowed, her throat working as she seemed to consider how to respond. "I don't think you murdered my parents."

"Good. Because I didn't."

"But I'm not ready to tell you yet," she added, her expression wary.

"Hmm," I hummed. Well, I supposed her response was better than simply refusing to tell me. Instead, she'd said she just wasn't ready to confide in me… *yet*. A key phrase, one that suggested she was considering opening up to me on her own.

I could bite her and learn all her secrets now.

But I'd rather earn it.

Because it's a challenge, I thought, smiling a little. *Something she knows I enjoy.*

"Will you one day tell me who gave you intelligence on me?" I asked, genuinely curious. "Because I've wondered who confided secrets to you from the very beginning of our courtship."

She fell silent for a long moment, then slowly nodded. "Yes. If you give me time to process everything, I'll give you the answers you seek."

"A deal?" I rephrased. "One that requires me to trust you not to run again?"

"Not exactly. You've already leashed me, Kieran. I'm not asking to be set free. I'm just asking for more time."

"Indeed," I agreed, because she was right—she hadn't asked me to release her at all. She was just requesting that I not push her for details.

Or bite her, I mentally added. Because we both knew I could mate her whenever I wanted to. She was fully healed now. All I had to do was sink my fangs into her pretty little throat, and she would become mine in every way.

But that wouldn't be as enjoyable as hearing her beg me to claim her.

Hearing her voice the truth with her mouth instead of via thoughts in her mind.

Making Quinnlynn—*the human part of her*—confess her desires to mate me with words, not just with her body.

Yes, I much prefer all that, I decided. "All right, little one," I told her. "I concede to this challenge."

Something sparkled in her eyes, a hint of excitement

twinged with arousal. "You do?"

"I do," I replied, my grip on her nape resolute as I tightened my arm around her slender waist. "You're worth the effort, Quinnlynn."

"Because of my bloodline?" she guessed.

I shook my head. "No, darling. Because of _you_." I brushed my lips against hers, my desire to kiss her a foreign concept in my mind.

I never kissed females.

It just wasn't part of the mating need.

But Quinnlynn... she made me want so much more. She made me want to taste and explore and learn every delectable detail about her. She made me want to bow and worship her, all while indulging in her submission as I taught her my own preferences in life. A conundrum that left me eager and slightly unhinged.

Only to be grounded by her presence once more.

"You're very brave." My words were quiet and underlined with the pride I felt warming my chest. "Honorable, too."

I released her nape to cup her cheek, wanting to look into her eyes while I spoke.

She responded by leaning into my touch, her pale cheeks blossoming with pretty pink shades.

"You handled our sector's wrath today like a Queen, never once cowering in the face of their disappointment and pain. Instead, you welcomed it and even excused it. There are not many who could be that strong, Quinnlynn."

"I did what needed to be done," she whispered.

"You accepted your punishment with grace and dignity." I drew my thumb along her cheekbone, allowing those words to swirl between us. "I'm proud of you, My Queen."

That blush on her cheeks deepened, her eyes searching mine for answers to questions she didn't voice aloud.

However, there was one I hadn't quite addressed— *"Why did you interrupt?"*

"To answer your earlier question, Quinnlynn, I interrupted our wolves because it was time for them to stop. I don't believe in going backward, only forward. They expressed their disquiet, you accepted their comments, and now we all need to focus on tomorrow. On our future."

She stared up at me with even more questions, her head shaking slightly back and forth. "You're not at all what I expected, Kieran O'Callaghan."

"Maybe you'll give me a chance to show you who I am, then, Quinnlynn MacNamara."

"Maybe I will," she replied, her voice soft as she continued to scrutinize me. "Part of me still worries that your kindness is all a ploy, a way to lull me into the real punishment to come."

"And what would that real punishment entail?" I asked, curious to hear her dark thoughts. "I've already told you that I remained faithful and I have no intention of taking another Omega."

"You could be lying," she whispered.

"I could be," I conceded. "But I think my actions should prove the veracity of my statements, Quinnlynn."

She started to nod, only to pause. "It's not easy to trust."

"No, I suppose it's not." Because I certainly wasn't ready to trust her yet either. "But are you willing to try?"

It took her a beat before she replied with a quiet "Yes."

"That doesn't sound very certain."

"I want to try," she admitted, the truth in those words reflected in her expression and her tone. "But it's been a long time since I could trust anyone other than Kyra."

My brow furrowed. "Kyra?"

Her eyes immediately rounded, the name obviously a slip of the tongue. "My... my..."

"Informant?" I guessed.

She didn't reply, but she didn't have to. I could see it in her concerned eyes. She definitely hadn't meant to give me that name.

Because I absolutely recognized it.

"A Vampire Omega," I mused, my lips twitching. "I suppose you would be friends, wouldn't you? She disappeared a few centuries ago, made her Alpha quite mad."

Quinnlynn still didn't speak.

"He died rather gruesomely, too," I continued. "But something tells me you already know all about that."

The blush in her cheeks had long disappeared into a pale shade that told me far more than her words ever could.

"I see." This was very interesting information. And it seemed I no longer needed her to tell me *who* had been talking to her about me. She'd just supplied me with the answer via a slip of the tongue.

Alpha Fare hadn't been a friend of mine, more of an acquaintance. Most vampires fell into that category. But he would have known enough about me to share important intelligence with a mate.

"Kieran..." My name left her mouth with a hush of sound.

"What do you think I'm going to do?" I asked her, slightly amused. "Demand that you hand Kyra's location over to me so I can give it to the vampires for retribution?"

Her skin seemed to pale even more, which shouldn't have been possible, given that she already resembled a ghost.

I released her lower back so I could cup her cheeks between both my hands.

"I don't play by anyone else's rules, love. Only my own." I pressed my lips to hers, my purr reigniting to soothe her worries. "I suppose my not being a hero works well for you in this case, hmm?" I pulled her into another hug, one she accepted with brittle arms.

Rather than say more, I simply held her.

She'd revealed yet another secret, and I would prove to her through my actions that she could trust me. Just as I would rely on her to show me that I could put my faith in her via her own choices.

I hadn't once felt her tug on my invisible leash, not even when the sector had descended upon her.

And the tug I'd felt the other day had been a misunderstanding between us.

Which meant she truly wasn't considering running. At least, not for the moment.

While I longed to believe that she would remain, I couldn't. Not yet.

Time would bolster our confidence in one another.

Or it would kill it entirely.

Only fate knew what came next.

But for now... "It's been a long evening," I whispered against her ear. "How about we go for that run?"

"A run?" she repeated, her voice hoarse.

I nodded. "Yes. A run. We can watch the sunrise together." I pressed a kiss to the throbbing pulse point on her neck. "Tomorrow's a new day, after all. And I would like to welcome it with you at my side." I straightened to read her expression.

Some of the color had returned to her cheeks, my purr seeming to be the antidote to all our troubles.

Or perhaps it was my lack of pushing her that had calmed her down.

"A run," she said again.

I arched a brow. "Yes, Quinnlynn. In wolf form."

Her chin came down a little, her nod shaky. "I... I would like that."

My lips twitched. "Your animal is demanding that you agree, isn't she?"

"Yes." She cleared my throat. "She's... she's demanding a lot of things."

That caused my mouth to twist up into a full smile. "Perhaps you can detail those things for me after our run," I suggested. "Whilst naked, preferably."

The sweet perfume of her slick graced the air, confirming she and her wolf very much liked that agenda for the evening.

"You'd better shift quickly, dear intended," I warned her. "Or I'll skip to the naked part now."

She shivered visibly. "I'm not sure I would object to that plan."

I nipped at her chin, my lips finding her ear again. "Then consider our run foreplay." I reached for the hem of her sweater and tugged it upward, revealing her breasts beneath. She hadn't bothered with undergarments—something that was typical for our kind. I found the trait very useful right now.

My sweater joined hers on the floor.

Then I went for her pants at the same time that she went for mine, her fingers bold as she met and held my stare. *There's my mate*, I thought. *My strong, beautiful, daring female.*

She'd crossed into my boundary to propose a betrothal, knowing full well that I could have taken her by force. Yet she'd been confident. Bold. Maybe a bit naïve.

Except she'd planned everything from the beginning.

And then she'd run.

"You asked me if it's your bloodline I desire." I tugged down her zipper. "But it's so much more, Quinnlynn. It's your courage I enjoy. Your fight. Your ability to outmaneuver and trick me."

She kicked off her boots, her eyes resembling black diamonds as she held my stare.

I knelt before her, my hands roaming over her legs as I divested her of the material. "Your talent for hiding all these years without me being able to capture you," I added, my mouth scant inches from her glistening cunt. "I only caught you because you chose not to run."

Her irises glittered, her lips parting to reveal her sweet little tongue.

"You once told me how much I enjoy a challenge, Quinnlynn." I leaned forward just enough to breathe the words against her clit. "You weren't wrong." I nuzzled her shaved mound and inhaled her alluring fragrance. "And you became my favorite challenge of them all."

I placed an open-mouthed kiss right against her damp flesh.

Her knees buckled in response, but I caught her and held her to me as I devoured her with my tongue. She clutched my head, her lips parting on a moan that turned into a growl when I brought her to the ground and said, "*Shift.*"

I released her to finish removing my own clothes, my gaze holding hers the whole time.

"See?" I murmured, prowling toward her again. "A challenge." I leaned down to nip her sensitive nub. "But we both know I can make you shift, Quinnlynn. So indulge me in a run, and if you're good, I'll eat this sweet pussy while the sun rises."

QUINN

My thighs tingled with memories of my run with Kieran and the way he'd made me scream for nearly an hour straight.

He'd damn near tortured me with his tongue.

And then he hadn't knotted me.

"I believe I owed you that after the other day," he'd said, referring to when he'd growled after I'd gone down on him.

While he wasn't wrong, I found myself craving so much more. Primarily his knot.

I squeezed my legs together, causing Cameron to tsk at me. "You're doing a poor job staying still, Princess."

"Sorry," I mumbled as he unfastened part of my dress at the back to tie it again.

It was a corset-like top, the ribbon going from my ass all the way up to my shoulder blades, and every time I moved, it offset his crisscross pattern.

I closed my eyes and tried to focus on my breathing while Cameron worked.

He'd already done my hair, choosing to keep it simple

by weaving a light blue ribbon through some ringlets. It gave my hair a lot of volume, the splash of color helping to highlight the depth and thickness of my mane—something I very much appreciated after decades of tying it all back at my nape.

I could have worn a crown.

But something about this felt better, like I was entering the betrothal dinner as myself, not a future Queen.

My parents had never been very flashy with their wealth or power, a trait I had admired and chosen to follow. It seemed Kieran had as well, at least to an extent.

He owned this entire building, but that wasn't about exuding his position or superiority over the pack. It was about security.

Kieran had entered this sector as an Alpha Prince, not the designated heir. The only reason he'd been welcomed was his betrothal to me. However, I suspected it ran so much deeper than that now. I'd seen the way the sector had bowed to him last night, their respect palpable, as was their shame at him chastising their behavior.

They considered him their Alpha now. Their *King*. Just like I'd wanted—like I'd *planned*.

I should be elated. Proud. Pleased that everything worked out the way I'd wanted it to.

Yet I didn't feel elated at all. I was... disappointed.

Disappointed that I hadn't been here to watch it all happen. Disappointed that I hadn't been able to help. Disappointed that I hadn't been a part of the journey.

Disappointed that I took too long to come home.

I swallowed, my mind spinning with conflicting thoughts.

This is how it needed to be.

I did everything right.

Then why does it all feel so wrong?

Kyra had provided me with ample updates over the years, but hearing the results was so much different from seeing them up close. Feeling the love and adoration the pack had developed for Kieran. Sensing their ire and displeasure for me.

None of it was what I'd pictured.

Mostly because I'd hoped to solve the mystery behind my parents' murder decades ago. I'd just gotten so caught up in helping the Omegas that I'd chosen to continue down that path.

Because Kyra had assured me that Kieran had everything handled here.

Which was all true—he'd absolutely established his control and had taken excellent care of Blood Sector in my absence.

But knowing that had been part of the reason I hadn't rushed home. *Everyone's fine. They don't need me.*

However, now I saw those phrases for the excuses that they'd been. I'd been running for so long that I'd forgotten how important it was to return home.

And now I would face the repercussions of that delay.

Deep breaths, Quinn. Deep breaths.

"Done," Cameron announced from behind me. His palms found my shoulders, the touch oddly warm. "Eyes open, Princess. Head high. Make your parents proud."

I exhaled slowly and did what he said, my gaze meeting his blue eyes in the mirror before me. "Thank you."

"Don't thank me, darl'. Working with your beauty was all the gratitude I needed."

"Careful, Beta, or I might choose to misunderstand your affection for my intended mate." Kieran's lethal tone cut through the air as he appeared right beside us, his power an avalanche of energy that heated my skin enough to lightly burn.

Cameron immediately dropped his hands. "I-I would never," he stammered. "I-I know she's... yours. My Prince." He bowed low, making me catch Kieran's gaze in the mirror.

Leave him alone, I said with my eyes.

He simply arched a brow back at me, almost as though daring me to make him.

All right, Alpha, I thought, facing him and taking in his black-on-black tuxedo. It fit him like a glove, revealing all that sleek and beautiful power beneath the clothes. I ran my gaze over him and allowed him to see my interest.

"You look very handsome, My Prince," I told him demurely.

"Do I?" he countered, his expression telling me I needed to try harder to distract him.

"You do." I ran my fingers up his vest to his tie and continued my path until I reached his collar. "Black is a good color on you."

"Hmm," he hummed, his hands still in his pockets as he stared down at me. But I caught the flicker of amusement in those midnight irises. He liked this game.

"It reminds me of your wolf," I whispered. "Maybe you'll let me see him later."

The beast in question overtook his gaze for a split second, his approval radiating from the inky depths of his pupils.

"I would very much like to pet him," I added as I pressed into him.

He finally moved, his hands leaving his pockets to grab my hips as he pulled me away from the mirror and backed me into a wall, his dark eyes radiating animalistic aggression.

There's my Alpha, I thought, allowing him to move me exactly where he wanted me.

But rather than stake his claim, he merely pushed me up against the flat surface and took a step back to admire me in a manner similar to the way I'd evaluated him seconds ago.

"Did you pick this dress?" he asked me. "Or did Beta Cameron find it for you?"

I drew my hand back down his chest, away from his collar, as I replied, "It was one of the dresses he suggested for me. I chose it because my mother's favorite color was blue." My arm fell to my side, my fingers curling into a fist at the admission.

But it was the truth.

My mother had loved midnight blue, as she'd said it reminded her of the Iceland sky on stormy nights. However, my father had always preferred the greenish hues of the northern lights, which could only be seen on clear evenings.

Polar opposites.

But that was what had made them so perfect for each other.

Kieran lifted one hand to fondle the ribbon in my hair. "And whose choice was this?"

"Mine," I told him.

"Instead of a crown?" he asked.

"Yes. I want to be just Quinn tonight."

"But you're not just Quinn," he replied. "You're Princess Quinnlynn MacNamara, the future Queen of Blood Sector."

"A Queen's title means nothing without the respect of her kingdom," I countered.

He studied me for a long moment, his gaze searching as he evaluated my words.

Then he did something that surprised me—he conceded with a nod.

This male is nothing like I anticipated, I thought. We'd spent a month together prior to my departure, and I'd been either blind or too focused on my task to notice his true nature.

Or perhaps I'd seen all these traits in him, which was what had allowed me to leave without much of a conscience.

But now... now I *saw* him.

And I very much liked the vision he presented.

"You're stunning, Quinnlynn," he finally murmured. "And you're right—a crown is just a statement. One you don't need because your beauty and presence speak for you."

My cheeks warmed beneath his praise. "Thank you."

He smiled and brushed his lips against my temple before facing the still-bowing Beta. "You did a fine job, Cameron. Of course, the canvas was already perfect, but you pleased my intended, and therefore you pleased me."

"Canvas?" I repeated, frowning.

"You," Kieran said, glancing at me. "I can't really compliment his work because you're already perfect as you are; a dress and an updo won't change that."

"Oh." And now my cheeks were on fire. Because that compliment was even better than his comment about my crown.

"You can stand up now, Cameron." Kieran uttered the words with a sigh. "I'm not going to punish you for complimenting my intended. Not when she so sweetly stroked my wolf's ego to save your hide."

My lips curled at the comment, causing him to look at me again. His own mouth mimicked my grin.

"Thank you, Cameron. You're excused."

"S-Sire," the Beta stammered, dipping his head and disappearing without another word.

"I very much like that smile," Kieran told me, his tone softer now that we were alone. "I want to see it more."

"You might not see it much tonight," I admitted, my mind shifting to the event ahead.

"Is our betrothal truly that troubling?" he asked, but the lightness in his tone told me he knew exactly what I'd meant. And it had nothing to do with our *betrothal*.

"They hate me, Kieran. And I can't fault them for it."

He stepped toward me again, his palm going to my cheek. "Neither can I," he admitted. "However, together we will lead them to a path that'll guide us all into the future."

How does he always know precisely what to say? I wondered.

"It'll take time, and tonight is simply one step, but it's an important one," he added, his words exactly what I needed to hear. "I'll be by your side at every turn and hurdle, Quinnlynn. We'll eventually find our way. I promise."

"How can you be so certain?" I whispered.

"I haven't survived this long by mistake, darling intended," he replied, his lips curling again. "And as I've been alive for well over a millennium, I've more than earned my confidence."

I studied his face, his chiseled cheekbones, thick lashes, and sharp jaw, and found his words to be true. He had earned his confidence and a hell of a lot more than that.

He's earned the right to learn the truth, I realized with a start.

All his actions, his decisions, his care and patience added up to the most obvious path for us to walk down.

He kept talking about the future, about leading the pack together and showing them how to move forward.

But it was so much more than Blood Sector.

We had to move forward.

And there was only one true way for that to happen.

I needed to tell him everything.

No. I needed to *show* him.

Because words wouldn't be enough. He had to see it to understand.

I'll take him tonight, after our dinner, I decided. *It's time to introduce him to the Sanctuary.*

KIERAN

Quinnlynn exuded elegance and grace as she walked along beside me, her hand in mine. She'd wanted to go on foot to tonight's betrothal dinner, her desire to see more of our home palpable.

I'd indulged her, mostly because it was the right decision.

Many of the humans had come out to see us, their curiosity a tangible presence in the air. They weren't invited to attend tonight's events, mostly for their own safety, but our meandering through the streets helped include them in a way they seemed to appreciate.

Quinnlynn smiled at everyone she passed, her movements carefree and friendly.

These were the mortals under our protection, the ones who helped us thrive by donating their blood as payment for our security. A mutual agreement, one that helped us all live in harmony. The wolves kept the humans safe, and their natural essence helped us thrive.

We could easily overpower them and force them into servitude—a method many of our vampire cousins had chosen to deploy—but I preferred the peaceful relationship between supernatural and mortal beings.

Perhaps it seemed more natural to us to exist in this way because shifters were partially human. Vampires were... *other*. Not dead. Not alive. Simply in-between. And they required a lot more blood than V-Clan wolves did to survive.

"You really have kept this place thriving," she said softly as she took in the newer infrastructure. "Thank you, Kieran."

I squeezed her hand. "I appreciated the challenge."

She glanced at me, her dark eyes reminding me of the midnight sky. Starless, yet glittering like black diamonds. *Beautiful.* "The last update I read said you had about ten thousand humans living in Reykjavik and a little under five thousand throughout the rest of Iceland. Is that still right?"

"Your numbers are a few decades old," I murmured. "We're closer to thirty thousand now. Mostly due to Cillian's penchant for saving mortals in need."

The Elite wolf materialized beside us with a snort, my words having been purposeful, as I'd felt his approach. "You told me to gather them from other areas of the world to ensure the procreation potential remained high. Something about needing more blood to ship to other V-Clan sectors?"

We both knew why I'd given him that task, and yes, it was for the sake of prosperity. But also because he truly did harbor a fondness for saving those in need. It was how Ivana had come to exist in Blood Sector and why she was so drawn to him.

But his passion for saving others kept him from committing.

"You're shipping blood to other sectors?" Quinnlynn asked, her gaze on me.

I nodded. "There are some who live in climates unsuitable for humans. They can't maintain their own flock as we have here."

A few mortals nearby frowned at my choice of terms. However, it seemed kinder than *cattle*.

Alas, the division between us was undebatable. Humans were the inferior species, and their blood resembled sustenance to our kind. End of discussion.

"Lunar Sector?" Quinnlynn guessed.

"Among others," I murmured. "They've expanded from Svalbard to Severnaya Zemlya, which is just uninhabitable for mortals." The entire former Russian archipelago was too cold and inhospitable for humans to survive. "So we send them nourishment as needed."

"Is Prince Cael still in command there?" she asked quietly.

"Prince Cael, Prince Tadhg, and Prince Lykos have all split the territory evenly between them," I replied. "Lunar Sector, Alpha Sector, and Glacier Sector, respectively."

"Prince Cael runs Lunar Sector, Prince Tadhg runs Alpha Sector, and Prince Lykos runs Glacier Sector?" she translated.

I nodded. "Yes."

"And what happened to Eclipse Sector?" It was a quiet question, one that suggested she already knew my response wouldn't be favorable.

"Destroyed," I answered flatly. "During the initial war provoked by the Infected Era."

She swallowed, her grip tightening on my hand. "Because of the humans."

"Because of the humans," I echoed, my tone causing a few of the mortals to duck back into their houses.

Eclipse Sector was a bit of a sore topic for me, considering it was my former home in Ireland.

The Infection had forced me to choose a territory to defend, and I'd selected Blood Sector because it was already equipped to survive. Not out of loyalty to the V-Clan wolves, or even to the throne. I'd simply chosen the most practical path to follow.

"I was able to relocate everyone in time," I told Quinnlynn. "There were no casualties."

"Other than the destruction of your home," she whispered, her gaze falling.

I stopped walking and stepped in front of her, my free hand going to her chin while my opposite remained curled around her palm. "This is my home now, Quinnlynn. *Our* home. I made a choice, one I don't regret. So never feel guilty on my account, because I sure as hell don't."

She gazed up at me, her focus intent. "Had I been here, we could have tried to save both."

"Not from that," I told her. "I likely would have died had I stayed."

Her jaw clenched, a rebuttal seeming to form on her lips.

"The mortals may be weaker, but their technology has proved deadly," I said before she could speak. "And while we now have security parameters in place to thwart such an attack, we didn't then."

That seemed to give her pause.

But I wasn't done.

"It's a lost cause to even consider the what-ifs. You asked about Eclipse Sector. I answered. Not to guilt you or to punish you, just to update you. Understand?"

She didn't reply for a long moment but eventually conceded with a nod. "I understand."

"Good." I released her chin to cup her cheek, my forehead meeting hers. "A lot has changed in your absence, Quinnlynn. But my desire to lead by your side has remained. You chose me. And now it's time to show the sector that I choose you, too."

My elusive Omega.

My devious mate.

My alluring challenge.

My Queen.

I gave in to the desire to kiss her, just for a second. A light meeting of lips. Then I pulled away to continue our walk while she moved alongside me in contemplative silence. I allowed it, my gaze flicking to Cillian on my other side.

He would tell me if there was anything I should know or be concerned about. Not just in regard to Quinnlynn, but to the wolves waiting for us up ahead.

"You rebuilt the entertainment venue," my intended whispered, her gaze taking in the magnificent structure before us.

"Yes, and renamed it The MacNamara," I informed her softly. "There are hundreds of tributes to your parents inside." I'd meant for that part to be a surprise, and also a punishment of sorts, but it felt right to warn her. Because it would be a bit of a shock when she stepped through those doors.

She paused to look at me. "Tributes?"

"From the pack," I clarified.

"Oh." Her lips curled. "They would have enjoyed seeing that." She resumed walking, her free hand going to the pendant hanging from her neck. "They weren't ones for being the center of attention, but they always respected our roots. That's why they built the park near their home." She slowed again. "Is that still there?"

"Yes," I confirmed. "There's a whole team devoted to the upkeep of that recreational area."

"But not to the home," she said, likely recalling our first run.

"No, not to the home. The sector felt that the MacNamara family would prefer it to be reclaimed by nature." It was meant to send a message to Quinnlynn that they considered her as dead as her parents.

Her nod now told me she'd received the message loud and clear. "I always preferred nature for a home," she confided softly. "But I think I could become accustomed to a building like yours. My wolf just might require frequent visits to the countryside."

"Ours," I corrected as I brought her hand up to my mouth. "That building is *ours*. And we can build a second home near your parents' estate, too." I kissed her wrist, my eyes on the group ahead of us.

I wanted them to know exactly where I stood as far as Quinnlynn was concerned. *Mine.*

A few of the males lowered their gazes in respect and understanding.

While a handful of females narrowed theirs, disappointment radiating from them.

One of them was Omega Miranda, a particularly forward woman who didn't seem to understand the meaning of the words "I'm not interested."

I knew she would cause an issue for Quinnlynn, and it was an issue I would allow my intended mate to handle. Because Miranda's pursuing of me was a direct insult to the throne. If Quinnlynn wished to punish the female for her behavior, I wouldn't stand in her way.

Just as I would punish—and likely kill—any male who was stupid enough to approach my female.

Lorcan appeared beside Quinnlynn, causing her to jump a little. She clearly wasn't attuned to the auras my

Elite tended to exude. That would come with time. Just as she would learn mine, too.

"How nice of you to join us, Lorcan," I drawled, glancing at my cousin.

He ignored me, his gaze on the crowd only twenty feet ahead.

We'd lived here for over a hundred years, and he still didn't trust many of our people. Cillian was much more at ease on my opposite side, but I knew he was scanning the minds of everyone around us, searching for any nefarious thoughts.

It made me comfortable enough to release Quinnlynn's hand and press my palm to her lower back instead. I intended to remain right beside her through each step, something I was telling her without words.

"Good evening," I said to those waiting for us. "I assume your presence outside means that dinner has yet to be served?"

A few of the shifters grinned.

However, Miranda replied, "We were waiting for you, My Prince."

"And my intended, yes?" I returned, not playing this game with her. "It is our betrothal dinner, after all."

Quinnlynn leaned into my side. "I think we all know they're here for you more than me, Kieran. But I appreciate the sentiment regardless. And I very much look forward to seeing the tributes made to my parents, the King and Queen of Blood Sector."

That last line was delivered with a hint of steel as she boldly met the offending Omega's gaze.

"Yes, your parents," Miranda replied coolly. "Not you."

Quinnlynn smiled. "I wouldn't expect a memorial for myself. Not only am I still alive, but I also haven't had a chance to prove myself worthy of one yet. My parents, however, have. And I appreciate you all honoring them. They would be very pleased by the gesture."

"Then let's see it, shall we?" I suggested, ignoring Miranda and whatever retort she'd considered voicing to my mate.

I didn't wait for anyone to agree, simply used my hand against Quinnlynn's lower back to guide us both through the crowd and into the building. All the walls were made of glass, but each one was etched with messages and memories devoted to the MacNamara reign. It told a story of greatness and respect, Quinnlynn's parents having left a legacy behind of love and affection.

They'd ruled Blood Sector for nearly a thousand years prior to conceiving Quinnlynn.

And their death had left a lasting impact, one that was evident in the stories written into these very walls.

I remained silent beside Quinnlynn as she paused to read every single one in our path.

It wasn't until over an hour later that she quietly said, "We should eat. But I would very much like to come back here to finish reading."

"You're welcome here anytime, Quinnlynn. This building was created in honor of your family. And it's *yours* as a result."

She shook her head. "No. This building belongs to the sector. It's a monument, one we should all cherish and visit."

That much was true, too. "But the fact remains that you can visit whenever you want."

"Thank you, Kieran." Her eyes smiled, the tears glistening in her dark depths reminding me of the ocean at night. "Thank you for creating this."

I returned her smile with a small one of my own. "It

was my duty as the future King, my dear intended. Consider it one of my many mating gifts for you."

I kissed her before she could reply, my desire to worship her overwhelming my instincts. This urge to press my lips to hers continued to override my mind, making me want to push her up against the wall and devour her with my tongue.

Not here, I told myself. *But maybe… maybe later.*

Kissing served no practical purposes. It had never appealed to me as an enjoyable form of foreplay, either. Not when there were so many other areas of the body that reacted to one's mouth and tongue.

But the more time I spent around Quinnlynn, the more I wanted to just kiss her. For hours. Days. Maybe weeks on end.

Do nothing more than let our tongues communicate in a secret dance, one meant for intimate lovers. *And mates.*

I released her before I gave in to the inclination, her eyes exuding a hint of disappointment in response.

But we had a dinner to attend.

I also had a speech to deliver.

It only seemed fair, considering she was the one who'd spoken at our first betrothal dinner. She'd pledged herself to me before the entire sector, stating openly that she desired to take me as a mate.

Tonight, I would return the favor.

Because they saw me as their leader now, and I needed them to understand that I'd brought their future Queen home.

And I intended to keep her here.

Forever.

QUINN

Dinner only reaffirmed my decision to share the Sanctuary with Kieran.

I wasn't solely impressed by the meal or how he'd arranged the tables—which I'd admittedly found fascinating. The entire sector had been seated at three long, rectangular tables, with Kieran and me right in the middle of the center row, eating family-style and sharing dishes with everyone around us.

Our backs had been to another group behind us, showing a level of trust among our wolves as we ate with ease and enjoyed civil conversation.

It was humbling. Natural. The way a pack should embrace leadership.

Because we weren't showing superiority or displaying our power over the sector. We were merely one of them, exactly as it should be.

But my admiration for Kieran went beyond the seating arrangements and general demonstration of trust. It was bolstered by the pack's reception of *him*.

They all looked to him for guidance, their respect and

adoration palpable.

Even now, as we finished our dessert, they stared at him as though he were a god meant to be worshipped.

Yet they openly conversed with him, asked questions, and spoke with him as though he were a brother. A companion. A true friend.

They love him.

As they should. He'd taken care of them all for over a hundred years. He'd rebuilt and fortified the sector during an apocalyptic event. He'd kept them all safe, developed a blood system that kept all V-Clan wolves thriving, and won over my people in the process.

Our original betrothal dinner had been met with a level of uncertainty that no longer existed.

At least where Kieran was concerned.

I, however, had a lot of work to do. Which I'd expected and accepted.

A few of the wolves made polite conversation with me, one of them being Ivana. She'd chosen the seat across from me, her easy candor making the meal a little lighter.

But I could feel some of the others watching me with disdain. Especially Miranda.

I ignored her. She wasn't worth the headache. None of the jealous Omegas were.

This Alpha was mine.

They could find their own princes.

I picked up my glass of wine, the crystal stem cool against my fingertips, and brought the drink to my lips. The red liquid was a mixture of fermented grapes and donated blood, creating a heady combination that I hadn't experienced in far too long.

Kieran glanced at me as I swallowed, a knowing glint in his gaze. He had to know that this was my first glass of blood in a very long time. I'd barely been sustaining myself, as evidenced by the way I'd disassociated from my wolf.

He picked up the bottle to refill my glass without asking, then stood with his own glass in his palm.

I frowned, wondering if he meant for me to join him, but he caught my shoulder with his free hand and held me in my chair as the echo of metal tapping glass sounded through the room.

He waited for everyone to quiet, his smile firmly in place.

He really is handsome, I marveled, his dimples flashing momentarily. *Incredibly handsome.*

"Good evening," he called out to the now silent room. "Thank you all for joining us tonight. Especially those of you who traveled from outposts and other distant areas of the sector."

He looked pointedly at Myon and the other Alphas seated around him.

Myon dipped his chin at the acknowledgment before settling his bright blue gaze on me.

The disdain I saw in his features yesterday had morphed into something a little less hateful. But I sensed that he still wasn't pleased with me.

Except he flinched as his eyes went to my throat, the pendant hanging from my neck a reminder that probably hurt him.

Sorry, I wanted to tell him. *I know you loved them as much as I did.* He and my father were best friends. Which likely explained his disappointment in my choices.

I'd never told him what had really happened.

So he thought I'd run.

An action he would very much look down upon.

Your father taught you better than that, he'd probably say.

But that was only because he didn't know the truth. *No one does.*

"As you all know, the purpose of tonight's event is to celebrate my betrothal to Quinnlynn MacNamara." He smiled down at me. "*Again.*"

A few chuckles followed that statement, as well as a series of irritated snorts.

I ignored them, instead choosing to give Kieran all of my attention. He was the future King. And he'd earned my respect above everyone else.

"But tonight is about so much more than a future mating. It's about welcoming our princess home." He gave my shoulder a squeeze before returning his focus to our audience.

There were at least a thousand wolves in the massive space, his voice only carrying because of our enhanced ability to hear. Otherwise, he would have needed a microphone.

But as he glanced at the long table behind us and the other in front of us, it was clear that everyone had heard him just fine.

"I know many of you are wondering where she's been and how I found her. And as you all know, I'm not accustomed to keeping information from the sector. So I'll tell you the truth."

My heart stopped. *What?*

"I found Quinnlynn in Bariloche Sector, where she was helping Omega captives heal after being brutally used as part of Alpha Carlos's slave trade," he continued before I could fully react. "Quinnlynn was nearly dead after putting every ounce of her energy into a dying X-Clan Omega."

I swallowed, the weight of everyone's stares making me feel even more scrutinized than before.

But it was the resulting gasps that made me flinch.

"Quinnlynn could have freed herself, but she chose to stay. To help. To heal. To protect. Because *that* is what royals do—they assist those in need of assistance, often at the expense of themselves."

His hand left my shoulder to go to my nape.

"I'm sure many of you have heard about the dismantling of Bariloche Sector. What you haven't heard about are the seventy-two Omegas that were saved that day. The majority of whom were only alive because of our future Queen."

Seventy-two, I repeated to myself. *There should be at least eighty-three. What happened to the other eleven?*

"She might not have been here for us when we thought we needed her, but she trusted me as her intended mate to lead us while she helped those who needed her more." He traced the column of my throat with his thumb, his touch reverent while also possessive.

I shivered, his words and presence making me feel both cherished and owned. *Because he's my Alpha.*

"So for those of you questioning how I can so easily forgive her for abandoning us, perhaps now you have a better understanding of my choice. Because I cannot fathom a stronger, more appropriate mate than Quinnlynn MacNamara."

He lifted his glass, his gaze returning to mine, his pride —not in himself, but in *me*—a palpable presence that left me breathless in my seat.

"Welcome home, Quinnlynn. I can't wait for you to rise and become our Queen." He made a show of toasting his glass, then brought the crystal to his lips for a decadent sip before bending to feed me the wine from his mouth.

I swallowed, the gesture so incredibly intimate that I momentarily forgot our audience.

Until they started cheering.

"To our future Queen," Cillian said, causing several others to echo his sentiment while Kieran's tongue slid into my mouth to sensually stroke mine.

It was quick.

An introduction.

A sinful promise.

Yet it was done before I even had a chance to memorize the feel.

The compulsion to reach for him and urge him to kiss me again overwhelmed my limbs, forcing me to my feet.

But he caught me before I could attack him with my mouth.

And shadowed me to the other side of the room just as music began to play.

I exhaled heavily, bewildered by the change and stunned by his impeccable timing. He'd either rehearsed this or had given explicit instructions to start the music the moment he shadowed.

Regardless of the *how*, it'd worked.

I felt as though I were dreaming as he twirled me around the room with expert steps, his hands moving all over me as he led me into one move after another.

At one point, he dipped me toward the floor.

In the next second, I was whirling around him, my mind spinning as fast as my feet.

I breathed his name, only to feel his lips brush mine, silencing me from speaking.

This is about feeling. About showing our sector that we are united. About proving our compatibility and demonstrating our future union.

We'd danced like this a hundred years ago, too.

Except everything was so much more intense now. *Real.* Because unlike then, I no longer planned to run.

Kieran spun me again, his chest rumbling with a soft purr that made my knees go weak.

"Mmm," he hummed against my ear. "Now that I know dancing is a way to seduce you, I'll have to engage the tactic more often."

He pulled away before I could reply, his eyes glimmering with dark promise as he bowed low in a gesture of immense respect.

The wolves howled in approval, making my cheeks heat beneath their appraisal and the way I'd essentially just melted on the dance floor before them all.

But at least they weren't glaring at me anymore.

Well, most of them, anyway.

There certainly seemed to be a few who despised me, and those few appeared to be led by Omega Miranda.

I ignored her again, choosing instead to take in the rest of the crowd.

When my gaze found Myon, he gave me a small smile.

I returned it.

Then Kieran led me specifically to see him first, which was in accordance with our last betrothal party, where we'd sought out Myon's approval before meeting with every other shifter in attendance.

At least half of the sector wasn't here tonight, but the words spoken among us now would travel to everyone not present.

I suspected many boycotted the dinner for obvious reasons. And others might not have been able to leave their posts.

While Kieran had thanked the few who had ventured into the capital for tonight's event, I knew he also hadn't allowed everyone to abandon the territory lines.

Protecting the sector was too important for such a mistake. We would make time to personally see those who hadn't attended and address any of their concerns then.

The overall hope was that the words exchanged now would ease the minds of others before we met with them.

"Myon," Kieran greeted. "Thank you for attending."

My former guardian nodded. "I wouldn't miss it." His light-colored eyes met mine, a hint of sadness in their depths. "I wish you would have told me, Quinnlynn."

I swallowed, uncertain of exactly what he meant. "I did what I needed to do."

He scrutinized me for a moment and pulled a box from his pocket. "These belonged to your mother. I think she would want you to have them." His gaze dropped to my neck. "They match."

My brow furrowed as I reached for the box. "They match?" I repeated slowly, lifting the lid.

I gasped at the earrings inside, the black crescent diamonds absolutely a match. Just like he'd said.

"I don't... I don't understand. How did you...? When did you...?"

"I believe what my intended would like to know—and I myself as well—is *why* you didn't hand this over sooner. After all, I imagine you've had them for quite some time." Kieran's tone sent a shiver down my spine.

Or perhaps that was from the power rippling off the diamonds.

I could feel it humming along my skin as I traced the familiar pendants.

"I imagine I received it in a way similar to you, Quinnlynn," Myon replied, his focus on me before shifting to Kieran. "And I'd intended to give it to her at her coronation, which was what I thought her mother would want. But the coronation never happened."

Kieran narrowed his gaze, clearly not appreciating that

response. "You knew I had her necklace. Why not mention the matching earrings?"

"I was removed from the royal detail before I could say anything about them." He shrugged. "So I waited for her to return, as they belong to the MacNamara family, of which you're not a member yet."

Kieran released a low growl. "Still doubting my worthiness even now."

"I'll always doubt you. That's my job."

"Not anymore," Kieran replied.

Myon took a step forward, his long hair moving like a wave along his shoulders. "My history with her family far surpasses your own, O'Callaghan."

Kieran stared him down, unmoved by the blatant display of aggression. "I don't live in the past, Myon. I live in the present. And my future is with Quinnlynn. *As her mate.*"

He pressed his palm to my lower back while he spoke, then turned us away from Myon before the Alpha could reply.

Cillian smoothly stepped in, keeping Myon from being able to follow us.

I glanced over my shoulder, my dark eyes meeting Myon's light ones. My throat worked, the temptation to thank him for the earrings riding my spirit.

But I couldn't.

Not when he'd so blatantly disrespected Kieran.

I slowly shifted my focus away from my father's oldest friend and found Kieran watching me without a single ounce of emotion on his face.

"You're right," I told him softly. "Our futures are tied, and I would rather live in the present with you than exist in the past."

Because the latter—*living in the past*—meant continuing

to hide the truth from Kieran. To continue being ridiculed for my choices and for running. To live a life alone, in pain, and unfulfilled.

And for what?

To not find my parents' murderer?

To continue killing myself in order to power the Sanctuary on my own?

I'd spent a hundred years trying to do this by myself, and what did I have to show for it?

I'd saved countless Omegas, yes.

But how many more could I have saved with Kieran by my side?

I glanced at Miranda and the group of unmated Omegas beside her. All of them were under Kieran's protection. And he guarded them without exuding much power.

Meanwhile, my soul continued to exhaust itself by trying to keep the shields alive around the Sanctuary.

For how much longer? Would I become so tired again that I disassociated from my wolf permanently?

I hadn't even realized how perilously close I'd been to losing myself until Kieran had found me.

And I'd thanked him by hating him. Fearing him. Wanting to escape him again.

I returned my focus to my intended mate and stepped in front of him. He watched without emotion, his gaze on mine as I started to kneel before him.

"You are my chosen future," I told him, aware of everyone in the room watching me openly submit to the future King of Blood Sector. "You are my chosen mate."

He stared down at me for a long moment, his expression still unreadable. Then he shifted his attention to the expectant crowd. "Memorize this moment," he told them all. "It's the only time you will ever see your future

Queen on her knees. Because she's meant to lead, not to bow."

He held out his hand for mine, and I immediately accepted his offer.

Only, he didn't help me stand.

He lifted my hand to his lips instead and kissed my wrist for all to see.

"I need to see to my intended," he murmured. "The festivities will continue with the coronation. And by that point, we will already be mated."

A cacophony of howls sounded, only to quiet as Kieran shadowed us back to his room, clearly having decided to end the evening early.

But I wasn't ready for our mating.

Not yet.

"I need you to let me shadow," I whispered as he pulled me up to my feet.

He frowned. "What?"

"I need you to let me shadow. It's the only way for me to show you."

"Show me what?" he asked, his brow crinkling with confusion.

"The Sanctuary," I breathed.

His irises flared, the only indication that he recognized the term. Maybe because I'd said it. Maybe because he'd heard about it or read about it in the family documents. I wasn't sure. And I couldn't focus enough to decipher it.

I needed him to *see*.

But that required him to release me and let me shadow, which was probably more than I deserved, given our circumstances. However, if he was truly the Alpha I needed, he'd agree to this request.

Not because I'd earned his trust.

But because he was the Alpha meant to protect the legacy behind my bloodline.

The heart of my world.

The true diamond of our kind.

"Please, Kieran. It's the only way. I want you to understand, to know the truth. But saying it... it's not the same as *seeing* it."

His expression hardened. "Quinnlynn..."

"Please." I squeezed his hand, then gradually loosened my grasp. "I need you to release my tether."

KIERAN

I STUDIED HER FOR A BEAT, my instincts telling me to trust her while my mind shouted every reason for me not to.

Why now? Why here? Why tonight?

"How about you tell me where to shadow you instead," I suggested.

Quinnlynn shook her head. "It's not that simple."

"Of course it's not." I couldn't help the sarcastic note in my voice. Of all the times to ask me to trust her, to release her, she'd chosen tonight. Right after our betrothal dinner.

Which was essentially the same night she'd disappeared a hundred years ago.

Did she think I was naïve? That a few well-placed comments would lull me into a state of trust?

I looked her over, disgusted with the very concept of her choosing now to betray me again.

"I mean it, Kieran," she said, her small hand clutching that box from Myon as though it was a lifeline.

Meanwhile, her opposite palm barely held on to mine despite my just pulling her up off the floor.

"It's not that simple," she repeated. "You have to be

taken there to know where it is."

I arched a brow. "Seems a little convenient, Princess."

She flinched at my tone.

But I couldn't help it.

Did she really think I was foolish enough to release her now?

Or does she truly want to show me something? I wondered, conflicted.

I released her to take several steps back, needing to think.

But she followed me.

"Kieran, I'm trying to tell you why I left. But it would be much easier to show you."

"Then perhaps I should make you tell me instead," I returned, feeling defensive. She was picking at old wounds, ones I didn't want to feel.

So much for living in the present, a dark part of me muttered. But was that really the same? She hadn't earned my faith yet. Not entirely.

And the memory of her disappearance tainted my ability to trust her.

Yet that memory intrigued me, too. It called to my feral side, to the beast that considered her ours.

It made me crazy with the need to take her. Mark her. Make her mine.

And yet, part of me wanted to trust her. To give her freedom and see what she would do.

Because that part of me *liked* the chase and wouldn't mind another challenge.

Except it would destroy our sector. We'd begun healing tonight. It would be slow, but I had faith in the process.

However, if she betrayed me—*us*—again, I might not be able to put the sector back together.

"It would be easier to show you," she whispered, her

eyes pleading.

"Why should I make anything easier for you, Quinnlynn? Haven't I done enough to prove myself worthy of being your mate?"

Fuck. I can't have this conversation right now. I need to think.

And I need to get out of these suffocating clothes.

I started toward the closet, my mind made up. At least on that one detail.

I'd shadowed us in here with the intent to kiss her. Make love to her. *Bite her.*

And she'd turned my intentions upside down with her request.

The one request I did not want to hear—"Release me."

All because she wanted me to trust her.

Well, fuck that.

And fuck me for realizing I'm not ready to trust her yet.

Which begged the question, *How can I mate her without trusting her?*

Quinnlynn made a frustrated noise behind me. "The reason I want to show you this is *because* I find you worthy. More than worthy." She growled then. "You... You're nothing like I anticipated, yet everything I need."

I paused at the threshold of my closet, those last three words piquing my interest. *"Everything I need."*

Everything you need for what, I wonder.

"I haven't been fair to you," she continued. "I... I didn't know who to trust. My parents..." She cleared her throat. "Kieran, I chose you because you weren't battling for me. That made me think that maybe you might be different. And you are. I just never realized *how* different."

I turned at that, my eyebrow winging upward. "Different from what?"

"Different from the Alphas who crave power." She swallowed. "I mean, you do crave it. But not for the same reasons as they do. Or at least some of them. Well, one in particular. I think. And not… not just power. But *access*."

My eyes narrowed. "What are you trying to tell me, Quinnlynn? Access to what?"

But I already suspected the answer—*her family secrets.*

"The Sanctuary," she whispered, using that term again and keeping it hushed like it was a sacred term. "I want to take you to the Sanctuary. Please."

"What is it?"

"A place you have to see to understand," she replied, her answer nowhere near convincing enough. "A place… a place you need to trust me to take you to."

My jaw ticked. She could very easily be playing me right now, the desperation in her scent caused by her need to flee more than her need to tell me the truth.

But that glimmer in her gaze, the one begging me to put the past behind us and trust her to introduce us to the future, was just enough to keep me from outright denying her.

I could simply fuck her. Mate her. Ransack her head for the truth.

However, that would break the tenuous bond we'd created over the last few weeks. And I didn't want our history to taint our destiny.

I wanted to believe in her. To trust her. To let her show me this truth.

Not steal it from her mind and fracture our fragile connection in the process.

She'd never forgive me for forcing her, not when she was on the verge of opening up on her own.

Assuming this isn't all a ploy, my pessimistic side murmured, my gaze going to that box again. It felt symbolic in a way I didn't quite understand. A token from the past meant to distort the future.

A ridiculous notion.

I pinched the bridge of my nose and blew out a breath. *Focus.* "What climate should I prepare for?" I asked, testing her.

A breath left her on an audible exhale, her pulse picking up several beats.

Was that relief because she thought I'd fallen for her trick?

Or relief at me trusting her?

"You'll release my leash?" Her question was soft, her expression far too hopeful.

"I'm not sure yet," I admitted. "Tell me the climate I need to prepare for first." *Stop stalling and give me a real answer, or I'll know you're lying.*

"C-cold," she stammered.

Not exactly the confident reply I'd been looking for, but I nodded anyway and disappeared into the closet to properly dress for the *cold*.

Quinnlynn entered the closet with her lip caught between her teeth.

I ignored her and hung up my jacket.

Then I unfastened my vest, tie, and shirt and turned to find her tugging at the strings behind her.

After a moment of letting her suffer—and finding it oddly endearing—I stepped forward. "Turn around, little trickster."

"I'm not trying to trick you," she muttered, obeying me anyway.

I leaned down and pressed my lips to her ear. "We'll see, won't we, darling?"

Goose bumps pebbled along her shoulders and arms, the reaction either a result of my whispering or a physical response to my words. It was hard to say.

But I helped her out of her dress anyway.

Then I grabbed her by the back of her neck and pulled her into me, my wolf demanding I stake at least some sort of claim.

Which I did with my mouth against hers.

Because I'd been dying to kiss her all fucking night, and if I was about to lose her again, then I was damn well going to steal this memory and use it as I saw fit in the future.

She gasped, her bare breasts meeting my chest as I tightened my grasp around her nape. My opposite hand went to her ass, my palm claiming her with an unyielding grip as I pulled her even closer.

Then I destroyed her with my tongue.

Taking more than giving.

Stamping my soul inside her without biting. Without marking. Yet possessing her so severely that there could be no question about who owned her.

Mine.

My mate.

My Omega.

My intended Queen.

I fucked her with my mouth, taking her in a way that she would never forget. Because I'd essentially just knotted her.

With my fucking tongue.

"Consider that a vow," I whispered darkly. "Betray me again, and you will regret it, Quinnlynn MacNamara."

I nipped at her lower lip, biting hard enough to hurt without making her bleed.

The next time I did this, I would break the skin, something I ensured she saw in my eyes.

"This game we've played is done," I told her. "Do you understand me?"

"Yes."

"Good." I released her. "Put on some warm clothes since we are going somewhere *cold*."

I turned to work on my dress pants, my cock so damn hard that I worried I might accidentally hurt myself. But thinking about the possibility of her deceiving me was enough to calm me down.

At least until I considered how I would chase her and punish her.

That had me hard all over again as I pulled on some jeans.

This woman is absolutely the most alluring challenge of my life. And the most frustrating one, too.

I yanked on some socks and boots, then grabbed a sweater before facing her.

She wore a similar outfit, only she'd added a coat to the mix. As well as her mother's earrings, which admittedly looked appropriate on her.

"Well, at least I know the clothes I procured for you fit," I drawled, glancing at the side of the closet that I'd designated as hers. "It would be a damn shame to waste all of this, wouldn't it?"

Quinnlynn reached around me to pull a fur-lined leather jacket off a hanger. "I'm not wasting anything, Kieran. We'll be back by morning."

I took the coat from her. "Don't make promises you might not keep, Princess."

"I'm not lying to you, *Prince*." She folded her arms. "But your reaction to all this proves my point—you're different. If you knew my secret, you'd be salivating for access."

"Is that so?" I asked as I tugged on her furry lapels.

"Yes." She sounded much more confident now, which increased my intrigue. "And you're going to apologize for doubting me once we're there."

"Will I?"

"Yes," she repeated. "I know I haven't fully earned your trust, but after this, there will be no doubts between us."

Well, that was certainly a promising statement. It could all be bullshit, but I rather hoped it was true. "All right, little one. You win."

Her lips parted. "I do?"

I nodded, leading the way out of the closet. "But I mean it, Quinnlynn. If you defy me again, I will make you regret it." Because it would destroy our sector, and I couldn't allow that to slide. "So think very carefully before you decide what to do next."

I unraveled my hold on her shadowing ability while I spoke, my back to her mostly because I wanted to test her.

But when I finished the process, she merely shadowed to stand in front of me, her eyes grinning with an emotion I couldn't easily define.

Happiness? Gratitude? A twinge of unease? It was an odd mix, one that had me lifting a brow.

"Are you having second thoughts?"

"No. It's just been a while since I last visited. And I'm really hoping their reception is better than the one I received here," she said, her cheeks reddening.

"Their reception?" I repeated. "Who are we going to visit?"

She grabbed my wrist. "You'll see."

"Quinnlynn." I grabbed her arm. "Tell me who we're going to see. Right fucking now."

I'd agreed to go to a place, not to be taken to an unknown group of people. I could handle myself, but Quinnlynn was a liability.

"Trust me," she whispered, the shadows already wrapping around us both.

Cillian. Quinnlynn is—

The world shifted, a sense of wrongness overwhelming me as power splintered the air between me and Quinnlynn. I stumbled, her arm seeming to disappear beneath my grip.

Her name left my mouth with a growl as I fought to see, the energy momentarily blinding me and sending me to the ground as though I'd physically been shoved.

Only there was no one there.

No other entity.

No mystical power of ability.

Just my bedroom.

With me on the floor.

And Quinnlynn…

Nowhere to be seen.

I blinked several times, trying to clear my mind, to process what had just happened. Everything felt momentarily numbed. *Wrong. Upside down. Denied.*

No.

Rejected.

The power had blasted right through me, *rejecting me.*

My jaw clenched.

Quinnlynn just denounced our betrothal with a goddamn spell. She'd fucking fled *again.*

And this time, she'd ensured everyone in the fucking sector had felt it.

As evidenced by my two Elites appearing only seconds after everything had transpired.

Cillian took one look around the room and cursed.

Lorcan narrowed his eyes.

While I… I let my beast react to our *betrothed's* very public rejection.

And roared.

QUINN

Ow. I curled into a ball on top of something soft as I tried to banish the ache from my head. *Ugh.*

It felt like I'd jumped off a cliff into a block of ice.

I groaned, everything splintering inside. *What did I do? Where am I?*

My mind resembled mush, my memories murky at best. Something about shadows.

Shadows. Shadows. Shadows.

Shadowing.

Hmm.

I swallowed, my throat resembling sandpaper.

Why am I on a cloud? It felt fluffy. Smelled sweet. Like home. I sighed, the familiar aroma making me dizzy with warmth. It'd been so long since I was last here. In safety. My nest. My safe haven.

Except...

Something's missing.

No. Not something. Someone.

"Kieran," I rasped, my fingers automatically searching for him.

"Not here, I'm afraid," a familiar voice said, making me frown.

What?

"The spell rejected him. Hell, it almost rejected you, which is strange, considering you created it. But maybe the magic is mad that you've been gone for so long? Fuck, I know I'm pretty mad about it."

Kyra, I realized.

"You went to Blood Sector before you came here. Can't say I'm not a little hurt by that, sis."

The nickname confirmed her identity but didn't explain how she was here. Or how I was here.

But then... then things started to roll back through my mind.

The betrothal dinner. Kieran. Dancing. Earrings. Convincing him to trust me. Shadowing...

My eyes flew open.

And immediately closed again. Because *fuck.* "Where did I land?" I asked, my voice as destroyed as I felt.

"Next to a seal," Kyra replied. "Scared the shit out of the poor thing."

I groaned as she chuckled, clearly amused by the memory.

"Fortunately, Fritz saw you. He was able to pull you out of the water. Then I did the rest by shadowing you here." Her hand whispered across my forehead. "You're not fully healed, but almost there."

"And Kieran?"

"Didn't make it through the spell barrier," she said, repeating what she'd already told me. "I imagine he's still in Blood Sector."

"*Fuck.*" I tried to sit up, only for her to nudge me back down.

"Oh, no, you don't. You need at least another day or

two of sleep."

I frowned. "What?"

"You've only had about three days so far, and given——"

"*Three days?!*" I tried to sit up again, this time my hands catching hers as she tried to hold me down. I fought her off, forcing her to let me finish the movement.

Only to be hit with a dizzy spell that sent me right back down with a groan.

"Serves you right, you stubborn arse," she snapped, her English accent thickened by her anger. "What the bloody hell is wrong with you?"

"Kieran," I breathed as I tried to open my eyes again. "He's going to kill me."

"Yeah? Then it's a good thing you're here with me."

I started to shake my head but couldn't complete the movement. "No. I promised. He's going to think…" I winced, my throat so dry that the words were coming out like harsh whispers.

"Here." A straw touched my lips, and I sucked it in until I choked.

"Easy, Quinn. It's not a knot."

I nearly growled at the bad joke, but I was too busy swallowing to make a sound.

When I finally finished, I tried opening my eyes again. Slowly. Starting with a peek that confirmed I was in my nest—the one I hadn't visited in decades. Yet it wasn't dusty, telling me someone had kept this place clean for me.

Probably Kyra.

She ran the Sanctuary in my absence.

Because we were partners. *Sisters,* I thought. Not by blood, but by purpose.

We shared a like-minded goal—to help save Omegas of all races.

I'd been born into this role.

267

And she'd sort of fallen into it after killing her Vampire Alpha mate.

It should have ripped her apart, the Alpha's venom an addiction for Omega females—they craved it during the feeding process and heat cycles. Something about the Alpha's bites and the whole exchange of power.

But Kyra was half V-Clan wolf.

Which allowed her to function differently from a typical vampire. She'd essentially inherited all of the best traits from each parent, and none of the weaknesses.

She handed me another drink, this one a juice box, and I drank it all before trying to sit up again. This time she didn't stop me, just gave me a look that expressed how she felt about me moving.

Such a matronly look, I thought, fighting a smile. Because Kyra was the opposite of matronly. Actually, she was the one Omega I would tell others to never trust with their pups. She'd have them cursing up a storm and playing pranks within minutes of meeting them.

Because Kyra didn't believe in rules.

She did, however, value loyalty.

"So why is your Alpha Prince going to try to kill you?" she asked. "Last I heard, he was so smitten with you that he was refusing every Omega who tried to tempt him to stray."

"You've heard that?"

"I've witnessed it," she corrected. "I kept an eye on Blood Sector, just like you asked me to. Something you'd know, by the way, if you ever bothered to call."

I grimaced. "I was stuck in Bariloche Sector."

"Until you weren't."

"Until I wasn't," I agreed. "Because Kieran took me back to Iceland and removed my ability to shadow."

"Is that why your entry was so fucked up?"

I shrugged. "Maybe. Or maybe because I tried to bring him back with me. You said the spell rejected him?"

"Yeah, I felt it."

"But he's my mate."

Her eyebrows lifted as her gaze went to my neck. "He finally claimed you?"

"Intended mate," I amended.

"Ah. Well, then that explains it—the spell won't let him enter because he's technically not part of the family bloodline yet. He'd have to drink from you first."

"But I've imbibed his essence before."

"Doesn't work like that, Quinn. He needs your blood." She gave me a look. "Don't you remember what happened with Livi after she was claimed? How her Alpha was able to break through the barrier because he'd bitten her?"

"Of course I remember that. I helped subdue him."

"Right. And it inspired all the defense training. But he was able to follow her and cross over because he'd swallowed her blood."

"Ugh," I grumbled, realizing she was right. I'd been so caught up in wanting to show Kieran the Sanctuary that I hadn't fully considered the magical barrier. I'd thought him being my chosen mate would be enough, especially since my family line had created and maintained the spell.

Apparently not.

"He's going to kill me." Not really. I was being dramatic. But he was definitely going to be mad.

My stomach churned with the notion, my heart skipping several beats.

He probably thinks I betrayed him. Again.

"I need to go back," I muttered.

"Uh, no?" Kyra replied. "You just said he wants to kill you."

"Because he'll think I left him again. I'll explain. It'll be

269

fine." *I hope.*

I pressed my palm to my forehead, my skull aching and sending tumultuous waves through my insides. I felt sick. Literally. Like I was going to vomit. And the spasm inside me didn't help.

Probably my wolf clawing at my heart, I thought dizzily. *Maybe she can sense her mate's ire.*

Except no, I couldn't sense Kieran at all. Not even his healing energy.

My eyes flew open—I wasn't sure when I'd felt them close—and my insides revolted again. "I can't feel him." I tried to find the strand that connected me to his power, to his *strength,* and felt nothing. "How…?"

Had he cut me off?

Is he hurt?

I started blindly feeling around me, searching for clothes. Because at some point, I'd lost my sweater and jeans.

"Quinn?"

"I can't feel him!" I repeated, frantic.

Had he broken our connection somehow? Had he taken another mate?

He'd promised I would regret it if I betrayed him again.

Had he… had he meant because he would disown me? Even after all that we'd shared?

Oh, moons…

It was what I would deserve, I supposed. But I hadn't betrayed him! "I need to go. I need to shad—"

I broke off on a cry of agony as my insides splintered.

"Quinn!" Kyra shouted.

But I could barely hear her.

Something was wrong. *Very, very wrong.* I could feel my soul splitting inside me, my wolf screaming in pain.

This was the opposite of healing.

This… this was torturous *hell*.

I burrowed into my nest, seeking the scents that I knew would heal me. Except they didn't exist. Because *he* wasn't here. My Alpha. My intended. My Kieran.

"I need to… to…" I couldn't finish the thought, another agonizing spasm reducing me to nothing but a writhing mess of moans and whimpers.

Voices sounded nearby.

Kyra. A male. Another female.

Names started to blur, memories whirling inside my mind, all of them starring Kieran.

He's punishing me, I realized with a gasp. *Doing something to… to reverse my healing. Hurting me.*

Because I hurt him.

I'd abandoned him.

Only, I hadn't. Not this time.

"Kieran," I breathed, tears clouding my vision as reality stirred with nightmares.

I was on fire, burning from the inside out, lost to this agony of solitude.

He hates me.

He's rejecting me.

He's… he's ensuring I know that we're done.

But I hadn't betrayed him. *I promise, Kieran. I… I tried to take you… with me.*

I sobbed, my body refusing to let me shadow, my mind fracturing as I fought to understand truth from fiction.

Maybe this was just a nightmare. Maybe I would wake soon to his familiar scent.

Or maybe…

Maybe this is my death. By my own mate's spirit.

I thought… I thought I could love you…

And now…

Now I see that you... you really are...
A villain.

More voices echoed. Kyra shouting. I only vaguely recognized her tones, her presence, something about *need*.

I whined, begging for Kieran. I needed him to understand. To forgive me.

To... to *accept* me.

My wolf mewled inside, the sound escaping my lips. Or maybe that was an alarm of sorts. I couldn't see. I could no longer truly hear.

I was lost to the aching sensation of loneliness.

Overwhelmed by the darkness.

Alone... in my nest... without... my mate.

My Kieran.

I'm sorry, I thought at him. *I never meant to leave you again. I actually... wanted... to stay.*

But he would never believe me now. I understood that. I *felt* it. This torment was my punishment.

And he was right.

I really did regret it.

Everything.

Trusting. Loving. *Falling.*

It wasn't fair. But life was never meant to be easy or kind. Life was a challenge.

Just like me.

His challenge.

And with each torturous spasm, it became clear that I was no longer a challenge he wished to pursue.

The villain had left me to suffer. Alone. In this nest. Without my intended mate.

Without his warmth.

Without his affection.

Without his purr.

Without his... *knot.*

KIERAN

My paws ran over the ice, my wolf pushing our limits as we sprinted across the glacier's surface.

It was dangerous.

Wild.

And exactly what I needed.

Or so I'd thought. Because that fucking pang in my chest continued to radiate.

She lied.

She betrayed us.

She rejected *us.*

That sense of being shoved to the ground hit me again, making me growl in frustration. I wasn't sure how she'd done that, and while part of me was impressed by the display of power, the other part of me raged about it.

I'd trusted her. I'd allowed myself to hope.

And she'd fucking used that faith to disappear. *Again.*

I'd won our game of hide-and-seek. How fucking dare she engage me in another round!

I'd proved my worth. I'd healed her. Helped her find her wolf. Fixed her disassociation. *Knotted* her.

Fuck!

I should have just claimed her and forced her to be mine.

Except then I would have overheard her agony at being trapped. I would have learned that everything she'd told me was a lie. And we would have spent the rest of our lives hating each other.

My wolf growled in protest, then pounded the ice even harder in response.

I was just along for the ride at this point, my beast having taken charge hours ago. I could rein him in, but I didn't want to. I felt feral. Alive. *Furious.*

Quinnlynn MacNamara had used me.

She'd betrothed herself to me. She'd run. I'd found her. And she'd fucking run again.

A dark part of me was thrilled by the prospect of another chase. But I worried about what that part of me would do when I caught her.

Because the entire sector now knew of her disappearance. Hell, I wouldn't be surprised if the other sectors knew, too.

Her rejection had been powerful, that spell sending a shock wave through all of Blood Sector. *Everyone* had felt her departure.

And I'd been too stunned to even begin to address it.

My job as the Alpha Prince of Blood Sector required me to soothe the pack. But how the fuck was I supposed to do that when I felt so utterly destroyed?

I couldn't let them see me like this.

Hence my run.

A run that had started *four* days ago.

A run I hadn't been able to stop.

A run that had taken me deep into the icy mountains

where food and life didn't exist. I'd eventually shadow back.

But not yet.

Not until my wolf's desire to *shred* everything in our—

Sire.

I growled at Cillian's unwanted disruption. *I don't care what it is. Fuck. Off.*

We've had a breach, he continued, ignoring me entirely.

Then deal with it. Because I wasn't in the mood for political bullshit.

It's not that simple. You need—

I need time, I interjected, aware that I was being a selfish arse and entirely incapable of fixing it. *Deal with it on your own.*

If I could shut him out, I would.

Alas, his telepathy overruled my desire to ignore him. *She's here for you, Kieran,* he said, my name resembling a whip across my mind.

I started to slow. *She?* My wolf perked up, excitement and anger creating an intoxicating mix in our blood. *Quinnlynn?* Had she returned?

No. Kyra.

I blinked, my pace nearly a walk now. *What?*

We've secured her in Lorcan's den. He paused. *Kieran, she has a vial of blood with her. Quinnlynn's blood.*

I froze. *Blood?*

She won't explain why. She says she'll only explain herself to you.

Which meant they'd tried to make her talk and she'd refused. *Do you think she used the blood to cross our boundary line?*

Quinnlynn had mentioned Kyra before, suggesting she was the source of her information on me. But she hadn't elaborated beyond that.

Was her blood something Kyra had used to enter our lands before?

No. She said the blood is for you and won't elaborate.

I frowned as I shifted back to my human form. *Did you detect her entry?*

No. I found her in your suite when I went searching for you.

My eyebrows lifted. *In my suite?*

Yes. She was pacing your room.

Meaning she entered without anyone knowing.

Yes, he repeated.

So how secure is she? Because if she could slip through all our security, I doubted we could hold her for long.

Honestly? I don't know. He sounded wary. *But she's being amenable for the moment.*

Amenable, I repeated incredulously.

She says if you make her wait much longer, then she's leaving and you'll never know what happened to Quinnlynn because she'll make damn sure you never see her again.

I growled at that. *I'm on my way.* Perhaps to kill the intruder who'd just dared to threaten my intended mate. Or perhaps to tell her to leave because I no longer wanted to care.

Yeah, it was definitely the former.

Because as mad as I was, I still cared.

Fuck.

I shadowed to Lorcan's closet and grabbed a pair of his jeans. We were the same size, so they fit.

Then I stalked out into his bedroom, opened the door, and headed toward his study.

He met me at the threshold, his gaze taking in the familiar pants with an assessing look. Then he backed up to reveal the woman sitting in his chair as though she owned it.

I cataloged her traits with a single sweep of my gaze.

Blue-black hair.

Catlike green eyes.

Pale skin.

Small.

Vampire.

Except she was so much more than that. She was part V-Clan wolf, too. An Omega of mixed genetics. Not necessarily uncommon, but I could feel the ancient energy wafting off her small frame.

This woman was powerful.

And she did indeed have a vial of Quinnlynn's blood. It sat on the table before her like some sort of fucked-up peace offering. The scent of it hit me like a drug, my wolf craving a taste of his intended.

Or perhaps it was my need for violence that had me salivating for the contents of that bottle.

"Where is she?" I demanded, not bothering to clarify who I meant. Nor did I clear my throat. The raspy growl in my voice seemed more than appropriate for this conversation.

"At the Sanctuary," she replied, not bothering to play games with me.

"Tell me where that is. Right now." Because I wanted to throttle my intended's pretty little throat.

"I can't. You need to drink that first." She pointed a sharpened nail at the vial on the desk. "But I'll warn you—I'm not sure it'll work."

I frowned. "Work for what?"

"Work for breaking through the barrier spell on the island. It requires you to be fully mated, but I'm hoping we can trick it by having her blood in your system." She pushed away from the desk and stood. "So drink up. Then I'll take you to her."

Lorcan stepped forward, his hand on my shoulder. It was his equivalent of a denial. Not that it was needed.

Because fuck if I was going to let this little blue-haired pixie take me anywhere.

I'd told her to tell me where to go, not to take me there like she was some sort of fairy escort.

"Why would I go anywhere with you?" I demanded. "I know all about your penchant for killing Alphas, Kyra. And I'm not about to become your next victim."

Some Alphas might laugh at the notion of fearing an Omega. But not me. I hadn't lived this long by allowing my ego to overrule logic.

This unassuming female had proved herself deadly decades ago. She was a proverbial black widow with powers no one knew anything about.

Her lips curled. "I only kill Alphas who deserve it, Kieran. Have you done something to earn my wrath?"

"I don't know," I admitted. "Have I?"

"You're starting to." She prowled around the desk, her movements all feline and matching the catlike shape of her eyes. "Your intended mate is injured and going into heat. If you continue to choose not to help her, then yeah, you're going to earn my wrath."

I stared down at her, the Omega over a foot shorter than me. She couldn't be taller than five feet. Yet I sensed the deadly aura circling around her like a dark cloak of enigmatic energy.

"She's my best friend, Kieran," Kyra continued. "And I left her screaming in her nest. So if you're not going to work with me, say it now. Because someone needs to comfort her, and even though it's you she wants, I can't just leave her to suffer alone."

My eyes narrowed. "She rejected me rather

spectacularly. So forgive me for not believing anything you just said about her *wanting* me."

"Did he lose his hearing when the barrier shoved his soul back here?" Kyra asked casually, her gaze going to Lorcan and then Cillian. "Because I swear I've already explained this."

"How about you try again?" Cillian suggested, his tone lacking emotion.

She rolled her eyes and looked at me again. "The *barrier* rejected you. Not Quinnlynn. And that spell damn near killed her as well."

"The spell she used to shadow without me?"

The feline-like Omega glared at me. "No, jackass. The barrier spell that protects the island. It knocked her out on her way in and caused her to crash into an ice block, which sent her rolling into the nearby water. Then she woke up and went into heat not too long after. And now I'm here because she needs you."

Lorcan and Cillian both growled at her tone and insulting nickname, but I was too busy deciphering her words to care about the nuances of how they'd been delivered.

"What is this barrier spell protecting?"

"The Sanctuary."

Obviously. "What is the Sanctuary?" I demanded, tired of this fucking riddle. "Tell me what it is, and I'll consider going with you."

"Kieran," Lorcan growled, his silence broken.

But I held up a hand to stop him, my gaze on the Omega. "Quinnlynn said she had to show me for me to understand. I don't trust her or you to do that, given everything that's happened. So tell me what it is instead."

"She never told you?" A hint of unease had crept into Kyra's features and tone, her eyes roaming over me warily.

"Obviously not."

"But she… she said she wants to mate you," Kyra said slowly, her expression morphing into confusion. "I… I'm here to help her. I thought. Unless… maybe it's the heat?"

She took a step backward, but Lorcan shadowed behind her, blocking her path and grabbing her hip to hold her in place. The Omega shivered in response.

His power licked at my senses, telling me he'd grounded her.

I guess she can be secured, I thought. *Just like Quinnlynn.*

Except Quinnlynn had tricked me into letting her escape.

Maybe, I thought. *Unless this female is telling the truth.*

"Tell us about the Sanctuary," I demanded.

"I… I thought you knew… She… she was trying to take you there. Why would she…?" Kyra blinked, confusion radiating from her. "It's been so many years since I last saw her. Maybe I misunderstood?"

"She told me it was a place I needed to see. Then she said only she could shadow us there, which was when I decided to trust her and she betrayed me with her rejection spell." Which might have been the *barrier* Kyra kept talking about. But I wasn't sure I believed her. I wasn't sure I believed anything at all as far as Quinnlynn was concerned.

"Why would she try to take him there if she wasn't planning to tell him the truth?" Cillian interjected.

"Or it was all a ruse," Lorcan muttered, speaking the words before I could.

Any other day and I would have gaped at him for breaking his silence *twice* in such a short span of time.

But I was too busy scrutinizing the Omega to focus on my cousin.

"It wasn't a ruse," Kyra said. "I felt her try to bring

Kieran with her. Then Fritz found her floating along the icy shore. He helped me bring her inside."

"Fritz?" I repeated. "Who the fuck is Fritz?"

"A Protector," she whispered. "The Sanctuary…" She trailed off, her gaze meeting mine. "It's a Sanctuary for Omegas. The MacNamara magic protects the island. And that magic serves as a barrier. Only Omegas can pass through. Or their mates."

KIERAN

My eyebrows lifted. "An island of V-Clan Omegas?"

She shook her head. "Omegas of all kinds."

I glanced at Cillian and then at Lorcan, their expressions of disbelief rivaling my own.

No wonder Quinnlynn wanted to show me rather than tell me.

Because it didn't make any sense.

How could an island of Omegas exist without others knowing about it?

The MacNamara bloodline protects it.

Her family secret.

The reason her mother and father were killed.

"That's why an Alpha murdered her parents," I whispered, all of it clicking together. "But how did murdering them provide answers? Because it weakened the barrier magic?"

Kyra shook her head. "No. The magic held because of Quinnlynn."

"Then what did their murder accomplish?"

"He didn't exactly murder them. He put a tracking enchantment on their jet, and the only way to thwart it was to land elsewhere. Except there was no safe place to land…

not where they were. Not without revealing too much. So they… chose to die at sea."

"That's what Quinnlynn meant," I realized out loud. "She said the culprit bespelled the plane and they had to crash it. But she didn't elaborate on why."

However, now I understood.

Had they not crashed, they would have given away their location.

And so they'd chosen to take their own lives to protect the Sanctuary.

Which explained so much about Quinnlynn. Everything she'd done was for the Sanctuary. "That's why she stayed in Bariloche Sector. Why she needed my healing powers. Why she ran."

She'd been searching for her parents' killer and taking care of Omegas in the process.

"She couldn't trust anyone," Kyra replied. "Especially not an Alpha Prince."

I nodded, understanding that now.

"But she tried to take you to the Sanctuary. And now she needs you more than ever. Not only has she gone into heat, but her healing is also slower than it should be, probably because all of her excess energy is used to power the shield."

That explained why she'd absorbed so much of my power when I'd been healing her. She'd felt like an empty void in need of far more vitality than anyone should ever require.

And it was because of her family legacy and the magic her soul empowered.

"I don't know if drinking her blood will get you through the barrier, but we need to try. The Sanctuary needs her. Fuck, the Sanctuary needs her Alpha, too. I've never seen her so weak. It's like she's using all her life energy to keep the magic thriving." The overconfident Omega was long gone, a concerned friend left in her wake.

Which side of her is real? I wondered. *Either way, she's an excellent actress.*

There's a way to force her to prove her loyalty, Cillian replied.

I glanced at him. *You have a suggestion?*

Yes. "We're not letting Kieran go anywhere alone with you," he said out loud, taking the lead on whatever idea he had concocted.

I didn't interrupt him.

I might be the leader here, but he was every bit as powerful and intelligent as me. If he had something to negotiate, I'd allow it.

Kyra growled. "Then you can't help me." She tried to pull free of Lorcan's grasp, but he held her in place.

"He's not saying Kieran can't go," my cousin told her, his voice low and menacing. "He's saying we won't let him go *alone* with you."

This time I couldn't help gaping at my always silent cousin.

But his eyes were on the Omega before him. "One of us is coming with you," he continued.

Cillian nodded to my left. "Yes. One of us will join you for Kieran's protection."

Kyra scoffed at that. "Have none of you been listening to me?" she demanded. "The barrier only allows Omegas and their mates."

"And you're unmated," Cillian replied, not missing a beat. "Since you killed your vampire mate."

My lips nearly curled. *A loyalty test,* I thought at him. *Clever.*

He was going to make Kyra prove herself by agreeing to mate one of my men. If she truly wanted to save her best friend, she'd agree to almost anything, including that.

Not that my men would follow through.

They just wanted to see what she would do and how she would react.

Oh, we fully intend to follow through, Cillian promised me. *You are not going anywhere with this female. And on the off chance she's telling the truth, then we need to get to Quinnlynn. This is our solution.*

I cut him a look. *That's not going to happen. If she agrees, we'll have our proof. And on the off chance she's an excellent actress, I can handle myself.*

Not in your current emotional state, he returned, his tone stern and brooking no argument. Then he dismissed me in favor of Kyra. "Mate one of us so we can cross over with you. That way, if Kieran still can't pass through, one of us can bring Quinnlynn back to him."

"You think I didn't try to bring her here?" Kyra demanded, arching a brow. "Because trust me, I did. But the barrier reacted, and Quinnlynn screamed so loud that she woke up the entire Sanctuary."

"Trust you?" Cillian asked. "I believe—"

"You haven't given us a single damn reason to trust you," Lorcan interrupted. "We found you lurking in Kieran's quarters with a knife."

"For my protection," she gritted out. "I'm not here to hurt anyone. I'm trying to help Quinn."

"And other than provide a few fancy explanations— that may or may not be true—you haven't given us any real reason to trust you," Lorcan countered, his Irish accent far more subdued than my own. Probably because he never used his voice. Yet this female seemed to have inspired a very talkative version of him.

"So you're giving me an ultimatum," she replied.

"No, we're giving you an opportunity to prove your loyalty," Cillian corrected her.

"By forcing me to mate one of you." She huffed a humorless laugh. "How chivalrous."

"You think we want to take a mate? Let alone one known for killing her last Alpha partner?" Cillian asked.

She narrowed her gaze.

But he wasn't done. "We're both well over a thousand years old, Omega. If we wanted a mate, we would have taken one by now. Our duty is to Kieran and Kieran alone. If it means taking an errant brat for a mate so we can guarantee his safety, so be it."

"That's true loyalty," Lorcan added. "We would die for him. Would you do the same for your supposed best friend?"

I gritted my teeth but remained silent. I'd let this continue until she voiced her response. Then I'd step in, tell them to fuck off, and allow this Omega to take me to the elusive Sanctuary.

Assuming she proved loyal in her decision, anyway.

Kyra growled at my two Elites. "You both know nothing about me."

"We know enough not to trust you, little killer," Lorcan replied.

I wasn't sure what shocked me more—the fact that this female's presence had miraculously unleashed my cousin's tongue, or that my two best friends were willing to mate a notorious Alpha-assassin for me.

Not that I intended to let it happen.

Don't, Cillian warned, obviously hearing my mind calculate a plan. *This is our due. Leave it be.*

You are not mating that assassin for me. I can fucking defend myself.

No, Kieran. He looked at me, his dark eyes oozing lethal energy. *It's not up for debate. She either agrees to this requirement, or she returns without you.*

I am not leaving my mate to suffer.

She's not your fucking mate, he shot back. *Not yet. Perhaps not ever. I felt the energy that put you on your ass. I'm not letting you near that fucking thing without backup. And neither is Lorcan.*

You can't fucking stop me.

I won't need to, he replied, drawing my attention back to Kyra and Lorcan.

She'd spun to face him, the two of them engaged in a verbal sparring match about loyalty and how neither one of them truly understood the meaning of the word.

"I don't fucking have time for this," the Omega snapped, her English accent stronger than before. "But you'd better believe that I will be handing you your arse when I return, *Alpha*." Energy shimmered in the air as Kyra tried to shadow.

Lorcan merely stared down at her, his expression cold and calculating. "Problem, *Omega*?"

She snarled at him. "Fine. You want a display of loyalty? I'll show you loyalty." She grabbed a fistful of his long hair and yanked him down to her.

Then she sank her fangs into his neck.

"Fuck!" I shouted, stepping forward, afraid she was about to rip his throat out.

But Lorcan growled in warning, his power whipping around her as he released a second growl, which caused her knees to give out.

He caught her with one arm, lifting her in the air, and returned the favor by sinking his own teeth into her neck. His dark eyes glittered with hunger as he swallowed her essence, their mating bond snapping into place.

Gods. "Have you lost your fucking mind?" I demanded.

"We're your Elites," Cillian interrupted. "Your life is ours to protect."

"Not at the expense of your own," I snapped.

"It's done," Lorcan replied, his voice deep and filled with need. Mating inspired sex. Which meant his wolf would want to fuck. Right now.

But my cousin released his new mate instead, his expression giving nothing away as he stared her down.

"She's telling the truth," he said after a beat.

"No shit," she muttered, her palm covering the bite mark on her throat. "At least I know your friend meant it when he said you didn't want mates."

Lorcan ignored her, his focus on me again. "We need to go. Drink the blood. If it doesn't work, I'll bring Quinnlynn back here."

My head was spinning, my wolf snarling inside at Lorcan's high-handed behavior.

Yeah, he was my cousin.

Which made him powerful and strong and capable of his own decisions.

But to take a mate in order to protect me?

"We're not fucking done with this discussion," I told him as I shadowed over to the table to retrieve the vial of Quinnlynn's blood.

"You can thank me later," he deadpanned, his behavior blowing my mind. It was so out of character that I was beginning to question whether or not someone had replaced my cousin with a double.

Or perhaps he'd been bespelled.

I eyed the Omega. *Or maybe bewitched.*

My jaw clenched, but I didn't have much of a choice here. If she was telling the truth about Quinnlynn, then my intended needed me. And I'd been wrongly pissed off the last few days.

"You'd better not be tricking us, Omega," I warned her as I unscrewed the cap of the vial.

"Pretty sure there isn't a worse punishment you could give me right now, Alpha," she returned through her teeth.

Lorcan glanced at her, his eyes flashing at whatever he overheard in her thoughts. But I couldn't find an ounce of guilt on him. He wasn't the type to regret a decision. He acted on impulse and did what he needed to do to survive.

As did I.

Rather than question the Omega further, I emptied the contents of the vial into my mouth.

And swallowed.

Belaboring the point would be a waste of time.

What was done was done.

Unfortunately, however, I didn't feel any different. Which meant drinking her blood hadn't mated me to my intended.

She needed my bite.

But maybe this would be enough.

It had better be.

"Take me to Quinnlynn."

"Us," Lorcan interjected, holding out his hand for Kyra. "Take *us* to Quinnlynn."

Kyra muttered something under her breath and grabbed his palm. Then she reached for me. "I hope this fucking hurts," she told us both. "*A lot.*"

KIERAN

THE WORLD SHIMMERED AROUND ME, making my stomach churn with unease.

At least I'm still standing, though.

My bare feet burned as I found my balance on the ice, my skin prickling from the frigid atmosphere.

Lorcan cursed nearby.

"Kyra?" a deep voice asked cautiously.

"It's fine," she gritted out. "He's here for Quinn."

"And the other?" the male pressed, causing me to blink in his direction. I couldn't see him. Not completely. But I guessed by his size that he was the Omega Kyra had mentioned. *Fritz.*

"Is someone I'll handle on my own," she replied dryly.

I closed my eyes and stole a deep breath. *Quinnlynn.* I could feel her everywhere. Her power. Her scent. Her presence.

She was definitely here.

But it was more than that.

This place is *her.*

Her family's energy swirled around every aspect of this

island's creation. I could feel the ancient vitality pressing against my spirit, demanding payment.

It caused my wolf to pace madly inside. He could sense the toll this place took on our intended mate, her soul's weakness fully exposed.

This island was draining her.

Completely.

I could sense the waves pulling at her being, demanding more. But my Omega barely had anything left to give.

"Does she often fall unconscious when she visits?" I wondered aloud, my eyes opening to take in the majestic outer walls of what appeared to be a fortress.

"No, but it's been a very long time since her last visit," Kyra answered, her tone wary. "She came here after your betrothal. Then she left to pursue a lead and never really returned."

I nodded. "The island is requiring her to make up for lost time." Or that was my guess, anyway. "Take me to her."

I could feel Quinnlynn's need, just like I could sense the barrier spell evaluating my presence. The enchantment lingered on my skin like a sticky substance, uncertain as to whether or not it wanted to allow me to stay. One wrong move and it would oust me. Maybe even kill me.

I needed to bite Quinnlynn.

Immediately.

Or I risked being tossed off this island.

The only reason it hadn't kicked me off yet was the blood from that vial.

And perhaps the minor weakness in the veil caused by Quinnlynn's exhaustion.

Which suggested that I might not be the only one capable of forcing my way through.

The sooner we were mated, the sooner I could help her.

There would be no questions. No punishment. No comments of any kind. Just my fangs meeting her throat and securing us together once and for all.

As soon as that was done, we could find our future path again.

"We need to walk," Kyra said. "I'm worried the shield will react to you shadowing."

I nodded, agreeing with her assessment.

Shadowing required me to tap into my inner strengths, which would disturb the magic around us. I needed to appear nonthreatening, like I belonged here. "This enchantment is unlike anything I've ever felt. How old is it?"

"Older than us," Lorcan deadpanned, his gaze on his new mate.

She glared at him. "Stop poking around in my head."

"No. Not until I'm sure we're safe here."

"You're not safe here," she countered.

"Exactly," he replied.

She clenched her jaw and turned on her booted heel. "I told you it's fine, Fritz," she muttered as she started toward the wall. "Open the door."

Magic shimmered ahead of us, allowing me to see the *door* she'd mentioned.

But it wasn't a door so much as a grand entryway made of fire.

Lorcan eyed it with interest while I took in the snow around it. Nothing was melting.

Interesting.

I'd have to evaluate the mechanics of that *after* I took care of my intended.

Kyra danced through the fiery portal, her blue-black hair waving us forward in her wake.

Lorcan followed.

Then he called out from the other side that it was safe, so I stepped through as well.

More of that tangible magic shimmered across my skin, the sticky residue leaving me uneasy. *No wrong moves,* I reminded myself.

A trio of Omegas stepped into the courtyard ahead, the icy landscape leading to a palace that glittered like crystals.

"It's fine," Kyra said again. "I'm not being coerced. And that's the future King of Blood Sector that you have in your sights, Jas!" She yelled the words at a sentry up on the wall with an arrow pointed right at my head.

I arched a brow, then purposely looked at Kyra and ignored the threat at my back. "How far away is Quinnlynn?"

Kyra pointed at the palace. "She's secured in her rooms there. Maybe a fifteen-minute walk from here."

"And if we run?" I asked her.

"I don't recommend it," Lorcan interjected. "The Omegas have an army, and it seems we're breaking their usual guest protocols. Which is why we have so many weapons pointed at us right now."

"Thank you for stealing information from my mind, *mate,*" Kyra said in a sarcastically sweet tone.

"Let's walk quickly," I suggested, ignoring the comments about weapons. I was more worried about the barrier catapulting me into the Arctic Ocean at the moment.

Kyra shot one more warning look at an unfazed Lorcan and started down the stone pathway toward the palace gates.

The courtyard around us was adorned in ice sculptures, similar to fountains with water and grass. Except everything here was frozen.

Still beautiful, though.

Just like the palace ahead with its decorative glass panes and ice-like spires.

The gates consisted of a synthetic metal that opened as we approached.

And the stairs ahead were made of white stone, similar to our current path.

More Omegas lingered here, many of them holding weapons.

But a signal from Kyra had them all standing down.

She clearly had power here. Which didn't surprise me if she was Quinnlynn's best friend. This all added credence to the stories about how Kyra had bled out her mate, too.

She was undoubtedly deadly.

Yet it seemed Lorcan had no interest in getting to know her. He actually looked like he was more likely to kill her.

Two sentries met us at the palace doors, their scents confirming they weren't V-Clan wolves but something else.

W-Clan, maybe?

They disappeared before I could properly evaluate their presence.

I almost asked, but a sudden whiff of Quinnlynn's fragrance had my wolf growling inside. *Slick.* She'd definitely gone into heat again.

That wasn't surprising, considering her last heat hadn't been complete. And I imagined the magic draining her here had pushed her into another vulnerable state.

My nose started leading me more than Kyra did, my inner beast tracking his intended.

The Vampire Omega didn't step in my way or direct

me otherwise, just walked beside me while Lorcan protected my back.

I trailed the scent through a door, up some grand stairs, and down an elaborately decorated corridor with crystallized glass framing the walls and ceiling.

The journey continued for minutes, to another section of the palace that seemed less populated.

Family quarters, I realized quickly as I pushed through another set of thick doors.

I no longer cared about Kyra or Lorcan, my focus entirely on finding my Omega.

Her whimpers echoed softly, her scent a beacon to my senses.

I didn't run, the thick magic in the air reminding me to remain calm, but I did pick up my pace.

More stairs sent me upward to a floor with three doors. No glass here. *Bedrooms.*

Quinnlynn's was at the end, her entryway partially opened to reveal an opulent space framed by windows that overlooked the mountains of snow in the distance. We were clearly very far north, on an island off the coast of either Greenland or Canada. Maybe even Russia.

But it didn't matter.

I only had eyes for the Omega curled into a corner bed, her dark hair splayed around her as she mewled in agony.

My energy immediately latched onto hers, giving her the vitality her soul craved and eliciting a sharp cry from her lips.

"What are you doing?" Kyra demanded from behind me.

I ignored her, my bare feet—which I'd lost feeling in some time ago—carrying me to my Omega.

"Kieran." My name left her on a whimper. "I'm sorry."

"Shh," I hushed her, joining her on the bed and kicking off my jeans in the process. "I'm here, little one."

She shook her head. "You hate me. This is a fever dream."

"Not a dream." I pulled her into me as I began to purr. "And I could never hate you, Princess."

She sobbed as her head met my chest, her cries breaking my heart. This wasn't my strong mate, but an Omega broken by the pressure of keeping this island alive. An Omega pained by going into heat without her Alpha. An Omega who had carried the weight of the world on her shoulders for far too long.

It was time to join as one, to lead *together*, not apart.

She needed my strength.

Just as I needed her truth.

This secret place was now ours to protect.

"You'll never be alone again," I promised her, my wolf humming in agreement.

I kissed her forehead and brushed her hair away from her beautiful face.

"Look at me, Quinnlynn," I whispered. "I'm not a dream. I'm real. I'm here. And I'm going to claim you."

"Kieran?" My name sounded so soft and fragile on her lips.

"I'm here," I repeated, purring louder for her and pushing more of my energy into her spirit.

It seemed to go right through her, the magic around us hungry for more. Hungry for *me*.

I no longer felt the elastic presence of the barrier, just a subtle brushing of curiosity, almost as though the enchantment were alive and possessed emotions.

That wasn't possible—magic didn't thrive on its own.

But it certainly felt like it was corporeal, perhaps because it was so heavily tied to my intended mate. A piece of her. *Her heart.*

She absorbed more of my strength, her nose pressing against my chest as she tried to claw her way into me.

I rolled us on her bed instead, taking her beneath me as I pressed my hips to hers. She finally dared to open her eyes, those beautiful dark irises immediately finding mine.

She blinked a few times as though stirring from sleep, her gaze flickering in and out of focus. "You're here?"

"I'm here," I said again.

"At the Sanctuary?"

I nodded. "Kyra brought me." I angled my head toward her, only to realize that she and Lorcan had left.

However, it didn't matter. Because Quinnlynn seemed to understand. "The blood worked."

"Yes." I balanced myself on one arm by her head while my opposite hand cupped her cheek. "But I need to claim you."

Her eyes glittered. "Yes."

"You're ready?" I asked, somewhat pleased to hear her agreement. Although, it could easily be the heat talking. But in the end, it wouldn't change what I had to do. She was mine. And it was time.

"I may never be truly ready," she whispered, her words sounding much more like the Quinnlynn I knew. "But it's what I want. What I *need*."

"To balance the power," I said, translating the *need* part of her statement.

But she shook her head. "To balance us. To… to move us… into the future."

That had been our conversation the other night— debating the past, present, and destined paths. Right before she'd betrayed me.

Or rather, right before I'd thought she'd betrayed me.

However, I knew the truth now.

She'd tried to bring me here, to show me her family's deepest secret. Because she'd decided to let me in. To trust me. To make me truly hers.

And now she *needed* me to complete the process.

"You want this," I marveled aloud, my gaze searching hers. "It's no longer a game or a matter of using me for power. You want *us*."

"I do," she confirmed, her eyes fully lucid now.

Then she tilted her head, exposing her neck.

And said the words I'd longed to hear from her.

For over a hundred years.

"Bite me, Kieran. Make me yours."

QUINN

Kieran had doused me in his energy and strength, pulling me back from the brink of insanity and into reality once more.

I wasn't sure how long it would last, the burn inside me growing hotter with each passing second.

But I was thankful for the brief reprieve.

It gave me the clarity I needed to understand. To believe. To *know* that he existed.

Not a dream.

Kieran is here.

He's on top of me.

Naked.

And about to claim me.

"Please," I whispered, wanting to feel his claim before I lost my mind with lust again. Everything was just so *hot*. A mess of sweat and tears and *agony*.

He pushed more healing power into me, making me sigh in contentment. His purr rumbled, his scent overwhelming my senses, his male presence a gift from the gods themselves, lulling me into a state of bliss.

Except I needed more.

"Bite me," I repeated, my head still rolled back to expose my neck.

"Just debating where I want to mark you," he murmured, his lips skimming my cheek on his way to my ear. "I'm struggling to decide if I want it to be in a place everyone can see. Or in a place only I know about."

He kissed my neck, his lips skimming my pulse.

"I want everyone to know we're mated, Quinnlynn. But above all, I want *you* to know that I've claimed you. That our souls are bonded. That you are finally fucking *mine*." He nipped my sensitive skin, teasing me before drawing his mouth to mine.

His name left my lips, only to be interrupted by his tongue as he devoured me in a kiss that had me seeing stars.

Because I forgot how to breathe.

This male consumed me. Owned me. *Claimed me without biting me.*

And I couldn't... fight him. Nor did I want to.

I grabbed his shoulders instead and held on while he mastered my mouth, destroying every thought I owned and introducing me to sensations that I'd only experienced with his knot.

Oh, moons... This male could kiss. No wonder he'd held back. This... this was... *everything.*

But it ended too quickly, his forehead meeting mine as he exhaled against my bruised lips. "Fuck, Quinnlynn. I feel like I could kiss you for eternity."

"Then do it," I said. "Kiss me, Kieran. Kiss me forever."

"My first and last kiss," he breathed, confusing me.

"First?" I repeated, not understanding.

"You're the only one, Quinnlynn. The only one I've ever kissed. The only one I've ever wanted to kiss."

"You've… you've never kissed anyone else?" I whispered, shocked by his admission.

"Only you."

Only me?

His mouth captured mine again before I could speak, his skilled tongue demolishing my stunned thoughts in an instant and driving me into a state of passion once more.

I dug my nails into his shoulders, my body lighting up in flames that threatened to burn me entirely if he didn't give me more.

He growled, making my stomach clench as dampness pooled between my thighs, coating his arousal with my own.

I was so ready for him, my heat having primed my body to unspeakable levels of *need*. I whimpered, part of that overwhelming urge to mate coming back to me and stirring a maelstrom of sensation inside me.

"Please," I mouthed against his lips, my oxygen nonexistent.

He was my air. My purpose. My *lifeline*. Only Kieran. Always Kieran.

His palm left my face, his hand drifting down my side to my hip. I parted my thighs even more, wanting him to touch me, to fuck me, to *complete* me.

"You want my knot, Princess?"

"Yes." I pressed up against him. We didn't need foreplay. Not when I felt like this. Not when I needed him as badly as I did.

But Kieran was a fucking tease.

Because he kissed me *again*.

His palm skimmed my side once more as he fully lay against me.

I could feel his cock against my clit, his shaft reminiscent of a brand against my slick flesh. I tried to move beneath him, to squirm, to convince him to take me, but he held me with ease as his mouth owned mine.

Teeth grazing my lower lip.

Tongue tasting. Plunging. *Fucking.*

I wrapped my arms around his shoulders, holding on for the ride that was completely controlled by Kieran O'Callaghan. My intended. My future. My chosen King.

He smiled against my mouth, both his hands suddenly exploring my body. Stroking. Petting. Stirring my desire into a frenzy that resembled molten lava in my veins.

I whimpered.

I pleaded.

I forgot my own damn name.

But then I felt his mouth at my neck, his teeth grazing my pulse again. "I don't need to mark you here," he whispered. "One look at you and everyone will know you're mine. They won't even need the crescent imprint of my mouth to prove it."

He started kissing a path downward, his tongue and mouth devastating and thorough.

"No, devious mate." His words were a low purr against my skin as he paused at my breast. "I want to mark you somewhere for *us*. Somewhere that you see every day. In a place you will always recognize as *ours*."

He took my nipple between his teeth, making me jolt on the bed, a strangled sound leaving my throat.

"Mmm," he hummed. "Maybe here, then." He bit down enough to taunt me but didn't break the skin before continuing his journey downward.

"*Kieran.*"

"Shh," he hushed. "The barrier feels better now. It's

likely my gift of power. We have a little time for me to pick the right place."

He paused to dip his tongue into my belly button, the sensation shooting off sparks behind my eyes.

"My heat," I panted. "I want... I need... I want to be... *aware*."

"And you will be," he promised as he doused me in another intoxicating wave of his healing essence. I practically melted, my inner wolf content and purring and reveling in her chosen mate's power. She saw this as an engagement gift of sorts. A display of intention.

A demonstration of worth.

I trembled, my stomach twisting with intensity as Kieran pressed an open-mouthed kiss to the most sensitive part of me.

His tongue nearly made me come with just a little flick, my body so ready to combust that I didn't need much.

But he took his mouth away, instead moving to my hip bone to nibble the flesh there.

And then down to my inner thighs.

His mouth and hands were everywhere, my skin blazing from his touch, my insides a fiery mess of exquisite insanity.

"You're punishing me," I accused, arching into him again.

"No, love, I'm worshipping you." His mouth returned to my overheated flesh, his tongue whispering hot words of adoration against my clit and forcing me to tumble into an oblivion of sensation.

It *burned*.

I screamed.

The world went dark.

And then I was alive and panting again.

Time ceased to exist; all that mattered was Kieran's mouth, his touch, his *growl*, and his control.

He was the Alpha here. The dominant one between us. The powerful wolf who always knew what to say and when.

I gave everything to him. All my faith. My heart. My soul. My *existence*.

Because I trusted him.

He would protect me. He would please me. He would claim me.

He's a worthy mate.

He's my mate.

My Kieran.

My Alpha.

"Yes," he purred against my damp center, his mouth scant inches from my throbbing bundle of nerves. "I'm yours and you are mine."

I must have spoken those words out loud, something his dark eyes confirmed as he stared up at me in approval.

He liked being called mine.

Or maybe it was the *worthy* part.

Perhaps it was everything.

He prowled upward again, his movements sleek and graceful and befitting his role in this world. All power and elegance. So perfect. Masculine. A tad bit feral. Yet utterly captivating.

"Mate me," I begged him. "Please, Kieran. I want to feel you inside me in every way."

He smiled, his mouth pausing right over my heart. "As you wish, My Queen." His canines bit into my flesh before I could correct him, his power hitting me like an avalanche and sucking me into a dark void of ravenous energy.

So. Much. Vitality.

So. Much. *Kieran*.

My world disappeared, yanked into the vortex of my mate, and annihilated every thought I'd ever possessed.

Only to suddenly be full of Kieran's mind.

Overcome by his thoughts. His desires. His emotions.

His loyalty.

Every word. Every statement. Every claim. It was all true. He'd never lied. Not even once. Always telling me exactly how he'd felt and what he'd desired.

He hadn't killed my parents.

He hadn't been after my family secrets.

He'd simply wanted me. *And my heart.* He'd wanted me to beg. To accept him for him, not for some nefarious scheme. But he'd wondered at my reasons for over a century.

And now he knew. Now he could see what had driven my choice that night.

It wasn't just about his lack of participation in the wards. It was about him. His power. His bad-boy status. His intimidating aura.

I'd known none of the other Alpha Princes would dare go against him. And those who did would perish.

Because he was fit to be a King. *My* King.

His power had lived up to my expectations. But I hadn't expected him to be this charming. This disarming. This... *perfect.*

He fancied himself a villain, and maybe for some, that was true.

However, for me, he was a hero. He'd led Blood Sector with the ease and skill of a King. He'd proved to be everything I needed and so much more.

He'd become the Alpha I hadn't even known I'd desired, and now I couldn't picture a life without him. A part of me was livid that I'd waited this long to feel so complete, so safe, so *at home.*

Yet I knew my journey to this point was part of what made us so right for each other.

I'd learned over the years how to appreciate every aspect and facet of life, and Kieran had learned how to be a King.

Together, we were stronger from our past, and we were heading into a future bolstered by our experiences.

He was older, wiser, and more powerful. But I understood other sectors, other supernaturals, and the beauty of maintaining a Sanctuary for those in need.

Our lives would forever be tied, forever strengthening the other, forever *thriving*.

This moment created such a beautiful collaboration that I wept.

And Kieran kissed away my tears.

Then he slid inside me and slowly made love to me. Not fast. Not hard. Just tender and right and *us*.

His mouth claimed mine, his tongue issuing marital vows against my own as he drove my body to new limits.

Gliding in and out.

Mastering me.

Cherishing me.

Honoring me.

I wrapped my legs around his waist, taking him deeper. Squeezing. Holding him inside. Begging for his knot.

But he kissed away my potential pleas, forcing me to accept his slow pace. His measured strokes. His hypnotic caresses.

His hands were memorizing my skin.

His tongue was speaking a love language with my own.

And my breast throbbed from his bite.

You claimed me, I marveled, engaging our mental link and loving how easily I found him inside my mind.

I did, he confirmed. Not that it was needed. I obviously

knew we were officially mated. But there was something intimate about exchanging words via our telepathic connection and not just with our mouths.

I could hear his desire. Could sense his darker cravings. And I could feel his need to make me feel loved, too.

Because he cared deeply for me.

Just as I did for him.

We were finally on our right path, our lives intertwined for the journey ahead and our hearts mingling as one.

My Alpha, I breathed, pressing up into him and clenching once more. *Give me my knot.*

Your knot? he replied.

Yes. My Alpha. My knot.

He chuckled, the sound deep and sexy and vibrating against my chest. "All right, devious one," he whispered against my mouth. "You win."

I didn't get a chance to ask what he meant because his knot exploded in the next second, driving me into madness.

It pulsated and throbbed inside me, forcing me to join him in the rapturous oblivion that followed.

Some distant part of my mind overheard his concern about not having taken another birth control pill.

A few weeks ago, that would have terrified me.

However, now... now I welcomed whatever life had in store for us.

We're on a new path, I told him. *Whatever happens... happens.* It was more of a delirious musing on my part, but that didn't make it any less true.

"Are you ready for me to release you back to your heat?" Kieran asked softly, his hands on my face again. "I suspect this one will last your usual thirty days."

I could feel my body agreeing with that statement. My

previous cycle had been a warm-up, a way to coax my soul back into our annual routine.

This heat was the real deal.

Roughly a month of fucking.

I ran my hands along the bedding beneath us, my legs still wrapped around his hips. "I'm going to need supplies," I told him.

"I think Lorcan and Kyra are already handling that."

"Lorcan?" I repeated.

Kieran shook his head. "A story for when your heat concludes. For now, I want to focus on fucking you."

My inner walls clamped down around his knot, eager for the promise in his words. "Yes, Alpha. Thirty days of fucking."

He growled. "I'm going to master every inch of you."

"Good." I smiled, very much liking the challenge in his gaze. "Now kiss me again. I want to lose my mind while I have your tongue inside my mouth."

I was giving him permission to ease me back into my heat, something he would know through our mental link.

So he didn't bother trying to clarify. He simply captured my lips.

And released me to my fiery instincts.

All of which led to me wanting to fuck him. *All month long.*

KIERAN

Quinnlynn stretched out alongside me, her mouth parting on an adorable yawn as she nuzzled into my side. I purred in response, content with my mate's satisfaction.

Four weeks of fucking had taken a toll on us both, but I sensed that Quinnlynn wasn't ready to surface yet. Not entirely, anyway. She'd been more alert these last few days, mostly as a result of her need to nest. It had taken priority over mating, her instinct to rebuild her safe haven driven by the bond forming between us.

Lorcan had shadowed in two baskets of clothing for me to give to Quinnlynn.

Fortunately, he'd left them outside in the hallway, the Alpha fully aware of my beast's possessiveness. Alphas were innately protective of their mating females, something that came naturally to us. And the scent of another male near the nest could send even the most in-control Alphas into a dangerous rage.

However, it had actually placated my wolf a bit to scent Lorcan's mated status. I hadn't felt the urge to rip his throat out as a result. Of course, that instinct could have changed in an instant. Thus, my cousin's decision to maintain his distance had been an intelligent choice.

I ran my fingers through Quinnlynn's dark hair, loving the way it contrasted with her alabaster skin. Her cheeks held a faint blush to them, telling me she was healthy and happy.

The Omegas had set up some sort of food delivery system here, making it easy for me to keep Quinnlynn fed. She hadn't fought me at all, something I suspected was due to her liking the offerings.

Which meant either someone had kept a list of foods all Omegas enjoyed during heat, or they had a catalog of preferences by person.

Either way, I intended to get my hands on that information.

It would come in handy in the future.

Quinnlynn yawned again, then buried her nose against my chest in a silent demand for *more*.

I smiled, my purr intensifying to meet her request.

She sighed in response, her leg sliding between mine as she let her body do all the talking for her.

We'd gone through enough cycles for me to know what came next.

A nibble.

Right over my pec.

Followed by kisses upward to my throat.

My lips curled as she did exactly what I expected, her lower half settling against me as she moved to straddle my hips.

I existed in a constant state of hardness around her, making it easy for her to seat herself on me. All the way to the hilt.

"You're so beautiful, Quinnlynn," I told her, loving the way she braced her palms on my chest as she sat up.

She hummed in response, liking my compliment.

It seemed my little Omega possessed a praise kink, something I very much enjoyed. She made it easy to compliment her, especially as she started to ride me.

Nice and slow.

Taunting.

Waiting for her Alpha to take control.

Some of the days, I had let her ride me for hours instead of minutes.

But I felt her coming out of her heat now, which made me eager to make this last time count.

I gave her a few more seconds to indulge her baser needs.

Then I slowly sat up, my gaze holding hers.

She encircled my waist with her legs, her wolf giving an appreciative growl deep inside. It was one I echoed as I wrapped my palm around the back of her neck and pulled her into a kiss.

Fuck, I love this. I love her. I was addicted to her taste. Her tongue. Her *lips.* Every embrace felt like the first time, which made no sense, as we'd spent the last month making out in her nest.

But I couldn't get enough.

I battled her with my tongue, loving how she matched me move for move.

I taught her that. Or maybe she taught me that.

It didn't matter.

We were mastering each other, learning our preferences, finding our balance, and spiraling into a heady world of intense pleasure together.

I palmed her breast with my free hand and gave her nipple a little twist right below my bite mark. She mewled, the action one I'd learned was a favorite of hers.

Just like she enjoyed my deep thrust—which I gave her

now—and the slight shifting of my hips that brushed her clit.

She trembled, her orgasm already close.

My responsive, gorgeous mate, I whispered into her mind. *I'm going to make you come so hard that you see stars.*

Yes, Alpha. Yes.

Kieran, I corrected her. *Say my name, love.*

Kieran, she repeated immediately.

Good girl, I praised her.

Her pussy clenched around my cock in response, her body vibrating with need.

That's it, Quinnlynn. Ride me, I told her, thrusting upward. *Take your pleasure. Make yourself feel good.*

Kieran, she moaned, our kiss growing ardent and vicious at the same time. She bit my tongue, then sucked it into her mouth to swallow my essence.

I'd return the favor against her neck in a minute.

I wanted to feel her soar first.

Mmm, you feel so fucking good, love, I praised her. *You're squeezing me in the best fucking way. I could stay here forever.*

Yes, she hissed. *Yes, Kieran. Please.*

Fuck you into oblivion and never stop knotting you. I nibbled her lower lip, then let her bite my tongue again. It hurt, but I liked it. Because I could feel the sensual gratification that it gave her deep inside to mark me so intimately, to taste me, to *claim* me. *Are you going to come for me, darling?*

She squeezed me impossibly tighter, her little body moving faster as she tried to fulfill my request. I felt her warmth spreading, her slick coating my shaft, her pulse racing. *Kieran!*

Now, Quinnlynn. Come for me now.

She did, her ecstasy erupting around me and *through* me in hot lashes of intensity. I could hear her joy via her thoughts, feel her rapture around my cock, and sense her orgasm as though it were my own through our mating bond.

Fuck, little one, I breathed, driving into her with a fierce punch of my hips.

I rolled us, putting her on her back, but kept her legs wrapped around my hips.

Then I took her the way I wanted to—fast and rough —and forced her into another climax that had her screaming my name.

"So fucking good," I told her, my lips going to her neck, my teeth primed to bite. This mark would heal. The other one would not. It was part of the magic that held our souls together, her body forever bearing my claim against her breast.

Just thinking about it made me harder.

Had me salivating.

My beast wanting to *taste.*

I gave in to the inclination, my vampire-like fangs sinking into the pulse point of her throat and spinning her into another euphoric cyclone.

She shook beneath me, her body on the verge of unconsciousness.

But I anchored her to reality with my knot, my own bliss overwhelming and intoxicating and downright *drugging.*

I felt dizzy from both my climax and her blood, my wolf sated, yet hungry for more.

I'm addicted to you, I told her. *I'm addicted to this.*

Mmm, she hummed, her agreement incoherent while also palpable.

We understood each other. We loved each other. We existed together.

My mate, I whispered, swallowing one more mouthful

of her delectable essence before slicing my tongue and feeding her my blood via a sensual kiss.

Mine, she echoed, responding to my claim.

Yours, I agreed, my palm going to her breast once more. *But also mine.*

She hummed again, her arms encircling my neck to hold me to her as we kissed each other through our shared oblivion.

My knot pulsed.

And pulsed.

And pulsed.

It was like my body knew she was on the verge of coming out of her heat, so I had to empty every ounce I had left inside her.

Meanwhile, she milked me in kind, taking as much of me as she could, filling her womb, and accepting every inch of me in return.

I purred, pleased with my mate and her willingness to play. To fuck. To do whatever I asked. To *trust.*

I'd felt her give in to my control weeks ago, having faith in me to keep her safe and just *existing* in the moment. *I've experienced many challenges in my life, Quinnlynn. But none of them compare to the joy you have brought me. Every obstacle was worth it for this moment alone.*

We would face the sector together soon.

Ensure them all that our love and bond were resolute.

And help them find peace in our destined paths.

My palm slid downward to her flat belly, my opposite hand still holding her nape.

Her dark eyes fixed on mine as I pulled away from her mouth, the knowledge in her depths rivaling my own. *New life.* It hadn't been planned. However, we both accepted our fate.

The royal bloodline would expand.

In the form of our future child.

An heir. Our heir.

The joy in Quinnlynn's features told me this wasn't an unwelcome gift but a blessing. I shared her sentiment, my wolf rejoicing at the creation warming our mate's abdomen.

It wasn't something I'd ever expected to desire.

But Quinnlynn had changed all my aspirations and provided new meaning for life.

Which was why I fully accepted and welcomed this new challenge. Because I would be embarking upon it with my mate by my side.

You're going to be an amazing father, she whispered, the lucidity in her response confirming what I already knew about her waning heat.

And you are going to be an amazing mother, I told her.

Then I kissed her again, my knot subsiding in preparation for a final round.

It would be slower again.

Thorough.

Everything we both needed.

Then I would bathe my mate.

Feed her.

And prepare us for tomorrow.

Where I hoped to finally be given a tour of the Sanctuary, as well as meet all the Omegas my mate held near and dear to her heart.

You're their King, she whispered as I kissed her soundly. *They'll welcome you with open arms.*

A far better welcoming ceremony than being the target for an Omega's bow, I mused.

Jas? she guessed.

That's what Kyra called her, yes.

I'm surprised she didn't take the shot. Jas hates Alphas.

315

Quinnlynn arched into me, taking me deeper, her dark eyes opening once more. *I'm glad she didn't, though.*

I'm glad she didn't either, I admitted. It wouldn't have killed me, but it certainly would have slowed me down.

Your magic protects them now. They'll grow to love you. Just like I do.

Maybe not like you do, I corrected her, sliding all the way to the tip before propelling myself forward again.

She trembled, her body meeting my movements with an upward thrust of her own. *Maybe not like I do,* she agreed with a groan. *But I mean it, Kieran. I do love you.*

I know. I nuzzled her nose, then kissed her before she could chastise my arrogance. However, I could hear her love inside her mind, could feel it in my very soul. Which was how I knew she felt mine, too. It was a thriving entity that existed between us, growing with each passing second.

This female had been made for me.

Just as I'd been made for her.

Our kind might not have believed in fated mates, but I did now.

Because of Quinnlynn.

There would be no one else for me. Just as there had been no one before her.

You are my existence now, I told her, the words surpassing love. *Everything I do will be for you.*

And our sector, she added.

I shook my head. *No, Quinnlynn. All of it is for you. It always has been. You needed an Alpha Prince to guide your people, and I accepted—for you.*

It was something I had begun to realize over the last few weeks. I'd already had power and a throne.

I hadn't needed Blood Sector.

But then an alluring Omega had broken through my security and essentially proposed marriage to me. A laughable affair. Yet that moment had shattered my shell of boredom and introduced me to a new reality. A new challenge. A new *game*. And I'd been so startled that I hadn't been able to deny my desire to play.

Then that Omega had taken the stakes to a new level, engaging me in a round of hide-and-seek that had caused my wolf to rumble in approval.

So I'd become the hunter.

She'd become my prey.

And all the while, I'd maintained her kingdom in her absence, not because I'd had to or because I'd felt a moral obligation to, but because I'd known all along that the only way to truly win my mate over was to ensure her home was stable and waiting for her when the game finally ended.

Since the day we met, everything I've done has been for you. It was a confession I would make to no one else. To the outside world, all my motives were driven by power. But with Quinnlynn, I would confide that my true motivations were out of adoration and respect.

And love.

Love for my intended mate.

Love for our future.

Love for the existence she represented.

She meant everything to our world, the very heart of our reality. Without Quinnlynn MacNamara, the world would be a much darker place.

Her magic was pure. Beautiful. All-encompassing.

And she used it for *good*. She used it to *protect*. A true hero.

I was just the villain meant to love her.

She didn't see me that way, but many others would. The dark Alpha Prince who'd kidnapped the princess's heart. A future King willing to destroy the world for his mate.

If she asked me to burn it all down tomorrow, I would.

But that was the key to Quinnlynn's beauty—she would never take advantage of such power. She simply embraced it and used it to better everyone around her. I could feel that in the lifelike energy keeping this Sanctuary alive.

You're an enigma, My Queen, I told her. *My enigma. And I am going to cherish you for eternity.*

Not a Queen yet, she whispered.

Official or not, you've always been a Queen to me, Quinnlynn, I confided. *Just as I've always been your King.*

She smiled against my mouth but didn't refute my statement. She simply kissed me harder, her body demanding that I stop talking and take her to oblivion again.

Such a demanding little thing, I teased, returning her kiss.

Fuck me, Kieran.

Now it was my turn to smile. *Are you begging?*

No. I'm demanding.

They say a King never bows for a Queen, I murmured. *But for you, Quinnlynn, I'll prove them all wrong. Because for you, I'll kneel.*

Rather than give her a chance to comment, I gave in to her demand.

Took her to the stars.

Made her scream so loudly that I was certain everyone in this Sanctuary heard her calling my name.

Only then did I knot her again.

And only then did I finally say... *I love you, too.*

QUINN

Kieran and I held hands as we moved through the palace's ice gardens, his gaze appreciative as he took in the details. "I suppose this is one way to make a glacier livable."

I grinned. "There's a whole team devoted to design and upkeep."

"And an entire army, too," he mused, his gaze drifting up to the sentries on the walls above.

"Not an army, necessarily. They call themselves the Protectors," I explained. "Kyra is their captain."

"Lorcan mentioned that during breakfast earlier this evening. Although, he called her a lieutenant, not a captain."

"That distinction doesn't mean much here," I admitted.

"No, I imagine it doesn't," he agreed.

"Kyra and the others felt it was important for Omegas to learn self-defense," I added. "Not all Alphas believe in cherishing Omegas."

He nodded. "Self-defense is an important skill. Especially in this world."

"It is. But we've learned that there is power in numbers here. And weapons help, too." I looked around, taking in the scenery and cool air. "They've grown a lot in my absence as well. It makes me sad that I've missed so much."

"You were pursuing your calling, saving other Omegas, and trying to find the culprit responsible for your parents' crash. The Omegas here understand, Quinnlynn." He paused, his hand going to my cheek as he forced me to look at him. "I can see it in the way they look at you. They admire you a great deal. And Blood Sector will, too."

"How?" I asked. "I can't tell them about this place."

"Perhaps not yet," he conceded. "But we'll find a way to win them over. Together."

"They think I abandoned them again."

"No. Lorcan and Cillian ensured that everyone knows you went into heat. And anyone who doesn't believe it will be proved wrong during the coronation." He released my hand to press his palm to my belly. "There's no refuting our time together now."

My cheeks warmed at the insinuation and pleasure in his voice.

I shared the sentiment, something he could no doubt hear inside my mind.

"I hope you're right about them forgiving me," I whispered. "Especially since the coronation is in three days." Cillian had told Kieran it was imperative to have the ritual sooner rather than later, particularly as Kieran and I were fully mated now.

My Alpha had agreed.

It seemed he wanted to set the record straight once and for all and move everyone out of the past and into the present.

No more doubts.

No more heartache.

No more claims of illegitimacy.

It was time for the V-Clan wolves to accept us as their King and Queen.

"Do you think whoever attacked my parents will be there?" I asked him.

"If it's an Alpha Prince, like you've suggested, then yes. We invited them all." He ran his thumb along my cheekbone, his gaze tracking the movement. "I imagine whoever you sensed in Bariloche Sector will be in attendance as well."

"They might even be the same wolf," I whispered, voicing the suspicion I'd maintained for years. "That's why I went down to Bariloche Sector initially—because I heard about a V-Clan Alpha visiting Alpha Carlos's, erm, *brothel*. I'd thought it could be the same Alpha. But then..."

Then I ran every time he visited, I thought, ashamed of my actions. I'd been so afraid of being caught that I'd given up on the one lead that had led me to Bariloche Sector in the first place.

My gaze dropped at my failure, only for Kieran to move his touch to my chin and force my eyes back to his. "Being afraid doesn't make you a failure, Quinnlynn. It means you were listening to your instincts. And to your *wolf*. Never feel bad for following her guidance."

"But it defeated the whole purpose of being down there."

"How many Omegas did you save?" he countered, his eyebrow winging upward. "How many of them would have died had you been caught?"

I swallowed, unable to answer that.

Because the answer was *many*.

"You might have gone down there in pursuit of a lead, but you stayed out of loyalty to the Omegas who needed you more. That's a difficult choice, Quinnlynn—finding your parents' murderer or helping those in need. However, I think we can both agree that you made the right decision."

"Except I still have no idea who sabotaged their plane," I muttered. "And you're right. I need to tell the sector the truth about their death. But I don't know how."

His grip tightened, his gaze intense. "We'll figure it out together."

"The way I should have done it from the beginning," I admitted in a whisper.

But he shook his head. "No, Quinnlynn. I had to earn your trust, just as you had to earn mine. This is exactly as it should be. No more regrets about the past. Only thoughts on moving forward. Understood?"

I stared into his midnight eyes, allowing his strength and assurance to bolster my own, and finally nodded.

He was right.

There was nothing I could do to change the past. I could only learn from it and accept it. But it went so much deeper than change, too. Because I didn't want to change my history. Everything I'd done had been done with a purpose in mind, and while I might have lost sight of my end goal, it had never truly disappeared.

"Do you have a plan in mind for the coronation?" I asked him. "A way to figure out who sabotaged the plane?"

"I have a few ideas," he admitted. "But there's one aspect to everything that I don't understand."

I frowned. "What is it?"

"Why did your parents fly when they could have shadowed? Why not crash the plane and shadow back to safety?" He paused for a thoughtful moment. "If the physical jet was what had been spelled, then why not ditch it and shadow out of it before the explosion?"

"Why have a plane to begin with when we can shadow?" I asked him softly, wincing at the memory of *why* my parents had needed to fly. "You took me home on a jet from Bariloche Sector when you could have shadowed me, right?"

"You were injured," he immediately replied. "That's why I brought the stealth jet—in case we needed to use it for transporting…" He trailed off. "Oh. They weren't alone on the jet."

"They were, but they also weren't." I cleared my throat. "My mom… was pregnant." And as Kieran already knew, it could be dangerous for a pregnant V-Clan wolf to shift or shadow. Which happened to be something we'd already discussed earlier this evening.

It was why I would have to be taken back to Blood Sector via his jet—a jet that Cillian had already personally inspected for enchantments. Kyra and Lorcan had shadowed there earlier today with the intention of piloting it back here because Kyra knew the way and Lorcan knew how to fly.

And since they were mated—something I still hadn't fully wrapped my head around—they could travel back here together without issue. Which essentially made them the perfect team. Although, they hadn't seemed all that thrilled by the pairing.

"So your father could shadow, but not your mother," Kieran said slowly, drawing me back to our conversation.

"Yes."

"Which is why they chose to die together rather than land the plane somewhere inhospitable and risk the culprit finding the location of the island." He sighed. "An honorable decision, one I wouldn't have understood a century ago but do now."

His gaze went to my abdomen, his touch leaving my chin to drop to my stomach.

I smiled down at his touch, my heart both happy and sad. But his questioning made me realize an important detail I hadn't considered before. "Whoever set up that plane knew my mom was pregnant." My lips curled down. "Did you know my mom was pregnant?"

He shook his head. "No, but I never dealt with the politics of our world. Some of the princes might have known."

"Maybe," I said slowly. "The sector definitely did; they could smell it. They also knew that was why my parents had to fly. So perhaps word spread to the others, but…" I trailed off, thinking through this detail I'd missed years ago. "But they wouldn't have had time to sabotage the plane, then."

"So either someone found out through a sector leak," Kieran started.

"Or it's not a prince at all, but someone from Blood Sector." My eyes widened at the notion. "No. That can't be right. The sector loved my parents."

"But it only takes one to dissent," Kieran replied, his mind far more skeptical than my own. "We need to warn Kyra and Lorcan." He pulled his phone out of his pocket, dialing before he even finished speaking. "Cillian. Check the jet again."

"They've already left," Cillian replied, his voice coming out through the speaker.

"*Fuck.*"

"What is it?" Cillian demanded.

Kieran quickly filled him in on what we'd just been discussing, including the bits about how we—primarily *Kieran*—questioned if the culprit was actually someone in Blood Sector.

I hated believing that.

But hearing him reiterate the facts had me thinking otherwise.

All this time, I'd assumed it was an Alpha Prince because of my mother's dying words.

"Don't trust the Alpha Princes. Not until you find out the truth, mo stoirín."

I'd assumed it was the power they'd sensed that had made them think an Alpha Prince was the culprit. However, now I wondered if I'd misunderstood everything they'd told me.

Although, I wasn't sure how. They'd been so adamant about not trusting those in power.

Why would they have done that if it wasn't an Alpha Prince?

I started to pace, my fingers stroking the pendant at my neck.

Why tell me not to trust the Alpha Princes when none of them could have sabotaged the plane that day?

My mother had been only a few weeks pregnant. The sector had known because they could smell it. But word hadn't spread yet. Not even Kieran had known about her pregnancy, his shock now telling me that he'd never been told.

Which suggested that none of the princes had known.

And the sector had chosen to keep it a secret.

"But it only takes one to dissent."

Kieran's words played through my mind, causing me to pace faster, my fingers continuing to brush over the pendant at my throat.

Someone had known that my parents had been heading to the Sanctuary. Someone had known to sabotage the plane. But how many people had actually known about their plans to travel that day?

Those who prepared the jet.

Those who prepared for their security.

I glanced at the phone in Kieran's hand as Cillian said something about locking down the sector. Because he was the current acting Alpha of Blood Sector.

As Kieran's Elite.

I stopped walking, the pendant flipping between my fingers.

"Don't trust the Alpha Princes. Not until you find out the truth, mo stoirín."

I'd alienated myself from all those in power as a result of that request. I'd hidden and denied all the proposals, allowed a war to rage for my heart, and went after the only one who hadn't tried to fight for me. And I'd only done that out of desperation.

Not for the reasons a princess should seek a mate.

To balance the scales.

To bolster my family's power.

To ensure the safety of this island.

My mother's statement had made me turn away all my suitors, to go against what a rising Queen should do in that situation. I'd chosen isolation... over a union of power.

"This is a token of power, mo stoirín. And it's yours now. Wear it for us. Wear it for you. Wear it when you kill our betrayer."

I frowned, my fingers stilling against the pendant. *A token of power.*

No.

It was a symbol for our family. A proverbial crown that defined a dynasty. A *purpose*—protection. The black diamond resembled the black rock hidden beneath the layers of glacier-like ice, the glittering stone a symbolic reference to the shimmering shield around this island.

It wasn't a token of *power*.

It was a symbol of our *purpose*.

I unclasped the necklace, confused by the memory it represented.

Then Kieran took the matching pendants from my ears, his mind having been tuned into my every thought. I wasn't sure where he'd put his device, perhaps back in his pocket, because he had an earring in each hand now.

"Give me that," he demanded, referring to my necklace.

I handed it to him without question.

And gasped when he shadowed out of the courtyard.

An explosion of power followed, sending me to my knees as a series of electric aftershocks rippled over my form.

Kieran! I shouted, my soul shattering beneath the wave of power that came next.

"Princess!" Fritz's voice echoed around me as I collapsed to my side on a spike of pain that went straight through my chest.

"Move," Kieran snapped, his Alpha aggression swimming over me as another shudder of fracturing power splintered inside me.

My head was suddenly against his chest, his purr a reverberation that did little to dispel the coldness growing inside.

But then he hit me with a wave of his healing essence, one that had me gasping as the shield around me almost immediately absorbed it.

"What the fuck is happening?" a female demanded. *Jas*, I vaguely recognized.

"A breach in the shield," Kieran gritted out. "We're fixing it."

We? I thought, delirious as my soul shuddered once more.

Kieran immediately hit me with another blast of his

power, causing me to gasp as my veins lit up with renewed vigor.

That was what he'd meant by *we*.

My magic was tied to the shield, which had just been hit by something powerful. Something *deadly*. The impact would have killed me slowly...

I frowned.

Killed me slowly... similar to... how I'd felt when I'd woken up a few weeks ago? I wondered. I'd felt so drained, my energy almost nearly depleted from the island's shield.

However, now I understood what had actually been happening, mostly because Kieran's mind was filling in the gaps.

The jewelry was enchanted, I heard him thinking. *Just like the plane. Perhaps they were even enchanted* on *the plane.*

The necklace and earrings had been countering the magic of the barrier in an attempt to create a back door of sorts, or perhaps just to act as a tracking beacon. Kieran's mind told me he wasn't sure. He'd simply shadowed outside of the barrier to see what the items would do.

Then he'd felt the vibration of power.

Tossed them away.

And the jewelry had exploded.

If we'd taken off on that plane... I couldn't finish the thought.

Because I already knew.

That explosion would have killed me.

And in doing so, it would have taken down the entire shield.

As well as left a beacon for whoever had created the spell.

How...? I asked, delirious from the energy exchange happening between me and Kieran and the barrier. *How is that possible?*

Whoever bespelled that necklace has been playing the long game, Kieran murmured. *Because you left it behind when you vanished.*

Because it didn't feel right to wear it yet, I admitted. *I was supposed to wear it when I found the betrayer.*

And you weren't supposed to trust any of the Alphas who could have potentially helped you find the culprit, he added. *Those words weren't from your mother, Quinnlynn. They were from someone trying to cover his tracks.*

KIERAN

It all made so much sense now.

Quinnlynn's avoidance of the Alpha war—all of which had been meant to secure her with the right mate for her ascension.

Quinnlynn's inherent distrust.

Quinnlynn's certainty that an Alpha Prince had been behind it all.

V-Clan Alphas were all about protecting and worshipping Omegas. None of the ones I knew would desire access to the Sanctuary. They would all respect it. Fuck, they would all volunteer their lives to *protect* it.

Why would an Alpha Prince be any different? We were all royalty for a reason, our powerful bloodlines the defining characteristic of our race.

We didn't need an island of Omegas; we received offers all the time for willing females and males.

There wasn't a single Alpha Prince I could name who would have killed the royal family for the purpose of stealing this island.

Hell, they'd all lost themselves in fighting each other to prove their worthiness of Quinnlynn.

Then she'd shunned them all, which was exactly what the real culprit had wanted.

Because had she been mated, the Alpha Prince would have learned the truth about her parents' death, and he would have helped her solve the mystery, while also bolstering the magic of this island in the process.

It was never an Alpha Prince, I repeated to her. *It's someone in Blood Sector. Someone who knows you and your family very well. Someone...* I met her gaze as she peered up at me with tired eyes. *Someone who knew you would not only accept those earrings but also wear them.*

Myon, she breathed.

Myon, I echoed.

But just as soon as I said it, her mind started to rebel against the notion, her memories of his friendship with her father making her question everything.

This has to be a misunderstanding, she was saying. *This can't be right.*

Who prepared your parents' jet? I asked her. *Who was the first to know about your mother's pregnancy, aside from maybe you and your father?*

A tear fell from her eye as she started to shake her head, denying the claim. However, her thoughts were already giving away her belief in the possibility of Myon's guilt.

He didn't approve of my betrothal to you, she thought quietly. *He wanted me to break it.*

I know.

I thought it was fatherly affection, him being overprotective, but now...

You realize it's because he saw me as a threat, I finished for her, my mind having already deduced the same line of thought.

There was a reason I hadn't allowed him to be part of

my Elite—I didn't trust him. Trust had to be earned. And he hadn't even tried to earn mine.

Unlike many of the others.

I'd chalked up his stubbornness to being tied to the old ways, or anger at me for "letting" Quinnlynn escape. Or perhaps even chasing her off.

I realized now that it hadn't been that at all. He hadn't wanted to get close to me because I might have seen through his bullshit.

But why? Quinnlynn asked, her mind quieter now. *Why would he do this? He was my father's best friend.*

Was he truly, though? I wondered. *Did your father ever tell him about the Sanctuary?*

Quinnlynn frowned. *Well, no. But it's a family secret.*

One you only shared with me when you considered me worthy of being part of your family, I pointed out. *One I've already shared with Cillian and Lorcan because they are so much more than my Elites. They're my family, too.*

It had also been a necessity, given the circumstances, but I allowed her to know that I would have told them anyway. Because they were truly my best friends.

If your father didn't confide in Myon, there was a reason for it. And I suspected it wasn't one she would like. *But if he was good at his job, then he likely had a feeling that this place existed. Or perhaps even found out about it.*

That could have been enough of a reason for him to react the way he had.

Or maybe there was a reason that went even deeper than that.

We wouldn't know until we questioned him.

It's a good thing I had Cillian lock down the sector, I thought, my lips brushing Quinnlynn's forehead.

Her magic had finally subsided, the barrier having taken enough energy from her to heal. Now her own soul was trying to rebuild its reserves, something I assisted with by pushing healing power to her via our bond.

She closed her eyes, her head resting against my chest as she allowed me to protect her.

There were several Omegas in the courtyard now, all of them staring at us with mixtures of wonder and respect. Even Jas—the one who'd seemed to be quite trigger-happy with her bow—appeared impressed.

I gave them all a soft smile that probably looked more like a grimace. I wanted to let them all know we were fine. Mostly because I wanted them all to fuck off.

If I could have shadowed my mate back to her room, I would have.

But the child growing inside her made that impossible.

I pulled her more firmly into my lap, my power running over her to check for any lasting damage. I hadn't expected the jewelry to explode; I'd just wanted to see how the barrier reacted to it.

Not well, apparently.

It was a miracle they hadn't combusted when Quinnlynn had arrived.

Perhaps because she'd shadowed here? With me? Had the shield been so focused on the wrongness of my approach that it'd let her pass, then used all its energy to thwart me instead of focusing on the jewelry?

I frowned. *No. The shadowing is definitely what saved her.*

Because I'd shadowed to the outskirts of the barrier and landed on the *outside* of it. Then I'd lifted the jewelry toward the shield, felt the buzzing energy, dropped the items, and shadowed backward before the gems could detonate.

So they were definitely meant to be worn on a plane.

Not via shadowing.

Which meant whoever had created them had done so for someone who they knew couldn't shadow.

Was your mom wearing those earrings and necklace when she left? I wondered, aware of Quinnlynn listening through my thoughts.

Yes, she replied. *She always wore them. Except maybe at night.*

Meaning she would take them off in her den... a place an Elite would have access to, but not many others, I thought, mostly to myself this time. But Quinnlynn heard it, too.

That's another piece of information that points to Myon's guilt, I said to her.

I know, she whispered, her mental voice sad.

Myon had been like a father figure to her, but she couldn't deny that he appeared guilty in this situation. For Quinnlynn's sake, I hoped I was wrong.

But I honestly doubted I was.

Because all the evidence pointed to Myon.

He must have gone to the crash site to retrieve the gems, I thought. *How long after your parents' death did you receive the necklace?*

It was a few days later.

I nodded. *Because, as an Elite, he would have known when they'd taken off. And then he would have been using the spell to track them.*

Which was how he'd known where it had crash-landed.

Because the stealth jets—even the ones back then—weren't traceable via technology. Hence the term.

He would have felt it crash, and as the enchantment seems to have not been broken—something I assumed since it had mostly worked while here—*he was able to retrieve the gems. Then he enchanted one to appear to you as though it was from your parents.*

An illusion would be easy to craft with the right sort of mental abilities.

I wasn't sure what Myon's unique talents were, but I

was betting that enchantments existed among his gifts. Perhaps something to do with hallucinations, too.

Although, given that it had taken a few days for the pendant to appear to Quinnlynn, it was also possible that Myon had sought out help.

But he had to know I wouldn't take a flight here, she said slowly. *So why give the earrings to me now?*

Maybe the spell on your necklace has worn off, or perhaps he worried it no longer works, I replied. *The earrings probably had a stronger tracking spell on them, which unfortunately means that he likely has the coordinates to the island now.*

Unless he needed the jewelry in his possession to follow the trace. That could be why he'd given the earrings to Quinnlynn, as he might have expected her to travel here and then return home, therefore giving him a trail to follow—assuming he could get ahold of the jewelry again.

Or maybe that was simply the backup plan—if the earrings and necklace hadn't exploded and taken down the barrier, then he could have stolen the diamonds and followed their enchanted trail back here.

If that was the case, then we'd just missed out on an excellent chance to trap him. We could have staged the jewelry to see if he came for them.

But that couldn't happen now that they'd detonated.

My pocket buzzed, causing Quinnlynn to jump. "It's just Cillian," I said, glancing at our audience again. They were clearly not going to leave us alone anytime soon.

I fought the urge to sigh and fished my phone from my pocket. Usually, I wore a watch. But I'd left it back in Blood Sector. Rather than bring me that with my clothes, Lorcan had brought me the phone. *Maybe he'll bring me my watch on the plane*, I thought, answering the archaic mobile instead. "Were you able to lock everything down?"

"Yeah," Cillian confirmed, sounding tired. "Just in time, too."

"What do you mean?"

"Whatever power bomb you just let off hit the sector. A few V-Clan Alphas tried to shadow. Not sure where they planned to go, maybe just home to their dens, but holding them down nearly put me on my ass," he muttered.

"Were any of them Myon?" I asked, ignoring his complaints.

"Yeah, why?"

"I want him detained until I get there to talk to him," I said. "In fact, put all the Alphas who tried to shadow in cells. But don't tell them why."

"You going to tell me why?"

"Sure." I looked down at Quinnlynn. Her eyes had fallen shut, her breathing evening out with sleep. The power explosion had clearly knocked her out.

"Why?" Cillian pressed when I didn't immediately explain myself.

"Because one of those assholes almost killed my mate," I told him. "Using the same spell that led to the death of Quinnlynn's parents."

This century-old mystery ended now.

The second I returned home, I would be demanding answers.

Answers that would likely lead to at least one death.

And then, I would finally take the throne with Quinnlynn by my side.

QUINN

My stomach twisted as the jet landed in Blood Sector. I'd practically broken Kieran's hand from clutching it so hard throughout the flight. He'd offered to help me *rest*, and I'd refused.

Because I needed to overcome this fear—a fear that was only made worse by knowing I couldn't just shadow myself to safety.

And yeah, I had no intention of doing this again. Ever.

So this flight had currently not provided any semblance of a cure. Not that I'd really expected it to, but I'd hoped to feel at least a little more confident or proud of myself.

Instead, all I felt was dread.

Because my reward for successfully surviving this trip was facing the man who might be responsible for my parents' death.

Kieran squeezed my hand, his appendage still somehow working despite my death grip.

"You'll have to try a lot harder to hurt me, love," he said, his eyes grinning with challenge.

But it was a musing I couldn't respond to. Not right now.

He used his free hand to cup my cheek, his thumb brushing my bottom lip. "You're one of the bravest wolves I've ever met, Quinnlynn. You've conquered more than most shifters do in a lifetime. I'm honored to be your mate."

I leaned into his touch and allowed his praise to wash over me, his mind accentuating his verbal claim. He meant every word. And knowing that made my heart beat that much harder for him.

This was what our lives were meant to become, this bond a love match similar to the one my parents had shared.

Thank you, I whispered to him. *Thank you for being mine.*

Thank you for sneaking into my sector and proposing to me, he returned, his comment breaking some of the ice surrounding my mind.

I almost smiled. *Almost.* But then the engines turned off, confirming our arrival. *At least we're on the ground,* I thought as Kieran released my face to unbuckle me.

I still hadn't let go of his hand, and he didn't seem at all bothered by it. Instead, he unclasped his own buckle, then pulled me up with him as he stood.

My legs shook, my balance questionable. But he held me still, lending me his strength until he was sure I could move on my own.

Lorcan met us at the door, his expression impassive. He'd chosen to return with us, leaving Kyra behind to guard the Sanctuary. I wasn't sure what deal they'd struck, but it seemed clear that Kyra intended to remain on her own at the Sanctuary while Lorcan stayed in Blood Sector.

They couldn't break their mating.

Which meant they were forever connected.

But neither of them wanted a mate—something Kieran had confirmed with a thought about Lorcan. And I knew Kyra had no desire to ever allow an Alpha inside her again. Not after what Alpha Fare had done to her.

Thus, she and Lorcan were simply going to remain in a mating of convenience where neither of them saw the other outside of random visits.

I supposed that worked for them.

As someone who had run from her betrothal bond for over a century, I also sort of understood it.

However, I would never run from Kieran again. He was mine. And I intended to ensure this entire sector knew that.

Just as soon as we dealt with the Myon issue.

Kieran squeezed my hand again and led me down the stairs of the jet.

Several pack members lingered near the tarmac, their expressions curious.

But the moment their noses caught a whiff of our scent, their eyes widened.

Not only could they smell our bond, but they would also be able to scent our heir.

A few of them exchanged looks. Others leaned in to whisper, their words drowned out by the wind. I didn't really care. What mattered was that Kieran and I were together now. For good.

He dipped his head to brush a kiss against my temple, his lips curled up a little in pleasure at the assurance of my thoughts. We could technically block each other, but I didn't see the point. I kept my mind wide open to him, and he did the same for me.

A display of trust.

A true mating.

We walked several feet before Kieran pulled me to a

stop. I frowned at him, not understanding his intentions until he drew me in for a kiss that nearly turned my world upside down.

It took me several beats to understand that this show of affection was not just for me but for our audience, too. He wanted the pack to understand our joint position.

Together.

Mated.

Forever.

His tongue dominated mine, his mouth leaving no doubt as to his desire and affection for me. I wrapped my arm around his shoulders and gave in to the display, aware that one of those observers was Omega Miranda.

This Alpha is mine, I was telling her and everyone else.

Kieran grinned, liking my possessive side, and allowed me to bite his lower lip.

His blood tasted sweet against my tongue, the flavor making me almost forget what had prompted my actions. I wanted to drag him back to his room and—

Our room, he corrected me, forever in tune with my thoughts. *If you don't like the building, we'll move. But it's our room, Quinnlynn.*

Our room, I echoed. *I need to make a nest.*

Yes, he agreed. *We can start right now, if you want.*

I almost consented to that plan.

But then I remembered the reason we'd come home earlier than expected. The coronation wasn't for another two days. We'd returned to question Myon first, as well as the other Alphas who had tried to shadow. Most of them had already expressed their apologies, their reactions having been to shadow to their mates or their homes to protect their young.

Cillian had let a few of them go, as he knew they weren't guilty as a result.

Kieran had neither agreed nor disagreed with the decision, his trust in Cillian resolute. Therefore, I trusted him, too.

But a handful of Alphas remained in custody, all of them on our interrogation list.

Or, in Kieran's case, *kill* list.

He was furious that someone had put not only my life but also the life of our child in jeopardy. And he wasn't taking that assault lightly. If we found out that Myon was behind it, he would die. There was nothing I could do to stop Kieran.

And I wasn't sure I would even try.

Someone had tried to kill my child. That was an unforgivable offense, even if the person hadn't realized I was pregnant. Knowing that wouldn't have mattered anyway, as evidenced by my own mother's demise.

No. Whoever was behind this deserved to die. I'd resigned myself to that.

I just kept hoping it wasn't Myon even though all the evidence pointed to the contrary.

The least he could do at this point would be to tell me why.

Although, Kieran already suspected he knew the answer—his ego had likely taken a hit after learning about the Sanctuary.

Which then begged the question of how he'd learned about it. *Who told him, if not my father?*

We'll find out, Kieran promised, his lips lingering against mine.

I opened my eyes to meet his dark gaze, the promise within it making me debate our course of events once more. *You're very distracting.*

As I should be, mate, he murmured, his irises glittering with intent. *May I bite you?*

My eyebrows rose. *You want to stake your claim?*

I do.

Then do it, I told him. *You don't have to ask.*

Consider me a gentleman, he replied.

I nearly laughed. *You are not a gentleman, Kieran.*

Then what am I? he asked, his lips ghosting along my cheek as he made his way to my neck.

Mine, I answered simply.

He grinned against my neck. *I like being yours, My Queen.* His canines sank into my flesh in the next instant, drawing a collective gasp from our audience. *Voyeurs,* he mused.

But I was too busy sighing at the intense endorphins to react to his comment.

His bite was pure euphoria, making my thighs clench with immediate need.

Fortunately, he didn't suck for too long, or I would have ended up coming in front of the sector.

Hmm, he hummed. *Something to consider for later.*

Don't you dare, I whispered, half-drunk from his bite.

It could be interesting. He considered it for another moment. *Except I would need to kill everyone in attendance afterward for seeing something that didn't belong to them. So perhaps not.*

I shook my head, feeling dazed from his teasing.

Except he wasn't teasing at all.

He meant every word.

It was then that I realized this whole display had been meant to distract me, to help me feel grounded, to reward me for being brave enough to fly from the Sanctuary to Blood Sector after everything I'd endured.

This male was taking care of me in his own way, all the while proving a point to the wolves surrounding us.

And he'd called me an enigma.

He was the true enigma here. Not the villain he liked to call himself. My version of a white knight. *My hero.*

His gaze narrowed. *Don't call me that.*

Offended?

Yes, he answered immediately, making me smile.

Okay, hero.

Quinnlynn, he warned.

Now I have a pet name for you, I continued, ignoring him. *You're my own personal hero.*

He growled, causing my smile to widen.

Don't worry, I whispered, my palm cupping his cheek. *Your secret is safe with me.*

His expression remained unmoved, his eyes still narrowed.

I love you, I added, nuzzling his nose. *Thank you for distracting me.*

He released a short purr in response, his wolf incapable of denying his affection even while the human tried to tame his reactions.

Then he responded by kissing me again, his adoration warming my thoughts.

"I think you've proved your point, Sire," Cillian drawled as he approached. "Word will absolutely spread now, and Miranda is practically beside herself."

Kieran continued kissing me for a long moment, then slowly stopped, all signs of his agitation having disappeared. *I love you, too,* he whispered before looking at Cillian. "You were the one who suggested we make our arrival known."

"Yes, I meant for you to announce your return so everyone knew you were back in the sector, Sire."

Kieran merely arched a brow. "Well, I believe they're all aware now."

"They most certainly are," he replied, his lips twitching. "Shall we?"

My mate released me, then pressed his palm to my back, and nodded. "Lead the way, Cillian."

Lorcan fell into step behind us, his presence silent and authoritative at the same time.

It made me feel secure, though. Because these three males were among the deadliest in existence. I could feel their power rolling over my skin like a hypnotic caress.

Cillian was exuding the most energy, his control over the sector somewhat surprising me. *He has everyone tethered.*

Yes, Kieran replied. *He was acting Alpha Prince in my absence, and I believe he's provided a rather thorough demonstration to explain how and why he was given that role.*

I nodded. *He's as powerful as an Alpha Prince.*

He comes from an ancient bloodline, just like me and Lorcan. Both of them could easily run their own sectors.

Why don't they?

Loyalty, he answered simply as we slid into a waiting car. I suspected the vehicle was for my benefit since I couldn't shift or shadow.

Lorcan selected the front passenger seat, while Cillian sat behind the wheel. Kieran and I settled into the back. Then we started on a journey that took us away from the airport—which was a good forty-minute drive from Reykjavik—and led us into the countryside. It didn't take long for me to realize that we weren't going to the capital, but elsewhere.

I didn't ask questions, as Kieran's mind held the answers I needed—we were going to a detainment facility away from the residential areas.

I laid my head against his shoulder and closed my eyes.

This was going to be a long night.

KIERAN

I DISMISSED two of the Alphas upon entering the dungeon, as well as a Beta. Their scents alone confirmed their innocence.

It wasn't just the terror wafting off them, but the anger, too. Particularly when they saw Quinnlynn and realized she was pregnant.

They weren't angry about the accusations, or angry at my mate for her previous behavior.

No, they were angry that someone had tried to hurt her and the future Blood Sector heir.

That reaction alone proved they were harmless. Given what Cillian had told me about their excuses for shadowing—they'd simply tried to shadow back to their dens for protection—it was easy to let them go.

But I added a subtle warning to the two Alphas as I did so. "You're Alphas. Good Alphas don't hide; they protect. Remember that next time you feel a power shift, or I might be inclined to remove you from my sector."

"Yes, My King," the one said, addressing me by a title I hadn't yet been given but had clearly earned. Then he bowed low before Quinnlynn as he said, "Welcome home, My Queen. We are pleased to have you back."

She smiled, her eyes misting a little as she replied, "Thank you, Odin."

He rose to his feet and excused himself with another polite bow toward me.

The other Alpha promised it wouldn't happen again before addressing Quinnlynn and expressing his gratitude for her return as well.

I suspected that would happen a lot over the next week.

It's the baby, she told me. *They're pleased I performed my duty to the bloodline.*

I scoffed at that. *That may be part of it, but deep down, they're grateful to have a powerful Queen protecting them. They all know that energy explosion was related to you. I daresay it scared the shit out of some of them.*

As it should have.

Quinnlynn might be an Omega, but she was a strong one with a bloodline that superseded everyone else in existence. Underestimating her would be their downfall.

She gave me a small smile. *Thank you for seeing me as more than a breeding tool.*

I grabbed her by the back of the neck, irritated by that statement. *You are much more than a womb to me, My Queen. Never doubt that.*

I don't, she whispered. *Just like you're much more to me than a knot.*

Her sassy little retort gave me pause, some of my agitation disappearing.

If you want to use me for my knot, I'm certainly okay with that.

"Sire," Cillian interjected. "What would you like to do with Myon and Orion?"

Those were our two remaining prisoners. *Kill them both so I can knot my Omega?* I suggested to him telepathically.

Quinnlynn narrowed her gaze in response.

Cillian merely sighed. *We can make this quick. I can read their minds.*

Yet you haven't been able to discern Myon's truths yet.

True, he agreed. *Because he's fighting me.*

And Orion? I pressed.

Seems to have a natural block.

What about the three I just released? I demanded.

His dark irises glimmered knowingly. *All innocent, but I didn't want to ruin your fun. Besides, I know how you enjoy a good show of power.*

Then it must have disappointed you greatly when I let them all go.

On the contrary, it rather proved my point, he murmured. *I already told Myon and Orion that you would be quick with your assessments. They now know I meant it.*

I see. I grinned at my oldest friend. *Maybe you should run Blood Sector more often.*

Please don't threaten me, Sire, he deadpanned. *I don't appreciate it after everything I've done for you.*

One of these days, Cillian, you're going to have to lead, I warned him. It was a conversation we had often.

Not today, Sire.

Not today, I agreed. I gave Quinnlynn's nape another squeeze and released her. "Let's start with Myon." He was the guilty one.

However, Cillian's comments about Orion made me curious.

He was an older Alpha. Unmated. And often kept to himself out in the countryside.

If he had an affinity for blocking powers, then I wanted to know more. He could prove useful. Particularly as a guard.

Cillian led the way to Myon's holding cell. He hadn't

handcuffed the Alpha with silver or anything, simply kept him leashed with his superior powers.

Just like Alphas could force others to shift, they could also control another's ability to shadow.

If Myon were stronger, he could fight Cillian.

But no one on this island outranked Cillian in power. That was how he'd managed to leash the entire sector. If he growled out a command to shift, everyone would comply.

Except for me and Lorcan. Just like our shadowing talents weren't impacted by Cillian's hold.

He had no dominion over me.

However, I also had no power over him.

That was what made us equal.

It was also what allowed us to hold Blood Sector's territory so easily—no one wanted to challenge us. We were essentially a trio of Alpha Princes.

I'd only won the higher title among us because I'd desired it more.

"Hello, Myon," I greeted.

I waved a hand to unlock the gate. It was magically charged by an enchantment Lorcan had taught us ages ago. Sort of like a complex logic puzzle that required the right degree of power and movement to make it unlatch.

It was nearly impossible for others to mimic.

Hence the reason we used it.

"You'll be pleased to know that Quinnlynn and I are officially mated," I continued as I entered. "She's also pregnant with our heir, as I'm sure you've deduced." I took a chair at the table across from where he sat.

"Congratulations," he deadpanned.

I smiled. "I'm glad you're not trying to play the sympathy card, Myon. I respect that."

I'd half expected him to try to plead with Quinnlynn

and claim immediate innocence. But instead, he just looked tired.

Did you work him over mentally at all? I asked Cillian.

No more than any of the others, he replied. *I think he's just resigned to his fate.*

Hmm. I can work with that.

"Why don't we just get right to it?" I offered. "You enchanted some jewelry with the hope of accessing a world that doesn't belong to you. And you failed."

He stared at me, his lips flattening into a straight line.

"Do you deny it?" I asked.

Silence.

"I see." So he wanted to play the quiet game. "I'm going to assume silence is compliance. Which means you enchanted those earrings and that necklace before giving them to my mate."

"Her mother," he clarified flatly. "They were given to her mother."

"So you admit to giving them to her?"

"They were a gift from Seamus. Not from me."

Seamus MacNamara, I thought.

That's true, Quinnlynn told me as she remained in the hallway. *My father gave my mother those diamonds centuries ago. Well before I was born.*

"When did you enchant them?" I asked, studying Myon.

"I didn't enchant them."

I arched a brow. "But you know they were enchanted?"

"Of course I do. All of Seamus's Elites knew."

I frowned. "All of them?"

"Yes. Seamus put a tracking beacon on them so he could locate his mate if she was ever taken." Myon spoke the words with clarity and no hints of lying. "And we all know how to access the enchantment, too. Which is why I tried to shadow to Quinnlynn when I felt the alarm."

"Felt the alarm?" I repeated.

"Yes. The one tied to the charm. It's enchanted with the blood of Seamus's former Elite. We all felt the call."

"But you were the only one who tried to shadow," I pointed out, both intrigued and confused by his story.

His expression darkened. "That's an issue you'll need to take up with the others. But I swore an oath to that family to protect them. And that's what I tried to do." His gaze went to Quinnlynn. "I'm glad you're okay, Princess."

He didn't sound very glad. He sounded angry.

But that could be because of the situation at hand.

Or perhaps residual anger at the other Elites for not trying to help Quinnlynn when the "alarm" had sounded.

"If you knew the jewelry was enchanted, why didn't you mention it?" Cillian asked.

He stood in the doorway behind me, while Lorcan lurked in the hallway, his silent objective to protect Quinnlynn.

"Because you should have sensed it yourself," Myon bit out. "But you're too concerned with protecting Kieran over everyone else. Something the jewelry more than proved."

I narrowed my gaze. "Cillian and Lorcan would protect Quinnlynn with their lives."

"I've yet to see proof of that," Myon retorted. "She was on her own for a century because she was too scared to remain here and tell you the truth."

"The truth about what?" I asked, genuinely curious as to what he thought she'd meant to keep from me.

"The Sanctuary." There was no hesitation in his reply. Likely because he knew I had access to her every thought now. Which meant I knew everything there was to know.

"And her parents' murder," I added, narrowing my gaze. "Because she was told an Alpha Prince did it."

"A necessary lie to keep her safe."

"From who?" I demanded.

"An unworthy suitor," he replied flatly. "Her parents wanted her to have a proper courting period, but I knew that wouldn't happen with their unexpected demise. So the Elites and I took matters into our own hands, to protect the dynasty."

"By enchanting a pendant and making up a story from her parents?" I couldn't help the incredulous note in my voice.

"That part wasn't my idea—the whole made-up story about them being murdered—but we needed her properly prepared to take on her duty for the Sanctuary."

"I don't understand," Quinnlynn said as she moved into the room. "What are you saying, Myon? That you manufactured a lie to... to protect me?"

"To motivate you," he corrected. "And to keep you from making a rash decision to mate. Your parents would have wanted you to take your time."

She slowly shook her head. "They'd already begun opening the courting process. They wanted me to mate an Alpha Prince."

"But not immediately. The courting process can take decades. Like it did for your mother."

"So you scared her off by making her believe her parents were murdered by an Alpha Prince?" I was absolutely not buying this bullshit, but I'd entertain him for a minute.

"Essentially, yes." He met my gaze. "As I said, it wasn't my idea."

"Then whose idea was it?" I asked, curious to hear the name of whoever he wanted to throw under the bus.

"Fritz's."

"*What?*" Quinnlynn demanded while I evaluated his interesting response.

He'd either heard that name from Seamus, read it somewhere, or actually knew the full truth about the Sanctuary.

Given that he couldn't access the island, it seemed doubtful.

But then again, Omegas could technically leave at will.

"Will Fritz corroborate that story?" I asked, my gaze narrowing.

"Only one way to find out." Myon didn't appear panicked at all, which told me that either he was confident and telling the truth, or he was a very competent sociopath.

"Lorcan," I called.

"He's already talking to Kyra," Cillian confirmed.

Good. "So if I'm following this correctly, then you're telling me the tracker jewelry was developed on purpose to ensure Kiana MacNamara's safety, and Quinnlynn's parents weren't murdered at all. Therefore, the story about the freak accident is true."

"Yes. The story about the jet exploding due to an engine malfunction is true." He leaned back in the chair, the picture of ease. "I have the black box."

My eyebrows lifted. "Where?"

"Already on it," Cillian replied, disappearing in a blink.

"You have a recording of my parents' death and never told me about it?" Quinnlynn demanded.

"You weren't ready to hear it, Princess," he said, the first inkling of sorrow coloring his tone and features. "It was sudden, though. They didn't feel any pain."

"Oh, well, that's nice," she spat as she approached the table on a wave of anger. "For the last one hundred years, you just let me think they'd been murdered instead. Made me chase a figment across the globe. Leave my sector behind. Not trust my intended mate."

Her cheeks were bright red with righteous fury, making me wonder if she was about to smite this poor bastard with a bolt of power.

I wouldn't stop her.

Fuck, I'd cheer her on.

"It's true," Lorcan said from the doorway. "The fake story about the murder was Fritz's idea."

"The Omega?" I asked, honestly surprised.

"He might be physically smaller than an Alpha, but the deadly Omega is a weapons expert," Myon replied. "That's why he's on the island. He's one of Seamus's former Elite."

"My father never told me that," Quinnlynn said. "Fritz is a Protector."

"He's the original Protector," Myon corrected. "He's older than all of us. Which is why I bowed to his wishes and enchanted the illusion to his specifications."

"And the explosion?" I demanded. "Was that part of the *specifications?*" Because if it was, I was going to kill that Omega, Protector or not.

Myon frowned. "No… That… I don't understand."

A truth, Cillian said, his presence nearby but out of sight as he materialized in the other room. *I can hear his confusion.*

Can you hear mine? I deadpanned.

You sound like murder, Sire. As per usual.

I grunted.

I'm going to listen to this video with headphones in another room. I don't want to disturb Quinnlynn, but I also want proof.

Let me know if it's true, I told him, not needing more details. Because if he provided them, then Quinnlynn would hear them. And I was not going to be the one to put nightmares in her head.

"The jewelry exploded when Kieran took it near the shield. If I'd been wearing those earrings, the blast would have killed me."

"Not possible. Those diamonds were enchanted to protect you." He frowned, his gaze turning toward me. "You took them to the barrier? From the inside?"

"The outside," I clarified, observing him intently.

His brow furrowed, then smoothed, a note of understanding seeming to overtake his features. "They weren't meant to protect you. They must have reacted to being close to the protective barrier without their rightful owner."

"Then why were they conflicting with the shield while Quinnlynn wore them?" I countered. "I could feel the barrier enchantment draining her energy as it fought the magic in those diamonds."

I stared at him, a hint of true confusion lurking in his expression. "That shouldn't happen. But maybe... maybe it's because the spell was meant for her mother, not for her?"

"So you gave her the jewelry without fully understanding how it would react to her?" I demanded.

"Quinnlynn is Kiana's daughter. I assumed that—"

"That word right there is your problem," I said, not bothering to hide my fury. "You cannot *assume* anything when it comes to my mate. And it certainly feels like you and Seamus's other former Elites made a lot of assumptions where my mate is concerned."

The recording is real, Cillian interjected quietly. *The jet exploded unexpectedly.*

I swallowed, my gaze going to Quinnlynn as I quietly shared the information with her.

She didn't outwardly react, her mind moving too quickly to decide how to interpret everything she'd just learned.

"Quinnlynn is our future Queen," I continued, my voice quieter now but no less furious. "She has a right to make up her own mind. A right to decide who she mates and when. A right to know the truth. And a right to be respected for her power and birthright, not handled as though she's made of glass."

I pushed away from the table, my gaze finding Myon.

"She will be the one to decide your fate because, unlike you and the other former Elites, I have faith in my Queen to make her own choices. I won't lie to her. I won't hide the truth from her. And I sure as fuck will never make decisions for her."

I faced my beautiful mate and bowed my head to her in a gesture of necessary respect.

Then I straightened and held out my hand. "Are you ready, My Queen? Or do you have more questions for your former guardian?"

The words were purposeful. A reminder to the Alpha in the room that he no longer protected this female; *I* did. And unlike him, I would be doing this the right way.

"I want to hear the recording," she said.

I nodded, expecting as much. I hadn't wanted Cillian's details because I refused to be the one to share those devastating facts with Quinnlynn.

But she had a right to choose for herself.

And if she chose to listen to those final moments, then I'd listen to it with her.

Afterward, I'd stand beside her as she questioned Myon. And if she so deemed it, I'd kill him for her, too.

Although, I already knew that wasn't a punishment she desired. Because part of her saw aspects of her father in

Myon, and while she didn't agree with what he'd done, she somewhat understood it.

That compassion was what would make her a brilliant Queen.

But it was also why she needed me.

Because I could be the villain when she needed one.

Just as I might choose to be one with Myon at some point, something I let him understand now with a glance.

Quinnlynn might choose his punishment. But I would be the one carrying out the sentence.

And I would not be kind.

Question Orion more about his gifts, I told Cillian. *Treat it like a job interview.*

Of course, Sire.

I stood. *And keep Myon comfortable. Our Queen will decide his fate at a later date.*

What about Fritz? he asked.

I suspect Kyra will deal with him. And if she doesn't, I will. After Quinnlynn delivered his sentence, anyway. I pressed my palm to her lower back as I led her from the room.

Understood. Consider everything taken care of here, Sire.

Thank you, Cillian, I said, meaning it. *You make a fine Alpha Prince.*

Fuck you, Kieran.

My lips threatened to twitch. *I can't wait for the day you take over a sector.*

He didn't reply.

Not that I expected him to.

But one day, he would lead. I was sure of it.

QUINN

THE RECORDING OF MY PARENTS' death haunted my thoughts as I stood in line greeting Alphas from across the V-Clan Sectors.

I'd dreaded this moment for so many years, terrified that I might accidentally shake the hand of my parents' murderer, only to realize it had all been a lie.

Not even that, but a ploy. A motivation. A way to keep me from mating an Alpha Prince "too early."

I felt betrayed in a way I didn't know how to define. People close to me—the ones I'd trusted to *protect* me—had lied to me.

And worse, I found out after all this that Fritz had been the one feeding information to Kyra about Kieran. Oh, she'd known of my mate through her own ties to Alpha Fare, but Fritz had been the one to tell her about Kieran's penchant for challenges.

Everything felt so manufactured.

So… so… *controlled*. Like I wasn't in charge of my own destiny.

And that infuriated me.

Kieran ran his finger down my exposed spine, my midnight-colored dress very different from the corset-topped one I wore to our betrothal dinner. He leaned down to press a kiss against my pulse, drawing me back into the moment before greeting Alpha Cael.

"You look radiant, My Queen," he greeted with a cordial bow.

"Doesn't she?" Kieran drawled, his palm going to my lower back in a proprietary move.

"Put the claws away, *King* Kieran. I have no intention of taking your mate." Cael winked at me, stirring a growl from my Alpha. "You certainly chose well, My Queen."

"I did," I agreed. *Except now I'm wondering if it was all planned out by a bunch of Elite males who felt the need to control my life.*

They certainly did not control mine, Kieran murmured back to me. *And if I hear you question our mating one more time, I'm going to fuck you in front of everyone here just to prove a point.*

You won't do that. You'd have to kill them all afterward, I reminded him, thinking of his threat from the other day.

Something I would gladly do in your honor, Quinnlynn, if it proves to you that we're together because we want to be, not because of a bloody lie and a pair of earrings.

His frustration was palpable and rivaled my own, just for very different reasons.

You're right. I'm not being fair to you.

This isn't about being fair, darling. This is about believing in us. Do you honestly think Myon wanted us together? He glanced at me, completely ignoring whatever Prince Cael was saying.

No, I really don't.

Then there you have it.

But Fritz apparently did.

All right, let's say he did, Kieran replied. *Are you truly upset by his choice?*

Of course not.

Then why are you torturing yourself like this? he demanded, holding up a hand to pause Prince Cael midsentence. "I love you, Quinnlynn MacNamara. That's all that matters, yes?"

Several people stilled around us, all of them waiting with bated breath to hear my response. "Yes," I agreed after a beat, deciding to be in the *present* with him as he was currently demanding.

No more past.

No more fretting over what-ifs.

It was time to exist together in the now.

Because regardless of Fritz's and Myon's meddling, I was here. Beside Kieran. The two of us having just been crowned King and Queen of Blood Sector. And politely thanking all the Alpha Princes for attending.

That was what mattered most.

The rest… the rest no longer applied.

An interesting moral lesson to learn, especially after years of being told how important history was to ensure that it didn't repeat itself. But truly, dwelling in the past only created sorrow.

And in my case, it created heartache and unnecessary pain.

My parents' jet had malfunctioned in a way no one could have anticipated. And the Elites had blamed themselves for not noticing. But they weren't aeronautical engineers or technicians. How could they have possibly known?

Yet it was clear they'd taken the blame upon themselves, which had led to them deciding to run my life as they thought my parents would want them to.

I still wasn't sure how to respond to all that.

Maybe I'd banish them.

Maybe I'd let them stay.

I leaned into Kieran, accepting his strength as we rekindled the conversation with Prince Cael. He gave me an assessing look, no doubt sensing my hesitation and internal conflict. But when Kieran gave a little purr that had me melting even more into his side, the prince smiled. "I've never been one for these types of affairs myself," he said conversationally.

"And yet, you were the one who told everyone I would be rescheduling this coronation," Kieran drawled.

Cael grinned. "It calmed them all down, didn't it?"

"It did," Kieran conceded, evaluating the other man. "Perhaps you'll return soon for a private dinner."

"That sounds more my speed," Cael replied. "I'll reach out to Lorcan to schedule a time. As he monitors my chatter, it should be relatively easy to do." He flashed a playful grin at Kieran before melting back into the crowd, causing my mate to hum in appreciation.

He reminds me a bit of you, I admitted. *A troublemaker.*

He dabbles and tries to play the game, Kieran replied. *But it's one I mastered centuries before his birth.*

Fair, I returned. *But I think he could be a strong ally.*

Indeed, Kieran agreed. *Assuming he's not the V-Clan Alpha who visited Bariloche Sector, anyway.*

He's not. I frowned, evaluating the room. *In fact, I don't think anyone here has the aura I felt there.*

A mystery for another day, then, Kieran drawled. *Perhaps I'll reach out to Ander and Sven, find out if there were any records in Bariloche Sector. Or perhaps one of the many Omegas can help us identify the culprit.*

We could send images to Ander to disseminate to them, I suggested.

Kieran nodded. *I'll task Cillian with it. I'm sure he'll be happy to handle the hunt.*

The Elite male in question met Kieran's gaze from across the room, his body shrouded in shadows as he remained inconspicuously out of sight.

He reminded me a bit of a chameleon, something Kieran's thoughts told me was common for the male. Apparently, he was frequently capable of hiding, even in a crowded room.

Is he agreeing to the request? I wondered.

Not verbally, Kieran replied as Cillian dipped his chin in a subtle nod. *A nonverbal agreement it is, then.*

Because he heard us talking about him?

Sort of, Kieran murmured. *From what he's told me, he can understand our tones more than our words. But it's muted when we speak to each other. However, our exterior thoughts give us away. Whatever that means.*

That's not very comforting.

No, it's really not, he agreed with a smile.

Cillian's lips twitched as well.

Then they flattened as he turned his head toward Ivana, who had materialized a few feet from him.

His jaw tightened at having been caught, but it didn't dissuade the bold Omega. She reached up to tug on a lock of his dark hair, then smirked at his scowl.

I can't hear her, but I imagine she's saying something like, "I found you. Do I get a reward?" Kieran mused.

And how do you think Cillian is responding? I wondered.

With a chastisement of some kind, surely.

"One of these days, you'll have to tell me their history," I said, choosing to speak out loud instead of into his mind as I pressed myself even more firmly into his side and placed my palm over his heart.

"It's not my story to tell," Kieran murmured. "But perhaps Cillian will enlighten you."

I smiled up at him. "Doubtful."

"Doubtful," he agreed, his hand traveling up my spine to fondle the curls in my hair. "I see Cameron did a fine job dressing you again. Should I be jealous?"

"Definitely not," I promised him. "He was an absolute gentleman."

"Was he now?" Kieran drawled. "A gentleman like me?"

"No, not a gentleman like you," I told him. "You're one of a kind." *My hero, remember?* I added that last part with a thought, as I'd promised to make that our secret.

His eyes immediately narrowed. *It's like you want me to punish you.*

I'm still not sure what that means, I admitted. *What is your idea of a punishment, Kieran?*

Push me and find out, he dared.

I grinned. *Well, now, that doesn't sound very heroic of you.*

Because I'm not a hero, darling.

Yes, yes, you're a villain. I made a show of rolling my eyes. *Yet I haven't seen anything villainous, Kieran. I'm rather disappointed. In fact, I'm downright bored.*

His eyebrows lifted. *Give me a dastardly task, and I'll see that it's done.*

I considered it for a few seconds, my lips pinching to the side. *I'm all out of dastardly tasks at the moment. How about a challenge instead?*

I'm listening.

How fast do you think you can get me out of this room while remaining politically polite? I wondered.

His lips curled. *Now see, My Queen, that is a task I can undertake. One that will show you just how villainous I can be.*

I said politically polite, I reminded him.

I don't do politics. And I certainly don't do polite, he told me. Then he looked at the crowd. "My Queen and I are retiring for the night. Enjoy the wine. It's spiked with blood."

He wrapped his arm around my waist and started leading me away from the room. "*Kieran*."

"What?" he asked, all false innocence. "You wanted to see how quickly I could get you out of the room. Now you know."

He pulled me right behind the throne area and through the back curtains.

Then he lifted me into his arms.

And started carrying me down the hall.

I couldn't help it—I laughed. Because of course this would be his method of avoiding the rest of our coronation ball. "We didn't even get to dance," I told him.

"I'll dance with you in our room," he replied. "Naked."

"Naked?" I repeated.

"Naked," he affirmed.

I considered that for a moment and nodded. "I accept."

"Well, that's good since you didn't have a choice in the matter."

"I thought you said I would always have a choice as Queen."

"And you will on almost everything except what we do in the bedroom," he replied, making my eyebrows lift.

"Is that so?"

"It is," he replied. "Consider that your *punishment* for making me wait a century to knot you."

I laughed again, incapable of arguing with him. I knew he was being serious, but I honestly didn't mind. If he wanted to control me in the bedroom, I'd allow it.

Because deep down, I trusted him.

I knew he would never push me too far. Never hurt me.

Never withhold pleasure—unless he meant it as a game. And most of all, he would never take me without consent.

This male was mine. My strong Alpha. My King.

I loved him.

Cherished him.

Respected him.

And vowed to be his.

Just as he vowed to be mine.

I would never run from him again. Unless it was a game. Whereby I would enjoy being chased. Mounted. And claimed.

His dark eyes sparkled with knowledge as he gazed down at me. "Thinking wicked thoughts, little trickster?"

"Plotting my next move," I countered.

"Hmm," he hummed. "It's too bad you can't shadow."

"Then I guess we'll just have to play hide-and-seek in the bedroom," I suggested.

"And what happens when I find you?"

"Whatever you want," I promised him.

"An alluring offer," he replied as he carried me out of the entertainment venue and onto the street. "I accept."

"But you have to dance with me first," I reminded him.

"Of course," he agreed. "Then I'll knot you in your nest."

I sighed, thinking of the new nest I'd started in *our* room. It was perfect because it smelled like Kieran.

No, it smelled like *us*.

A safe haven where I could hide from the past and the nightmares that haunted the present.

A protective burrow where decisions didn't matter.

A soft space to make love to my Alpha, to join as one, to be together and alone and exactly as we were meant to be.

"You were right," I whispered, leaning my head against

his shoulder and pressing my lips to his neck. "Their influence wasn't what really brought us together. Our wolves did."

"Our souls did," he corrected.

Which was truly the same as our wolves, yet somehow deeper.

"We were fated, Quinnlynn. I felt it the moment we met. Your devious ways called to my inner spirit. And my penchant for breaking the rules called to yours."

I almost made a joke about it being his heroic side that had called to my soul, but I didn't want to spoil the moment.

It was too perfect.

Too right.

Too *us*.

"Take me to the nest and make love to me, Alpha," I whispered several minutes later. "I no longer wish to play games."

"As you wish, My Queen," he replied as we entered his building. "Everything I do, I do for you."

"I heard you say that once," I admitted softly. "Something along the lines of being willing to do just about anything for me. I thought it was a dream."

"It wasn't," he confirmed, the elevator dinging as he called it to the lobby area. "It was the truth."

"I believe that now." I kissed his neck. "Thank you, Kieran. For accepting my betrothal and becoming my King."

"Thank you for teaching me how to live again," he returned, his purr rumbling in his chest. "Now be a good little challenge and slicken those pretty thighs for me. I have plans for that beautiful pussy of yours."

"How romantic."

"I never claimed to be romantic, Quinnlynn."

"No, I suppose you didn't." Just like he claimed not to be a hero.

But that didn't make him any less of one in my eyes.

"I love you, Kieran O'Callaghan. Just the way you are," I promised him.

He smiled and stepped out of the elevator and into his suite. "And I love you, Quinnlynn MacNamara. Now strip."

I laughed as he set me down.

Then did exactly as he demanded.

And led him straight to my new nest.

"Knot me, Alpha."

"With pleasure, Omega."

EPILOGUE

KYRA

"HAS Quinn decided on her punishment for us yet?" Fritz asked by way of greeting.

I glanced up at him from my bed and arched a brow. "If she did, do you think I'd tell you?"

"Yes."

"After you essentially betrayed her by using me to do it?" I pressed.

"We both know that's not what happened." He leaned against the door frame, his muscular arms flexing as he crossed them over his broad chest. He was pretty big for an Omega male, standing a little over six feet tall, making him a good foot taller than me.

If I didn't know his true nature, I'd call him a Beta. Not an Alpha, though. He wasn't growly enough for that.

However, his penchant for playing games was all Omega.

"You fed me information about Kieran, knowing I would recommend him to Quinn," I reminded him. "That's betrayal, Fritz."

"Some would call that accurate matchmaking," he corrected.

"Yeah? And what about that bullshit murder story you concocted? What do you call that?"

His jaw clenched. "A necessary trial."

My eyebrows lifted. "A trial for what?"

He blew out a breath and ran his fingers through his long blond hair. "We both know Alphas can be evil, Kyra. I was trying to steer her away from the mating games by making her wary of them all."

"While also driving her toward Kieran," I pointed out.

"Because I knew he was good for her."

"And all the others were bad for her?"

"Some of them are," he hedged, his cagey response making me wonder what he was hiding. "But Kieran was meant to be hers. They're perfect together."

"Okay, Mister Matchmaker," I drawled, unimpressed by his finagling.

"You and Lorcan are pretty good together, too," he added, making me narrow my eyes.

"Are you trying to convince me to kill you? Because I gotta tell you, Fritz, I'm already halfway there. You might not want to push me much further over that line, or I'm liable to put a blade in your heart."

He grinned. "Flirt."

I rolled my eyes. "Get the fuck out of my room, Fritz." I wasn't ready to forgive him yet. I might eventually, but not anytime soon. Quinn was my best friend. My loyalty went to her first.

However, that wouldn't stop me from recommending she go easy on Fritz.

While I didn't at all agree with his meddling, I knew he'd meant well deep down. And he'd saved my ass enough times for me to feel pretty strongly about keeping him alive.

Fortunately, Quinn wasn't the killing type. She was more forgiving and believed in moral lessons over lethal ones.

I supposed the whole *opposites attract* methodology applied to friendships, too. Because I absolutely preferred the murderous method to the compassionate one.

"Do you think she'll ever forgive me?" Fritz asked, ignoring my demand to leave.

"Honestly? I don't know," I admitted.

He nodded, his blue eyes holding a touch of uncharacteristic sadness. "I can't really blame her. But I did it to protect her."

"Sometimes we don't need others to protect us, Fritz. We have to learn how to protect ourselves." It was about as morally correct as I could get, but it sounded like something Quinn would say.

"I'm starting to realize how true that is," he admitted, disappearing into a shadow and leaving me alone in my nest once more.

I sighed and lay down again, my gaze on the ornate ceiling above. It didn't matter how long I stared at it; the visual would be replaced as soon as I closed my eyes.

Because all I could do was dream of *him*. My dead mate. The Vampire Alpha who had kept me captive for nearly twenty years, sharing me with his friends and proving just how vile Alphas could be.

Vampire Omegas had a rare blood type that could sustain Vampire Alphas for far longer than any human could. Our blood was like a drug to them, mine even more so because of my mixed V-Clan genetics.

And worse, once mated, Vampire Omegas were reliant

on their Vampire Alpha's venom, making it a vicious cycle of giving and taking that proved intoxicatingly addictive.

I shuddered just thinking about it.

Kyra? Lorcan whispered, his intrusion in my mind distractingly welcome.

Which, of course, had me snapping, *What?* in response. Because I *hated* how his mental voice seemed to calm me instantly. I did not want to be addicted to another Alpha ever again.

I sensed unease.

I'm fine, I told him.

All right. Good night.

He left just as swiftly as he'd arrived, his respectful demeanor unnerving. He did this almost once a day, just checking in before retreating and giving me the space I desired.

Because he didn't want a mate—a fact Cillian had claimed about both himself and Lorcan, but I hadn't actually believed it until I'd heard the truth of it in Lorcan's mind.

He truly did not want anything to do with having a mate. It was a trait we shared. And it was the primary reason I hadn't killed him yet.

Oh, I'd planned to off him before I'd even bitten him. I was going to lure him back to the Sanctuary with Kieran, ensure Quinn's safety, and then stab Lorcan right in the heart.

Only, the clever bastard had hidden all the knives in my room before I could find one that worked.

Then he'd pinned me to the bed and told me that if I kept fantasizing about killing him, he'd be forced to lock me in a cage.

A. Fucking. Cage.

I'd growled.

He'd growled back.

Then he'd released me and informed me that he had no desire to consummate our mating bond. It was sort of a lie because I'd been able to sense his arousal and interest, but I'd also overheard his mental resolve not to touch me.

He would never take a female by force. Nor did he want one of his own.

"Once Quinnlynn and Kieran are ready to return to Blood Sector, I will go with them. Our interactions going forward will be minimal," he'd stated flatly.

I'd been stunned by his proclamation.

"What about my heat cycle?" I'd asked him.

His dark brow had lifted slightly. "What about it?"

"You're not going to offer to see me through it?"

"Would you like me to offer to see you through it?" he'd countered.

"No."

"Then no, I'm not going to offer my assistance. Besides, it would require me to leave Blood Sector for an extended period, which is not something I wish to do."

The whole conversation played through my mind as it often did, my shock still palpable. Because he'd meant every word. And aside from his casual check-ins, he left me alone.

Although, I suspected he was responsible for my shortened nightmares lately. I kept waking in the middle of the day, covered in sweat and shaking. Only to be lulled back into a dreamless sleep.

It was like he'd woven a spell to help chase away my day terrors.

I swallowed and closed my eyes, feeling oddly safe knowing that Lorcan might be the figment protecting me from afar.

It was a silly notion.

But it helped me fall asleep.

Only to immediately yank me into my memories of *him*.

The Vampire Alpha who haunted my mind and spirit.

I shuddered, curling into a ball, desperate to escape him.

Except the visual changed a little, revealing my room. The lights had flickered off, which was strange because I always kept them on. Primarily because of the nightmares and my need to be surrounded by light after so many years of living in the pitch dark.

I reached for my lamp, desperate to flick it back on.

Only to touch something cold.

Inhuman.

Impossibly real.

My blood ran cold.

This isn't real. It's a dream. I'll wake up soon.

I squinted my eyes closed, willing it to disappear.

But the air swirled around me, the Sanctuary a tangible presence.

It's my mind playing tricks on me, I told myself. *You're fine. There's no one here.*

Except my hand was still against that cold, unmoving object. And it certainly felt fucking real.

As did his fingers as he brushed my hair from my face.

And his lips that he pressed to my ear in a falsely tender kiss.

The hairs along my arms danced in response to his nearness, his familiarity, his *presence. Not real. Not real. Not real.*

"Hello, pet," he greeted, his voice silky and lacking the typical gravel of my nightmares. "I think it's time for you to come home, hmm?"

My eyes flew open, the room around me light with bright color.

My nest, I breathed, my palm landing against my sweat-soaked shirt. *Thank fuck.*

Except on my pillow, right beside my head, was a wilted black flower.

And next to it was a note written in blood that read, *Let's play…*

The V-Clan Series continues with *Night Sector*, featuring Lorcan and Kyra

NIGHT SECTOR

I never wanted a mate.

Especially not *her*—the notorious assassin known for killing Alphas.

But as fate would have it, she became mine.

Fortunately, we have an agreement. One where I rarely have to see her and she pretends I don't exist.

Everything's fine.

Until she's kidnapped by a sadistic Vampire Alpha hell-bent on turning her into his own personal Omega blood bag.

Now I'm the only one who can hear her screams. And I'm really f-cking pissed off.

I might not want her as a mate. But she's mine.

Mine to protect.
Mine to avenge.
Mine to *hunt.*

Don't worry, little killer.
I'm coming for you.
And when I find you,
I'll hand you the silver blade,
And watch you slay.

Author's Note: This is a standalone dark shifter romance with Omegaverse vibes—A, B, O dynamics with kn*tting, nesting, and biting. Check the trigger warnings in the introduction for more details.

LEXI C. FOSS

USA Today Bestselling Author Lexi C. Foss loves to play in dark worlds, especially the ones that bite. She lives in Chapel Hill, North Carolina with her husband and their furry children. When not writing, she's busy crossing items off her travel bucket list, or chasing eclipses around the globe. She's quirky, consumes way too much coffee, and loves to swim.

Want access to the most up-to-date information for all of Lexi's books? Sign-up for her newsletter here.

Lexi also likes to hang out with readers on Facebook in her exclusive readers group - Join Here.

Where To Find Lexi:
www.LexiCFoss.com

ALSO BY LEXI C. FOSS

Blood Alliance Series - Dystopian Paranormal

Chastely Bitten

Royally Bitten

Regally Bitten

Rebel Bitten

Kingly Bitten

Cruelly Bitten

Blood Alliance Standalones - Dystopian Paranormal

Blood Day

Crave Me

Dark Provenance Series - Paranormal Romance

Heiress of Bael (FREE!)

Daughter of Death

Son of Chaos

Paramour of Sin

Princess of Bael

Captive of Hell

Elemental Fae Academy - Reverse Harem

Book One

Book Two

Book Three

Elemental Fae Queen

Winter Fae Queen

Hell Fae - Reverse Harem

Hell Fae Captive

Hell Fae Warden

Immortal Curse Series - Paranormal Romance

Book One: Blood Laws

Book Two: Forbidden Bonds

Book Three: Blood Heart

Book Four: Blood Bonds

Book Five: Angel Bonds

Book Six: Blood Seeker

Book Seven: Wicked Bonds

Book Eight: Blood King

Immortal Curse World - Short Stories & Bonus Fun

Elder Bonds

Blood Burden

Assassin Bonds

Mershano Empire Series - Contemporary Romance

Book One: The Prince's Game

Book Two: The Charmer's Gambit

Book Three: The Rebel's Redemption

Midnight Fae Academy - Reverse Harem

Ella's Masquerade

Book One

Book Two

Book Three

Book Four

Noir Reformatory - Ménage Paranormal Romance

The Beginning

First Offense

Second Offense

Third Offense

Underworld Royals Series - Dark Paranormal Romance

Happily Ever Crowned

Happily Ever Bitten

X-Clan Series - Dystopian Paranormal

Andorra Sector

X-Clan: The Experiment

Winter's Arrow

Bariloche Sector

Hunted

V-Clan Series - Dystopian Paranormal

Blood Sector

Night Sector

Vampire Dynasty - Dark Paranormal

Violet Slays

Crossed Fates

Other Books

Scarlet Mark - Standalone Romantic Suspense

Rotanev - Standalone Poseidon Tale

Carnage Island - Standalone Reverse Harem Romance